Praise for *I Invited Her In* by Adele Parks

"A smart, suspenseful tale about love, betrayal, and the illusion of happiness."

—*Kirkus Reviews*

"Tightly plotted, brilliantly conceived and totally gripping."

—Lisa Jewell

"Gripping, twisty and heartbreaking, this standout story is a triumph."

—Isabelle Broom, *Heat*

"Unpredictable and gripping until the end."

—*The Lady*

"The plot twists and turns… The reader is left frantic to know how it's going to work out."

—*Woman*

"Twisty, unputdownable and utterly engrossing."

—Jenny Colgan

"The secrets, lies and suspense kept me engrossed."

—*Daily Mail*

"Convincing, sensitive and rich with emotional intimacy."

—*Daily Express*

Look for Adele Parks's next novel
LIES, LIES, LIES
available soon from MIRA.

I invited her in

ADELE PARKS

mira™

Recycling programs for this product may not exist in your area.

ISBN-13: 978-0-7783-8926-2

I Invited Her In

Copyright © 2019 by Adele Parks

This edition published by arrangement with Harlequin Books S.A.

For questions and comments about the quality of this book, please contact us at CustomerService@Harlequin.com.

Mira
22 Adelaide St. West, 40th Floor
Toronto, Ontario M5H 4E3, Canada
www.Harlequin.com

S.A.

For Alex King, Marguerite Weatherseed, Emma Woods and Cary Rudolf, with love.

I
invited
her
in

CHAPTER ONE

MELANIE

Monday, 19 February

While the girls are cleaning their teeth, I start to stack the dishwasher. It's too full to take the breakfast pots—I should have put it on last night. There's nothing I can do about this now, so I finish making up their packed lunches and then have a quick glance at my phone.

I'm expecting an email from my area manager about the results of some interviews we held last week. I work in a high-street fashion retailer that everyone knows. There's one in every town.

Our branch needs another sales assistant, and as assistant manager, I was asked to sit in on the interviews. Dozens of people applied; we interviewed six. I have a favourite and I'm crossing my fingers she'll be selected. Unfortunately, I don't get to make the final decision.

I skim through the endless offers to invest in counterintuitive home-protection units or pills that promise me thicker and fuller hair or a thicker and fuller penis, and look for my boss's name. Suddenly, I spot another name—ABIGAIL CURTIZ—and I'm stopped in my tracks. It jumps right out at me. Abigail Curtiz.

My first thought is that it is most likely to be a clever way of spreading a virus; the name is a coincidence, one just plucked out of the air by whoever it is who is mindless enough and yet clever enough to go to the effort of sending spam emails to infect other people's gadgets.

But Curtiz with a *z*? I hesitate before opening it, as it's probably just trouble. However, the email is entitled It's Been Too Long, which sounds real enough, feasible. It *has* been a long time. I can't resist. I open it. My heart thumping.

Normally, I skim read everything. I have three kids and a job, my default setting is *hurried*, but this email I read carefully. "No!" I gasp out loud.

"Bad news?" asks Ben with concern. He's moving around the kitchen, looking for something. His phone, probably. He's always mislaying that and his car keys.

"No, it's not." Not exactly. "I've just got an email from an old friend of mine. She's getting divorced."

"That's sad. Who?"

"Abigail Curtiz. Abi." Her name seems strange on my lips. I used to say it so often, with such pleasure. And then I stopped doing so. Stopped talking to her, stopped thinking about her. I had to.

Ben looks quizzical. He's one of those good husbands who tries to keep up when I talk about my friends, but he doesn't recall me mentioning an Abigail. That's not a surprise. I never have.

"We were at uni together," I explain carefully.

"Oh, really?" He reaches for the plate of now-cold toast in the middle of the kitchen table and snatches up a piece. He takes a bite, and while still chewing, he kisses me on the forehead. "Right. Well, you can tell me about her later. Yeah?" He's almost out of the door. He calls up the stairs, "Liam, if you want a lift to the bus stop, you need to be downstairs five minutes ago."

I smile, amused at his half-hearted effort at sounding like a ruthless disciplinarian, hell-bent on time-keeping. He blows the facade completely when he comes back into the kitchen and asks, "Liam has had breakfast, right? I don't like him going out on an empty stomach. I'll wait if needs be."

We listen for the slow clap of footsteps on the stairs and Liam lumbers into the kitchen right on cue. He grew taller than me four years ago, when he was just thirteen, so it shouldn't be a surprise that he now towers above me, but it absolutely is. Every time I see him, I'm freshly startled by the mass of him. He's broad, makes an effort to go to the gym and bulk out. He's bigger than most boys his age.

I wonder where my little boy went. Is he still buried somewhere within? Liam is taller than Ben now, too. Imogen, who is eight, and Lily, just six, are still wisps. They still scamper, hop and float. When either of them jumps onto my knee, I barely register it. I have to stretch up now, to steal a hug from Liam.

I also have to judge when doing so is appropriate and acceptable. I try to get it right because it's too painful to see him dodge my affection, which he sometimes does. He's outgrown me. I must respect his boundaries and his privacy; I'm ever mindful of it but I can't help but miss the little boy I could smother with kisses whenever the desire struck me. Now, I wait for Liam's rare but generous hugs, mostly contenting myself with high fives.

Today he looks tired. I imagine he stayed up later than sensible last night, watching YouTube videos or playing games. When he's docile, he's often more open to care and attention. I take advantage, ruffle his hair. Even peck him on the cheek. He picks up two slices of toast from the plate I'm proffering. Shoves one into his mouth, almost in its entirety, unconcerned that it's cold. He takes a moment to slather the second slice with jam. He's always had a sweet tooth.

"Thanks, Mum, you're the best."

I don't spoil the moment by telling him not to speak with his mouth full; there really are only so many times you can remind someone of this.

He turns to his dad and playfully asks, "What are you waiting for? I'm ready."

They're out the door and in the car before I can ask if he has his football kit, whether he's getting himself home from training this evening or hoping for a lift, whether he has money for the vending machine. It's probably a good thing. Me fussing that way really irritates him. I usually try to limit myself to just one of those sorts of questions per morning.

The girls, however, are still young enough to need,

expect and even accept, a barrage of chivvying reminders. I check the kitchen clock and I'm surprised time has got away. I gulp down my tea and then shout up the stairs. "Girls, I need you down here pronto."

As usual, Imogen responds immediately. I hear her frantic footsteps scampering above. She starts to yell, "Where is my hairbrush? Have you seen my Flower Fairy pencil case? Who moved my reading book? I left it here last night." She takes school very seriously and can't stand the idea of being late.

Lily is harder to impregnate with any sense of urgency. She has picked up some of the vocabulary that Liam and his friends use—luckily nothing terrible yet, but she often tells her older siblings to "chill" and she is indeed the embodiment of this verb.

I drop the girls off at school with three minutes to spare before the bell is due to ring. I see this as a bonus but honestly if they're a few minutes late, I don't sweat it. I only make an effort with timekeeping because I know Imogen gets stressed and bossy otherwise.

I'm aware that it's our duty as parents to instil into our children a sense of responsibility and an awareness of the value of other people's time, but really, would the world shudder if they missed the start of assembly?

I wasn't always this relaxed. With Liam, I was a fascist about timekeeping. About that and so much more. I liked him to finish everything on his plate, I was fanatical about him saying please and thank you and sending notes when he received gifts. Well, not notes as such, because I'm talking about a time before he could write. I got him to draw thank-you pictures. His shoes always shone, his hair was combed, he had the absolutely correct kit and equipment. I didn't want him to be judged and found lacking.

It's different when you're a single mum, which I was with Liam. I met Ben when Liam was almost six. Being married to Ben gives me a confidence that allows me to believe I can be two minutes late for school drop-off and no one will tut or roll their eyes. I didn't have the same luxury when Liam was small.

Suddenly I think about Abigail Curtiz's email and I'm awash with conflicting emotions.

There are lots of things that are tough about being a single parent. The emotional, physical and financial strain of being entirely responsible for absolutely everything—around the clock, a relentless twenty-four-seven—takes its toll. And the loneliness? The brutal, crushing, insistent loneliness? Well, that's a horror. As is the bone-weary, mind-wiping, unremitting exhaustion.

Sometimes my arms ached with holding him, or my back or legs. Sometimes I was so tired I wasn't sure where I was aching; I just felt pain. But there were moments of reprieve when I didn't feel judged or lonely or responsible. There were moments of kindness. And those moments are unimaginably important and utterly unforgettable. They're imprinted on my brain and heart. Every one of them.

Abigail Curtiz owns one such moment.

When I told Abi that I was pregnant, she was, obviously, all wide eyes and concerned. Shocked. Yes, I admit she was bubbling a bit with the drama of it all.

That was not her fault—we were only nineteen and *I* didn't know how to react appropriately, so how could I expect her to know? We were both a little giddy.

"How far on are you?" she asked.

"I think about two months." I later discovered at that point I was officially ten weeks pregnant, because of the whole "calculate from the day you started your last period" thing, but that catch-all calculation never really washed with me because I knew the exact date I'd conceived.

Wednesday, the first week of the first term, my second year at university. Stupidly, I'd had unprotected sex right slap bang in the middle of my cycle. That—combined with my youth—meant that one transgression was enough. And even now, a lifetime on, I feel the need to say it wasn't like I made a habit out of doing that sort of thing. In all my days, I've had irresponsible, unprotected sex precisely once.

"Then there's still time. You could abort," Abigail had said simply. She did not shy away from the word. We were young. The power, vulnerability and complexity of our sexuality were embryonic, but our feminist rights were forefront of our minds. My body, my choice, my right. A young, independent woman, I didn't have to be saddled with the lifetime consequences of one night's mistake.

There had been a girl on my course who'd had a scare in the first year. I'd been verbose about her right to choose and I'd been clear that I thought she should terminate the pregnancy, rather than her education. The girl in question had agreed; so had Abi and pretty much everyone who knew of the matter. She hadn't been pregnant, though. So. Well, you know, talk is cheap, isn't it?

She's the chief financial officer of one of the biggest international fast-moving consumer goods corporations now. I saw her pop up on Facebook a couple of years ago. CFO of an FMCG. I Googled the acronyms. She accepted my friend request, which was nice of her, but she rarely posts. Too busy, I suppose. Anyway, I digress.

I remember looking Abi in the eye and saying, "No. No, I can't abort."

"You're going ahead with it?" Her eyes were big and unblinking.

"Yes." It was the only thing I was certain of. I already loved the baby. It had taken me by surprise but it was a fact.

"And will you put it up for adoption or keep it?"

"I'm keeping my baby." We both sort of had to suppress a shocked snigger at that, because it was impossible not to think of Madonna. That song came out when I was about five years old but it was iconic enough to be something that was sung in innocence throughout our childhoods. The tune hung, incongruously, in the air. It wasn't until a couple of years later that the irony hit me: an anthem of my youth basically heralded the end to exactly that.

"OK then," she said, "you're keeping your baby."

Abigail instantly accepted my decision to have my baby and that was a kindness. An unimaginably important and utterly unforgettable kindness. She didn't argue that there were easier ways, that I had choices, the way many of my other friends subsequently did.

Nor did she suggest that I might be lucky and lose it, the way a guy in my tutorial later darkly muttered. I know he behaved like an arsehole because before I'd got pregnant, he'd once clumsily come on to me one night in the student bar. I was having none of it. I guess he had mixed feelings about me being knocked up, torn between "Ha, serves the bitch right" and "So, she does put out. Why not with me?" I tell you, there's a lot of press about the wrath of a woman scorned, but men can be pretty vengeful, too.

Anyway, back to Abi: she did not fume that I was being romantic and shortsighted, the way my very frustrated tutor did when I finally fessed up to her, nor did she cry for a month, the way my mother did. Which was, you know, awful.

She made us both a cup of tea, even went back to her room to dig out a packet of Hobnobs, kept for special occasions only. I was on my third Hobnob (already eating for two) before she asked, "So who is the dad?" Which was awkward.

"I'd rather not say," I mumbled.

"That ugly, is he?" she commented with a smile. Again, I wanted to chortle; I knew it was inappropriate. I mean, I was *pregnant*! But at the same time, I was nineteen and Abi was funny. "I didn't even know that you were having sex with anyone," she added.

"I didn't feel the need to put out a public announcement."

Abigail then burst into peals of girlish, hysterical giggling. "The thing is, you've done exactly that."

"I suppose I have." I gave in to a full-on cackle. It was probably the hormones.

"It's like, soon you are going to be carrying a great big placard saying, *I'm sexually active.*"

"And careless," I added. We couldn't get our breath now, we were laughing so hard.

"Plus, a bit of a slag, cos you're not sure who the daddy is."

I playfully punched her in the arm. "I do know."

"Of course you do, but if you don't tell people who he is, that's what they're going to say." She didn't say it meanly, it was just an observation.

"Even if I tell them who the father is, they'll call me a slag anyway." Suddenly, it was like this was the funniest thing ever. We were bent double laughing. Which was odd, since I'd spent most of my teens carefully walking the misogynistic tightrope, avoiding being labelled a slag or frigid, and I'd actually been doing quite a good job of balancing. Until then. It really wasn't very funny. The laughter was down to panic, probably.

The bedrooms in our student flat were tiny. When chatting, we habitually sat on the skinny single beds because the only alternative was a hard-backed chair that was closely associated with late-night cramming at the desk. The room that was supposed to be a sitting room had been converted into another bedroom so that we could split the rent between six, rather than five.

We collapsed back onto the bed. Lying flat now to stretch out our stomachs that were cramped with hilarity and full of biscuits—and in my case, baby. I looked at my best friend and felt pure love. We were in our second year at uni; it felt like we'd known one another a lifetime. Uni friendships are more intense than any other. You live, study and party together, without the omniscient, omnipresent parental influence. Uni friends are sort of friends and family rolled into one.

Abi and I met in the student union bar the very first night at Birmingham University. Although I would not describe myself as the life and soul of the party, I wasn't a particularly shy type either; I'd already managed to strike up a conversation with a couple of geology students and while it wasn't the most riveting dialogue ever, I was getting by.

Then, Abigail walked up to me. Out of nowhere. Tall, very slim, the sort of attractive that girls and *Guardian*-reading boys appreciate. She had dark, chin-length, sleek, bobbed hair with a heavy, confident fringe. She was all angles, like a desk lamp, and it seemed remarkable that she was poised to shine her spotlight on me.

She shot out her hand in an assured and unfamiliar way. Waited for me to take it and shake it. In my experience, no one shook hands, except maybe men in business suits on the TV. My dad was a teacher; he sometimes wore a suit, but mostly he preferred chinos and a corduroy jacket. I suppose he must have occasionally shaken the hands of his pupils' parents, but I'd never seen anyone my age shake anyone else's hand. Her gesture exuded a huge level of jaunty individuality and somehow flagged a quirky no-nonsense approach to being alive. Her eyes were almost black. Unusual and striking.

"Hi. I'm Abigail Curtiz, with a *z*. Business management, three Bs. You?"

I appreciated her directness. It was a fact that most of the conversations I'd had up until that point hadn't stumbled far past the obligatory exchange of this precise information. "Melanie Field. Economics and business management combined. AAB."

"Oh, clever clogs. Two degrees in one."

"I wouldn't say—"

She cut me off. "That means you are literally twice as clever as I am." If she believed this to be true, it didn't seem to bother her; she took a sip from her wine glass, winced at it.

"Or half as focused," I said. I thought a self-deprecating quip was obligatory. Where I came from, no one liked a show-off. Being too big for your boots was frowned upon; getting above yourself was a hanging offence.

Abi pulled a funny face that said she didn't believe me for a moment; more, that she was a bit irritated that I'd tried to be overly modest. "OK, that's the bullshit out of the way," she said with a jaded sigh. She didn't even bother to introduce herself to the geology students. I glanced at them apologetically as she scoured the bar. "Who do you fancy?" she demanded.

"Him," I replied with a grin, pointing to a hot, hip-looking guy.

"Come on then, let's go and talk to him."

"Just like that?" I know my face showed my astonishment.

"Yes. I promise you, he'll be more than grateful."

She made me laugh. All the time. Her direct, irreverent tone never faltered, never flattened, not that evening or for the rest of the year.

We did talk to the hot, hip guy; nothing came of it, I didn't really want or expect it to, but it was fun. We spoke to him and maybe ten other people. It quickly became apparent that Abigail oozed cool self-belief; she thought the world was hers for the taking, and it was a fair assessment. She was charming and challenging, full of bonhomie and the sort of confidence that is doled out in private-school assemblies. The best bit was, she seemed happy for me to hitch along for the ride.

It was Abi who persuaded me to join the debating society and she was the one who insisted we went to the clubs in town, rather than just limit ourselves to the parties that bloomed in the university common rooms.

She did all the student things like three-legged pub crawls and endless themed parties but she also insisted we did surprising stuff, like visit the city's museums and art galleries. Some people whispered that she was pretentious; they resented the fact that she only enjoyed listening to music on vinyl and was fussy about the strength of coffee beans; she refused to drink beer, sticking exclusively to French red wine; she rarely ate. She was, by far, the most interesting person I'd ever met.

We became close. She wasn't my only friend, or even my best friend, but she was my favourite. I sometimes found it a bit exhausting to keep up with her and while she signed up for the university's dramatic society, I was content to sit in the audience and watch her play a shudderingly shocking Lady Macbeth. I joined her on the coach to London and protested outside Parliament over something or other—I forget what now—she waved her placard all day, whereas around noon, I slipped off to Oxford Street for a quick look around Topshop.

She was the first person I told about my pregnancy. By the time we'd munched our way through almost the entire packet of Hobnobs, Abi commented, "Bizarre to think there's an actual baby in there." She was staring at my still reasonably flat stomach.

"I'm going to get so fat," I said laughingly. Weirdly, this seemed a matter of mirth.

"Yeah, you are," she asserted, sniggering, too.

"And no one is ever going to want to marry me." Suddenly, I wasn't laughing anymore. I was, to my horror and shame, crying. The tears came in huge, uncontrollable waves. I gulped and gasped for air in pretty much the same way I had when I'd been laughing, so it took Abigail a moment to notice.

"Oh no, don't cry," she said, pulling me into a tight hug. She smoothed my hair and kissed the top of my head, the way a mother might comfort a child that had fallen over. Abigail was beautiful and sensuous—everyone wanted to touch her, all the time—but she generally chose when any contact would happen.

"Who will want to marry me when I have a kid trailing around after me?" I hadn't actually given much thought to marriage up to that point in my life. I wasn't one of those who'd forever dreamed about a long white dress and church bells, but I'd sort of assumed it would happen at some stage in the future. It frightened me that the undesignated point seemed considerably more distant and blurry, now that I was pregnant.

"You'll still get the fairy tale," Abi said with her usual cool confidence. "I mean Snow White had seven little fellas hanging off her apron and she still netted a prince."

This caused another round of near-hysterical laughter. I laughed so hard that snot came out of my nose. It was embarrassing at the time. A few months on, I became much more blasé about wayward bodily fluids.

She hugged me a little tighter. "They will call you a slag, but it will be OK," she assured me.

"Will it?"

"Yeah, it really will," she said cheerfully.

I felt a wave of something like love for Abi at that moment. I loved her and I believed her.

That feeling has never completely gone away.

CHAPTER TWO

ABIGAIL

From the moment Abigail first saw Rob, she had found him completely irresistible. It wasn't an exclusive club; he was to many. Bad boys often were. That had always been their problem.

Irresistible. Such a silly word. It didn't get near it.

It tore at her. What she felt for him back then ripped a hole in her and she knew no one could plug it but him.

There were several undergraduates vying for his attention in those early days. Nubile, brilliant, interesting, beautiful young women by the busload. He'd flirted with a whole string of them. At least flirted.

She wasn't someone who was accustomed to being turned down, to being told no, and she wasn't prepared to settle for what the others did: heady evenings at the pub, one night of fun and thank you, move on. She had to have him. Make him hers. For real. Forever.

He'd been studying for his PhD when she was just

an undergrad. He took tutorials. Taught and formed young, willing minds and yet, as he was still studying himself, he was somehow one of them at the same time. He drifted around the university, unique and glamorous, enigmatic and brilliant. There was an element of power, otherness; it was very attractive.

Her body leaned into his when he walked into a room, like a compass pointing north. Her throat dried up; everything else was wet. She pulsed, beat like a huge heart.

It sounded ridiculous these days, so romantic. Too romantic. All these years on. But at the time she thought she'd been peeled back, stripped bare. That she wasn't anything more than a huge, bloody, exposed heart. Beating for him.

It was hard for Abigail to recall that in her current life, that intensity, that certainty. It had been smothered. Years of living together had normalised them. Respectability and maturity had dampened the fire. Put it out. Layer after layer of ordinary things: shopping for groceries, one telling the other they had food stuck between teeth, listening to overfamiliar stories, worrying about promotions, deadlines, accolades, choosing wallpapers and cars. Those things build layers around a pulsing heart—at once protecting it and smothering it.

And the baby thing. And the other women.

Combined, those factors meant it was impossible to recall the unadorned longing, the wanting.

But back then, he was everything. She couldn't see or think about anyone else. The boys that were buzzing around her, undergraduates, she swatted them away like flies. Rob was seven years older than she was. Enough of a gap to make him seem far more interesting than he probably was. He seemed more confident, knowledgeable, erudite. He was athletic and toned although not overly worked-out. Tall. He took her to fancy restaurants, the theatre and arthouse cinemas.

They talked about politics, novels, travelling. He was fiercely ambitious and focused. She couldn't deny that ambition and focus had panned out for him. He was, undoubtedly, a success, as he'd always wanted to be, as he'd always said he would be. She couldn't deny that she'd enjoyed the fruits of his labours. He provided an enviable lifestyle.

When they'd first met and he was messing about with a few undergraduates, he explained to her he was owed a bit of crazy time. He'd not so long ago split up from his girlfriend of five years. They'd split because that girlfriend had fallen pregnant and he hadn't wanted the baby. They'd agreed on an abortion but, afterwards, there wasn't much hope for them as a couple. They'd both found it hard to move past what had happened to them, past what they'd done. The ex maintained it was an accidental pregnancy. So many pregnancies in those days were. Fertile young people. Rob had never quite believed her story about throwing up the pill after eating dodgy takeaway. He'd felt trapped. He'd felt the net fasten around him.

"She was just about to haul me onto the fishing boat and bash my brains out," he'd said laconically, as he pulled on his cigarette or took another swig of Merlot. "We simply wanted different things." These words, delivered with a shrug, somehow made it sound as though he was the victim and Abigail ought to feel sorry for him. Which she did.

He did choose her in the end; she became his official girlfriend. It took quite some months. Months of strategising, teasing, being in the right place, saying the right thing. But she did it. She was so happy, delirious, although never quite sure why she was the one he'd picked. She wanted to know.

She thought if she knew exactly why he had chosen her, she could maintain whatever it was that had attracted him. If only she could pinpoint it exactly. Yes, she was attractive—she knew it then and she remembered it now—but many of them had been attractive. She was also buoyant and independent and confident.

Those things were harder to recall.

Maybe, she was simply the most persistent. The last woman standing.

Or just the most foolish.

Maybe the others got bored of his petulance, his pretentiousness, his unwillingness to commit. They settled for nice guys in their own year, even if those boys thought a great night was eating pizza from a box while watching *Futurama*. One day those boys would talk about political affairs and Booker winners. Everyone grows up eventually.

So that was what it was. She saw it clearly now. Her twenty-year commitment began on the back of another woman's heartache.

And now, it ended in her own.

CHAPTER THREE

MELANIE

I don't work on Mondays, which today I am particularly glad about. I can't wait to get home from drop-off and reread Abi's email.

Dearest Mel,

Well, I'm sure I'm a blast from the past and the very last person you'd expect to see pop up in your inbox. I know we haven't managed to stay in touch as much as we'd both perhaps have liked, but we are friends on Facebook and I've always enjoyed reading your posts. Although why don't you post more pictures?! I'd love to see how your family have grown. I flatter myself to think you might have caught one or two of mine over the years and have perhaps kept up with my news. The truth is, I've been thinking of you so often recently. I just had to reach out. It felt like the right time.

Things aren't going as well for me as one might hope.

In fact, things are bloody awful. Naturally, when things are bloody awful you turn to your old friends, don't you?

Rob and I are divorcing. There. I might as well just say it (or at least write it). I'll have to get used to admitting it, I suppose. I imagine it will get easier to do so, although right now my heart is breaking. I mean that sincerely, no hyperbole. I can feel it crack. Have you ever felt that, Mel? I hope not.

It's the usual story. Tragic only in its repetitiveness. He was having an affair. With his (much!) younger PA. I found them together in our bed. Can you imagine? It's not like he couldn't afford a hotel. It was just cruelty. I can only assume he wanted me to find out.

I am at a loss. I can't go into work as he is, to all intents and purposes, my boss. I'm sure you know about our careers. I find most of my English friends keep up with what's going on with me. He exec-produces my show; practically owns the channel, as a matter of fact. The humiliation. Everyone must have known before me. The wives are always the last to find out.

I've decided to travel home to England. Maybe find some work there. I need a change of scene. I have nothing to keep me here in the States. We never had children so I'm not tied by schools or whatever. My plans are vague. I'll call in on my mother—

my father died four years ago. I wanted to look up my old friends. I thought perhaps we could meet for a drink. Wouldn't that be lovely? Reminisce over old, less complicated days.

I'll be arriving in London on 20 Feb. Where do you live now? I'm guessing London, everyone does. Let me know. Phone number below.

Love, Abigail

The kettle has boiled by the time I've read the email through twice. I make myself a cup of tea, add a spoon of sugar, which I rarely take. I need something sweet.

She is right, I have never imagined I'd see a note from her in my inbox. True, we are Facebook friends—I remember sending her a request on impulse one evening a few years ago. I'd had a glass of wine or two, otherwise I'd probably never have done it. Her name was suggested to me because I'm Facebook friends with a few people from my days at uni. I'd been a little surprised when she accepted it. Surprised and flattered.

Abigail Curtiz's attention is still to be coveted. Perhaps more so now as she is famous. Not A-lister-movie-star famous but someone who makes her living by appearing on TV—that seems glamorous enough to me. As far as I'm aware, she has never "liked" any of my posts. I haven't liked hers either. Doing so would seem impertinent, pushy.

She's right about something, though: I have kept abreast of her news via Facebook. And Google. And

Wikipedia. And the occasional celeb mag search, if I'm honest. Of course, I looked her up.

She married Rob Larsen. They've been together since we were at university. A good innings, some might say. An absolute tragedy therefore that it's ended the way it has. I'm sorry for her. Truly. Her heart is breaking. She aches. The confession, so bold and frank, moves me. It shows a level of trust and confidence in our old, neglected friendship.

I wonder whether Rob has had affairs throughout their marriage. Perhaps. I've long since thought he was arrogant. Cold. It must be a dreadful position to be in.

Abi isn't exaggerating in her letter. Her career is entirely wrapped up in his, I know from all my searches. They are a golden couple of TV, with the Midas touch, stronger together, bigger than the sum of the parts. Until now, I suppose.

When we were undergraduates, he lectured in business studies with an emphasis in marketing while he was still studying for his PhD. A peculiar position to be in, straddling both roles—a staff member and a student, albeit a postgraduate one. He was fast on the uptake with new media and positioned himself as a bit of an internet and digital marketing expert, the things that the older lecturers were afraid of. I didn't pick the media module so I was never taught by him, but he was a bit of a legend within the university. Charismatic, bold, far younger than most of the other members of staff. Lots of girls had a crush on him, Abi included.

They started hooking up at the end of our first

year. It was a clandestine affair to begin with. A chaotic on-off sort of thing. She never knew where she stood with him or the university. What were the rules? Them having a relationship wasn't expressly forbidden, but it was certainly frowned upon.

Truthfully, I think Abi enjoyed the sneaking around, the drama, his inaccessibility, his power. This combined with his good looks meant he was irresistible. I gather from Wikipedia that they emigrated to America a couple of years after she graduated. He was offered some fancy job in a big advertising agency. Then, in a move I don't quite understand (but no surprises there as I'm hardly the big businesswoman), he somehow managed to get involved in TV production.

He now owns an enormous and extremely successful production company. He seems to have shares in actual TV channels and investment in several other media companies. The photos I've seen online always show them both to be more groomed, wealthy and glossy than anyone else I know. Shrouded in success. She's become much thinner, not that she was ever heavy. He's got bigger, broader, more substantial.

This is not just a case of a pretty woman piggybacking on her successful husband's career. She's worked hard. Chosen that life over a family life. Yet, it seems her career belongs to him. What a mess. Now, she has nothing to tether her if she floats away. Nothing to cushion her if she crashes to the ground.

That bit in the email about her father dying. That's sad. I met Abi's dad two or three times. He was very nice. Surprisingly unassuming, considering the daughter he reared. Luckily, my parents are in hale health; Ben's dad died before I met him but his mum, Ellie, is well. Abi's bad luck makes me feel oddly guilty about my own good fortune.

I haven't seen Abi for seventeen years. She came to visit me once when Liam was a couple of months old, which was more than most did. It was an awkward visit, even though we both did our best for it not to be. Liam was born in June, around the time most of my friends were finishing second-year exams. Most of them had plans to be backpacking around Europe that summer, so I didn't invite them to meet my baby to spare them the embarrassment, and me the hurt, of them refusing. Abi wasn't backpacking though. She didn't want to leave Rob alone in Birmingham. She just showed up.

She brought Liam a cuddly goose. It was one of his favourite things for a few years. He inaccurately called it Ducky. I kept it. It's at the bottom of a box in the attic, along with his first romper suit and a few other bits and pieces that I've hung on to for sentimental reasons.

She chatted about our friends and tutors, brought me up to date on who was house sharing with whom, who was dating whom, who had done well in their exams and who had just scraped a pass. I was still talking about going back to uni and maybe if my degree had been a three-year course, I might have done. But it was a combined course, four years. I was only halfway through. Despite what I said, I think I already knew I wouldn't be going back.

My boobs leaked milk during her visit because

I did not want to feed Liam in front of her. I didn't mind getting my baps out—I was already becoming accustomed to that. It was more complicated.

I didn't want her to go back to uni and remember me as a feeding mother, pegged to the sofa, stewing in front of daytime TV, someone whose best friends were the six New Yorkers on the sitcom of that name. My breasts became miserably heavy, and I could smell my own milk leak onto my padded bra, then my T-shirt. Eventually, Liam woke up screaming. He was blissfully unconscious of my need to preserve some fragment of the old me in my friend's memory. He hungrily rooted around my chest, staring at me with confused and furious eyes. Why wasn't I feeding him?

In the end, his loud and insistent crying drove her away. She made vague promises that she'd visit again but I didn't hold her down to a date. The moment the door closed behind her, I collapsed into the chair and pulled out my boob, fumbling. I squirted milk into Liam's eyes and nose before I found his mouth.

Do I want to dredge all that up again? Is it wise? The twentieth, that's tomorrow.

A small part of me would like to meet her for a drink. I'm not sure which force is driving me the most. Curiosity or kindness. It doesn't matter, because I don't live in London. Funny that she should think I do. She clearly hasn't read my Facebook profile in any detail.

I'm based in Wolvney, on a housing estate that's sprouted up halfway between Coventry, where my parents live, and Northampton, where Ben works. I suppose it's not entirely out of the question that I go to London to see her for an afternoon. It's only just over an hour on the train. We sometimes take the kids there for a daytrip at the weekend but we tend to only do so for a special occasion. The last time we went was to see *Matilda* the musical. It was Imogen's birthday. We all loved it, even Liam. Bless him. It would take a bit of organisation to hoof down there on my own but I'm sure Ben wouldn't mind holding the fort up here if it was something I really wanted to do.

But is it?

It's been a long time. Too long? Long enough? I don't know.

Suddenly I have a better idea. Or is it a worse one?

I could invite Abi to come and see me here in Wolvney. That way she'd meet the kids and Ben. I've never had the urge for her to meet my family before, quite the opposite, but now she's made this move, and under these circumstances, it seems the right thing to do.

She probably won't accept anyway. I can't imagine her coming all this way out of London. Not that it's far but there are certain types that think anywhere out of zone three is abroad. Is she that type? I won't know unless I invite her.

Before I change my mind, I draft a quick email back to her.

Hello, Abi,

Wow, it's so lovely to hear from you, although I'm sorry it's under such awful circumstances.

I would love to meet up. Actually, I don't live in London, I live in Wolvney, urban sprawl outside Northampton. It's just a zip on the train. It can take as little as 51 minutes if you get the fast train, no changes. I was wondering, would you like to come here? You could meet my family. I could pick you up from the station or you could get a taxi—there are always plenty available. You could come for the day or stay for a weekend. Well, whatever works, stay as long as you like!

Love, Mel

I read through my message once and wince at the slightly needy, girlish tone I fear it strikes. I feel disloyal referring to Wolvney as urban sprawl; it makes it sound much worse than it is. It is in fact a very well thought through, quite attractive housing estate, a mile from a pretty village. I guess its biggest crime is that it's ordinary.

I find a certain comfort in conforming; an unplanned teenage pregnancy can do that to you. Our house was built ten years ago and is identical to seven others in our street; a four-bedroom (well, three and a box room) semi-detached, its best feature the quite spacious walk-through kitchen diner. Still, I like to think it has warmth and integrity.

However, for some reason, I feel I need to undersell it so that when she sees it, she's more likely to be pleasantly surprised. *If* she ever sees it. Also, do I sound desperate? All that detail about the travel arrangements. Possibly, saying "stay as long as you like" is a bit over the top. A bit keen. I hope she doesn't think I've turned into the sort of person who is being particularly nice because she's famous now. I'm really not. I'm being particularly nice because she's going through a difficult time. I'm not some nosy curtain-twitcher, desperate for the gory details on the death of her marriage.

I consider redrafting but don't. I press Send without overthinking the invite.

She probably won't accept. After all, she *is* famous, I don't doubt she has countless people she would rather stay with. More exciting people than me. Trendy, waiflike women, men with groomed beards and abs. Don't get me wrong: I love my life, I adore my family and am proud of our home, our own little enclave, but when all's said and done, we're not especially interesting to anyone other than each other. We like it that way.

I have loads to do today even though I'm not working. My at-home days are far busier than the ones in the shop. Even though I have two full-time members of staff and three part-timers reporting to me in a thriving store, it's never as much work as being at home.

However, I find that as I am cleaning the kitchen floor, loading and unloading the washing machine and scrubbing the hard water marks off the shower door, I can't get Abi out of my mind. I have thought of her often enough over the years, but usually when I've done so, I've deliberately pushed thoughts of her away. She is intrinsically linked with such a difficult time. No matter how fabulous the result of that time is (and Liam really is a fabulous son), it isn't easy thinking about being pregnant and having to leave university. I've never wanted to think about her. Her path was so different to mine, I just found it easier not to dwell on what might have been.

But everything is different now.

Throughout the day, I keep checking my phone to see if she's responded to my email at the same time as telling myself she absolutely won't have. A shiver of excitement skitters through my body when I see her name once again in my inbox and I feel jubilant when I read her reply.

Mel, Angel!

I'd love to visit! Send me your address. I'll be with you on 22 Feb.

All love, A

A. Just *A.* I remember that's how she'd sign off her notes when we were at uni. Assumptive and intimate all at once. The twenty-second. Thursday. Just three days away.

Wow, I'm flattered and excited. She's coming to see me more or less straight away. A pit stop in London and then up to see me. I can hardly believe it. Thursday isn't an ideal evening to have guests—the girls have ballet. Oh well, I suppose they can skip a week.

My eyes dart around the hallway where I happened to be standing when I checked my phone for emails. There is a jumble of boots, shoes, sandals and wellingtons tumbling out of an overfull wicker basket in the corner; they look as though they're making a bid for freedom. We have five coat hooks on the wall, one each. There are about five coats hung and slung on and over each hook.

The light grey carpet was a mistake. Who chooses light anything for a family hallway? Well, I did because I saw it in a lifestyle mag and it looked amazing. In all the time we've lived here, we've never had the carpets cleaned. That's probably a mistake, too. The paintwork could also do with a freshen-up. We've got cats—they rub against the walls, which over time leaves grubby marks. In fact, because of grimy handprints or general wear and tear, most of our rooms look like they've been stippled, an effect that hasn't been popular since the 1980s—and with good reason.

I'd better get to work.

CHAPTER FOUR

ABIGAIL

Abigail was always honest with herself. She'd had enough life experience and counselling to understand and appreciate the value of developing a high level of self-awareness. It was essential to be completely truthful with herself because there was no one else with whom she could ever be completely so. She found people were less enamoured with the truth than they believed themselves to be.

So, as she packed her suitcases, she had to admit Rob had never lied to her or misled her. Not about the baby thing. He'd always been very clear, laid out his stall. No babies. Not then, not ever. She'd accepted as much, even told herself it was what she wanted, too. She decided to work hard at her career instead. That was fulfilling. Very much so. For a time. Quite some time. But that hadn't panned out exactly as she'd thought it would. How she deserved it to. A gap had opened up in her life.

She caught sight of her reflection in the mirror, puffy eyed, gaunt. She really needed to pull herself together, put some make-up on. She was likely to be recognised at the airport. She was a face. Someone.

Maybe not a name—people didn't always remember her name—but certainly a face.

People were forever saying, "I know you from somewhere. No, don't tell me." She'd smile, wait a beat and then she would tell them because it got awkward if they really couldn't place her or, worse still, mistook her for someone who worked in their hair salon or whatever. That had happened once or twice. So, she'd smartly say, "Oh, you've probably seen me on TV." Although she'd say it in a way that suggested nonchalance, as though she couldn't think of anything more obvious, more dull, than the fact she worked in TV. Then they'd whoop or hug her or squirm, self-conscious about their own ordinariness and her extraordinariness. They'd invariably ask for a selfie.

People would kill for a job as a chat-show host, a TV presenter. Admittedly, it was only state-wide TV, not nationwide. Abigail's show ran in the afternoons, rather than at prime time—breakfast or evenings—but still, people would do anything for that job.

You had to, in fact. Do anything.

And she had. Anything and everything Rob had asked of her.

When Abi arrived in the US, she was seen as nothing more than Rob's wife: a young, extremely attractive, clever-enough wife. Even if she'd had the combined IQs of all the CEOs of the FTSE 100, she probably wouldn't have been noticed for anything other than her looks—Rob and Abigail didn't mix with the sort of people who wanted anything more from women than beauty. They thought she was charming. That's what they said, often: "she's so cute," "so charming," "so sweet." It was a good thing that the Americans had always loved British accents. It gave her an edge. Stopped her falling into obscurity. Rob's colleagues and their wives lapped it up. "Say vite-a-min," they'd demand. "Say sked-ual—no, say tuh-maytoe." And she would. She was doing her job. Cute, charming, sweet corporate wife. Even though it wasn't the 1950s.

"Vitamin, schedule, tomato."

"Isn't she just adorable? She should be on TV. Rob, put her on TV," they'd say.

They never asked Rob to perform like that, yet they hung on his every word. So, he wrote the scripts, she read them. She didn't resent that. She loved it. She was grateful when he did as they suggested, when he put her on TV. The higher he rose, the higher she did. It was a mutually beneficial relationship. She was always telling herself as much.

He wrote the script for their private lives with the same autocratic approach, and she regurgitated it. Now, with hindsight, as she scrabbled around his desk drawer to retrieve her passport, she wondered whether she was overly willing to be repressed. It worked, for quite some time. But then it stopped working because her time ran out. To have had a chance at longevity, she would have had to secure an anchor job with one of the five major US broadcast television networks by the time she was thirty.

She didn't manage that. There were younger, thinner, leggier, keener women waiting in the wings. Always.

She couldn't resent it; it was a system she'd played. She'd given it her best shot. It hadn't panned out. Suck it up.

Rob was doing very well for himself. He was not subject to a time limit; men could get old and stay successful, interesting.

At that point, he was concentrating on syndicating out his shows, although her particular show was never picked up. On occasion, she privately wondered how much effort he put into selling it. He often reminded her that it didn't really matter whether her show got picked up or not—they didn't need the money and he did need her at home.

Or at least, she liked to think he did.

She'd have had to have been way bigger for the chance to grow old gracefully in front of a TV audience. Katie Couric, Barbara Walters and Diane Sawyer had been allowed. That was about it.

It was her own fault. Sometimes she'd lie awake at night, alone, even though he was sleeping next to her, and she'd admit that she'd never had the necessary commitment to her career. Not one hundred per cent. She'd drawn lines. She had principles.

She wouldn't, for example, appear on TV shows that were solely designed to humiliate people. She hadn't gone to university to rip the shit out of those with less education, money or fewer chances than she had. She played fairer than that. And although she did watch her weight (that was just common sense, right?), she wasn't prepared to starve herself. Eating tissues was not her idea of fun, and while she'd had Botox, that was to help with her migraines (mostly). She'd resisted plastic surgery (at least on her face) and had only had a little augmentation to her breasts. She was not prepared to sleep with anyone other than Rob, because she loved him and respected herself.

But it limited her career options in a business where the casting couch was still being bounced upon. In the past couple of years, she'd found she was not even willing to go to absolutely every party she was invited to, to make small talk with strangers, on the off-chance one of them (out of, say, fifty thousand) might offer her an opportunity. It was exhausting. Soul destroying. She found that neither the canapés nor the conversation ever quite filled her up.

She used to do that sort of eternal mingling and mixing willingly, hopefully. She couldn't really explain it, but more and more, she found she preferred to stay at home and snuggle up with a good book (which was handy really because there was rarely the option of snuggling up with Rob—he still seemed to like the parties). Now, as she pulled the door of her luxurious LA home shut behind her and clumped down the path towards the waiting taxi, she wondered whether maybe she should have gone to the parties. Dragged herself there.

The question of other women had raised its ugly head time and again throughout their relationship. As he became increasingly successful, increasingly powerful, she became increasingly paranoid, increasingly jealous. He said there was no reason for her to be like that. To check through his emails, his phone records, to hire private detectives. But he would say that, wouldn't he? He would say that she was the only woman he'd ever truly loved or wanted. It didn't have to be true. Just convenient.

It sometimes felt it was like an incredibly fast version of that arcade game, Whack-A-Mole, where moles appear at random and the player must use a mallet to hit them back into their holes. Other women kept popping up. She'd have to slam them down. Bash them back into their places. Thwack, thump, slap. Take that.

It was exhausting. She'd had enough.

CHAPTER FIVE

MELANIE

"What are you doing?" asks Ben as he carefully edges in the door, through the hall, past the paint-splattered sheet that I've put on the floor to protect the carpet. It's a thoughtful act. Lily walked right over it and inadvertently stood in some wet paint; paint that is now trailed throughout the kitchen and sitting room. I'll get a wet cloth and sort that out later.

He loosens his tie, a gesture I always think of as sexy. At least, part of me thinks that he looks sexy, another part of me clocks that he looks worn out; unfortunately, both of those things are overwhelmed by my own sense of panic and exhaustion. Ben is a financial director in a small software company. I'm certain what he does is important, crucial maybe—it's just not very comprehensible, at least not to me. Even so, I do normally ask how his day has been.

Today I snap, "What does it look like I'm doing?"

"Painting the hallway."

"Give the man a prize."

"But why?"

"It needed painting."

"Have the kids been fed?"

"I asked Liam to do some fish fingers and beans for the girls."

Ben makes his way into the sitting room. I hear a blast of CBeebies as the door opens and then the excited shouts of the girls as they fling themselves at him, demanding cuddles, desperate to offload their news.

I wasn't very receptive to their chatter about the trials and tribulations, triumphs and trade-offs that occurred at school today. When I picked them up, I more or less frogmarched them home, then stuck them in front of the TV until Liam arrived back and could take over. He's a good kid. I feel a bit guilty that neither my kids nor my husband got the welcome they deserve today.

I have nearly finished a first coat on the hall walls. The jackets, scarves, hats, gloves, shoes and other debris from the hallway are now in the sitting room in a huge untidy pile. I'm at the stage of the job when you just wish you hadn't started.

Ben knows me well enough to leave me to it. He takes over from Liam with looking after the girls. He listens to them reading, gets them bathed and into bed. Liam does his homework, then goes out to meet his girlfriend, Tanya.

While the paint in the hallway is drying, I start to thoroughly clean the sitting room. This largely involves picking up an endless stream of newspapers, books, toys, stray socks, hair clips, Lego, cups and plates, etc., looking at these items helplessly for a moment and then throwing them into the kitchen sink, a cupboard or the girls' bedroom.

I run out of paint halfway through the second coat. I'm a little snow-blind anyway. It's late, there's no natural light and in the electric light it's hard to see where I have layered the second coat and where I haven't.

I admit as much to Ben and he comments, "That suggests a second coat is unnecessary. Come on, love. I've made you a cheese and pickle sandwich. You should eat something. Come and sit down for five minutes and tell me what the rush is."

It's too welcome an invite to resist. I collapse into a kitchen chair. Ben squeezes my shoulder and I lay my cheek on his hand. He feels warm, smooth, comfortable. "We're expecting a guest," I explain.

"We are?"

"Yes."

"My mother?" He looks a bit aghast as he places the sandwich in front of me.

"No."

"Who then?"

"My friend, Abigail Curtiz."

He sits opposite me, scrunches up his eyes the way he always does when he's trying to recall someone. "Oh, the woman who emailed this morning?"

"Yes."

"When is she coming?"

"Thursday."

"This Thursday?"

"Yes."

"And you're redecorating because someone is coming to dinner?"

"She's staying with us for a few days."

"How long is a few days?" he asks suspiciously. Ben is a social man, he'll accept pretty much any invite that comes our way and we reciprocate, too. However, he has his limits. He likes waking up in his own bed and he doesn't like entertaining before breakfast, so he's not a big fan of stayovers.

"I'm not sure. As long as she needs," I reply, vaguely.

"But why?"

"I told you, she's getting a divorce." I realise this doesn't address the question he is asking. Why would I invite someone he's never heard of until today to stay with us? We rarely have house guests. Theoretically we have a spare room but it's incredibly small and currently stacked with boxes full of Christmas decorations, old clothes, files and photo albums, as well as unused gym equipment and the ironing board. "I think it will be nice," I say breezily.

"How will it be nice? It will be cramped."

"Cosy," I insist. I start to devour my sandwich. I hadn't realised how hungry I was until I stopped painting. Besides, with my mouth full I can't answer any difficult questions.

Ben studies me. "Will it be OK, her staying here for a few days?"

"What do you mean? Why wouldn't it be OK?"

"It's just I haven't heard you talk much about this

Abigail Curtiz over the years. At all, actually. I didn't realise she was a particular friend, not the sort you offer our spare room to indefinitely. I mean, who is she?"

"Well, we were once very close. People lose touch." I hope Ben won't push. I can't bring myself to articulate exactly why we had to go our separate ways. Why me having Liam made it impossible for me to continue to be her friend. He must understand our lives went in very different directions.

While I was trying to secure a place for Liam at nursery, Abi was stepping onto the stage to receive her certificate that confirmed her first-class honours degree. While I was spooning goop into Liam's mouth, Abi was being interviewed for her first job in TV as the assistant to Piers Morgan's assistant.

"No big thing. We just drifted," I say with a shrug. "You'll like her. I promise. Everyone does." I stand up, lean across the table and kiss him briefly on the lips. He stands, too, and puts his hand on the back of my head, kisses me hard and long. Even after all these years, that particular manoeuvre makes me melt.

"I have cleaning to get on with," I mumble, breaking away.

"We'll be quick." I can hear the smile in his voice. "Liam's out and the girls are asleep. Why wouldn't we?" He's kissing my neck now.

"What's got into you?" I ask, giggling. "It's a Monday night."

"It must be the paint fumes," he replies. He slips his hand up my T-shirt and works his thumbs under my bra strap. My body leans into his; instinct, habit, pleasure. I'm aching from painting and tidying all day but suddenly I realise this is what I need, what I want. It delights me that Ben knew as much before I did.

"You are not suggesting doing it on the kitchen table, are you?"

"I thought that was why you cleared the clutter."

"Are you mad?" I ask, laughing.

"About you," he replies cheesily.

We compromise and do it on the sofa in the sitting room.

CHAPTER SIX

ABIGAIL

Tuesday, 20 February

Neither airports nor aeroplanes particularly excited Abigail; she'd become accustomed. She didn't bother looking at the tax-free luxury products that were available because she could afford to buy them at full price, if she pleased. She didn't grab the in-flight entertainment brochure and get excited by the movies that were showing because often she'd been to early screenings, even premieres. She wasn't interested in the glass of champagne that was complimentary in business class, because alcohol was dehydrating and it was important not to look drained after a flight.

Today she visited duty-free, bought the first perfume and lipstick that came to hand, put it on his credit card; she'd have bought more but they were calling her flight. And while she did still ignore the in-flight entertainment, she put herself in danger of becoming it, as she helped herself to four glasses of champagne and knocked them back swiftly, ignoring the slightly concerned looks on the flight attendants' faces.

Abigail felt cheated.

He'd stolen from her. Her dignity, her youth, her opportunities, her time.

Him, and that woman. She wasn't going to take it lying down. She was going to even up the score. She was owed. And she was going to collect.

CHAPTER SEVEN

MELANIE

Thursday, 22 February

Abigail insists that she'd get a cab to ours rather than allow me to go out of my way to pick her up. I'm grateful because it gives me a bit more time to dash around the house, making last-minute adjustments.

The box room has been cleared to the extent that it is now at least possible to see the sofa bed. The musty old boxes have been shoved into the attic. I promised Ben that I would sort them one day, maybe when all the kids leave home and go to university. I've put the exercise bike, which I insisted upon buying about a year after I had Lily, into Liam's room.

He wasn't best pleased but I pointed out he could throw his clothes over the handlebars, rather than on the floor, which means I won't have to stoop so much when I'm picking up his dirty washing. I've squir-relled away the rest of the rubbish wherever I could.

Along with the house, I've benefitted from a mini makeover. I've taken care with my make-up, I had my hair blow-dried and I'm wearing a new shirt. I'm wearing accessories: hooped earrings and multiple bracelets. I'm now worried that rather than channel-ling hippy chic, I'm more gypsy fortune teller.

I've bought scarlet gladioli, because they're dra-matic and impactful but don't break the bank. I'm just hunting out a long thin vase—I know we used to have one; I think it may be in one of the boxes that I've just moved up to the attic—when the doorbell rings.

Abigail. She is even more glamorous in the flesh than either I remembered her or the photos on the internet revealed. She is five foot eight, four inches taller than I am, and yet seems somehow dainty, frail. Maybe it's because she's been through something so awful recently. Her skin is pale, cool and smooth. No spots, no freckles, no lines or creases. She looks brand new. I fight an urge to caress her cheekbones. They are so sharp, I might prick my finger and draw blood, like people do in fairy tales if they touch a spinning wheel. Her hair is sleek, slightly longer than she wore it at university, blunt-cut at the shoulder. Glossy. With her arrives a waft of something exotic, a shiver of something exciting.

After all this time, it's good to see her.

"Darling." She flings her arms around me and hugs me close to her. I feel her collarbone and can smell her perfume and cigarettes. I'm surprised she smokes. I thought it was practically a criminal offence in LA.

"You look amazing," she gushes. Her voices oozes—I think of amber syrup sliding off a spoon.

I almost believe her. I mean, she sounds sincere but I have mirrors and "amazing" is a stretch.

She holds me at a distance, her hands on my upper arms and her head tilted to one side. "Amazing," she repeats. Breathily. And now. Yup, despite the evidence, I believe her. She flicks her eyes at my newly purchased bay trees that stand proud and neat in pots, either side of the door. Yesterday, when I dragged the girls to the local garden centre to purchase them, I'd thought they were the most perfect things. Now, under her gaze they look a little try-too-hard. My fault, not hers.

"Come in, come in," I say. "Go right through to the kitchen. I've baked."

"You've baked!" She repeats this as though it's the most astonishing thing she's ever heard. In truth, it is quite astonishing. I only bake about half a dozen times a year and four of those occasions are to make birthday cakes.

The scent of dough, butter and cream drifts through the hallway. Tempting and comforting. Suddenly, I feel a little shy about admitting to baking. It seems like too much of an effort; I doubt Abigail ever eats cake anyhow. She can't possibly, not with a figure like hers. Still, she makes all the right noises; she insists it smells like heaven and that she can't wait to try them.

Lily is bouncing around her like a puppy. Imogen is holding back a little but is clearly transfixed. Abigail is possibly the most glamorous and beautiful woman they have ever seen in real life.

"Where shall I put this?" The taxi driver startles me. He's coming up our garden path pulling the most enormous suitcase.

"Oh, I'll take that," I say.

"That's twenty-eight fifty."

"Right, right." Abi is already in the kitchen. I can see Lily has climbed onto her knee. It would be a shame to disturb her when she's just got settled. I reach for my purse and pay the man.

I pull the enormous case into the hallway and leave it at the bottom of the stairs. Ben or Liam can move it later. In the kitchen, I turn to Abi with a beam. "I can hardly believe you are here, in my house," I say excitedly.

"Nor can I." She has only a hint of an accent now. Of course she does. She's been living in the States for over a decade but as a result I can't quite read her tone. Obviously, the circumstances that have brought her here mean she's not going to be feeling ecstatic. "Have you paid the taxi?"

"Yes."

"Did you ask for a receipt?"

"Oh, no. I didn't think." I'm not in the sort of business that you can claim back expenses so it never crossed my mind.

"Never mind." She bends to root in her bag and I expect her to reach for her purse to reimburse me; instead she pulls out a packet of cigarettes. I should tell her about our non-smoking policy. I don't. I'm not exactly sure why. I don't want to make her feel uncomfortable. I don't want to seem unwelcoming. I rummage around in a cupboard until I find a saucer that will act as an ashtray.

"What would you like to drink?" I glance at the Krups coffee machine which I'm disproportionately proud of. Ben bought it for me last Christmas and it makes a mean cup: Americano, cappuccino, espresso, caffeinated, decaffeinated. It's pretty cool. However, just in case Abi isn't a coffee drinker anymore, I've also bought a variety of herbal teas: chamomile, peppermint, lemon and ginger.

"Oh, I don't mind. I'm happy with red or white. Or a G&T, if that's your thing. Whatever."

My eyes compulsively slide to the clock on the wall. It's just after four. I don't know what to do. I have a rule that I don't drink before seven. It's something I introduced when Liam was a baby because otherwise there was a danger I'd start drinking at 11:00 a.m. or something. I also limit myself to just one glass during a weeknight.

Suddenly, these rules seem a bit shaming and provincial. I pull a bottle of white from the fridge and pour two glasses. I hope it is still OK—I think we opened it on Sunday.

I place one glass in front of her and nurse mine self-consciously. Imogen whispers in my ear, "I'm going to tell Daddy." I bat her away.

"So, tell me everything," I say with an expansive wave of my arms.

"Like I said in my email, I found out Rob was having an affair, the bastard. I couldn't stay with him for another moment."

I glance nervously at the girls. They are wide-eyed, agog. "Oh yes. You must tell me everything about Rob, but I meant other things, more general things."

Abi looks confused. Clearly for her there aren't any other conversations to be had right now. There is nothing else on her mind.

I try to give her some prompts. "What was it like living in America?" I regret the question immediately. I sound so naive. It's not like I don't know anything about the States. We have been there. To Orlando. Once. Although, obviously, I realise that Disney World isn't representative. It doesn't cover it. It's a big place. Huge.

Abi shrugs. "I couldn't possibly say. I don't know where to start."

It's odd because I know more about her than she's told me. Well, she hasn't told me much. That's the weird thing about Googling people. It forces a false one-way intimacy. I glance at Abi and am shocked to see she is pressing the bridge of her nose, dewy-eyed—she's obviously trying to stem tears.

"Oh no, Abi. You poor thing. I'm sorry." I want to kick myself. I always say the wrong thing. I'm nervous. It's odd having her here after so long, and exciting, too. My demand that she "tell me everything" was far too flip. Now, she's crying. I've made her cry. That's the last thing I wanted to do. I'm embarrassed and sad for her, yet also flattered that she's letting her guard down in front of me. Her emotions are so real, and expressing them is a true testament to our friendship. It's as though the long years, since we last saw each other, have been swept aside.

"No, *I'm* sorry."

I should have been more careful, more tactful. Just because she looks stunning doesn't mean she's not suffering. I sit forward in my seat. I want every ounce of my body to demonstrate that I'm here for her, that I want to help her.

"It's just been so hard. Such a shock," she mutters, staring at me, her big black-brown eyes filled with incomprehension. *How could this have happened to me?* she's asking, as about a zillion women before her have asked.

Ben is a faithful sort of man, and for that I'm infinitely grateful. His father played around and then eventually left Ellie when Ben was fourteen; he swore he'd never cause the same hurt. But just because my husband is faithful it doesn't mean I don't have a clue about men who are not, of which there seem to be very many. Working in a dress shop gives surprising insight; once women are inside the changing room, they think they're in a confessional box. People tell me stuff. A lot of stuff. It's rarely good.

But Abigail *is* surprised it's happened to *her*. I reach towards her and gently put my hand on her arm because I'm not capable of finding the correct words.

"Married affection," she corrects herself, "married love, is often undervalued just because it's reliable. That's a tragedy, isn't it?" I nod. "It's a tragedy that we don't value reliability. If our fridge breaks, we throw it out. We don't try to fix it and we don't care what becomes of that fridge, if it's left to rot, if it makes the earth bulge. Landfill." She's warming to her metaphor. "People treat their marriages like that a lot of the time. I think I'm an old fridge. He's got himself a new model, the sort that dispenses ice and has a fancy drawer to keep vegetables fresh."

"You've lost me," I murmur.

"Yeah, I'm dragging out the comparison, but you see my point. I'm on the scrap heap."

"Don't say that."

"Why not? It's true. It was Valentine's Day. Did I tell you that?"

I gasp and shake my head. Ouch, that's cruel.

"He hadn't mentioned any plans for the evening, which was unusual. Normally we make quite a thing of Valentine's night, a celebration, you know?"

"Mmm," I mumble, not committing. To be honest, Ben and I are not big celebrators of Valentine's Day. We might remember to pass one another a card across the breakfast table, or we might not. Valentine's Day often falls in the half-term holiday, and we're usually more wrapped up in balancing childcare. The most romantic thing Ben can do for me around then is work from home.

"Last year, we went to Hawaii. It seems like five minutes ago. I can still smell the flora and fauna. I can still feel the warm, tranquil waters. It really is a breathtaking place. We had a candlelit dinner on the beach, prepared by the islands' top chef and served to us by a butler."

"Wow." I know she's telling me about the romantic gestures of a man she found with his pants around his ankles, but wow. It's hard not to be a tiny bit impressed.

"One year, he flew me to New York and we went

ice-skating in Central Park, then drank hot chocolates in a cutesy log cabin café. Another year we had a helicopter tour of LA at night. He always sent me two dozen red roses. We always did *something*. This year he hadn't mentioned what we'd be doing. I just thought he'd planned something extra special. I wanted to be prepared, so as soon as I finished at the studio I dashed to the beautician. Had the usual: a manicure, pedicure, a Brazilian. You know?"

I do not know. I mean, of course I know in theory that this is what women do to prepare for a special night but I can't remember the last time I went to a beautician. I can paint my own nails and, as for the other business, well, let's just say Ben has learnt to love the retro look. He's lucky if I pluck my eyebrows. I just find life busy and tricky enough without having to inflict extra pain on myself for an aesthetic that precisely one person is going to benefit from. I mean, I'd never ask him to put hot wax on his best bits. Ben has never complained about my lack of grooming in that area; it's not as though he needs help finding his target.

I don't interrupt Abigail to tell her as much. I know she'd be shocked and think I'm slovenly.

"I popped to the salon for a blow-dry and it was just chance that my stylist was running ahead of schedule. What were the odds, on Valentine's Day? Normally there's a backlog. I was just going home to get changed, and then my plan was to return to the studio so that he could meet me there. I wanted to look fresh and fabulous but without admitting to making the effort. When I saw his car on the driveway, I was excited. That's the worst of it, Mel, I was actually excited to think he was home. I thought maybe we'd have a little afternoon delight, sod the blow-dry."

I realise that she means the sex she was planning would be the sort to mess up her hair. It's a bit more detail than I need.

"I knew there was something wrong the moment I went into the house. I could smell her."

I glance nervously at the girls. Ostensibly they are playing with their Aquabeads, making coasters or something, caught up in their own worlds, but I'm never certain—they both have big flappy ears and love eavesdropping on my conversations. I throw a significant nod in their direction to give Abi a warning to be careful of what she says in front of them, but I don't think she catches my drift.

"I could smell her perfume. And there was music playing. Unfamiliar music. Rob usually listens to Oasis or Blur, stuck in the 1990s, hasn't bought a track since, but I could hear this heavy pounding beat. Hip-hop or something. I didn't call out, I carefully closed the door behind me and crept up the stairs. Knowing what I was going to see but praying that I was wrong."

"But you weren't wrong," I murmur gently. I reach for the cake plate and offer her a chocolate brownie. I hope that's enough for today—she can tell me more later. I'm dying to hear more, I'm so flattered that she's being open with me, but I'm also terrified that she doesn't have a filter and the girls are going to hear too much.

"I sneaked up the stairs, like a criminal in my own house. The bedroom door was open, and I could see clothes on the floor. They were at it like animals."

I glance at the girls again. It's unlikely they understood that.

"He was taking her from behind." Or that. "Her breasts were swinging, practically in my face." But that I think they got. "He didn't even notice me until after he climaxed."

"How about another glass of wine?" I say, jumping to my feet.

Abi's eyes follow me. Dejected. Distraught.

Hearing about Rob's infidelity isn't pleasant but it isn't a surprise to me, as it is to her. I've long since thought that he's an arrogant, untrustworthy creep. One of the reasons Abi and I haven't stayed in touch is that I really didn't like being around Rob. I get no pleasure in being proven right.

The girls have abandoned the coaster making and migrated towards Abi and me. I can't decide if it was the lure of the brownies or if they did hear enough of her conversation and feel curious. It's awkward. Obviously, Abi isn't used to being around kids and self-censoring. They stare at her, transfixed, somehow able to sense—even at their young ages—that they are in the presence of something, someone, truly exciting.

Abi watches them as they cram cake into their little pink and pouty mouths. She can't help but be enchanted, too. Even in their little sweatshirts, grubby from a day at school, they are adorable.

"I should have brought gifts," she says with a sigh.

"No, no," I insist. I didn't expect gifts. Although the girls might. They shouldn't. It's not something I approve of or encourage. However, we are pretty lucky. On the whole, when people turn up for dinner or lunch, they invariably arrive with a bottle of wine for me and Ben and chocolates or sweets for the kids. It doesn't matter that Abi hasn't thought to bring a little something. Yes, she's staying with us for—well, actually I'm not sure how long she is staying for, it hasn't been discussed—some time at least, but that doesn't mean we should expect gifts.

All that said, the girls hover, none too discreetly, over her handbag. They are clearly hoping she's bluffing and that she might produce something any moment now, like a magician produces a rabbit from a hat. She does seem rather magical.

Abi sees them loiter with intent and takes the hint, but it's obvious to me that she really hasn't brought anything. She roots around her handbag, pulls out a half-eaten packet of nicotine chewing gum.

"I was trying to quit. Until all this happened," she explains. For a moment, she seems to consider gifting the gum to them but then thinks better of it. "Ah, here we go!" She pulls out a duty-free plastic bag and then passes Lily a Clinique lipstick and hands Imogen a bottle of Chanel No. 5.

The girls look stunned, not because of the brands, which mean nothing to them, but because someone has just handed them make-up.

"Oh no, they couldn't accept those," I say hastily.
"Why not?"

I don't know how to reply. I can't explain that the

gifts are inappropriate and clearly unintended for the recipients; those objections seem rude. Nor can I say they'd be more greatly appreciated if she gifted them to me. I get new perfume once a year, Christmas, off my mum and dad. They buy me Eternity by Calvin Klein. They've bought the same one for years. I love it but can barely smell it on myself anymore, I'm that used to it. I suddenly imagine the excitement of wearing a new scent and want to grab the box off Imogen.

But the objection that the gifts might be more dearly appreciated by me is null and void, since Imogen and Lily are openly ecstatic. They are both wearing a gash of scarlet lipstick somewhere in the vicinity of their mouths. Imogen has ripped the perfume box open and is liberally spraying the scent around the room as though it's air freshener.

"Don't waste that, Immie. It's expensive."

"Oh, they're happy," says Abi. Again, I can't quite compute her tone. Maybe she's making a delighted observation or she could be inferring I'm a nag and that I should leave them alone.

"What do you say, girls?" I hate it that I have to prompt them. They are normally quite well mannered but I think the adultness of the gift has overwhelmed them. They mumble none-too-convincing thank-yous. Embarrassed, I mutter, "You know how kids are."

I wonder, does she? How much contact has she had? Other than the people who turn up on her chat-show sofa, does she have any interaction with kids? Is she a godmother to anyone? She must be, right? She's perfect godparent material.

At that moment, I hear the front door bang against

the hall wall and a rucksack being dropped. I look out of the kitchen window and notice that the street lamps are on, the sky has turned a deep indigo; it will be black as a bruise in another hour. "Liam's home," I announce. "He's been at football practice."

Liam lopes into the room and I am, as always, so very pleased to see him. Liam has an easy, cheerful manner, besides which he manages his two younger sisters with flair and effective ease; he'll probably be able to retrieve the lippy and scent. I know Abi will be impressed by his height and his manners—all my friends always are.

"Liam, come and meet a friend of mine." I jump up and rush to him. I thread my arm through his, just resisting presenting him with a *ta-da*. "This is Abi— we went to university together."

He was expecting her, or at least he should have been; the house has been turned upside down by her imminent arrival and yet he looks surprised. Typical boy. It's possible that he's forgotten we've a house guest staying for a few days. Still, his manners are as perfect as ever. He leans forward and extends his hand for her to shake. She reaches for it and at the same time gracefully pulls herself up to standing.

"Oh my God. I wouldn't have known him."

"Well, you haven't seen him since he was about two months old," I point out, laughing.

"He's—" She pauses, remembering that he's in the room. "You're all grown up," she murmurs, obviously shocked that in a blink of an eye my baby has turned into this. Looking at Liam no doubt makes Abi feel old in a way that even birthdays can't. I totally understand. Kids are like egg timers. Time slips through your fingers like sand, as you stand back and watch them grow.

"A-levels this year," I say proudly.

"Really? What subjects?"

"Maths, philosophy and politics," Liam reels off his subject choices.

"Wow, clever as well." I'm grateful that she hasn't spelt out exactly what he is, besides clever.

He's handsome.

There's no doubt about it. Quite particularly so. But he's young and absolutely hates it when my friends say as much, even though they are only trying to pay him a compliment. Even now, under her gaze, he blushes a little bit. He keeps his head down, his blond, sleek, straight fringe falling over his eyes. His eyes are arguably his best feature. Deep, dark blue pools. Framed with long, thick lashes. I already pity the girls who are going to feel the heat of his gaze once he fully understands the power of it.

I suppose there will be quite a few. He has been seeing Tanya for eight months now; it's serious but it can't be *it*. He's too young. There were girls before her, and there will be others after.

"Yeah, he's smart," I say, not being able to hide my pride. "Wants to change the world, does our Liam. Don't you, love?"

Liam shrugs. He thinks I'm being flip about his ambitions to become a politician, to champion the rights of those without voices, to find a way of doing the right thing in a world where doing the wrong thing seems to pay, but I'm not. I'm proud of him.

A little daunted, to be honest. His ambitions seem so big.

Liam turns to his sisters, engaging with genuine interest. "What have you got on your face?"

"Lipstick," they chorus, giggling proudly. They fling themselves at him and cling like limpets. Although he is too old to comfortably accept a hug from his mum, I'm pleased to say he still cuddles his younger sisters with genuine zeal. Well, really, they don't give him any choice.

"Have you two had your tea?" he asks.

I glance at the clock guiltily. It's past six. I normally feed the girls by quarter to five. I've been distracted by Abi's arrival. "Wow, no, no, they haven't. You must be starving, girls." Although probably not—Abi hasn't touched the brownies and yet there's only one left on the plate. "What do you want?" I ask.

Liam sees my panic and somehow senses my desire to stay put and chat with Abi some more. He waves his hand. "I'll do it. No problem. What's it to be, girls? Scrambled egg or beans on toast?"

"No, honestly, love, I'll do their tea but if you could just go and see they wash their hands. Perhaps listen to them reading for school, while I put something on for us all."

Liam leads them out of the room. Abi and I smile at one another as we listen to their chatter and laughter trail upstairs.

"He's quite something."

"Thank you."

"You did a fine job, Mel." She looks me in the eye and nods.

"Thank you. I didn't do it on my own. Ben is a brilliant dad and my parents have been such a help."

"Yup, I don't doubt it, but it's mostly you."

I nod and accept her compliment because it's what I like to believe. Not that I mostly did the bringing up. But that he is mostly me. He's a fine boy and he is mostly mine. Nothing to do with the boy I had a one-night stand with, someone I hardly knew; he is irrelevant.

Suddenly Abi looks serious and intense. She reaches for my hand, looks me in the eye and says, "Thank you for having me. You've saved my life."

"Don't be daft." It's an expression, right? I mean, I know it is, except that her eyes are all dewy.

"I'm not being daft. I'm one hundred per cent serious. If you hadn't responded to my email, I don't know what I would have done. I really don't. You, inviting me here, it gave me a purpose."

I pat her hand and mumble about being "Happy to help. It's the least I can do." And it is. It really is.

CHAPTER EIGHT

ABIGAIL

Abigail lay in the funny box room on the lumpy sofa bed and wondered how her life had come to this. It was humiliating, unfair.

Her suitcase barely squeezed into the room. There certainly wasn't space to hang everything she'd brought with her, even though she'd only brought a fraction of what she owned. She hadn't known what to expect. Not exactly, but whatever it was, it was not this. On her plane journey to England, she had thought of the last time she saw Melanie Field, now Melanie Harrison. She'd been a nursing mother. Drab, tired, strangely ashamed. Abi hadn't known what to say to her then. It had seemed easier not to say anything at all. For years.

But here she was, invited back to the very bosom of Melanie's life, on the back of just one email after seventeen years. It was almost too easy. So, Mel hadn't been able to resist throwing her doors wide open, despite holding them fast shut for so many years. Was it because Abi was famous? People loved her celebrity. Or was it pity? Guilt? Abi had laid herself open in the email. It would have taken a hard woman to ignore the plea for friendship and support, at such a difficult time. Mel had never been hard. She'd been determined, resilient, sometimes even selfish, but not hard. Abi had counted on it.

Yes, here she was, in the very heart of the family. Naturally, Abi had friends in Los Angeles who had families, but they also had nannies and pools and space. Melanie had none of that.

Abi's senses had been assaulted all evening as she was absorbed into their home. The house was shabby, cluttered, noisy, chaotic. There were things everywhere. Just so many things. Toys, books, ornaments, cushions, candles, pens, cards, pictures and clothes, which came in every variety: clean, dirty, ironed, crumpled.

Hilariously, Ben said Mel had been manically tidying in anticipation of Abi's visit; she couldn't even imagine what it must have looked like before. They didn't have much money to throw about, that was obvious. With the notable exception of the hallway, which had been recently (badly) decorated, every other wall was in dire need of a freshen-up. Carpets were worn thin on the stairs, there was a stain on the sofa, the crockery was pretty but she'd spotted two bowls with chips.

Also, it was so loud. The TV was always on, even when no one was in the sitting room, the same went for the radio in the kitchen; besides that, the girls squealed, shouted, sang, argued or laughed pretty much all the time, literally non-stop. Mel and Ben took it in turns to yell up the stairs as they tried to capture someone's attention; only Liam had any sense of serenity.

And the smells. Obviously, Mel had lit a few candles before Abi arrived but underneath that were the scents of the family bashing and clashing up against each other in the house. She could smell the baking that had taken place in her honour, the tomatoes, basil, fried mince in the bolognese sauce, the substrate in the hamster's cage, the urine in the cats' tray. She could also smell the people. The little girls' bubble bath, Ben's aftershave, Mel's hairspray, Liam's youth.

Abi was dizzy with the energy in the family home. The mystery as to why Melanie didn't post much on Facebook had been solved though: there was nothing much to brag about.

Except.

Well, they all looked good. Not Mel. She had once been pretty but was now diminished; she didn't take care of herself as she ought. Ben, however, was quite something. Undeniably handsome. And the son. Beautiful. Youthful. Perfect. The girls were a treat to look at, too. Adorable. And while the house was shabby, cluttered, noisy, chaotic, it was also so obviously fun. Happy. Loving. While it was noisy, the sound that was heard most often was laughter. And the smells: a vibrant, potent contrast to the sterility of her own home, that rarely smelt of anything other than cigarette smoke or cleaning fluids (on a Tuesday and Friday when the maid visited).

Melanie's house was ugly. Yet, on some level Abi loved it.

Melanie's house was beautiful on so many levels. Abi hated it.

CHAPTER NINE

MELANIE

I was never ashamed that I had sex. It wasn't like Liam's father was my first—he was my third as a matter of fact, if you're the type that counts. I was more ashamed at the carelessness I'd demonstrated by having *fruitful* sex. There was no need for an accidental pregnancy in October 1999. It was the turn of the millennium. We had science and everything on our side.

"Haven't you heard of condoms?" My brother spat out this question, unable to meet my eye—whether through anger or his own embarrassment, I was never certain. It was a fair question.

I was also ashamed that I couldn't soften the blow by introducing a lovely boyfriend into the mix, someone who was willing to stand by me and at least show up at the prenatal scans or, better yet, make an honest woman of me as my mum so blatantly wanted.

And it was awful, the way it happened. I hate thinking about it. Even now, all these years on when the result of the dreadful night has turned into such an overtly wonderful thing: a decent, intelligent, kind young man. Just thinking about that night always makes me start mentally humming random tunes so that I don't delve too deeply into my thoughts. Into my memories. He didn't force himself on me or anything awful like that. Liam wasn't a product of rape. He was the product of selfishness and irresponsibility. On both sides. Honestly, he deserves a better providence story.

I was drunk. And, he—well, he was hot. It was as simple as that. So drunk and so hot that I thought that withdrawal seemed a reasonable option. I was the one to suggest it. He'd have been happy with a blow job. Of course he would: biology is designed to give men a leg up and to stomp on women. It was me who pushed for more. I wanted him inside me. However fleetingly, I wanted it absolutely.

I remember my dad pleading, "But you must have a name. Can't you tell us his name?" I really wished I could.

On about the hundredth time he asked, I finally replied, "Ian." I know my tone was snippy. Awkwardness often manifests itself that way with me.

"A surname?" He probed gently, fighting his frustration, yet sensing a breakthrough, sniffing at it like a bloodhound. Aware if he moved too suddenly, he might scare me off; a terrified rabbit.

"I didn't catch it. It was a loud club," I muttered sulkily.

Dad hung his head in his hands. Rubbing his eye sockets with the heels of his palms, he aged in front of me. Suddenly, his head snapped up, fortified by a new idea. "But he's studying at your university. We could get in touch with the chancellor, or what have you, and demand they look at their records. We could track down all the Ians that are registered." He seemed momentarily hopeful. It was sad, in the true sense of the word, not the way Imogen uses it now.

"What and do an identity parade?" I snarled, sarcastically.

"Do something!" Dad yelled. Dad is not a shouter, so this upset me, but I couldn't let him pursue this warped version of Cinderella, chasing across the kingdom of Birmingham University to see if the shoe fit. I did the only thing I could think of that would put an end to the business.

"He doesn't go to my uni. He said he was visiting a friend. Freshers' week, you know. It's packed. People float through. He came from down south somewhere. I don't think he ever said exactly where." It was safe telling my father that the man responsible for my downfall was a southerner. An intelligent man and reasonable in most ways, largely devoid of prejudices, my dad was and is irrationally unsettled by the south: its size, its smugness, its slickness. It suited him to believe all forms of trouble came from down south. Why would this trouble be any different?

Still, he pursued the matter. "What friend? Did he at least give you the name of the friend?"

"No. He didn't."

Dad sighed—it was like all his breath was coming

out of him. "There doesn't seem to have been much talking," he commented sadly.

"No, not talking," said Mum, eyeing my tightly rounded belly with poignancy. I couldn't drag my gaze to meet hers. In fact, I spent months looking at people's shoes.

Abigail also thought we ought to pursue my partner in crime. She insisted on returning to the club I'd said we met at, in the hope he'd be there, or at least, I'd recognise his friend. It was mortifying.

It was loud, thumping, strobe lights sweeping the room, making me feel dizzy. It was packed, heaving with noisy, sweaty gangs of people looking for a good time. Dancing, kissing, drinking, laughing. They seemed alien to me. I held my hands in front of my belly, protecting my bump from the raucousness.

"Where do we start?" yelled Abi above the throb of music that was banging and thrashing through the club. Even she looked slightly defeated. I couldn't believe she'd ever held any hope. She must have been expecting crowds this large and dense. We'd come here together often enough.

I sighed, looked up and gave a cursory look around. "Nope, he's not here—we might as well go."

"Not so fast. You can't just give up like that. This place is huge. We need to have a good scour about. You do want to find him, right? That's what you said."

I nodded. Yes, that's what I'd said. That's what everyone had expected me to say. But I knew I would not find him there. I was one hundred per cent sure of it. "It's been months. He was visiting a friend."

"Yes, you've said." Abi's stare was penetrating.

"Why do I get the feeling you're not telling me everything?"

"Can we just go home? My back is aching."

This was all a long time ago. I do not associate Liam with that mess, that anger and disappointment of those early months. Not anymore. He's nothing but a joy. A funny, good-looking, bright kid. He's turned out just fine.

So why have I invited this reminder of that time into my home? Someone who knew me from before? Abigail Curtiz in particular.

Why am I pressing the bruise?

CHAPTER TEN

ABIGAIL

Friday, 23 February

Abi was pleased that Melanie had taken the day off work. It wasn't popular with her boss, apparently, as Friday was a busy day at the dress store. Abigail said she really didn't have to inconvenience herself but Mel insisted, as Abi knew she would. Being with Melanie reminded Abi of how things had been when she was at the peak of her career, when she was twenty-eight, twenty-nine, and people liked doing things for her.

Then, they sent her invitations to their parties, and cars to ensure she got to said parties in comfort, then they'd send flowers the day after, a thank-you for her attendance. The attention had been dwindling for some time, but Abigail hadn't realised how much she missed it until Mel started to make a fuss of her. Although Mel's motivations were quite different from those who used to fawn around Abi back in the day. Mel didn't want a job or an introduction to Rob or even the chance to be snapped at her side by the paparazzi.

What did she want? Abigail believed everyone wanted something.

They caught the train to Stratford-upon-Avon. It was a chilly but dry day, which was as much as you could hope for the last week in February in England. They wandered about, visiting the notable houses of Shakespeare's womenfolk, his wife and daughter. They dipped into tiny boutique shops and bought small treats: handmade chocolates, a lime green scarf, a bottle of organic grapefruit tonic. They then went for a cream tea at a smart hotel. Abi noticed that Mel was bright with excitement. She was easy to seduce.

"Isn't this wonderful?" commented Abi, glancing around the dining room, which was tastefully decorated in light greys and awash with a sense of gentry: white linen tablecloths, the clink of a spoon against bone china, delicate cakes stacked on tiered plates. "I adore your family. But just the two of us having this time together is such a treat."

Mel agreed with more enthusiasm than was seemly for a woman who loved her husband and kids to distraction. She admitted, "I can't remember when I last did anything so intrinsically indulgent."

Abigail insisted that Mel eat the last salmon sandwich and have both the little chocolate cakes; when Mel demurred—making embarrassed, reluctant comments about her weight—Abi tutted, swept them away and insisted that Mel was beautiful. Blushing, Mel tucked in. "I'd forgotten quite what it's like to have a bestie girl friend," she giggled.

Obviously Mel meant she'd forgotten what it was like to be picked out as Abi's friend. Abi had a talent of bathing those she singled out in a unique sense of importance. She knew the power of her intense interest. She knew it was flattering and motivating. Look what her attention had done for Rob. Without her, he probably would never have gone as far as he had. In Abigail's company, Mel unfurled, as she always had. She became more vivid, stronger and wittier than usual. More daring. More entitled.

"Oh, come on, you must have loads of friends," Abigail insisted. Although she wasn't sure. If Mel did have friends, would they have let her become so dowdy? Real friends would surely have encouraged her to visit one of those women who told you which colour suited you most. Beige was not Mel's colour.

"I'm friendly enough with the people I work with, but mostly they're young."

"We're young."

Mel laughed. "You, maybe. You look about twenty-seven. I'm wearing all my thirty-seven years; these girls I work with are just out of college. You know, eighteen. They work for a couple of years at the shop and then move on. Mostly, I feel motherly towards them, as they're closer to Liam's age than mine."

"Don't mums make friends at playgroups and such? I always thought that's why we lost touch, because your life was so full of new people. New mums."

Mel's colour intensified. "I did join a couple of mother-and-baby groups when I had Liam, but people kept assuming I was the au pair. As such, they thought I couldn't relate to them, share their conversations and experiences, so largely they ignored me. When they did discover I was his mum, they were shocked at my youth."

"And presumably your lack of partner?" said Abi, bluntly.

"Well, yes, that, too. So, they continued ignoring me." Mel shrugged.

"But it must have been different with the girls."

"Yes, then I could have made friends and—to an extent—I did. However, people generally assumed that Imogen was my first baby. Once they discovered I had a son nine years older, the playdates tended to dry up."

Abigail forked the tiniest scrap of Victoria sponge into her mouth. "Why?"

"Nine-year-old boys are energetic, cheeky. Sometimes hard going. Mums of newborns don't appreciate that—they thought Liam was a pain. I never could stand to be anywhere where it was obvious other people would prefer him not to be."

"Which mum could?"

Mel smiled. "Thanks, Abi."

"For what?"

"For getting that. Ben and my mum always thought I was being overly sensitive and that I should cut the first-time mums some slack. But I became bored of the endless comments such as, 'Gosh, he doesn't know his own strength, does he?' Or 'If only little boys came with volume control buttons.' Liam, for the record, was a perfectly normal little boy in terms of energy levels and probably slightly better than average when it came to obedience. I will admit he was pretty noisy."

Abigail laughed. "Should we upgrade this afternoon tea?"

"Upgrade?" Mel looked at the array of goodies spread in front of her, and no doubt thought of the ones she'd already chomped her way through. She probably couldn't imagine how it could possibly be made any better.

"Let's order a glass of champagne. What am I thinking about? We're on the train. Let's order a bottle."

Mel demurred for less than five seconds and then agreed, as Abi knew she would.

As she sipped, Mel talked more about her friends, or lack of them. "My closest school-gate friends are Becky Ingram and Gillian Burton. They've daughters Imogen's age and I've known them a few years now, since reception class. We sometimes carpool, we sit through adorable but clumsy ballet performances together. That sort of thing."

"Fun," said Abi. Mel gave her a look that suggested she doubted Abi could mean this, but Abi did. What could be dreamier than watching your daughter skip about in a tutu?

"We go to a book club together once a month. They also go shopping and to the tennis club on a weekly basis."

"I know the type."

"They're very kind," said Mel defensively. "We bail one another out if there's a problem with child-care at pickup time. Truthfully, they bail me, as neither of them have jobs, other than the one of raising a family, which seems like a luxury to me. They're never late for pickup."

"They sound lovely," commented Abi, although she withheld any conviction from her voice, because she secretly wanted Mel to understand—and then confess—that they were quite ordinary friends.

Mel obliged. "They are kind to me but ever since Taylor Swift and her bunch of leggy girlfriends started promoting themselves as the ultimate girl gang—you know, arms slung across each other's shoulders, snaked around one another's waists—I've had a niggling feeling that I'm missing out on the whole female friendship thing."

Abi smiled encouragingly. "Girlfriends are cool."

"They are," said Mel firmly. "How had I forgotten that?" She sipped her champagne and became more confessional. "I guess because I spent my twenties wiping various baby fluids and singing nursery rhymes, the friendship rituals—that I know other women enjoy—took a back seat."

Abi reached forward and squeezed Mel's hand. Mel necked her glass of champagne and Abi quickly refilled it.

"I've never had a friend who would drive a hundred miles, armed with chocolate and wine, to avert my personal crises." Mel paused. Something hit her, not just the alcohol content of the Moët. "At least, not since you, Abi."

Abi had never actually had to drive one hundred miles—they'd shared student accommodation when they were young—so it was an untested theory but it was a lovely idea.

"I have held back your hair as you've said a second hello to your dinner and cocktails. Twice, I think," said Abi. She wasn't certain. She had a strong stomach; she had done this for many friends at university; Mel might have been among them. Or maybe not. Mel laughed and didn't contradict her, so Abi assumed she must have.

"I suppose you have a lot of close friends." Mel sounded almost sulky.

"Absolutely!" Abi lied. "I need them to help me forgive my embarrassing mistakes and appalling faux pas."

"I can't imagine you have many of those."

"I've had my share." Abi shrugged.

"That's what friends do, though, don't they? Forgive your moments of crazy recklessness or selfishness," Mel declared with intensity.

"If they can," said Abi. For a moment, there was a silence between them. Heavy and layered.

Mel gulped back the champagne and looked longingly at the bottle. Then she seemed to shake herself. "Oh, I don't know. I mean even if, in some alternate universe, Gillian or Becky were interviewed for *Hello!* magazine, I'm pretty sure they wouldn't use the opportunity to declare that their very survival is dependent on my friendship, the way Taylor Swift's friends might," said Mel with a sad sigh.

Abi remembered this about her now. She became

emotional on alcohol. Abi leaned across the table. "Maybe not, but you know I would, right? I mean, what you've done for me, scooped me up, invited me into your home. It's so generous. Above and beyond. I'm more than grateful."

Mel smiled and blushed. Abi had thought Mel might have grown out of the blushing by now; it was almost cute on a teen but a little dispiriting on a woman who ought to be more confident.

"Well, if anyone is going to be interviewed by *Hello!* it's you!" pointed out Mel laughingly. Then, more soberly, she added, "I know it's crazy because we've only been reunited for twenty-four hours, but Abi, it's like we've never been apart, isn't it? And you know, I'd do anything to make things better for you. I really would."

"People say anything, but they don't really mean it," said Abi.

Mel looked crushed. "Well, I mean it. Anything at all," she insisted.

Abi smiled and nodded. It was exactly what she wanted to hear.

CHAPTER ELEVEN

MELANIE

I've never fallen in love at first sight. I'm a slow-burn sort. My boyfriends before Liam's father were mates before they became dates. I was never in love with Liam's father; just in lust. And Ben? Well, he had to woo me in the old-fashioned way because, basically, I was terrified he was going to hurt me—or more important, Liam—by bouncing in and then out of our lives. His good looks worked against him; it took a long time for me to trust him.

Yet, I remember back to that first moment I met Abi, I had flutters in my stomach. An instant spark, a feeling that we were meant to be together. And now, I feel it all over again. I'm not coming out here. I don't fancy her. I'm just saying being with her is intense, wonderful, uplifting. I've missed her.

I can't wait to get the girls to bed. They sense it and play up. Ben's no help because he sees Abi's visit as an excuse to pop to the gym and then no doubt he'll undo the good work as he'll nip to the local for a cold one; he rushes out the door at seven thirty.

"You've got yourself a good man there," says Abi as she waves to him from the sitting-room window. Ben waves back and grins at her as he dashes down the path. "Where is he from?"

It's a strange non sequitur comment. "Newcastle."

"His parents?"

"Newcastle." I know what she's getting at and even when it's Abi asking, it's annoying. It's hard to see her enquiry as anything other than outright prejudice. There's an implication that he's somehow not exactly British, even though he was born here and his parents were born here. "His grandparents are Jamaican," I add, because this is what she's asking and because we're proud of the fact.

"How fascinating. How wonderful. Do you ever go there for holidays?"

Her obvious enthusiasm makes me relax a little. I feel a bit ashamed that I thought she was being off. It's just that mixed-race couples still raise an eyebrow and we shouldn't. But I should never have imagined Abi would be so small-minded. "No. His mother once went to visit her aunt and uncle but Ben doesn't know anyone there," I explain. "I'd love to go one day. Take the kids, so they get to know a bit more about their heritage."

"You certainly don't have a type, do you?" she muses.

"What do you mean?" I ask carefully. I'm smiling because I don't want this to be a thing but I sense it is.

"Well, Liam's father, what was he called? Dean?"

"Ian."

"Yes, Ian. Well, he can't have looked much like Ben. Liam is so blonde."

"I think he gets that from my mother," I reply, not prepared to confirm or deny whether Liam's father was blonde. It's been a long time since I've had these sorts of conversations. I start to head towards the kitchen.

"Maybe. They do say certain genes skip a generation."

"Shall we try that grapefruit tonic?" I offer.

"I hope you mean with gin."

"Absolutely."

"Then yes." As I pass her the drink, she asks, "Does Liam mind?"

"Mind what?"

"That he doesn't look anything like the rest of you. Does he feel separate? Isolated?"

What an odd question. It's true that the rest of us all have brown hair and eyes. Ben is black and the girls have beautiful sepia brown skin. I pick up quite a good tan in the summer, although I'm a ghostly white right now; my hair has a definite kink to it; the girls and Ben have big, confident afros. Liam's hair is poker straight. He's pale and blonde, as Abi mentioned. Blue-eyed.

"We've never really dwelt on the matter." I know I sound prickly. I'm trying not to be but I am.

I nervously flick my gaze at Abi. I don't see any likenesses between Liam and his biological father, but then I can hardly remember the face of the young man who impregnated me. For me, Liam's providence is an ancient story, a closed book. Ben is his dad. And an exceptionally good one. I never feel comfortable talking about the man who brought him into being. It reflects badly on me. I worry that Liam thinks it reflects badly on him, too. Obviously, it doesn't. But kids see things weirdly. They blame themselves for things that are way out of their control.

Abi looks abashed. "No, no, silly of me to have brought it up. You do know I didn't mean anything odd." She reaches out and grabs my hand, squeezes tightly, like a child might. Impulsively, I bring our hands to my lips and kiss her knuckles. Weird, but she permits intimacy, somehow demands it.

"Of course," I reassure her. I want to move on. Get off this topic. She smiles at me, eyes glistening with relief. I matter to her. My good opinion matters to her.

The evening races by, shimmering with laughter and shared confidences. Our lives are obviously very different, yet we find things in common. We find we watch a lot of the same TV shows and we have the same view on them, we've read some of the same novels and I make a note of others Abi recommends. Abi has been to several places on my bucket list and it's fascinating to hear all about them first-hand. She strengthens my resolve to travel more, when the kids are all a bit older and when there's a bit more spare cash floating about.

Abi shows me her Instagram account. It's full of stunning, glistening, gleaming images. Her in exotic locations, in fabulous restaurants, at gigs, shows and the theatre.

"Don't you have an Insta?" she asks, not even self-conscious about the casual use of the abbreviation, as though she was sixteen. She is so confident.

"No, but maybe I should get one." I don't really mean this. Or at least I do, right now, but I won't in the morning after I've slept off the effect of the G&Ts. What would I post? I think about the food I prepare. Liam wolfs it down—there would be no time to photograph it. The girls pick and poke; in the end, everything I prepare looks like a Jackson Pollock on a plate.

"Oh, don't bother," says Abi, sounding bored. "It's so time-consuming."

"That's what Ben says. He's not a fan of social media. He thinks it's desperate and deadening. Basically, I think he just doesn't like his boss knowing too much about his personal life."

"Is that why you never post photos?"

"I suppose." I take a sip of my G&T.

Abi nods thoughtfully. "Ben's quite right. Very dignified."

Hearing her compliment Ben encourages me to add, "I've always been careful with what I post. Liam didn't grow up in an era where social media dominated childhoods. When he was very tiny, I still had photos developed at Boots. By the time every Tom, Dick and Harry was equipped with a smartphone and everyone fancied themselves to be the next Annie Leibovitz, Liam was at the age where he point-blank refused to let me take his photo, let alone allow me to post pictures of him."

Abi smiles and nods.

"I never got into the habit. I still prefer printing the shots and putting them in albums. The girls grumble about this on a regular basis. They'd love to be plastered all over the internet."

"You're a very special person to have such standards. It's unusual, Mel, to have such a high regard for privacy. You know the thing I don't like about social media?"

"What?"

"The fact that no matter how many photos I post of me meeting pop stars, politicians or the Dalai Lama—"

"You've met the Dalai Lama?" I interrupt excitedly.

She nods, smiles and carries on. "Yes, but even so, I'm in a competition I can't win."

"*You* can't possibly suffer from FOMO."

"It's more FOMOOM. Fear of missing out on motherhood," she says sadly.

"Oh."

"Social media is nothing other than an echo chamber. People are forever posting pictures of their children. Just children doing perfectly normal things, often as not—but I can't join in. Here's little Elliot or Harriet in a sandbox or in a hat, in the bath. It's so ordinary, there's a plethora of these shots, at any and every point, on my feed." Abi sighs, then straightens her back, which was unusually bowed, sniffs bravely and admits, "It's exquisitely, painfully inaccessible for me. From bump to junior school, people post practically every moment."

"I'm so sorry, Abi. I had no idea you felt this way." Why would I?

She shrugs and then tries to make a joke. "Although I do notice the photos tend to drop off once a kid gets a bit older. I guess the cute factor wears a little thin then. Not quite so appealing."

"They do go through an ugly stage," I say with a laugh. I don't mean it. I think my babies are and were beautiful every single step of the way, but I feel a sudden need to detract from their perfection. It makes no sense but I suddenly feel aware of my glut and her lack and I'm drenched with a wave of guilt. Stupidly, I think of that fairy tale—"Sleeping Beauty"—where the witch left off the invitation list swoops in and brings all sorts of trouble. I stare at my G&T glass.

It's empty. I need to slow down. My thoughts are bonkers. If anything, Abi is the fairy godmother who gets Cinderella to the ball, not a bad fairy.

"Did you hear about that man who photographed his son every day from the boy's birth to the day he turned twenty-one? He made a time-lapse video with the 7,500-odd photos. That's what I'm up against," declares Abi. "Baby worship. It's an epidemic."

"It must be hard," I admit. I love Facebook—even though I don't post pictures, I love to read other people's euphoric posts. The ones wishing the "sweetest, kindest, funniest boy/girl a happy birthday." Oblivious to the fact that everyone else is claiming the same of their child. These utter and complete testaments of love have always delighted me. Now, I see it from Abi's point of view. The vanity behind the posts. The insensitivity.

Abi shoots me a look that suggests she is irritated, if not outright angry. It is difficult to know what the right thing to say is, exactly. She juts out her chin and says firmly, "Still, I'm an absolutely awesome PANK."

"PANK?" I ask, not certain I want to know the answer.

"Professional Aunt, No Kids."

"Oh yes, you are, the girls are already totally under your spell."

"And Liam, too, I hope."

I'm not sure Liam has actually noticed Abi's existence; teens live in their own very small world but saying so to Abi would only sound as though she's ignorant of how big kids tick. The last thing she needs to hear, right now. I nod, and then ask tentatively, "Did you and Rob ever try for children?"

"Rob was the biggest child in his life. He didn't want kids."

"Oh. I see."

"He hated the idea with a vengeance."

I shift uncomfortably in my seat as she starts to brew up a new wave of invective. I wish I hadn't brought Rob up. What was I thinking? I try to cut her off. "You have plenty of time for a baby," I say encouragingly.

"I don't have plenty of time. I'm thirty-eight. But I do have *some* time. Friends of mine are getting pregnant in their forties. There are options. But first I need to divorce Rob and then meet someone new. Then get pregnant. Let's not pretend. It's not going to be easy."

We sit in silence for a moment. Both sobered by the truth of her words. Suddenly, Abi laughs. "Oh, listen to me. I sure know how to kill the mood, right?"

Coughing, I say the most honest thing I can. "You're entitled to."

She stares at me for the longest time. "Yes, I am, aren't I?" Then she asks, "How did we ever lose contact?"

I feel warmth seep through my stomach at her comment, the meaning implicit: how could we have let something so important fall by the wayside? Simultaneously, I feel sadness, guilt, grief. It's confusing.

"Well, I had Liam. You had your studies," I murmur, scratching the surface.

Abi brightens. "Bring me up to date. What have I missed?" she says with a burst of enthusiasm and excitement.

"Where to start?"

"Show me the pictures. Take me through every lost year. You said you have albums, right?"

"Well, yes, but—" I can't believe she'd be prepared to sit through them. I mean, how interesting can they be to her?

"Come on. You get the albums, I'll fill the glasses."

CHAPTER TWELVE

ABIGAIL

Despite her suspicions that Rob sometimes strayed, dallied, Abigail had never felt so inclined. She told herself that he wasn't being unfaithful, it was, at worst, just sex. Someone once told her that sex was like drinking a large G&T. Pleasant at the time, forgotten once swallowed. She didn't imagine there was ever any emotional commitment to these women, therefore there wasn't any emotional betrayal of her. Overall, he was careful, discreet. There were hints, whispers but no evidence, no facts.

Anyway, even if he was indulging himself that way, then *she* certainly wasn't going to compound the issue by also doing so. She had opportunities. If not endless, then certainly countless. But a marriage was a marriage. Vows were vows. If they weren't taken seriously, then what was the point? You could just buy a white dress and throw a party, you didn't need the solemn oath bit. That's what she'd always thought. But now she was questioning her own decisions, mourning the opportunities she'd missed. Now, she knew just how deep the betrayal ran.

When she found out, was faced with indisputable evidence, facts, she'd howled. She wanted to kill him, rip him piece from piece. A bolt of visceral violence surged through her being. She'd been lied to and cheated upon. It was wrong, it was cruel, it was unfair. She screamed, roared. Like a lioness.

Rob was passive, almost sanguine. That hurt her more; he couldn't see why she was so devastated. He said their marriage was dead anyway.

"No fucking way is it dead. Don't say that," she'd yelled.

"It is," he insisted. "You killed it with wanting a baby more than anything else. You stopped wanting me ages ago. I was a means to an end and when that didn't work out for you, you didn't want me at all."

"No, no, that's not true. That's not true!"

"When did we last have sex, Abi?"

She wasn't sure. It was months, probably, maybe a year. She didn't like to think about it. That wasn't how she saw herself, how she saw them. She was sexy. He was sexy. People assumed there was a lot of sex. But the truth was she'd started to go off it a while back.

She glared at him. How dare he say *when that didn't work out for you*, as though their childless state was some awful dollop of unluckiness. It wasn't that way. She felt fury swirl through her body, gushing like blood. She knew when she'd started to go off sex. She could give him an exact date. He should be able to work it out, if he cared to. It was the day he came home with a slight limp, told her he'd been to the hospital and had a vasectomy. Just like that, without even discussing it.

When she threw a dinner plate at him, he'd been surprised. "We agreed no kids, we agreed that forever ago." He'd said it as though it was no biggie.

No one understood. She had been thirty-six at the time; he was forty-three. When she complained to her girlfriends, they commented that he was being thoughtful, considerate, taking away the burden of responsibility from her. One or two of them leaned in and whispered to her that a man getting a vasectomy was an indicator that he wasn't planning on throwing over the first wife and starting again with a younger one. She should be pleased!

She just saw a full stop. An end. A blank. If their marriage was dead, it was because he killed it when he had that operation. Indiscreetly fucking other women? No longer being considerate enough to try to be careful? That was just a matter of scattering the ashes.

Besides, she also suspected that the vasectomy was not a considerate act designed to take the burden of responsibility away from her, it was so there would never be the chance of an accident. Either with her or, she supposed, with any of his other women, who all had the potential to turn out to be gold-diggers.

He'd always been disproportionately concerned about unplanned pregnancies. She was on the pill and she took it regularly, never daring to skip a day because he was right, they had agreed no kids, and it wouldn't be decent to try to trick him. Now, she regretted playing so fairly. Even though she had always known it was unlikely she would get pregnant while she was taking contraception, she always believed there was a chance, an infinitesimal hope. Then, after the vasectomy, she knew it was all over. She cried in the bathroom every month that she had her period.

So yeah, maybe things had become a bit snoozy in the bedroom, maybe even comatose. It would be impossible to exist in that crazy mental early stage, when all they wanted to do was grab one another and rip each other's clothes off. Truthfully, she could barely remember that stage when they couldn't see anything other than each other. When nothing else existed.

She wanted more. And he wasn't allowing her to have it. He was blocking her. It was only when she walked in on him, discovered his horrid, dirty little secret and started to yell at him—really scream, swear, shout—that she remembered feeling passion. Her indignation was so violent, her fury, her hurt so absolute that she felt something like passion. She couldn't remember wanting to rip off his clothes. She couldn't remember thinking the world was populated by just the two of them. It was a relief, in a way. It would hurt so much if she could.

She wished he was dead. Then people would have sent cards and flowers. They'd have respected her, sympathised with her. As soon as news of their split leaked out, people started to avoid her, cancelled coffee dates, didn't listen to her at production meetings, scattered to the corners of a busy room when she walked into the centre of it. They were embarrassed for her. She was drenched in shame and it should have been him. He was the shameful one.

She'd been robbed. Opportunities had been stolen from her. Years had been squandered. She'd been a fool.

But she wasn't going to be anybody's fucking fool again.

CHAPTER THIRTEEN

MELANIE

Saturday, 24 February

On Saturday evening, Abi offers to take Ben and me out for dinner as a thank-you for our hospitality. She even thinks to invite Liam along, which is so kind. He declines, preferring to spend the evening with Tanya, but it was nice of her to think to include him. We pay him and Tanya to babysit the girls and the three of us set off to Golden Orchid for Thai—it's the nicest place in the local area.

As we leave the house, Abi giggles, "Isn't that weird for you?"

"What?"

"The fact you've basically just paid them to have sex on your sofa."

"Oh my God, Abi. That is not what I have done," I laugh.

"It sort of is," Ben points out as he climbs into the front of the taxi and Abi and I scramble into the back.

"No, I paid them to see that Imogen and Lily clean their teeth and go to bed. If they have sex on the sofa, that's their business. There are some things it's best not to think about too closely."

"I just can't believe you have a son old enough to be in an adult relationship," says Abi. "I still feel like we're eighteen, don't you?"

I nod and smile. I guess I do, when I'm around Abi at least, I get glimmers of it. But until this weekend, I'd say I felt the full weight of my years. I'm not complaining, I'm just saying, I'm a mum of three.

Tanya is slight, blonde, clever and generally calm and smiley. I see her as a very positive addition to the family dynamic. The girls adore her. Almost as much as Liam does. Liam has had girlfriends before Tanya. Interchangeable, pretty, feral girls in tiny denim cut-off shorts and thick black tights, the sort who couldn't look you in the eye but could certainly roll their eyes. None of them lasted longer than six weeks and they all came with a huge dollop of teenage emotional trauma and drama.

There isn't any of that with Tanya. They are simply content and confident in one another's company. They go to the same sixth-form college and see each other most Friday and Saturday evenings—she often stays over and joins us for Sunday lunch.

I sometimes wonder what's going to happen to their relationship when they go to university. Tanya wants to be a vet and really must go where there are courses, which are few and far between. Liam wants to go into politics and is very keen to study in London—he already has a place confirmed at UCL, providing he gets the right grades.

Their one chance of avoiding a long-distance relationship is if Tanya gets accepted at the Royal Veterinary College, University of London. She won't find out for another month or so. I'm crossing my fingers for her. If that doesn't work out, I don't know how they plan to manage. It's their business and not mine. If Liam, or even Tanya, decides to discuss the matter with me, then it becomes my business, but until then I'll keep my nose out of it.

We have a great night at the Golden Orchid. Again, it flew by. Again, I get a little bit drunk, I don't know how. It sort of creeps up on me. I wonder whether it's down to that thing Abi was saying in the cab? There's something about being with her that makes me feel as though I'm eighteen again and can knock back drinks without any consequences. I want to use chopsticks in front of her, and not resort to a fork, so I don't manage to line my stomach as efficiently as I should.

Abi is a little worse for wear, too. When we are drinking our second bottle of wine, she reiterates the story of finding Rob in bed with his PA, for Ben's benefit ostensibly. Although, the way Ben squirms on his chair, I think he'd have been happier not to get the details. I discover that Abi did indeed self-censor when she told me the story in front of Imogen and Lily. In the Golden Orchid, she is less discreet, which is a little tricky because it's not a big place and the tables are quite tightly packed.

"Sneaked up the stairs," she slurs, "like a criminal.

In my own home. At it like dirty animals, they were. Tits practically hit me in my face. Slapping her arse as he came. Filthy bastard."

Ben shifts uncomfortably, coughs and then suggests we might want coffee, in much the way I offered cake when I first heard the sad story. Ben and I are not prudish. We have a good sex life. There just comes a point when that sort of thing doesn't seem appropriate conversation. My conversations with Gillian or Becky centre around OFSTED reports, not orgasms. Honestly? It's often the same conversation at the school gate; we use one another as a check and balance. Are we doing enough as parents?

I suppose Abi talks more openly. More honestly.

Abi accepts the coffee and stops talking about sex but can't seem to get away from the subject of Rob's infidelity.

"The problem is, I'm left exposed, financially *and* emotionally. What a fool I've been." She shakes her head, still stunned. "Everything I've ever done was for him. The move to America, the type of work I took on, the size of our family—or rather the non-existence thereof—were all his decisions."

Ben and I murmur sympathetic noises but don't quite commit to words.

"How has it ended up like this?" Abi wails, disbelieving. "You know I had such promise," she says, eagerly grabbing Ben's arm. "There was such possibility when we first met at university. I could have had *anyone*. *Been* anyone. Couldn't I, Mel? Tell him."

I nod because it's true.

"There's nothing more heartbreaking than squandered promise," she adds.

I glance at Ben and indicate, with an almost imperceptible shift of my head, that it might be time to get the bill. I don't feel comfortable with her laying this all out in this tiny restaurant, in this small town; I know that big ears are always flapping.

"My mother never liked him," Abi tells Ben. "Said that he'd turned my head." Ben smiles. "What?" Abi demands.

"Nothing. It's just a funny turn of phrase."

Abi laughs but she doesn't sound amused, more bitter. "You are right," she says, poking his arm, one jab per word. "I always imagine a cartoon character with its head spinning comically. But it's not so funny now because that's how I feel. Foolish, distorted. Two-dimensional." She pauses and then adds, "Terrified."

Abi starts to cry. Tears curl and swell; her long lashes can't harness them. They trickle down her face. She's a very beautiful crier.

Ben looks about and grabs a clean napkin from a nearby unoccupied table, offers it to her. She takes it and dabs her eyes. I rub her back and try to stare down the rubberneckers. I can't intimidate them—Abi is too much of a draw. It is impossible to hope that they'll even pretend to stay in their own conversations.

"I just want to undo the moment. To just rewind or wipe it out. You know?" Abi sighs and adds, with a stale air of defeatism, "I'd even settle for it happening but me not knowing about it. How pathetic is that? I want to be an ostrich. I'm willing to bury my head in the sand."

But, it's not possible to do such a thing. She can't scrub it out, she can't unknow. That's why it matters so much what you tell people, what you do to people. Some things can't be undone. Not ever.

Abi suddenly turns from upset to angry. She's always been mercurial, and drink doesn't help. Nor does an adulterous husband. "I've always feared it might happen. I've never really trusted him. He wasn't the sort you could trust." She stares at me, fuming. "How had I forgotten that?"

"I guess because you've been together for a long time," comments Ben gently. "Obviously, this is really hard."

"Yes! Eighteen is no age at all to make a decision as gargantuan as who you should spend the rest of your life with, but I did." Abi is swaying on her chair slightly. "The thing was, besides my mother, who doesn't really like anyone, everyone adored him. Didn't they, Mel?"

I shrug, unsure I can agree but feeling she really expects me to.

"You know her husband?" Ben asks, surprised.

"Yes, absolutely she does," confirms Abi. "He was studying for his PhD when we were undergrads. He tutored some of our classes."

"Not mine," I chip in.

"His power was very magnetic. Plus, he was absolutely beautiful. Wasn't he, Melanie?" She nudges me with her elbow.

"Erm, well, you remember him far better than I

do," I mutter, embarrassed. I don't want to fortify the image of Rob as an astoundingly sexy, desirable but ultimately unobtainable man. It's too sad.

"He was!" she insists. "Irresistible."

I nod—it's just easiest to go along with her.

"You know what you need, Abi," says Ben lightly. "You need to get back in the saddle."

"Nice thought," I mutter, glaring at him.

He ignores me. "Seriously. Give yourself a treat. Even the score," insists Ben.

Abigail stares at him from under her damp eyelashes but doesn't comment. I put my hand in the air and wave at the waiter, make the universal sign that asks him to bring the bill. Ben doesn't mean to be insensitive but at the risk of generalising, women just aren't like men. We don't move on so easily.

It's a long night. When we finally get home, Abi suggests we all have a nightcap. Tanya says she can't stay but will come back for Sunday lunch tomorrow. Liam walks her home, just ten minutes away. I don't want to be rude—Abi so obviously wants company—and so agree to a quick one. Ben stays up with us as well.

It's a relief when Abi stops being maudlin and instead makes us laugh with stories about her old colleagues; the way she tells it, every one of them was a marvellous character. Liam returns and delights me by not shuffling off to bed but instead settling down to hear Abi's stories and drink with us, although he sensibly stays off the hard stuff and just sips on beer.

We only call it a night at two in the morning. I can't remember when I last stayed awake until that time, let alone stayed up drinking. We polish off the whisky Ben got from my parents at Christmas. I think I suggested we start on the brandy, but Ben says he can't find it. I'm pretty sure it's in the kitchen, in plain sight, on the tray where we keep spirits. I wonder if he is really drunk and honestly can't see it or if he wants to pull the night to a close? I'm too drunk to bother to look myself and something in the back of my head is saying it's probably a good thing since, if I drink the brandy, I'll feel even worse tomorrow.

Ben and I haul ourselves upstairs, Abi says she's going outside onto the patio to smoke a cigarette. I see Ben, an avid anti-smoker, shake his head but I'm just relieved she hasn't lit up in the sitting room. Liam, the angel, starts to clear away the glasses.

"You're a good kid," I say, but am surprised that it comes out as a bit of a slur. "I'll increase your pocket money." This is a joke we still run. Liam doesn't have pocket money anymore—he has a part-time job in Costa and earns a bit through babysitting—but whenever he does anything helpful or kind, we joke that he's doing it for economic reasons and that we'll increase his pocket money.

"Do I get extra if I bring you water and paracetamol in the morning? I think you're going to need it." There's nothing a teen likes more than teasing a parent because they're handling their alcohol poorly.

"I'm on it," laughs Ben, holding up a glass of water.

Abi stumbles back into the kitchen. "God, he's amazing, isn't he? Tends to your every need." Then she suddenly pulls me into a tight hug. "I love you guys," she says with the absolute conviction of a drunk. I don't care if this affection is alcohol induced. I feel warm and glowing when she adds, "You are the best." She hugs Ben and then Liam, too, with equal ferocity.

I go to bed knowing all is right with the world.

CHAPTER FOURTEEN

ABIGAIL

Abigail lay on the sofa bed, her long, tanned limbs stretched out in front of her. The room was not dark enough—the girls preferred the landing light to stay on during the night and the bedroom door didn't quite fit as snugly as would have been ideal, so light flooded under and over. Also, the room was too hot. She'd tried turning the radiator down but it didn't seem to make any difference. She got out of bed and flung open the window. The cold night air rushed in, a relief.

Ben's words floated around Abigail's head. *You know what you need, Abi. You need to get back in the saddle.*

Back in the saddle. Giddy-up.

People wanted her to move on. They were bored of her mooning. Rob had stopped loving her, and chivvy along now, she had to stop loving him. Giddy-up. The thought made her smile. It was a good idea. Ben was right; there was no time to waste. No more time.

You know what you need, Abi. You need to get back in the saddle.

She wondered, just briefly, was it a suggestion or an offer? They seemed like such a happy couple but who knew? No one ever really knew what went on in a relationship.

Abigail checked her emails. Even though it was a Saturday, Rob had sent her two: one from him and one from his lawyer. He must have his lawyer working on this around the clock. Naturally he had; he knew he was in trouble. Being caught having sex is pretty damning evidence of fault. She planned to take him to the cleaners. Make him pay in every way she could.

His email suggested they could make this divorce quick, clean and as painless as possible. Fuck that. She saw that offer for what it was: a man who knew he was going to be paying through the nose, running scared. She opened the email from the lawyer and looked at the details of the proposed settlement. It was fair enough, some might say; not exactly generous, but reasonable. She typed her response.

Fuck you.

She was drunk enough to think this was hilarious and bold. She was sober enough to regret it the moment she pressed Send. She wondered whether it was possible to recall emails and Googled it. She wasn't sure, even after she'd read the chat forums debating the issue. It seemed it was but the recipient would know you'd done so. That was just as bad. Worse. She'd rather Rob think she was bold and rash than cowed and insecure.

She started to cry. She hated crying, it was ageing and hopeless, defeatist.

She heard a quiet knock at the door, so quiet she hardly dared call, "Come in." Slowly the door opened just a couple of inches.

Ben put his head around. "I thought you might need water, too?"

Abi hurriedly brushed the tears away; she didn't want him to see them. "Oh, thanks, yes."

He handed her a glass of iced water. Thoughtful, not tepid from the bathroom tap. Their fingers brushed together.

You can't make some things up, you can't imagine them, even if you want to wish them away or even if you plan to ignore them. There was a flicker of electricity. It shot through her arm, her shoulder, her chest and then down into the pit, the core of her body. She hadn't felt anything like it for years.

She met his eye, acknowledging the flash that had just lit between them. Those things were always two-way, weren't they? She felt it, he must have. A bee sting of sexual attraction.

He looked her in the eye and no doubt noticed she'd been crying. "Get some sleep, Abi," he instructed as he closed the bedroom door behind him.

And she did sleep. She dreamed she was riding a horse over a prairie. She was riding it hard, could feel its size and strength beneath her; between her legs, she felt its muscles ripple next to her thighs. She was breathless and free. Excited and able. It felt real, as she bumped up and down on the warm, leather saddle.

CHAPTER FIFTEEN

MELANIE

Sunday, 25 February

I look up from chopping carrots as Ben walks into the kitchen. He's wearing the Paul Smith shirt that I got him for his birthday, like I told him he should, with new jeans (that still look a little stiff) and his Ted Baker brogues, which he normally keeps for the office as he generally prefers Adidas trainers at home.

He's handsome, no doubt about it. When I'm walking in the streets with him, out shopping or whatever, I always feel secretly pleased, smug. I often see women check him out. He either doesn't notice or pretends not to, for my sake. Bless. Today he puts me in mind of the new, neat bay trees outside our front door. A little too formal, out of place and stiff.

"Maybe you should put on a T-shirt," I suggest.

"You told me to wear this," he replies with a confused and slightly frustrated shrug.

He glances about. I have the lunch ingredients out of the fridge but nowhere near in the oven. Even though I've been up since six thirty when Lily came into our room and asked if I wanted to see a puppet show. There are approximately a hundred things—including toys, homework, stray socks, breakfast pots and a hairbrush—scattered across the table. I'm obviously not what anyone would describe as on top of things. My head aches and I'm so pale I'm transparent. I'm too old to stay up drinking until 2:00 a.m.

One of the very many lovely things about being married to Ben is that we are a partnership. I don't have to nag him to help out or do his share. If he sees something needs doing, he invariably does it. Maybe not exactly as I might have done it, but he gives it a go and I'm grateful. Normally, he lends a hand with notable affability; right now, he gathers up the debris from the kitchen table and then clatters down the cutlery in a distinctly irritated manner. He didn't like me suggesting what he should put on today and, having complied, he likes me changing my mind even less. I can hear his frustration in the clinking of the knives and forks.

"I know I did but—" I'm about to say it looks a bit over the top, when Abi interrupts.

"You look fabulous, Ben, ignore her."

"Oh, Abi, I didn't realise you were there." I'm embarrassed that she's caught our conversation and wonder whether she noticed the slight testiness in the air. I want everything to look effortless, seamless and—most of all—blissful. Nagging my husband about the formality of his wardrobe is none of those things. It's too late to get Ben to change now. I shouldn't even expect it. Her compliments make me feel shallow. I'm also embarrassed that she's here before I've managed to transform the kitchen. I wanted to have set it with a vase of tulips, a bowl of olives and wine. I have a very specific image of how I want to present things for Abi.

Clearing the breakfast pots would have been a start.

She looks around, too. Her gaze is unreadable. She might be thinking we're charming, or she might be thinking we're revolting. "Can I do anything to help?" she asks with convincing gusto.

"Oh no," I reply automatically, although why? When another pair of hands would obviously be useful. Instead I find myself saying, "Ben, why don't you show Abi our holiday photos from last summer?" Turning to Abi, I add, "We visited the Edinburgh Fringe." Ben looks startled.

"Are you interested?" he asks Abi with some scepticism. "It's a bit throwback. People haven't actually thought it was entertaining to show others their holiday snaps since circa 1979, have they?"

"Yes, yes, she is interested," I insist.

Abi backs me up. "I love the way Mel still goes to the effort of printing photos and putting them in albums. With the tickets of the places you visited and maps and such. Works of art, really. History in the making. Who does that?"

"Who indeed?" says Ben, mildly amused. He thinks my photo albums are a bit of a waste of space and money and prefers keeping things digitally, but he indulges me. He has even promised that if there is a fire or flood, after the kids and the cats, he'd save my albums. Exactly how he'd do that isn't clear, since I have about two dozen.

"I've shown Abi loads of old albums already," I say.

I'm eager to encourage them both to get out of the kitchen, so that I can rush about and pull the place into some semblance of order. I want the kitchen to myself. I don't feel up to coordinating making lunch and having a conversation.

Somehow, when the doorbell rings at one o'clock, lunch is almost ready and the table is dressed with our best glassware and pretty paper napkins.

"Will someone get that?" I yell. No one reacts. "It will be Tanya." I hear Liam gallop down the stairs with enthusiasm.

"Someone's keen," says Abi, amused; she and Ben have wandered back into the kitchen, ready to take their seats or at least refill their glasses.

"I'll say. The only other person who can get him to move as quickly as that is the pizza delivery man," jokes Ben.

Lunch is loud and lively. I've put the meat and multiple vegetables in bowls on the table so everyone can help themselves. There is the inevitable hassle when Lily says she'd rather die than eat peas but I put them on her plate anyway. Again, Abi entertains us all. This time with stories about famous people she's met and interviewed. Her stories are hilarious, informative and sometimes risqué. The girls—giddier than ever because they have both Tanya and Abi to play to—are near hysterical when she tells them she's met Selena Gomez. They squeal at a constant, high pitch and, for fun, I join in.

Ben jokily covers his ears and yells at us all to shut up. "I can't hear myself think."

Quick as a flash I say, "You think with your head? Wow, you are quite a special man." This gets a big laugh from Abi and Tanya, the girls, too, although they probably didn't even hear the joke, let alone understand it.

Smiling, Ben turns to Liam and bemoans the fact they're outnumbered. "More than ever. We're going to need to get soundproofing."

"You can't say that," says Liam with a distinct note of embarrassment. "You two are so politically incorrect." He can be an outspoken kid and his opinions are generally quite well researched but normally he keeps his discussions and deliberations for the college debating society; today he seems to want to peacock in front of Tanya.

"Can't say what?" asks Ben, genuinely mystified.

"Mum can't say that men think with their…" He glances at his sisters, who are hanging off his every word. He corrects himself. "She can't say men think with anything other than their heads. It's sexist."

"It was a joke," I say, still giggling. Quite pleased with myself.

"It's a cliché," replies Liam. "What are you saying? All men are dumb, led by instinct rather than intellect. Clichés always lead to sexism."

I sigh because this may be true but it's so damned sad. "Clichés used to lead to jokes, I'm pretty sure of it. We used to be better at laughing at ourselves," I comment, defensively.

"Sexist jokes. I'm surprised at you, Mum."

Teens do have occasional forays into bouts of self-righteousness. Normally, I ride them out. Today, I wish Liam hadn't decided to so abruptly change the atmosphere. We were having fun. I pick up the tureen that still has some roast potatoes left in it and offer them to him—he can usually be sidetracked by roast potatoes, but he shakes his head impatiently. "And Dad, you're no better, implying that women are nothing but pointless chatter and noise."

Ben looks horrified. "Mate, I'm pretty sure that's not what I said."

"The thing about soundproofing."

"I'm not being sexist. I'm being accurate." Ben winks at me and I throw a balled-up napkin at him. "The women in our family are more garrulous and the men more circumspect, on the whole."

Although not right now. Liam seems determined to make his point. Ben is walking the thin line of taking him seriously and yet fuelling a debate that would be better closed down. "We work in a world full of clichés and assumptions but there's nothing wrong with that. Those things are stabilising, helpful. We need to be able to categorise and order," adds Ben.

Liam shrugs because he can't bring himself to agree. He's too young for such heavy-handed certainty. He still sees nuance and complication everywhere. His world is delightfully in flux. "I bet you never relied on cliché, Abigail, when you were interviewing and stuff," Liam declares.

I smile inwardly. He may be feeling argumentative with his parents but he's remembered to be polite to our guest.

"I'm sure I'm guilty of slipping one in on several occasions," admits Abi diplomatically.

"Abi used to be a TV presenter in the States," I explain to Tanya, in case Liam hasn't told her.

"Less of the past tense, if you please," says Abi. I can hear that she's trying to sound amused but isn't.

"Oh, sorry," I mutter, colouring.

"You've gone red," Imogen points out unnecessarily.

"It makes the stripe in your hair look totally and absolutely white," declares Lily. I want to kill her.

Instead I run my fingers through my hair and try to sound unconcerned. "I meant to pick up a kit yesterday when I was in town but work was hectic. I only got a thirty-minute lunch break."

"A kit?" asks Abi. Then she understands. "Oh. Wow. Do you dye your own hair?" Her tone is incredulous. I'm embarrassed but maybe my expression comes across as one of irritation because Abi quickly changes her tone. "Oh my God, that is so impressive. I honestly thought you must pay a fortune in some fancy salon. You look amazing."

I do not enjoy the process of dyeing my hair. I don't like the smell or the waiting around, plus I'd like to be the sort of woman who can afford to go to a salon for the job, but mostly I feel cheated that I'm already turning grey, even though I'm still in my thirties. It doesn't seem right. Grey hair is for grandmas and I am nowhere near that stage. No rush at all. I've no desire to age gracefully; I do what I can to push back the inevitable.

Tanya, bless her, picks up the conversation. She asks the girls which is their favourite Disney song. Soon, everyone joins in. My grey hair and home dye kits are forgotten as people shout out, "Let it Go," "A Whole New World," "Circle of Life."

The rest of the lunch passes without incident. My sore head is easing but probably only because I've had two glasses of wine.

"A Sunday roast. Just what the doctor ordered," comments Abi as she puts her knife and fork together and leans back in her chair. This is the first hint she's given that she might have been even a tiny bit hungover; I'm in awe, she's a superwoman.

She's the last to finish—she had the most stories to tell and besides, she eats the tiniest bites. Lily and Imogen have been waiting patiently, nailed to their seats through years of training that you can't leave the table until everyone finishes.

Lily immediately seizes the opportunity to hop down from her seat and climb on Liam's lap. I see Tanya melt when he wraps his big arms around his tiny sprite of a sister. Lily likes sitting on his knee because when the adult conversation gets too boring for her to follow but she doesn't feel ready to slink off on her own, he keeps her amused by whispering in her ears. Silly jokes and sounds that send her off into peals of giggles.

"I was wondering, how long are you staying, Abigail?" Ben's question is shot over the clatter of my gathering up the used plates. I shoot him a quick look of reproach, one I hope he sees but no one else does. He doesn't catch it because he's determined not to; he's staring at Abi, not me. He's smiling. He looks affable enough. There's only me who would know he's asking her to pack her bags.

I get it. I know what he's thinking—it's been a fun weekend but tomorrow is Monday; we should get back to being normal. "We have a busy week ahead of us," he adds, as though it's a simple observation.

Abi smiles—if she's picked up on his hint, she doesn't seem bothered by it. "Really? What's going down?"

Ben must have checked the family calendar before we sat down to eat because he rattles off our commitments with impressive confidence. "It's Imogen's Brownie investiture."

Abi pulls her face into a picture of awe to show she's impressed, Immie beams back, thrilled to be centre of attention.

"Lily has a school trip to a working farm and Mel is a parent volunteer, so is going along, too."

Abi gasps excitedly and claps her hands in glee, as though she can't imagine anything more fun.

"Liam needs to practise for his internship interview." Ben's list obviously isn't simply a point of information; he's hinting she needs to get out of our hair. I shift uncomfortably in my seat. I wish he'd drop it. "Mel has also got an extra shift to do at the shop because she needs to make up the time from Friday."

"OK, Ben." He's being rude now.

"And I'm in the middle of a big audit at work."

He turns to look at me, reminding me of as much, I suppose. I assumed Abi would stay for the weekend but she hasn't made any noise about catching a train tonight or tomorrow. I suppose we do need to know her plans so that we can make our own, but I can't stand the idea of shooing her out the house.

"I haven't quite decided," says Abi. "Mel, so sweetly, said I could stay as long as I needed."

"Of course, you're so welcome," I gush. I mean this, at the same time as I know it really isn't a helpful thing to say. I throw Ben a look that's begging for his understanding. He relents.

"Yes, absolutely. I'm just saying we've a very busy week next week. I hope you don't think we're rude if we're not around too much to look after you."

"Not at all," Abi assures him with the broadest smile. It's inscrutable. "I'm pretty self-sufficient. So, Liam, what is this internship?"

"I'm hoping to work in the Houses of Parliament."

"Wow."

"But it's really competitive."

"Well, you are gorgeous and principled and have the confidence to question your parents' passive, institutionalised sexism—I'd say you'll cut through the competition."

"Abi!" I squeal, laughing as I know she's joking. Liam reddens.

"Just kidding." She turns back to Liam. "Maybe I could help with the interview practice," Abi offers.

"Really?" I ask.

"I'm not saying I'm an expert but..." She laughs. "But my entire career is based on interviewing peo-

ple. I do know how to carefully solicit particular information, even when a person doesn't want to give
it." She beams encouragingly at Liam; he's looking
at the table. "I know how to then present that information to make someone look erudite, original. I can
coach you."

Of course she's an expert. This is great news. What
an advantage. I glance at Liam to see if he hates the
idea of Abigail helping but he shrugs, seemingly OK
with the suggestion. I have a feeling Abi might be
able to provide the zing and edge; help him stand
out. I'm grateful.

"That's so kind," I gush.

"Well, that's settled then, I'll stay until after Liam's
interview," she says enthusiastically.

I daren't look at Ben—the interview is not until
the week after next. Instead I say, "Now, who's for
pudding?"

"Oh, me please, I can diet tomorrow," Abi says
with a careless giggle.

Everyone, even Lily, says in unison, "You don't
need to diet, ever!"

CHAPTER SIXTEEN

ABIGAIL

It was vital to behave perfectly normally, not to alert Mel in any way to whatever it was that was bubbling. Because something certainly was bubbling. Was it in her imagination? Was it one way? She watched him carefully. When he smiled at Mel, it was an oblique, faintly perplexed smile. When he smiled at the girls or Tanya, it was uncomplicated, amenable. When he caught her eye, he didn't smile at all. He looked like he wanted to lick her. Taste her. So, she was almost certain.

While Mel tidied away after lunch and put the kitchen to rights, something about having to iron the school uniforms, too, Abi spent the afternoon playing Barbie with the girls. They sat on the floor in the middle of the sitting room, surrounded by tiny plastic shoes, handbags and semi-clad dolls with tangled hair. If she had daughters, she would not buy them

Barbies. To be fair to Mel, the girls had Doctor Barbie and NASA Barbie, but even so, her physical proportions were crazy and were probably the root cause of all sorts of unrealistic body expectations.

Ben, Liam and Tanya were sprawled out on the two sofas watching sport with varying degrees of enthusiasm. There wasn't much room for six people. She was just centimetres away from his feet. She was aware of him. His proximity. If she moved just a couple of centimetres to the left, she could bump up against him. What would he do? Move away?

The girls were forever getting up, walking in front of the TV, causing everyone to move around them to get a view, stumbling as they sat down again. On one occasion, Abi took advantage. She reached for the box of Barbie accessories and allowed her shoulder to bang up against his knee. He didn't flinch; if anything she thought he moved towards her. An infinitesimal transfer of energy and focus but she was sure of it.

She waited a few more moments to see if he would yet move away. He didn't. The heat from his leg could be felt through her shirt. She became emboldened. She spilled out the Barbie accessories onto the floor and under the cover of all the mess she ran her hand over his foot, tentatively. A move that she could deny, could be dismissed as an accidental brush. Or not. She dared to glance at his face. He continued to stare at the television; he did not say, "Oh sorry, am I in your way?" and move.

She was pleased. Professional. Unfazed. She squeezed his foot deliberately. Boldly. It had begun.

Abi liked being part of a family. She had imagined

it often enough. Back in America, she found herself looking at other people's babies. Not just babies, their children, too, and wondering what it was like to have such a mass of noisy energy living in close proximity all the time. If a woman pushed a stroller past her in the street, she'd strain her neck, as surreptitiously as possible, to see if the baby was asleep or gurgling; did it have a pacifier in or thumb?

She'd gotten into the habit of sitting near mothers and children in coffee shops. That was almost certifiable—the chances of spillages increased tenfold. What was wrong with her? She lingered outside play-parks (she'd told herself she had to stop, it was only a matter of time before someone made a complaint). She thought her adult-only gym sleek and stylish—with state-of-the-art Olympic-size pool, divided into neat columns to allow the most efficient length swimming—was soulless because she wanted to see kids splash around, to make noise and play on inflatables.

It wasn't just the cute and smiley ones she liked. If she heard a baby scream, she didn't want to run in the opposite direction, she wanted to pick it up and comfort it. Once she had gone so far as to swap seats with a passenger on a flight from LA to NY to move closer to a mum with a toddler in tow.

She was so achingly broody.

The obvious, adult thing to do was to sit down with Rob and explain how she felt. She had tried to do that. She really had. The conversation always went the same way.

"No, no, Abi. A baby? What are you saying?"

"I'm not saying I want a baby right now."

"Good."

"I'm just saying, I'd like the subject to go back on the table, maybe." She wished she hadn't added the word *maybe*; it sounded defeatist.

"It's not fair, Abigail, you can't just change the rules. We agreed," he'd insisted, sounding not unlike a child himself. "You know what I think. How I feel. We agreed."

Fair or not, the deal they had struck, the demands he had made, were no longer acceptable to her.

"I think I feel differently now." What was wrong with her? She did feel differently, she shouldn't have said she *thought* she felt differently. It was too subservient, too deferential.

It was hard; because he was older than she was, because he'd been studying for a PhD when she was a mere undergraduate, she'd never quite asserted herself. Most of the time they were fine, they were equals—in bed for instance—but when they talked about current affairs, art, literature or even money, he seemed to be in control. She was cast into the role of deputy.

He hadn't even finished his damn PhD!

She supposed it was these conversations that hurried him into the vasectomy. She supposed he thought he was so clever. She felt such rage. Pure, unadulterated, fiery rage. She had nowhere to spend it. No way to dissipate it. He didn't want to listen to her. She couldn't tell anyone else. Her friends, her mother, Mel. It was too humiliating.

So, the rage flung its way around her body, ricocheting off her heart, bouncing around all her vital organs, spreading through her veins and arteries up to her brain. It intensified, multiplied. It ravaged her from the inside, while outside she had to keep smiling.

CHAPTER SEVENTEEN

MELANIE

"She has a lovely way about her, don't you think?"

"She's nice." Ben has his back to me, unbuttoning his shirt.

We both feel tired after the busier than usual weekend. "She's more than *nice*." The word is almost an insult used in reference to Abigail Curtiz. "She's charismatic," I say firmly. I wash my face and then slap on a bit of moisturiser. I know I should gently smooth in the cream in long, even, upward strokes but it's never been my way. "The kids *loved* her stories. She's met everyone."

"I'm not sure that Lily and Imogen actually know who half the people are that she talked about."

"Oh, they probably do. They loved hearing about Selena Gomez."

"Abigail only happened to be at a party that she was at. They didn't speak to one another."

"Have you been at a party Selena Gomez has attended?" I ask, amused. Ben shrugs. I think the effects of lunchtime drinking are making him feel a bit grumpy and out of sorts.

He's been acting moody all afternoon. "Tanya and Liam were certainly impressed," I point out. "I mean, she's interviewed three people from *Game of Thrones*."

"There's a cast of thousands," he murmurs as he walks into the bathroom to put his clothes in the laundry basket. "Do you think Liam and Tanya are OK?"

"Liam and Tanya?" I put toothpaste on both our brushes. "They seem as happy as ever."

"Really? I thought Liam was tetchy today. Not himself."

I shrug.

"You know, a bit spiky."

"He was just being a teen." I'm irritated that Ben seems to be looking for problems. Creating them. My experience is that enough come along without me going to the bother of hunting them out. Why can't Ben just chill, enjoy this exciting little interruption to our lives? I mentally hum as I clean my teeth, relaxed, content. I spit and then say, "Have you noticed she seems to put people at their ease? I think it's because she's comfortable in her own skin, you know? Accepting of herself? So much so, that she finds it easy to be accepting of others."

"Tanya?"

"No, Abigail."

"And you got all that from this weekend, did you?

After a seventeen-year hiatus in your friendship," he asks, raising his eyebrows.

I finish my ablutions and climb into bed; Ben turns out the bathroom light and follows me. "Obviously, she's still in pieces over Rob but she did well today, I think."

"Uh-huh."

"She's really brave. I don't think I'd be able to get out of bed for a month if I found you doing that." Suddenly, I feel scared. Stupid of me because Ben's fidelity is something I've always believed in and counted on. I trust him, he trusts me. We're just not the sort to cheat on each other, to have affairs, to skulk around. We haven't the energy, for a start. As I haven't turned off my bedside lamp, Ben picks up a supplement from the Sunday paper. I don't reach for anything to read. I want to chat.

"It's nice being around her," I observe.

"Because she's met famous people?"

"Because she's exceptional."

Ben looks over the top of his magazine. "I've never seen you like this with anyone else before."

"Like what?"

"Giddy. Eager. You seem eager to please her. Why?"

"Why what?"

"Why is she so important to you?"

"What do you mean?"

He holds my gaze.

I shrug. "It's just fun having a friend stay."

"Why didn't Abi come to our wedding?"

"I don't know. I don't remember," I mumble

133

vaguely, suddenly deciding I do want to read after all. I look at the floor beside the bed—as usual there are about half a dozen books scattered about. I grab the nearest one and open it on any page, start reading immediately.

"Did you invite her?"

"I suppose I must have."

"But you can't remember why she couldn't make it."

"No."

He's silent for a moment. "She says she wasn't invited."

"You've talked about it with her?" My heart speeds up.

"It came up when we were looking through the albums today."

"Well, I suppose I can't have invited her then, if she says not. We didn't have a huge wedding, did we? It's a long time ago. I can't remember exactly who could or could not attend and why." I hope he believes me. I hope he lets the matter drop.

"I just wondered why I haven't met her before and yet now you're all my-home-is-your-home with her."

I don't know how to explain it to him but I know I need to say something. After a while I admit, "I feel I owe her."

"Owe her? How?"

I put down my book and turn on my side to face him. "She was kind to me when it mattered."

"In what way?"

So, I tell him the story of how Abigail was the first person I told about being pregnant. Sat in the tiny, utilitarian student bedroom in our scruffy student flat in Birmingham. As I tell him, I drift back there. I see the *Buffy* and *Trainspotting* posters on the walls. The door to the skinny wardrobe is ajar, clothes are falling out and onto the floor; I've never been naturally neat. The positive pregnancy test is in the bin under my desk. The air is scented with my perfume (Flower by Kenzo); I squirted it around the room because I was sure I could smell the urine from the stick. Missy Elliott is playing. My heart is banging against my chest. It's too much.

I pull myself back to the here and now. This room. This bed.

"She didn't make me feel stupid or doomed," I explain. "She told me I could still have a fairy tale. She said even Snow White got her prince and she had seven little fellas hanging on her apron strings, not just one. It was that. That kindness." I know I'm not explaining this fully or even well when Ben's look of confusion just deepens.

"So she's here because she made a joke about dwarfs?" he asks. His reaction annoys me. I'd hoped he'd get it.

"Kindness," I reiterate. "She made me think that the pregnancy was just something that was happening, an experience, part of me, obviously, but not defining." Ben doesn't look convinced and nor should he be. The truth is, my teenage pregnancy did define me, for good and ill, whether I like it or not.

The pregnancy was the reason I never managed to complete my degree but instead work in a clothes shop on the high street. Certainly a good job—but not the one I'd been expecting. The pregnancy was the reason my parents practically kissed Ben's feet when he proposed to me, they were so grateful that he'd "taken on" their fallen girl. Ben always says he felt their gratitude was excessive; it wasn't meant to be insulting but sort of was—their surprise that he'd fall in love with me and Liam. Insulting to everyone.

Ben runs his hand through my hair and murmurs quietly, "The pregnancy did define you, sweetheart, you know it did. But that's not a bad thing. It's a brilliant thing. The pregnancy is the reason you're Liam's mother, fact."

"Well, obviously."

"You know, the way you were as a single mum was one of the reasons I was so attracted to you in the first place. I admired you. You were so strong and determined. So focused and selfless."

I shrug off his hand that is stroking my hair. I like it but this sort of talk embarrasses me. I don't deserve praise for just getting on with the mess I'd made.

"You were so unlike any other twenty-five-year-old I'd ever dated, so unlike me at the time," he says.

True. Aged just twenty-seven when I met him, Ben was still pretty hedonistic back then. He was leading a life full of corporate meetings (where he shone), high-end holidays (where he surfed) and fun dates (where, more often than not, he shagged), but even so, from the moment I met him, I knew he was a good man. When he proposed to me, he said he hoped he could be a better man, and he thought Liam and I might help him become just that. I already thought he was perfect but I understood what he was saying.

We all want to be better. None of us can really forgive ourselves for being human.

Ben leans into me and kisses my lips. Softly. Tenderly. As he pulls away, he says, "I don't care what defined you. I love you fiercely, Mel. You and the three children you've given me. You're the best things that ever happened to me."

I don't quite know what to say to this. Ben and I liberally bandy the word *love* around our house. We say it to each other and the kids many times a day. This shouldn't mean that it's lost its currency as a word but it has, a bit. "Love you" said at the end of a phone call or as you are dashing out of the house doesn't hold its potency. This declaration was designed to hit the mark, to send tingles up my spine. Odd then that I just feel a little weighed down by it.

"You know, it's great you have a friend staying with us, but you don't owe her anything for being nice to you," he says carefully.

I shake my head. I do owe her. I can't explain.

He continues, "Hers was just the normal reaction. It was the other clowns that were odd."

It's true, everyone else wanted me to be ashamed. I roll away from him and turn out my bedside lamp. It's worse than that; on some deep and long-buried level, I was ashamed. But saying so out loud would be a horrible betrayal of Liam.

CHAPTER EIGHTEEN

BEN

Friday, 2 March

The week proved to be just as busy as Ben predicted. It was the sort of week where he and Mel only managed to see each other at handovers, conversation never developed beyond swapping of essential information: Who had eaten what? Who needed to be where? What had to be packed in a school bag or a lunch box? Abi, true to her word, took time out to help Liam prepare for his internship interview. Time out from what exactly, Ben couldn't say.

Abi wasn't the sort of guest who pitched in generally. She'd wait until everyone was home from work and school, then ask, "So what's for dinner?" rather than think of boiling some pasta and heating a tomato sauce. She lounged, while they scurried. She was always underfoot, as Ben's mum would say. Abi spent her time calling London friends, ranting about her ex-husband and drinking coffee and wine with his wife. There was a lot of that because no matter how harried they were, Mel always had time to pause for a joke or a chat with Abi. It was different with him; he couldn't expect the type of manners that were reserved for visitors. There was no time for coffee. Or anything else, for that matter.

He was trying with Abi, he really was. Putting himself out, small courtesies to make her feel welcome, accepting her need to be tactile, when really he thought all her hugging and touching was a tad excessive. He wanted to make her feel at home. He liked her, on the whole; she was undeniably attractive, physically, it was just that he didn't like her quite as much as Mel seemed to.

Mel adored her. And Abi seemed to adore Mel; in fact she was oddly possessive about her. That was a bit irritating—after all, Mel was *his* wife. Abi was forever talking about their time at university, "Before your time, Ben," she'd say, waving her hand dismissively. A hand that usually held a cigarette, and although she followed house policy to the letter of the law and did not smoke in the house, she often hung out of the window or lingered by the open patio doorway. Letting the heat out and the cool air and clouds of smoke in.

It seemed that Abi had countless stories about their undergraduate antics. Stories she retold with great panache and relish, stories that caused Mel to sigh and giggle and blush. It was obvious that Mel had managed to have quite a lot of fun in her brief time at uni. He was glad of that and, also, a bit surprised. He hadn't heard these stories before. When Mel talked about her time as an undergraduate she was always a little reticent; there was some level of embarrassment and disappointment. Hers? Other people's? He wasn't sure.

It appeared that Mel wasn't the only person Abi had kept tabs on; she seemed to know about everyone they'd studied with. This showed a level of interest in others, a friendliness, which was something, he supposed, considering she'd moved abroad and was so successful. Since she was "a Famous," as Lily kept saying, he'd have understood if she'd let old relationships slide. It was admirable that she hadn't.

She was always saying, "You must remember him" or "How could you forget her?" Mel nodded along but didn't commit to a comment, and Ben knew that Mel didn't have a clue who these people were. If they had ever been friends, then they had fallen by the wayside a long time ago. Apparently, according to Abi, everyone they'd ever studied with was "just absolutely brilliant," "totally marvellous" or (this was her favourite) "very, very successful." This accolade was delivered with reverence, often in a whisper and the information accompanied by a wink.

Other than Abi herself, Ben had never met a single person from Mel's university years. They must have all been so absolutely brilliant, totally marvellous and very, very successful that they couldn't send a Christmas card. It might have been different if she'd kept up her studies, but it had proven impossible; not enough hours in the day, not enough pounds in the bank account. And since? Well, they connected from time to time on Facebook at best.

He used to resent the way these people had let Mel slip out of their lives. He felt angry that they hadn't valued her enough to want to stay in touch. Now, Abi had found her way to their door, it was churlish to wish she hadn't bothered.

Fact: there was just not enough space, they were falling over one another. Last night he came home to the house and assumed it was empty. Mel took the girls to ballet on Thursdays, Liam usually went round to Tanya's. As he pushed open the front door he heard it—silence. He mini-punched the air. It was such a relief. Abi, he guessed, had gone along to the ballet class.

He loosened his tie, kicked off his shoes. He didn't have any plans to hog the TV and remote, he just wanted to clear some emails that he hadn't managed to get to as his day had been full of meetings. Not a lot to ask. That nirvana now seemed within his grasp. However, he no sooner set up his laptop on the kitchen table than Abi dawdled in. It was only just seven but she was dressed in a silky robe; her bare legs and painted toes distracted him more than they should.

"I was just taking a bath. I didn't expect you home yet," she commented, as though he was the interloper. "Normally you aren't back until after eight." This wasn't true—normally he tried to get home by six, preferring to spend a bit of time with his family, even if it meant working late at night after the kids were in bed. Since Abi had been visiting, he'd found it more efficient to stay in the office a little longer. More efficient and more comfortable.

"I thought I'd have the house to myself. I've some things I still need to plough through." He knew he was being tactless, rude, really. He couldn't help himself. It was her legs, and her skin, soft and flushed from her bath—they agitated him. Made him snappy. Abi moved to the fridge and pulled out a bottle of Chardonnay.

"Do you want a glass?"

"No, thank you, I need to keep a clear head."

She shrugged. The cold wine shivered into her glass; he wished he'd said yes. Ben tried to turn his attention to his work, hoped Abi would take the hint, go and sit in the TV room, leave him to it. She didn't. She sat down and then swung her tanned, toned legs up onto the chair next to his. She let her head flop backwards—her hair dangled down behind her, damp. She closed her eyes but her mouth parted. A little wet gap.

"I'm sorry, Ben," she said suddenly. He was startled. Looked away quickly. Did she know he'd been staring?

"What for?"

"Well, for being here. Being in the way." She sat forward now, eyes wide open. She clasped at the neck of her silky robe. It pulled the material across her breasts, somehow making her seem less respectable, not more.

"Not at all. No," he said, without conviction. She waved away his objections and he was too honest to continue to protest.

"I'm a complication you don't need," she stated flatly.

"I wouldn't say that."

"Why not? It's true. I can see you are a busy man.

Conscientious at work, a good husband, an involved father of two."

"Three. I have three children," Ben corrected.

"Yes, of course. I only meant you have two little ones. Liam is grown up."

"Well, not entirely."

"Three. Right. I didn't mean anything."

Ben knew he should leave the matter—she probably hadn't meant anything by her comment; a slip of the tongue. Still, he found himself saying, "One ready-made, the other two needed popping in the oven and baking." It was a crass explanation.

Why had he put it like that? He was always jokey in public when anything deep was being discussed; he was not the sort to wear his heart on his sleeve— he kept that for Mel alone. But suddenly his explanation for the evolution of their family seemed wrong. Next, he'd be telling Abi he'd bought one and got one free, that Mel was a BOGOF.

Abi obviously thought he was vulgar, too; she looked faintly disturbed and murmured, "Quaint."

Ben turned his attention back to his emails. It was probably best not to get into this. He didn't have the time or inclination. Unfortunately, Abi obviously had other ideas.

She smiled. She had very white teeth, red lips. "You're so obviously a wonderful man, taking on another man's son, that's quite something. I'd hate to disturb the delicate balance that relationship needs to thrive."

Ostensibly, it was a compliment but Ben felt wrong-footed. Neither his relationship with Mel nor

Liam was delicate. They were sound. Real. Huge. They couldn't be sent off-kilter just because an old friend visited. He didn't know how to say as much, at least not politely. He wondered whether he had to remain polite.

"I suppose everything that Mel was before she met you must seem like a bit of a mystery," mused Abi.

Ben felt a prickle of irritation run along his spine, the hairs on his body stood up, shuddered. "Not really," he lied. "It's not as though she's secretive about it. She often talks about the early days of motherhood, filling me in on what I missed."

"I didn't suggest she was being secretive," Abi laughed, sounding surprised. Again, Ben felt he'd said the wrong thing. "I was just thinking it must be very hard to imagine her as a carefree student, razzing around campus. Or to understand her years as a single mum, because you weren't there."

It was a fact but it sounded like an accusation. Together, Ben and Mel had been through two births, done all the family stuff that is the privilege and pain of any normal family. They'd made dashes to the A&E to check out bumps and breaks, they'd tended itchy heads with fine-tooth combs, they'd changed pungent nappies and pulped carefully prepared organic dinners to mush (just to see it smeared across foreheads and over high-chairs). They'd sat in the audience at school shows and held their breath through ballet exams. They'd talked to their kids about manners, bullies, stranger danger and exactly how it was possible for Father Christmas to circumnavigate the world in one night.

He knew what it was to be a parent with Mel, but

yes, Abi was right, he couldn't imagine what it was like for her doing all that on her own.

He'd tried to. He wanted to. He regretted that he wasn't there.

It struck him once, in the middle of the night, when Imogen was about eighteen months old and sick with a particularly vicious tummy bug. Now, they took turns with getting up to comfort whichever child was having a nightmare or throwing up or running a temperature; back then, when the kids were tiny and appeared painfully vulnerable, they got up together. Dashed towards the heart-searing shrieking.

That night, they'd stripped Immie's bed, cleaned her up, soothed her until she fell back to sleep. Then they crawled back to their own bed—the usual routine, familiar to every parent—only to be disturbed thirty minutes later when she threw up for a second time, then a third. Together they bathed her, stripped sheets, frantically searched the internet and then called the NHS helpline, just in case it was something more than a regular tummy bug. They took turns in cradling her hot little body, soaked with sweat and tears. Sponged her limbs to try to lull and cool her. They felt the waves of emotion wash over and through them in unison: sympathy, frustration, panic, fear and then finally relief.

When they eventually sank back into bed, only an hour before the alarm was due to go off, Mel noticed Ben was quiet and distracted. No doubt she presumed he was just shattered and worried, but he turned to her and confessed that his heart was aching. Those were the words he used.

"My heart is aching."

"It's OK. She gave us a bit of a fright but she's fine. She's asleep now," Mel murmured sleepily.

"No, it's not Immie."

"Then what?"

"It's the thought of you doing that on your own for the first six years of Liam's life. You know, I'd literally give anything to turn back time and be with you both from the very first moment. It isn't a biological thing. You know I don't care that I didn't physically bring Liam into being. It's an emotional thing."

Mel had shrugged. "Some things just can't be changed, though. We're fine as we are."

He knew that. They were fine. But it was just how he felt. When the girls were very little and reached milestones, a tiny part of Ben found he couldn't one hundred per cent enjoy those moments because he knew no one had shared the equivalent occasions with Liam and Mel. He'd sometimes admit, "I just wish I'd seen Liam stumble through his first steps or utter his first words."

"It doesn't matter," Mel insisted. It was irrational of him, but he couldn't help but think he'd somehow let them down by not finding them sooner. "You can't beat yourself up about stuff that happened before we met."

"I know. I just mean, I wish I had been there. I wish you hadn't had to do it alone."

He'd liked it when they hit Liam's firsts together, not walking and talking, but joining cubs, being picked for a football team. He liked it when the girls got to an age when he and Mel could look back and say to one another, "Do you remember when Liam first went ice-skating/did a sleepover/cut a big tooth?" It felt solid. He loved them all to distraction. He didn't believe he loved or raised his girls any differently than he had Liam, and Mel would say the same.

"Mel and Liam share such a special bond, don't they? I noticed it straight away. It's very precious," said Abi, bringing Ben out of his memories and back into the kitchen. Abi stood up, poured herself a second glass of wine. She tilted the bottle towards him. "You sure?" This time, he nodded. What the hell. Ben sipped his wine and didn't answer. Didn't want to.

Well observed, Abi. He thought that had to be something to do with her job; she was a people reader. She scrutinised, delved. It was true: the love Mel felt for Liam did seem to be different from the love she had for the girls. It was not more or less—just distinct. Mel was too much of a feminist to mother differently depending on gender. It was because they had been alone together. He knew that. The deep, impenetrable closeness that there was between his wife and son was mysterious. There was something so intuitive about their relationship, almost animalistic.

He'd seen flashes of primitive instinct throughout their married life. They'd never had any teenage problems with Liam, well, other than that dreadful time with Austin, but no one could have predicted that and they'd dealt with it as well as possible. They'd had a relatively trouble-free ride because his mother knew him inside out. She pre-empted every crisis, avoided every disaster. They talked a lot, practically all the time, way more than the average teen and mum, and even when he couldn't articulate what it was that was on his mind, Mel somehow knew.

"It's his grades."

"It's a girl."

"It's his hair."

"It's Austin."

She was always able to identify exactly what was niggling him, whereas however hard Ben tried (and he did try) all he could see was a distressed teen, unable or unwilling to say what was up.

Liam was more like Mel in temperament than either Lily or Imogen were, even though he didn't look much like her. They had the same weird, sharp, slightly teasing sense of humour; this normally delighted the other three but, just occasionally, it rattled. Ben was more of a pun man and the girls got giddy over knock-knock jokes. He remembered Liam at Imogen's age—he was pretty sure the boy was already too sophisticated for knock-knock jokes by then, although he'd always laugh politely when Ben told them.

Liam got his good manners and kindness from Mel, too. They had the same reaction to politicians who outraged them (fury, swiftly followed by a brief dose of depression, then an energetic rally of local do-gooderism). They had the same reaction to movies that moved them (raw passion). OK, they were different movies—Liam's favourite was *Inception* and Mel preferred *Brokeback Mountain* (they agreed that *Toy Story* was awesome but Ben didn't read too much into that; everyone loved *Toy Story*). They were both horrendously impatient about slow internet connections or traffic jams but always had time to strike up conversations with tardy serving staff in a restaurant.

They liked and disliked the same people, often drawing their swift, unshifting character appraisals within minutes of meeting. They finished one another's sentences. Sometimes they didn't even have to speak but still seemed to understand each other's plans as though they were passing symbiotic signals. It was like they were locked in their own little world.

Best to think of it that way, because no one ever wanted to be locked out.

Not that there was anything wrong with Ben's relationship with Liam, far from it. His relationship with Liam was phenomenal. He thought so, Liam thought so, everyone thought so. It was often commented upon; how close they were. Ben had found it easy to fall in love with Liam from the get go. There hadn't been a power struggle between the man and the small boy; Liam had clearly been looking for a dad, whether he was aware of it or not. Ben was more than willing to be that.

They had their things, too. Some of the happiest times of Ben's life were when he was stood on the sidelines of a footie game on a Saturday morning cheering Liam on. Mel never came to the matches and although both the girls had been encouraged to play football, neither were interested. It was Ben and Liam's thing. As were podcasts, supporting Aston Villa, Marvel superheroes and Lego (although Lily did show some interest in sharing the latter two with them).

Ben stared resentfully at his now-drained glass, which had gone down far too quickly, and then at

Abigail. Why were his thoughts going in this direction? It was as though she was making him think these things, feel these things. What things, exactly? Like an outsider. A little out of step.

He reached for the bottle of wine; Abi did, too. Their fingers touched one another. He let go of the wine instantly. She was making him feel uncomfortable in his own home. She smiled, a slow smile that started on one side of her mouth, the other taking a moment to catch up; then she picked up the bottle and poured wine into both their glasses.

"Wow, we've made light work of that," she commented, staring at the now-empty bottle. Ben told himself that he must not drink that second glass. "This is nice, isn't it? You and I getting to know one another a little." He didn't comment. What could he say? Abi stood by his elbow. Close. Too close. "So, what are you working on?" She stooped a little to read what was on his screen. Her left breast was just centimetres away from his ear.

"Just emails." He shifted his body away from hers.

She was certainly eye-catching. Quite incredible, actually. It was impossible not to notice.

Ben loved his wife. He thought she was beautiful. Her beauty was subtle, delicate perhaps, even faded if he was brutally honest. Or at least submerged because she didn't have time to take care of herself as well as she ideally might.

There was nothing discreet about Abi's attractiveness. She had big eyes and boobs, long legs and lashes, glossy hair and lips. She was a TV presenter; her larger-than-life shininess came with the territory.

Those sorts of people had to be glistening and out there. But she had to be kidding, right? This was a seduction prototype for dummies. Flush from a bath, silky robe, sharing a bottle of wine. Or was he imagining it? Was he fooling himself? Flattering himself? Maybe she was just being friendly.

Someone coming on to him happened from time to time. He knew how to close it down. He knew the importance of doing so. He was not the sort to flirt or experiment with infidelity. Loyalty was a choice.

He closed his laptop and stood up. "You know, I think I'm going to have to pop back to work."

"What, now?" Abi looked amused, as though she knew he was running away from her. As though she expected it.

"Yeah, now. I've forgotten a file I need." He knew his excuse sounded weak. What file? Was he living in the last century? Obviously, anything that he might need was on his computer.

"You've had a glass of wine," she pointed out. "You can't drive."

Ben held his computer across his chest like a shield, picked up his jacket and headed towards the kitchen door. "I can get a cab, or even a bus." He planned to sit in the pub around the corner for half an hour. He was relieved to hear his wife's and daughters' voices just the other side of the front door. It swung open and they fell in, chattering, laughing, bringing with them a sense of reprieve, escape. The girls simultaneously started to tell Ben about their day. Mel kissed him quickly on the cheek.

"Oh, you're home. Great. Have you put tea on?"

"No, no. I didn't know what time you'd be back."

Mel shrugged. "Same time every week. What shall we have? How many are we?"

"Ben's just heading back to work, actually," said Abi as she emerged from the kitchen.

Mel look confused, a beat as she looked from her husband, agitated, twitchy, and her friend, languorous, semi-clad.

"No, no, I don't have to," said Ben quickly. "Madness at this hour. I don't know what I was thinking."

"Right." Mel turned away from him, started pulling off Lily's shoes.

"So, we're five, Liam's out," added Ben quickly. As he said so, Liam came clattering down the stairs.

"I thought you said he was out," chastised Mel playfully as she made her way to the kitchen. "Abi, you missed the cutest thing."

He never heard what it was that Abi had missed because his wife's voice was lost in the white noise of their domestic setup. Water gushing into a kettle, the girls and Liam chatting, the sound of the TV being switched on.

And blood whooshing around his ears.

His son had been upstairs. She'd practically waved her breasts in his face. Proffered herself on a plate and his son was upstairs. He'd never have done anything. Never, he told himself.

And yet he felt sick with guilt and uncertainty. The room quivered with a sense of relief at escaping a close call.

CHAPTER NINETEEN

MELANIE

Thursday, 8 March

I like my body. Not in a wow-I'm-a-hottie way. Far from it. I like it because it functions well. I rarely catch a cold, I have never broken a bone and most awesome of all, I've given birth to three healthy babies. But facing facts, I'm not the sort of shape that's considered typically desirable. I only stop traffic if I press the button and the lights change. Undeniably, I have breasts, hips, tummy, bum, even a hint of bingo wings—all the curves. Some of them are in the right places, some are certainly surplus to requirements. I've just mentioned, three babies. Have some understanding.

My body has been through the biological equivalent of the hokey-pokey. In, out, in, out, shake it all about. The first time, I snapped back into shape. After all, I was still nineteen when I had Liam, but the last two (and the constant eat-up of fish fingers, pesto pasta and shepherd's pie) mean Ben definitely has more to love; that's the way I look at it and, as I say, I'm fine with that. I like my body.

Or I did, maybe not so much now Abigail's body is so present.

I know, it's immature to compare. Counterproductive and pointless. But! She's so tight and toned, it's unnatural. Abigail has tits. No way would anyone look at them and think of calling them anything as motherly as breasts. They are (literally) outstanding tits. The sort that men dream about. Maybe not her actual husband, as things have turned out. Poor woman. But other men, I'm pretty sure, must appreciate them.

Ben said that she's most likely had some work done. I know he said this to cheer me up but it didn't cheer me up, it just highlighted the fact he'd noticed her amazing bod, too. How could he not? He swears that toned, tight, surgically enhanced bodies don't do it for him but, obviously, he's lying. Her body does it for me and I'm a confirmed heterosexual, I never so much as had a crush on the head girl. Actually, I went to the local comp, we didn't have a head girl. But you get my point.

Abi is hot. Her boobs are pert and full and forward pointing. Like they know where they are going in life. I don't for a second think anything would ever happen between Ben and Abi. I trust him. I trust her. Even if she is prone to drifting around the house in her scanties. I see that as a compliment; it shows she's relaxed with us.

Just this morning, I bumped into her on the landing, dashing from her bedroom to our bathroom wearing nothing other than a towel (which I'm sure was intended to be a flannel). We have two bathrooms in our house but I couldn't ask her to share the kids' one—there is no telling what she'd find, plus it would make Liam uncomfortable. It's awkward enough for him that his sisters are constantly banging on the bathroom door when he's in there, demanding to know, "Why does Liam take so long to poop, Mummy?" A question I'm not sure I can answer.

So, Abi has had to use our en suite. I admit this is awkward at times. She needs to come through our bedroom to get to it. It was no problem at first because she isn't a fan of early mornings and so Ben and I had cleared out to work before she needed to shower, but the past few days she's started to get up with us and the kids, so it has become a little more problematic. She often knocks at our door, but doesn't wait for an answer, just trails through our bedroom before we're out of bed. This is tricky on a couple of counts. One, we tend to sleep naked and Ben gets hot at night so doesn't always stay under the duvet. Obviously, we've now started to wear pyjamas. Two, Abi has a tendency to stay in the bathroom for over an hour. Once she's woken us up, Ben and I are hostage to nature and so have to scramble to the kids' bathroom for a wee.

At least she usually wears a robe (hers is silky and floaty, she looks like a 1920s starlet in it) but this morning, she just had the tiny towel to protect her modesty. It didn't. I was taken aback and you should have seen poor Liam's face. He just happened to stumble out of his room at that point. He turned scarlet, practically climbed into the airing cupboard to get out of the way.

I must say something to her about appropriate dress in front of the children, even if doing so will make me sound provincial, a nude-prude. Still, I ought to tackle it. Since Liam's interview is done, now Ben has started mumbling about when Abi will be moving on. I don't want that, I like having her to stay, so I need to keep the peace.

My boobs. What can I say? Think sports socks with a cricket ball pushed to the toe. Hanging, loosely, forlornly. Swinging about, likely to take an eye out if you come at them from the wrong direction. I blame breastfeeding. True, none of my kids suffer from allergies or food intolerances but sometimes, secretly, I wonder was it worth it? I mean yes, yes, absolutely I know it was worth it but, well (whisper), was it?!

Imogen was practically attached to me twenty-four-seven for fourteen months; I had to prise her off. I was worried that I'd have to go into her primary school to give her a top-up at break time. Yuck. Not judging, just saying, not my thing. Why couldn't she have been a little more temperate? Forget I asked that one. Temperate and Immie are not two words that ever go together.

This is something Abi points out while we are sipping coffee in the kitchen. I've just returned from school drop-off, accessorised with a red face and generally frazzled demeanour that advertises the fact Imogen and I struggled through another tussle at the school gate. Abi has witnessed enough tussles over the past two weeks that the moment I walked in through the door, she flicked the switch on the kettle. Thinking about it, Immie seems to be kicking off more frequently of late. I know she adores Abi being here, but at the same time it's somehow unsettling. She's a little more hyper and my mind isn't really in the game as much as it is when we don't have guests. Obviously, I mean, it's just maths. I have one more person to think about, cook for, talk to. Immie doesn't like sharing my attention.

Abi asks, "What was it today?"

"I made the mistake of kissing her goodbye."

"Doesn't she usually kiss goodbye?"

"Yes, she kisses me. That's the point. She didn't like it that I kissed her. It's a phase she's going through, I know that—I just momentarily forgot."

"She certainly likes to be in charge. On the bright side, she's never going to be anyone's fool," says Abi breezily.

"Right," I agree, reaching for one of the biscuits that Abi has set out on a plate. The plate belonged to my great grandmother and I don't generally use it, it's more for show. I stop myself saying so because no one wants to be known as the sort of person that keeps things for best; it shows a lack of self-confidence. I should think that having coffee and biscuits with my friend is occasion enough to use the plate. I'll just be very careful with it when I'm washing up. "Immie is extreme. She's passionate and stubborn and furious and adorable, all on the flip of a coin. I'm already saving for all the professional psychological help that will be needed to see her through her teen years. Help for me, I hasten to add."

Abi laughs loudly, like I'm extremely funny. I love her for it. Her reaction encourages me to carry on. "She redefined the terrible twos, leapt up the Richter scale. Other mums used to complain about the tantrums their kids had and then Immie would put that in perspective for them."

"How so?"

"Maybe she'd think her T-shirt was too scratchy, or say someone picked up her purple sippy cup by mistake, then she'd put on a show. Why be a storm when you can be a tsunami? I found it mortifying. The other mums looked at me with a naked expression of horror and condemnation, the expression that so obviously said, 'Oh my gosh. My kid is a saint in comparison to yours. Where did you go wrong?'" I pause; this time Abi does not laugh. I'm not funny—what made me think I was? "Sorry, I do go on about my kids a bit."

"No, no, not at all, I find it interesting."

I doubt she does. I mean, I bore myself sometimes and she hasn't even ever been through it. Still, it is nice of her to pretend. She has always been a very polite person. Great at parties, a master of interested and interesting small talk. I sometimes doubted she really did think that French film noir was fascinating but I remember her talking about it for hours with Rob, when she was first trying to secure his attention.

"Was Lily the same? Liam?"

"Lily was a little doll. No trouble at all. Everyone loves her. In fact, I think that's part of Imogen's fury at the world. Sweetie Lily came along just as Imogen was approaching the notorious terrible twos. It must be a bit like feeling menopausal and your husband running off with another younger wo—hell, I'm sorry." I feel the colour flush up my face and neck. Sweat prickles under my arms. I've made the joke about feeling grumpy and then displaced, many times to my mum friends, and it always raises a laugh. I've just never said it to someone who has actually been displaced. "I'm so, so sorry, I didn't mean, I didn't think," I gush.

Abigail waves her hand coolly. Calmly. She doesn't appear to be particularly offended or affronted. Her aloof, confident demeanour is so infinitely impressive. The thought of boring her embarrasses me, the thought of hurting her wounds me. "Anyway, no, in answer to your question, Lily didn't play up in the same way, she was much more self-contained," I manage to stammer.

Abi nods. "I'm so glad I'm getting to know the girls, but I feel I missed out with Liam. What was he like?"

I never know where to start when I talk about Liam's babyhood and early childhood. Illogically, it seems so much bigger than either of the girls'. I'm not saying I love him more; I love them all with equal ferocity. It's just that Liam's childhood memories are somehow more vulnerable than the girls' because I'm the only custodian of them. The vulnerability, I guess, makes them more precious. I've a responsibility to remember everything carefully and accurately, almost formally, because I can't allow myself to colour the memories with my own inflection. I must keep them true, it's a duty. For example, if I say Lily was two when she got her ten-metres swimming certificate, Ben might dive in and insist she was three.

"Really?" I'll ask sceptically. "Yes," he'll say firmly. "Early, though," I'll insist. "Yes, early," he'll agree.

Or if I said Imogen wouldn't go to sleep without her cuddly cat, he'll gently remind me it was a cuddly raccoon, because he'll know. We remember and recall and capture together.

But with Liam there was only me.

He got his ten-metres swimming certificate aged three and four months; by five he could swim a hundred metres; his favourite game was hide-and-seek, which I always cheated at. I kept my eyes open when he was hiding so I knew where he was and (this is the worst bit) sometimes I didn't bother looking for him until, say, after I'd made a cup of tea, and even then, I'd do it really slowly, just because it was nice to get a few minutes to myself.

"Liam?" Abi prompts.

"Off-the-scale cool and cute, an extraordinary kid," I blurt, without really considering how gauche this makes me sound. Abi laughs. "I know, every mum thinks the same about their child," I admit, blushing.

"Oh, I believe you. I'm fully briefed on his achievements."

I look at her quizzically.

"The interview prep I helped him with. He seems like a genius to me," says Abi, laughing. "No one could fail to be impressed."

I nod, gratified. Then I demur, because it's the law. "Kids are impressive nowadays. They do so much."

"So, what do you mean when you say he's an extraordinary kid?"

"I suppose they'd call it emotional intelligence now. He was always thoughtful. Perceptive."

I don't know how to explain it and having tried a few times over the years, I now know it's better not to bother; it just leaves me sounding weird, pushy or deluded. But from an early age, he really did seem to understand way more than other kids did, many of whom seemed a bit glassy-eyed and interchangeable to me, if I'm to be perfectly frank.

"He was born with an old soul. It was as though he knew and understood far more than he should, or possibly could, for his age." I glance at Abi. If she's outright sceptical, she's managing to hide it. I rush on. "It wasn't just me who thought so. My parents, other mums and the nursery teacher made the same observation."

His difference was simultaneously a source of pride and pain for me. I figured it was almost certainly the result of the fact he had one fairly inadequate parent to muddle through with, instead of two competent ones, which was what he deserved. He had to grow up quicker than most other kids.

"Liam isn't your usual teenager, is he?" Abi muses. "I was talking to him about parties and drinking. He doesn't seem that interested."

"No, he's not really," I agree.

"He doesn't seem to have many friends."

I freeze. I know Abigail doesn't mean to criticise

but it's a sensitive subject. "He has friends," I say, a little snappily. "He has the guys he plays football with and—"

Abigail puts a hand on my shoulder. I relax. "I didn't mean anything. It's just a guy like him—handsome, funny, clever, you'd think there would be mates knocking on the door all the time."

"Tanya takes up a lot of time."

"I suppose."

"He's never been the sort to need a big gang of pals," I add.

"Always had you?"

"Yes, and well—" I break off. It's hard to talk about. It's hard for people to listen to. I rush at it. "He had a best friend throughout primary and secondary school. Austin. They were inseparable. But he's gone."

"Did they have a fallout?"

"No."

"Did he move away?"

"Austin died two years ago."

"Oh, Mel, how awful. I'm sorry."

"He ran out in front of a car. Liam was there, actually."

Abi turns pale. People do. It's devastating. The worst thing a parent can ever conceive. Losing a child. It was a dreadful time. Dreadful. Stupid word. It doesn't cover it. Words don't, I found. Not at the time when I was trying to comfort Liam, not when I was offering my sympathy to Austin's devastated parents, not now two years later. Never. "It really

CHAPTER TWENTY

ABIGAIL

Thursday, 15 March

Abigail, a chameleon, easily settled into the Harrisons' home. She'd been with them for three weeks now, turning a deaf ear to Ben's increasingly frequent hints that he could help her look for flats in London if she needed a second opinion, instead choosing only to hear Mel's enthusiastic extensions on her hospitality. Abi had started to recognise, then expect and finally understand their routines, their habits and humour.

She knew that Imogen woke first and that she couldn't resist giving Lily a nudge to get her out of bed, too. She heard their whispers and giggles, then their feet clatter down the stairs, cupboards opening and closing as cereals pitter-pattered into bowls. Their mother would dash downstairs the moment she heard them stir; pulling her drab, bobbled dressing robe around her, make-up smudged beneath her eyes, morning breath. The one time she didn't get to the kitchen before her daughters, they came down to a carpet of Rice Krispies. They were spilt across every surface in the kitchen—spilt or thrown, they never really got to the bottom of it. Ben liked to shower and shave before he emerged. Smart, groomed, dashing, some might say.

Abigail, for instance, she'd say so.

And Liam? Well, he preferred to stay in bed, keep out of the way of all the morning anarchy, if he could. This was easiest on Tuesdays and Wednesdays because he didn't have timetabled lessons first period. The other days he loped down the stairs in whatever garment first came to hand. Sports shorts, more often than not. He didn't bother with a top. Liked to show off his broad chest and developing pecs. Something that often elicited comment from Ben.

"No one wants to see your hairy pits, mate, put on a T-shirt."

The level of noise cranked up a notch once they'd eaten, then the hunt for a lost shoe or book would begin. The girls argued as they cleaned their teeth, Abi stood back from the bathroom door as their toothbrushes swished and then they spat, enjoying feeling part of this domesticity. School uniforms would be hunted, at least twice a week something needed a hasty last-minute iron, and eventually school shoes were tracked down. The goodbyes casually flung, the door banging behind them.

She knew the dance in reverse, too, the sounds of them returning. Their chatter as they fell through the door, how long it took from key in the lock to TV on. She could tell what after-school snacks Melanie was dishing up, just by listening to whether it was a cupboard or the fridge that was opened. She loved both anthems, the family setting off, the family coming home. The girls were easy to read; they paraded their emotions with the entitlement of youth.

"I'm tired."

"I'm hungry."

"I love you."

"She started it, I hate her."

It was enviable, their instinctual prerogative to say what they thought about everything; to have everyone listen and care and respond.

Liam was harder to read. To reach. Obviously. He was well past the age where an ice cream or some extra gaming time could solve everything. He wasn't a child anymore. Although Melanie couldn't see it. She patronised him, closeted him.

Suffocated him.

Abigail saw the ram in him, butting against the fence, wanting to get into pastures new.

And Ben. Well, Ben was a turn-up for the books. Not what she'd been expecting at all. More, she supposed. She'd thought perhaps he might be just a man Mel had settled for. He wasn't. He was a man any woman would strive to attract, go all out to net. He was a pleasant surprise. Quite exciting to be around. Added an extra layer. Sharpened things.

Through the day, when the house was empty, she liked to familiarise herself with their things. Nothing odd in that, basic nosiness. It could get boring on the days that she had to stay at home alone. It wasn't snooping because Mel had made it clear that nothing was off limits to Abi. She'd been more than keen to show her the family photo albums.

The filing cabinet where Ben carefully stored bank statements, the tool shed and their underwear drawers were just a step on from photo albums. Just another layer of family life. The beat of their lives was her lifeblood.

Melanie took it all for granted. She did not see it as the beautiful symphony that Abigail recognised. She sighed impatiently when the girls couldn't decide whether they wanted plaits or ponytails; sometimes as they clambered on her lap, she moaned that her back or legs ached after being in the shop all day; she yelled at them if they left out toys. She didn't appreciate what a privilege it was to be a mother. Sometimes, Abi thought that Mel didn't deserve everything she had, everything she took for granted.

They all had secrets. Abigail didn't like secrets. Hated them, in fact. Families shouldn't have secrets. They were little fissures, cracks, that eventually became great gaping wounds.

Melanie weighed herself every Monday morning and made a note of it in a little book she kept in her make-up bag; funny, because she was always saying that she wasn't in the least bit bothered about how fat she'd become. The notebook exposed the fact she never lost weight but had put on three pounds in six months.

Imogen kept a broken Barbie in the back of her wardrobe, under a bundle of old dance kit—it belonged to Lily. Lily still occasionally wet her bed. Mel knew this of course—she changed the sheets—but it wasn't something she'd told anyone else; it didn't fit with the image of Lily being a go-getting tomboy. Abigail had to assume something was bothering the child.

But they were only babies; Abigail wasn't interested in their secrets. Ben watched porn on his laptop on the first Wednesday of the month when Melanie was at book club. Poor man, Mel really needed to get a better social life—at least that way her husband could masturbate with a little more regularity. Since she so obviously wasn't seeing to his desires herself.

And Liam? Well, he kept the best secret of all.

And Abi knew it.

CHAPTER TWENTY-ONE

MELANIE

Wednesday, 21 March

Ben comes home and finds Abi and me sat at the kitchen table.

"Hello, ladies," he says with a quick smile that frankly looks like it took a bit of effort. I notice his eyes drop to the bottle of Bordeaux. I see him taking in the label, Château Deyrem Valentin Margaux, and recognising it as his.

Usually, the wine we buy is just *ours*, no one claims ownership, but this bottle was bought by his mate as a thank-you because Ben spent an entire weekend helping him clear his garden. It costs twenty-five quid in the supermarket; when we spotted it on the shelf, we nearly died of shock. I'd balk at spending twenty-five quid on a bottle of wine in a restaurant; it would have to be a very special occasion. I know I shouldn't have opened it without him being there to enjoy it, as he did sweat for it, but it was that or the cheap bottle we won on a tombola at the school Christmas fair. Neither of us have touched that as it's likely to be vinegar. We should probably throw it out, but I'll most likely donate it back to the school for the summer fête raffle. I wanted Abi to know I recognised a decent wine when I saw one.

Luckily, Ben is not the type to be funny about this sort of thing. At least, he's unlikely to comment in front of guests, which Abi is, even if she has been here a few weeks now and acts like a member of the family in many ways. He reaches for a glass and pours what's left of the bottle. It makes a half measure. He shrugs, knocks it back.

"Any food left?" He glances at the tureen that has the last remnants of a lasagne, not even a third of a serving. There are a couple of sad tomato halves and wilted lettuce leaves left in the salad bowl but he's not a fan of salad at the best of times.

"Liam came back for seconds," I say apologetically. Ben knows that we can't feed our teenage boy enough. He says he's hungry as he's finishing dinner.

"My fault," giggles Abi. "I just love his appetite. I encouraged him to eat as much as he could. I think he saw it as a dare. It's so different from my experience as a teenage girl. I agonised over every morsel I consumed. He's a delight to watch. I'm rather envious."

Ben opens the fridge, closes it again, letting out an almost imperceptible sigh. I need to get to the supermarket and stock up. I haven't done a big shop this week. Abi and I tend to dash to the M&S Foodhall that's attached to the local petrol station and I pick something up on a day-to-day basis. Prepacked meals are an expensive way to feed six but it's fun. I don't want to waste time shopping and cooking.

Ben opens a cupboard. "I'll heat up a tin of soup."

I feel guilty. I should whip up something a bit more substantial. I think I could manage to pull together eggs, bacon, toast. It isn't that I worship at the altar of the 1950s housewife, but I know Ben would make food for me if I came home from work at eight thirty.

The thing is, I'm at that stage of drunk when I feel a bit lazy and lumpy and can't really be bothered to dash about. The kitchen is a mess. The bin needs emptying and the recycling box is overflowing. The traces of our supper are sprawled over the kitchen table: a chopping board with a half-eaten loaf, the butter dish, a sticky ketchup bottle, glasses, crumbs, drips and splodges. I don't know how it's the case, when we have a dishwasher, but we also seem to have a perpetual sinkful of dirty dishes, too. I tell myself it looks relaxed and cosy rather than squalid. Funny to think of all the effort I put into preparing the house for Abi's arrival. Since she's been here, I've been incredibly lax.

I don't stand up to heat his soup but instead continue to flip through a magazine with Abi; she's looking for ideas for a new haircut. She's set up some meetings in London tomorrow and Friday and is keen to make sure her image is bang up to date. Abi has been mining her contacts this side of the pond. From what she's told me, her initial approaches to various producers and TV companies have been well received. Everyone wants to take her for lunch, to talk.

When I first heard about her meetings I felt almost disappointed, which was stupid of me, selfish.

"You're leaving us?" I asked, shocked. Aghast.

"Well, we can't go on like this forever, can we?" she said, with a sweet smile.

Of course not. Abi must start to piece her life back together. Get back out in the world. She didn't come to England to stay with me and my family. We were only ever a stopgap.

I reminded myself that at least Ben would be pleased to hear there were moves afoot for Abi to move on. He's an easy-going guy but even so, I know he's found having a constant house guest a bit of a bind. He's brought up the subject of when Abi was planning to leave on a number of occasions. I've dodged the matter, refusing to ask Abi outright, because I don't want her to leave. I like having her here. So, I felt a little flattened to hear she's got one foot out of the door.

Ever sensitive to other people's feelings, Abi tried to comfort me. "It's just a few meetings. They may not come to anything." But they will and they should, because Abi is amazing.

She's full of creative, innovative ideas and she's no longer content with just being a presenter, she wants to produce her own shows. I'm certain she's going to be incredibly successful, as soon as she gets her ideas in front of the right people. I'll miss her, though.

"It's just London," she pointed out. "That's way closer than LA." Abi put her arm around me. "Imagine dashing down to visit me in London for a weekend of shopping, drinking cocktails, maybe going to the theatre. We can be the British version of Carrie and Samantha." She giggled. I did, too. It was a seductive idea.

Before Abigail cropped up on my doorstep, my life was full. I was busy. Don't doubt that for a minute. I spent my time wishing there were more hours in the day so that I could finally get to the bottom of the ironing pile, take a long bubble bath instead of a speedy shower or maybe go for a run. Things that inevitably fell to the bottom of my to-do list. Not only was I busy but I definitely had a life that everyone would agree was full of meaning and purpose, not just ironing. I have a husband who loves me, whom I love, three healthy children. I'm living the dream.

It's just. Just that.

Sometimes. Look, I'm not moaning here, but sometimes I am a tiny, tiny bit lost. Or ignored. Even in a full room. No one asks how my day has been. And if they do ask, they don't listen to the answer because they are already shouting stuff like, "Have you seen my goggles?" (Answer: "Yes, they are packed in your swim bag, Lily.") "Who moved my tutu?" (Answer: "No one has, it's on your bedroom floor where you left it, Imogen.") "What's for tea?" (Answer: "Spag bol/lasagne/meatballs, Liam.") "How was your day?" (Not asked, but if it was, answer: "Fine, thanks, I put on three loads of washing, did a big shop, paid bills and oh, you've all left the room.")

Now, I have Abi.

Ben finishes his soup and then says he's exhausted,

he's going to have a shower and an early night. He kisses me on the forehead, says goodnight to Abi as he heads out the door. I can almost hear him counting down the minutes until Abi says she's packing her bags, but I know she'll have no idea he feels that way, he's incredibly polite.

Abi shakes her head, her face a picture of admiration. "Did you date many men before you met Ben?"

"A few," I admit. "I forget about them now. None of them were a big deal at the time and once Ben came along, the few-and-far-between contenders were blown right out of the water."

"You're so lucky."

"Yes." I agree because I *am* lucky that Ben came along and that we fell in love. I didn't feel lucky when I was enduring single-mum dating. I think there were half a dozen abortive attempts. Not a lot of dates, over a period of six years. Most women between the ages of nineteen and twenty-five score higher.

I see that Abi is waiting for me to elaborate. "It was tricky. Liam made potential boyfriends nervous. They all assumed I was looking for a daddy for him—in reality I just wanted a cuddle, not a little box from Tiffany's. I remember first mentioning Liam to one guy and he responded, 'Look, we all have things that we don't want to draw attention to, I wear calf-enhancing socks.' I laughed. I thought he was joking. He was not. I couldn't decide what put me off him most, the fact he thought my son was 'something I didn't want to draw attention to' or that he introduced me to the concept of calf-enhancing socks."

"Noooo!" Abi squeals.

I'm encouraged to go on. "Another guy asked if 'it had all sprung back into shape.' At first I thought he meant my figure—lack of sleep made me slow to process—but then he elaborated, 'Is it all tight, down there? I don't want it to be like throwing a welly down a tunnel.'"

"Oh no, that's horrible," Abi shrieks, giggling.

"It was but you know, it's a long time ago. I just made the decision that it was naps before chaps. Until Ben came along, that is."

"You are so lucky, Melanie. To have such a good man." She must be serious because she rarely calls me Melanie. "You hang on to him." I don't know how to respond. I know that Ben is a good man but agreeing with her sounds smug. Luckily, she isn't waiting for me to respond. "I'm not sure Rob was ever a good man," she muses.

I freeze. The only thing that I find difficult about having Abi here is when the conversation inevitably traverses this way. She has found quite a few ways to call the man a bastard and I don't think she's anywhere near running out of them. I don't disagree but I don't think it's good for her to dwell. She's left him. He's in the past. She needs to move on. That's always been my modus operandi.

She retells the story of finding him with his PA over and over again. It gets more and more elaborate with every telling. Not that I'm suggesting she's exaggerating—she wouldn't; I just mean she's allowing herself to relive it in extreme detail now. I wonder how wise that is.

She's described how the light from the afternoon

sunshine fell on the younger woman's hair, how their clothes were sprawled all over the floor, how she watched as though in slow motion, as her mind untangled what she was seeing. "They didn't even draw the curtains. It was as though they wanted to be seen," she wailed, on one retelling of her story. On another occasion she said, "Maybe they didn't even notice the curtains, maybe they were so consumed with one another."

It's my duty to listen to things I already know. That's friendship. Sometimes she goes days without referencing Rob. Unfortunately, but understandably, he comes into her mind most when Ben is around, especially if he does something she sees as particularly thoughtful, like listening to the girls reading or taking Liam out for some driving practice. Things I appreciate but feel are part of the deal and so rarely compliment Ben on. I mean, no one thinks to congratulate me if I do the same parenting tasks.

Tonight, however, she doesn't say anything more about Rob, she's too involved in her plans for London. She asks me to help her pick out clothes to pack, we watch her showreel and check her train tickets so we can calculate what time she should set her alarm for. I take this as a positive sign. She's heading in the right direction. She'll mend, she'll learn to live without him. Thrive without him. Why not? I'm pleased for her. And for myself.

CHAPTER TWENTY-TWO

BEN

Ben was still awake when Mel came to bed. She looked surprised as it was past eleven and he'd gone up ages ago. Had she expected him to be fast asleep? He wasn't as knackered as he'd made out, he just didn't want to stay downstairs with her and Abi. He didn't have an opinion about whether Abi should have a "lob" that "channelled Emma Stone." Mel could probably work this out, if she stopped to think about it, but she wouldn't think about it.

Mel looked at him with something like guilt. She hadn't had much time for him of late. The kids took the lion's share of her attention (which Ben didn't resent) and Abi sponged up anything she had left over (which, yeah, he did resent). The only time Ben and Mel got to catch up was when they were in bed.

He was reading a sci-fi novel. She gamely asked, "Good book?"

"It's OK." He took off his glasses and rubbed his eyes. He sometimes told her the plots of the books he read in quite some detail. Truth was, she had no interest in sci-fi and on the occasions when he did describe the plot or offer up a review, he often thought that she tuned out, probably thinking about what she needed to pick up at the supermarket. Still, he usually told her anyway, in the vain hope that one day she'd demand to read the book after him; it was one of those little dances that married couples performed to keep things ticking over. Tonight, he didn't even bother.

She went into the bathroom, washed her face and cleaned her teeth.

"Enjoyed the wine, did you?" he asked.

"Yes. But ill-advisedly we also cracked open that tombola bottle after you went to bed. There really was nothing else. Mistake. I can already feel the effects under my eyes, on my neck, in my head."

She'd been knocking it back since Abi arrived but he didn't comment. He didn't need to; Mel was a grown-up.

"I probably should cut back and get more sleep. I won't drink when she's in London. That will give my liver a few days off."

Ben knew that Mel should have done all this a long time ago. Late, gossipy, boozy nights. He realised she was making up for lost time.

"Was it a good night?" he asked, as she threw back the duvet and climbed in next to him.

"Yeah."

"Lots of chatter?" He didn't mean to but he could hear it himself—the way he'd said the word *chatter*, he'd made it sound like an illicit activity. Something slightly shady or at least giddy. He wasn't trying to convey implicit disapproval, but he had.

"Yes," Mel replied simply.

"You are certainly warming to your role as confidante." He said *confidante* in a silly way, too, emphasising each of the syllables. It was just a bit weird. He didn't know what was the matter with him. He wasn't being himself. Abi put him on edge. Since that evening in the kitchen when he thought she was coming onto him he'd avoided them being alone together, whereas she seemed to seek it. Was he being a dick, imagining it? Who did he think he was? Idris Elba? He hadn't mentioned the incident to Mel, she'd probably laugh her head off. But if he wasn't wrong, and Abi was making a play for him, then maybe he should talk about it with Mel.

Before he found the words, she said, "We watched her showreel."

"Oh yeah, she showed me and Liam that, too."

"What did you make of it?" Mel asked excitedly. "I thought she was amazing. She was so in control. She made people look charismatic and charming or she could expose them as bigoted fools. Very clever."

His wife was practically in love with this woman. He didn't want to burst her bubble with his half-formed suspicions. Still a note of caution, realism couldn't hurt. "Well, naturally Abi has put together her best work. Her funniest, most flattering interviews, to impress. It is a showreel after all."

"Abi always had a sort of throwaway candour that people find refreshing and dazzling. She's managed to harness that in a way that makes her an enticing but also probing interviewer," Mel concluded.

Ben sighed, exasperated. "I don't think there's anything disposable about her candour at all. She's an actress. A controlled, tight professional."

"Wow, that sounds a bit harsh."

Ben shrugged. "I'm not being harsh. But it's her job, right?" He decided not to say any more. Mel didn't probe. She'd clearly decided that there were times in a marriage that if you know your partner is trying to hold something back, you let them. You respect their decision to exercise self-restraint. It's not always good to talk. She turned out her bedside light but he didn't follow suit.

"I was wondering how much longer you think she might be staying for." He sounded politely guarded. It was a new thing between them. Normally, they were totally frank with one another; they saved their Sunday-best manners for people they didn't love and trust quite so much. "It will be four weeks tomorrow since she arrived."

"Has it? That's flown by. I feel so sorry for her," Mel said sadly.

Ben reached out his hand and found his wife's under the covers, squeezed tightly. "It's a terrible situation to be in. I don't mind helping out your friend. Naturally, I want to," he murmured. She looked at him, waited for the *but*. There so obviously was one. "But an open-ended invitation is not easy to negotiate. Our home life is so disrupted."

"How so?"

Ben was terrified to be alone with her, the girls

were becoming wild, Liam seemed changed, too. Ben couldn't say exactly how—harder to reach, not insular, maybe aloof. Ben couldn't find a way of articulating any of that so he stuck to the facts.

"Well, the smoking." Ben loathed smokers. He couldn't understand it. Why poison yourself? He resented passive smoking and was angry that the kids were being polluted.

Mel nodded. "I'll reiterate the no-smoking-in-the-house rule."

"She hogs the bathroom."

"She's started to use the kids' bathroom more, so as not to get in our way, but I'll keep an eye on it."

"Plus, she's not careful about what she says in front of the girls. Yesterday Lily said, 'You're the bitch' and then high-fived me because I tied her shoelaces."

"Ah."

"Not a suitable expression of joy for a six-year-old, I think you'd agree."

Mel looked infuriated, as though she thought Ben was the pain in the arse for bringing these things to her attention, rather than Abi being at fault for doing them. "Abi hasn't had kids, she doesn't have the same sensitivities. Is this really about me being out for tea yesterday?" she asked huffily.

"Yesterday and twice last week. The kids can't live on restaurant food." Ben knew he sounded like a bit of a wanker, a throwback. He wasn't sure why he couldn't present his case more pleasantly and convincingly. He just needed Abi to leave.

"They can," Mel pointed out.

"OK, well, we can't afford constant restaurant

food, plus you stayed out late and had to get a cab home."

"I'd had a drink, you couldn't want me to drive home."

"No, I'd never suggest that. But because you didn't get up early enough to retrieve the car the next day, we got a parking ticket. An eighty-pound fine."

"Sorry about that." She didn't sound particularly sorry. "Next time we'll walk there and plan to get a cab back."

"That's not really my point."

"But it is a solution."

They both fell silent and stared at the ceiling. Ben thought that if Mel dwelt on the points he'd made, she'd see that they were all reasonable.

"I'm really tired," Mel mumbled. "I just need some sleep. I have work in the morning and no time for this."

"Time to sink two bottles of wine, though," he snipped. He hadn't meant to say that but seriously, tired? Who was to blame for that?

"You are not to be pacified, are you? I suppose I should be pleased you're not falling under her substantial charms. Other women might have to worry about that." Mel said this with a smile in her voice. She was trying to avoid a row. He didn't want a row either but her comment just embarrassed him. He couldn't explain.

Instead he asked, "She has a meeting in London tomorrow, right?"

"Yes, she does. A couple, I think, from what she

was saying. She's setting off early to get her hair cut and then she's meeting an agent on Friday."

"What's her proposed show about then?" Ben asked. They were still holding hands; hers felt a bit clammy now. Uncomfortable.

"I did ask but she was vague."

"Did she think you wouldn't get it?"

"Ben!"

"Or is it top secret and she felt she couldn't tell you? Both explanations for her ambiguity are a bit insulting, wouldn't you agree?"

Mel snapped impatiently, "What is the matter with you? Don't you get it that sometimes it's not helpful to be reductive? She has many ideas. She's very creative. Nothing is set in stone yet."

"So, these meetings are brainstorming sessions, rather than actual pitches?" He wanted to come across chilled and cool but he knew he was behaving like a dog with a bone.

"There's a lot of interest," Mel replied firmly.

"Good." Ben wiggled a little closer to his wife; the length of his body was warm, pushed next to hers. "It's good that she seems to be in demand. I don't think it's going to be too tricky for her to find work again." His point being that as soon as she was back in work, their lives would go back to normal. "I guess she'll want to get settled in London now things are hotting up for her."

"Well, she will be down there for a day or two but she'll be back at the weekend."

"Hasn't she got meetings next week, too?"

"Yes."

"Wouldn't it make more sense to stay in London?"

"It's expensive to take a hotel for the whole weekend."

God forbid Abi should actually spend any money. "Couldn't she catch up with some of her other friends?" He felt exasperated.

"She hasn't mentioned anyone and London is just an hour on the train from here. Why wouldn't she come home?"

"Home?"

"You know what I mean. Anyway, we're going to the cinema on Saturday evening. Do you remember? I asked if you were OK with looking after the girls or if you wanted to come with us, in which case I'll get Liam to sit."

"Will Liam be around?"

Liam was off to Scotland tomorrow for a visit to the Scottish Parliament. His politics teacher had organised the trip. He was excited about it.

"Yes, he'll be back Saturday afternoon."

"What are you going to see?"

"That one with Meryl Streep."

He considered it. "No, you go without me. Liam won't want to sit. He'll want to be out with Tanya after being away in Edinburgh."

"Are you going to turn your light out?" Mel asked. "I'm really knackered."

He did as she asked and they lay in the darkness, Ben's eyes open, his mind whirling. "How are Abi's finances?" he asked.

"Wow, Ben, you can't ask that."

"I can, considering she's staying with us, rent free."

"She's a friend, a guest. You can't think I'm going to ask her for rent."

"No, I realise you'd never do that, you're far too generous for your own good, but I thought maybe she'd offer, or at least do a shop or something. I mean, if she's going to stay much longer."

"She bought me a bunch of flowers the other week."

"Supermarket flowers. If I'd bought you those, you'd have thrown them back at me."

"I would not." She would. They both knew it. He waited patiently for her to answer his question.

"Abi has made one or two references to money since she's been staying with us. Nothing specific, but enough for me to gather she's a bit short at present."

Ben tutted.

"It's just a matter of cash flow. Once the divorce is settled, she'll be in a better position, really quite wealthy. Her assets are currently tied up."

"When you say her assets, you mean Rob's, don't you?"

"Which is practically the same thing."

"I don't know if his lawyer would agree."

"Obviously she's not as well off right now as she was, but she says she likes rising to the challenge of economising."

Ben snorted.

"What?" asked Mel.

"Well, no one who is ever really broke likes 'rising to the challenge of economising.'" He repeated

the words, couldn't resist dipping them in heavy sarcasm. "People who are genuinely broke hate it. They
stress and worry about it."

"I never said broke. It's cash flow. Look, Ben, talking about money with Abi—or any of my friends—is
a bit icky-making."

"That's odd, because you happily talk about breast
exams, bodily fluids, the colour and consistency of
children's poop. I've heard you. You are not normally
known for being shy."

"Yeah, but that's different."

"Doesn't she have any savings? Isn't Rob giving
her anything? He must be. It's the law."

"I don't know all the ins and outs of her finances.
Obviously, her lifestyle is going to be adversely im-
pacted by the separation but she's a strong woman
with skills and talents—she'll get back on her feet.
The last thing she needs now is any pressure from
her friends."

"Yeah, but we can't go on indefinitely. We need an
end date." Ben just wanted Abi out of the house, he
wanted them to be a tight little family again.

"Don't you like her? I can't see why you don't
like her."

"It's not that I don't like her," he replied carefully.

"That's a lot of negatives."

"Just two. The correct amount for a positive." But
he knew he didn't sound positive.

They lay in awkward silence. The tension in the
air, overpowering. Mel yawned ostentatiously. "Look,
tomorrow, when Abi is in London and Liam is out,

maybe we should do something, just us and the girls. Or even just us."

Eventually, he mumbled, "Maybe."

"A takeaway? Thai? Fish and chips? Or I could cook. Beef fillet? It will be nice. Now, let's get some sleep."

Ben agreed, "OK, I'll make sure I'm out of the office dead on five."

CHAPTER TWENTY-THREE

MELANIE

Saturday, 24 March

We never managed the takeaway or the beef fillet, I didn't even get to see the Meryl Streep film. Instead, I spent Friday and Saturday at my parents' home, the result of a call from my mum saying she and Dad had both come down with what she described as a "nasty sickness virus"; they needed me, to see they kept hydrated, to change sheets, to nurse them as well as I could.

Ben took the reins with the girls and I swapped my Friday shift for Sunday, gambling that my parents would be on the road to recovery by then, or a worst-case scenario, Ben would take over from me. Obligingly, my parents had stopped vomiting by Saturday evening and were even able to eat some soup and crackers. I played with the idea of stopping over but just before midnight I made the decision to drive home. I wanted to get back to my family and Abigail; I could always return if they needed help tomorrow.

As I pull the car onto the drive, I see that the house is in darkness. I sneak in the front door, quietly closing it behind me. I'm totally knackered but also a little bit wired and feel in need of twenty minutes' reading before I go to sleep. As a working mum who is always busy and in demand, there is a secret quiver of freedom attached to being awake when everyone else is tucked up in bed. I don't feel hurried or observed. I feel like I'm breaking the rules. I don't want to disturb Ben so I get a glass of water from the kitchen and then head into the sitting room.

"Gawd, Liam, you scared me." I jump out of my skin, spilling water down my top and jeans as I catch sight of Liam in my peripheral. He's lounging in the saggy leather armchair that I think of as the cats' chair.

Sometimes when I see Liam unexpectedly, it takes me a fraction of a nanosecond to recognise him. His size and width always surprise me. I still expect to see—well, not a little boy—but maybe an eleven-year-old, skinny shouldered, knobbly kneed. Liam has broad shoulders, definition around his chest, and his legs are like tree trunks. Him growing up shouldn't be a surprise to me, but it is. I don't understand how I can have grown this giant.

"How was Edinburgh? What are you doing sat in the dark?" I glance at the clock—it's half past midnight and he's not watching YouTube videos or playing video games. I flick on a coffee-table lamp.

Obviously, it's tricky to impose bedtimes as such on people who are six foot plus, but normally Liam has taken himself off to bed by now or is glued to his PC.

"Who is my dad?"

"What?" The question is so stark and unexpected that for a moment I don't understand it at all. It's late. It's been a long night. My mind is still with my parents. They were asleep and peaceful when I left but will they be able to keep down supper? "What?" I ask a second time, dumbly.

"It's an easy question. I mean, I'm hoping you have some idea. Who is my dad?" It's impossible not to hear the aggression in his voice.

"Ben is your dad," I say firmly.

"You know what I mean. Who is my father?"

I put down my handbag, take off my jacket and shoes. These actions buy me precisely thirty seconds, not long enough. "Why do you ask?"

"I'm not allowed to ask?"

"Of course you can ask. It's never been a secret. You've just never shown any interest before so, I mean, why are you asking now?"

He shrugs. I sigh and sit down on the sofa opposite him. I don't flop back but instead perch awkwardly, leaning towards him. I reach forward to put my hand on his knee; he shifts out of my way.

The last time Liam asked about his biological father he was seven years old. Ben had just proposed to me and I'd said yes, provisionally. I'd said I needed to check with Liam first. It wasn't that I was asking Liam's permission, exactly—and even if I had been, I was certain he'd give it because he adored Ben from the get go—it was more that I felt it would be weird to present the situation as a *fait accompli*.

I took Liam to a café for his tea, just the two of us. I remember he was actually put out that Ben wasn't joining us. Ben always did this daft little trick with his drinking straw if it was in a paper packet. He'd rip off one end of the paper and then blow so that the paper wrapping shot off, often into Liam's face. Liam used to laugh his socks off over that. Ben still does the same now for Lily and Imogen; they never laugh as much as Liam did.

"Where's Ben? Is he coming?" Liam demanded, looking about expectantly.

"Well, today it's just the two of us because I have something big I need to talk to you about," I explained.

"OK," said Liam, not looking especially interested, let alone concerned. I explained to him that Ben had asked to marry me, that he wanted to be Liam's daddy.

"What do you think?" I asked. "I mean, I'd like to marry Ben, but only if you want it, too, because we both have to want this."

"Would he live with us?"

"Yes. He'd probably sell his flat and we'd move out of ours. We'd probably buy something new for all of us. A house, hopefully. A small house."

"That's cool," Liam said, smiling. "I'd like to live with Ben. And would I get to call him Daddy?"

"Yes, angel. If you want to."

"I really want to. I think you should say yes quickly."

I started to smile, said we should order milkshakes

to celebrate and assured Liam I would say yes as quickly as possible.

"You don't want him to change his mind," said Liam with some concern.

"We can text him if you like!" I laughed.

"Do that." And then Liam reached across the table and put his chubby, sticky little hand on mine and whispered, "Does this mean the daddy who made me can never come back and take me now?"

I was shocked. He'd never hinted that he believed this to be a possibility. "Angel, that's never going to happen," I said quickly, hoping to reassure him.

"Why not? Doesn't he love me?"

My heart stopped. That's what it can be like, having a child. One minute you are euphoric, certain you are making their world a happier and better place. The next minute you are crashing, realising you've messed something up. What was the right answer? "He doesn't know about you, Liam, my sweet. I am sure if he did he would love you more than anything in the world."

"Why doesn't he know about me?" Liam, by this point, was drawing on the corner of his menu. He was drawing a robot, his favourite doodle at the time.

"I didn't tell him."

"Why not?"

"I didn't know how to." I am not a trained child psychiatrist. I have no idea if this was the best answer to give my angelic seven-year-old, it was just the best I could do.

"Why not?"

"Because I didn't know where he lived." What else could I say? How else could I explain it?

"Well," said Liam, smiling, "what he don't know can't hurt him, as Nana always says." I suspected my mum used this expression when she secretly gave Liam jam sandwiches for tea. "If my first daddy doesn't know about me, I don't think he'll mind if Ben is going to be my daddy now," said Liam finally. "I'll have a strawberry milkshake, please, Mummy."

From that day onwards, Liam called Ben Daddy and Ben *was* Daddy. He has never, ever asked anything about his biological father, even when he was studying sex education or genetics in biology or when he had to draw a family tree for social studies. Sometimes, in our home, we might comment that Imogen has my temper, or that Lily is messy like I am. Liam sometimes jokes that he gets all his good qualities (his patience, his logical reasoning, his ability with tech) from Ben. We never allowed the fact of his biology to get in the way of what we wanted to believe. Liam never showed any curiosity about his father, and I suppose, I allowed myself to believe he was an irrelevance.

I glance at Liam now. He's not looking at me. He's looking at his hands. Large hands, angular, long, tapering fingers. They are nothing like the chubby hand that reached across the table to squeeze mine, all those years ago, in the café. A lot like his father's hands, if my memory serves me correctly. "What do you want to know?"

"Who he is."

"I'm sorry, Liam, I don't know, not exactly," I stutter, uncomfortably.

Liam stares at me now. I recognise the look; it's just I've never seen him throw it, and certainly never my way. It cuts. The look says he thinks I'm a slut. I rush on, trying to correct his perception. "I mean, I know who he is but just not his name. Least not his full name."

"Explain. What do you know about him?"

"His name was Ian. We met one night at a club when I was at uni. We hit it off." I stop. I wonder how much detail Liam can possibly want. Not too much, surely. No one wants to think about their mother in that way. No one can really imagine their mother young and irresponsible. Wild and impetuous. Wrong. "We only ever… It was just… It was a one-night stand," I admit.

Liam looks disgusted with me. I'm surprised—he's not normally the judgemental type.

I've left this conversation too late. How could I have fooled myself into believing he wasn't giving this any thought? Over the years, Liam and I have had an open relationship and we talk about most things freely: alcohol, drugs, sex. I suppose we've just never talked about sex in conjunction with me. Normally I'm the one lecturing him to be careful, considerate. We've had awkward convos—ones about porn and specific consent. Now I feel dirty and inexperienced. Wrong.

"You have to bear in mind, Liam, I was only a year older than you are now. I wasn't thinking clearly. He was gorgeous." I smile half-heartedly, trying to win him over by telling him something favourable and true about his father.

"Did the condom split or something?"

"Erm." There is no good answer to this question.

"I know it happens. You read it on the packet. Ninety-eight per cent safe. Was I the two per cent? Am I the product of a reckless liaison and a Durex failing?"

Oh wow, I feel sick. I've just told my son that he's the result of a one-night stand? Can I also tell him that I did not practise what I preach? I didn't use a condom. If I do, I have the small comfort of knowing it's the truth, but I'll probably lose his respect forever and I'll certainly lose my right to offer any moral orienteering tips in the future. I wish Ben was here. He'd help me out. He'd find a way of making this crap origin story seem bearable.

Liam doesn't wait for me to respond but pushes on. "What's his surname?"

"I don't know."

Liam sits forward in his chair and glares at me. "How can you not know? When you found out you were pregnant, didn't you track him down? Tell him? How did he respond?"

"I never saw him again. Not after that night. He wasn't a student at my uni. He was visiting." It sounds brutal. It doesn't get any easier to say. Not even all those years on.

My son stares at me, weighing up what he's been told, then he flings himself back in his seat and spits, "I don't believe you."

"What?"

"You're lying."

"Liam!" I've had several responses to my story over the years. At first people were shocked, angry, frustrated and judgemental. Some people were sympathetic, embarrassed for me. Others thought they could solve the problem, suggesting that I go on Facebook and try to track him down that way. I'd explain it was a needle in a haystack. A common name. No surname. Not even sure of where he lived.

No one has ever doubted my story.

"I don't believe you," repeats Liam. "You would never have given up that easily. It's not your style. I've seen you put weeks of effort into tracking down a lost swimming towel, Mum. You'd have found a way of tracking him down."

"No, Liam, how could I? How could I possibly have done that?"

"You're hiding something. I know you better than anyone and I don't believe you."

"Liam, honey, you just don't want to believe me. It's a different thing." I don't manage to finish my sentence because he stands up and roughly pushes past me.

"I'm going to bed."

CHAPTER TWENTY-FOUR

MELANIE

Sunday, 25 March

The alarm clock goes off and I know I won't get a chance to talk to Ben about Liam's outburst because I must get to work, nor do I get a chance to speak any more with Liam himself because, naturally, he's still in bed when I set off; not that I'm sure what I might say. I'm glad when Abi turns up at the shop and suggests we have lunch together. She says she wants to tell me all about her meetings in London and she wants to know how my parents are.

However, when we sit down together at an outside table at Pret, I find myself blurting out the details of the scene with Liam. It's all I can think about. I've been anxious and stressed all morning. Years ago, I discovered that my children's moods colour my own, dictate them, actually. If they're happy, then I'm happy. If they're not, well… She's not as sympathetic as I'd hoped she would be. I think she's trying to help but it comes out wrong.

"I guess he'd rather believe his mum is a liar than a slut," she says bluntly.

"Oh, thanks very much, Abi. That's comforting."

She takes a drag on her cigarette. "Sorry, I didn't realise I had to sugar coat it." She smiles.

She's right, she's entitled to be brutal. Real friends tell it as it is. She's helping. Or at least trying to. She doesn't know how awful rowing with Liam makes me feel.

It's always been that way. When there was just the two of us I hated it if—on the rare occasions that he had a tantrum or I had to bring him into line over something—we fell out with each other. If we did, then who did we have? He'd run into his bedroom, turn and face the wall, refuse to look at me. His little body, clad in dungarees and Bob the Builder T-shirt, quivering with anger, hurt or temper—the particular brand of outrage that only preschoolers can feel. I learnt that there was no use in pursuing him. Our flat was so tiny that my trying to coax him back into a good humour just made him feel trapped and cornered. Instead, I'd stay in the kitchen, waiting for him to reappear when he was ready.

It's been different with the girls. If they ever feel stroppy with me, then Ben or Liam can play the good cop and cajole them around. There are more options. Liam and I had very few options. It's another luxury denied to single parents. So, fallouts felt massive and they still do, even though we now have Ben and the girls to cushion the blow. Liam's anger at me is rare and so painful, it's almost debilitating.

"What are you going to tell him?" Abi asks.

"There's nothing I can tell him," I say, keeping my eyes trained on my tuna and cucumber baguette. I push it to the side. I don't have an appetite. "I wonder what brought it into his head?" I ponder.

"Me," says Abi.

"You?" I ask, startled.

"I guess, you know, having me, someone from your past, in your home. It's a first, right? My presence must have made him start thinking about all this stuff."

"Oh, yes. I see." I'm relieved. "I thought you meant you'd talked to him about it."

"Why would I?"

I don't answer. I just drop my head into my hands. "I feel so dreadful."

"He'll get over it. He'll get used to his pretty desultory paternity story soon. Luke Skywalker heard worse." I appreciate she's trying to make me laugh but she can't. Suddenly I have a need to explain it to Abi.

"The issue is, I'm always playing catch-up with him."

"What do you mean?"

"I created Lily and Imogen with a perfect man—or as near as damn it. I gave them a doting, reliable father from the off. I picked well for their creations. I can't claim the same for Liam, so I guess I always feel I need to make things up to him. That I owe him." I glance around the busy street, full of harried, careworn shoppers; momentarily I can't see anyone looking bright and optimistic. Life can be tough. "I feel I put him into this race but tied his legs together, gave him a handicap."

Abi is staring at me. It must be the dazzling spring sunlight, unexpected and bouncing from the aluminium table between us into her eyes, because the way she's squinting causes her face to curl up into a hideous expression. For a split second, she looks disgusted. But then her expression changes and I know I imagined it. She pats my hand and says, "Don't worry, you'll think of something to say to him. You've always been good at explaining things away." She's beaming at me, but it doesn't sound like a compliment.

It doesn't sound like an admirable skill. Just a convenient one.

Abi stretches her hands into the air and then lets her head fall first to the right and then to the left, unfurling like a cat in the sunshine. It's an expansive, inflated gesture. It demonstrates an entitlement to space, energy and attention. I notice two or three bypassers glance in her direction.

I guess I'm tired, and stressed over this business with Liam, because an incredibly uncharitable thought comes to mind. I remember a passage in one of my favourite novels, *Pride and Prejudice*; Miss Bingley persuades Elizabeth Bennet to walk around the room and Darcy scathingly dismisses her actions as a clear attempt to draw attention to her figure. I can't help but think Abi's stretch shows the curve of her boobs, the length of her neck, the narrowness of her waist to their greatest advantage. Calculated to draw admiration.

I must talk to her about running around partially clothed in the house and I owe it to Ben to mention the smoking, the swearing, the hogging of the bathroom and all the other little things that were bothering him, but I just can't face them right now. They're not important. Now, I just want to sip my coffee, close my eyes, feel the heat of the spring sunshine on my eyelids. I don't really want to think about all the niggles of home. I turn the focus on Abi so that I don't have to.

"You look well after your break in London," I comment.

"Yes, it's where everything happens."

I avoid Abigail's eyes. It is not where my everything happens. My everything happens here, in Wolvney; mostly inside the four walls where my family dwell. I thought she'd got that. I thought she liked that. I think my studious avoiding of her eyes gives her pause to think.

"Oh, I don't mean… I don't want to sound ungrateful. It's just that's where my new agent is and the meetings. My contacts." She trails off. Stops digging her own grave.

"Of course it is, no offence taken," I say, waving her comment away. "Now, tell me about the meetings with the producers. How did they go?" I pick up my paper cup of coffee and beam at her. "I'm all ears."

"Oh, no, well, there's nothing much to report."

"Do you think they went well?" I'm disappointed by her lack of excitement.

"What?"

"The meetings."

She pauses, reaches for the sachets of sugar and stirs a spoonful into her espresso. I've never noticed her take sugar before. "Actually, they were cancelled. I did meet with my new agent, though."

"Cancelled? All of them?"

"Both of them. There were only ever two," she says a bit snappily. "Well, postponed, actually. You know these things happen. I'm dealing with very busy people. Much in demand. Their diaries are constantly in flux."

"Oh, I'm so sorry." I imagine her disappointment and embarrassment. Trailing all the way to London only to be told at the last minute that the meetings were cancelled. Postponed. I'm just thinking about whether I should offer for us to get a takeaway tonight, a sort of cheer-up treat, when she glances up to me and beams.

"But you had a good time, right? You're smiling," I say, relieved. "It was worth it to secure the UK-based agent, I take it?"

"No, not that," she giggles.

"Then what?"

She instantly covers her face, much the way Lily does if there's too much adult kissing on the TV, embarrassed but a bit thrilled. "I went on a date."

"No!" I squeal excitedly. Abi laughs at my reaction. "Tell me all," I demand.

"There's not much to tell, really." She shrugs. I'm unconvinced. I mean, she's grinning from ear-to-ear.

"Who is he? Where did you meet him? Was it Tinder?" She shakes her head. "One of the other dating sites then? Give me details," I demand. There is obviously loads to tell. This is great news, just the diversion I need to avoid having to think about what

I'm going to say to Liam. Abi laughs again and then relents.

"Yes, one of the sites."

"What's he like?"

"Funny, clever, tall, blonde. A lot like Rob, as it happens. I think *I* do have a type."

I want to get her off the subject of Rob. She should be moving forward, not looking back. It's much better that she concentrates on the here and now.

"What does he do for a living?"

"Something in education," she says vaguely. Again, this sounds like Rob when she met him; maybe she has a professor thing. I try another angle.

"So, what did you do together?"

"Nothing much, we just wandered about London, mostly walked around the Southbank area, talking. Non-stop talking." She's staring at her hands.

"And?" I demand. There is so definitely an *and*.

"There was this amazing chemistry between us." Her voice is low and lush, the bitterness that sometimes means she clips her words has completely vanished.

"Did you kiss him? Are you planning on seeing him again? Come on, details!" She looks up now but at a spot above my ear. She is struggling to meet my eye.

"The kiss, it was—" She breaks off, shakes her head as though confused. "Just wonderful. He kept his eyes open and looked at me like he'd never experienced such bliss."

"Oh my gosh. You had sex."

She bursts out laughing. "Well, yes, actually we went back to my hotel."

"No! Yes!" I mini-punch the air. "I want to know everything."

Abi glances at her watch. "Yup, obviously, I can't wait to fill you in but, right now, no can do. You were supposed to be back at work five minutes ago."

"Bugger!" I jump up from my chair, causing a clattering and nearly upsetting my barely touched coffee. "We'll have to continue this conversation later," I say regretfully as I'm already dashing up the street. I turn and call over my shoulder, "What's his name?" I'm desperate to show that I am interested and pleased for her.

"Stud," she trills back.

"For real?" I ask.

"No, of course not." Giggling. When we were at university we used to distinguish between different potential boyfriends by calling them things like "Kilt" or "Mr. Shakespeare." She called Rob "Prof." It was because we knew a lot of men called Matt or Mark, Rob or Bob. Her giving this man a nickname brings to mind those heady days. The anonymity is somehow invigorating.

"Well, I want the full low-down later." I speed off, almost knocking over an old dear with a pull-along shopping basket because I'm not really looking where I'm going.

My manager glances purposefully towards the clock on the wall when I dash through the door. I ignore her, I don't care. I'm full of excitement and happiness for my friend. She's really cheered me up.

CHAPTER TWENTY-FIVE

ABIGAIL

He had no body consciousness. He moved with such carelessness. He just pulled up his T-shirt and scratched his belly in front of her. She saw it, the narrow provocative line of hair that pointed down. His jutting pelvic bone and the thin, almost delicate skin that stretched across the cavity, like a tablecloth strung out. She stared at him. She was wild about him. His body was beautiful. Compelling, available. He was generous with it. Invited her to enjoy it.

She gripped the smooth hotel pillow in her fists and felt his breath behind her, the burning air on her shoulders, her back. He straddled her, confidently. Entered her with a neat, self-assured efficiency that surprised her. Then backwards, forwards. A rhythm. Their pace. She started to sweat, slip between his thighs. She was glad he couldn't see her face, normally so calm, cool and composed. Now red, wild, puffed up with passion.

It was boldly back to front. Main act and then post-play that became foreplay as he started again. First one way, then another. He flipped her over. He didn't seem to care that her face was ablaze; his was steady, concentrating. That surprised her. He seemed more concerned with her pleasure than she might have imagined, than she remembered Rob ever being. He held her nipple in his mouth, cradled her other breast in his palm, his other hand seeking out the heat of her. She couldn't get enough of him. She slid up and down, discovering him, introducing herself. His neck. Her nipples. His stomach. Her thighs. She licked him, salty, on her tongue. She felt her wetness slipping on his skin.

She was exhausted and aching but she didn't care. She didn't want to waste time by sleeping. She was owed so much. And she was collecting. Every moment counted. She wanted him to exhaust her, numb her, change her. She wanted his weight on top of her.

"Like this?" he murmured. A question. As though he was inventing something. And he was. She nodded.

There was no end to it, no end to the new things. When he finally collapsed on top of her, they stayed like that, slick, exhausted, spent, splendid until the weight of him eventually became too much and she crawled out from underneath.

She felt the scales swing, adjust, find a new point of balance. This much she was owed.

CHAPTER TWENTY-SIX

BEN

Ben was in the kitchen with Abi and the girls when Mel got back from work. They were making a Lego city; it stretched across the table and covered most surfaces. The project had taken all afternoon; no one wanted to stop and pack away. Ben caught his wife's mood, flighty like a spring breeze carrying cherry blossom. She dashed around the kitchen, pulling crockery out of cupboards, opening the fridge and breadbin, grabbing anything that came to hand, then slamming them closed again.

He sensed that she wanted him and the children out of the way, that she wanted to talk to Abigail alone. He resented it and rather than accommodate her obvious need for a gossipy chat, he contrived to interrupt it. He sometimes went for a run at teatimes but he chose not to today, instead he offered to help make tea, taking a strange delight in ostensibly being the helpful husband but in fact being a bit of a pain in the backside. His wife should want rid of Abi, she should want to spend time with him, he thought.

He put tomatoes in a colander, ran them under the tap, started to make a salad because it looked like his wife was doing pasta. "You must be so tired, Mel, after a day on your feet in the shop," he commented, throwing a glance at Abi. She could have offered to lend a hand but hadn't. Rarely offered, never actually helped.

He saw Mel catch Abi's eye and wink. "Me? No. *I'm* not the one that hasn't had enough sleep."

Abi giggled, like she was a teen. It irritated him. He wasn't a fool, he could take a wild guess: Abi had shagged someone. So what? Put out the bunting.

"I thought, after being at your mum and dad's, you'd be whacked. I know you never sleep well there." He put a hand on Mel's shoulder and squeezed. He knew she needed him to cuddle in to.

Mel didn't acknowledge him, other than to mutter, "I'm fine."

"I called them," he added.

"Who?"

"Your parents."

"Oh." She had the decency to colour. She should have called them at lunchtime—how could she have forgotten?

He was aware he was point scoring, he just couldn't stop himself. "They're on the mend. They've eaten scrambled eggs on toast today."

"Oh, thanks." She didn't seem that grateful. She was still bouncy and scatty. Untethered. She fried some mince and onions for a bolognese sauce. "Where's Liam?" she asked.

"Not sure, at Tanya's probably."

"How was he today?"

"Great. Why?"

"Happy?" she asked tentatively. Casting a quick glance at the girls, who were ostensibly still playing with their Lego but really, as always, just hanging about, listening in.

"Seemed it. Very much so. Full of the joys of spring actually," Ben confirmed. He noticed his wife didn't seem as delighted by this news as she usually was, as he'd expect her to be.

"Just me then," she muttered.

Ben found Mel's secretive and skittish mood particularly irritating. Since Abi had started to live with them, he wasn't unused to feeling a little sidelined or out of the loop. Conversations did sometimes stop when he walked in the room; it was rude. This evening Abigail and Melanie both seemed to be particularly restless, sharing meaningful glances; he found it childish.

By the time they'd put the girls to bed, Ben wasn't in the mood for anything other than sitting in silence and watching TV. However, it wasn't even possible to do that much, since Abi's phone kept vibrating, as texts pinged through. Each time it did, she seized it and immediately tapped a response, which caused Mel to smile and Ben to tut. Whether Abigail was responding to Ben's barely concealed irritation or Melanie's barely concealed nosiness was unclear, but at about 9:00 p.m., she stood up and announced that she was going to take a long bath and get an early night.

"Yeah, you must be knackered after your trip to London," Mel commented with another giggle. Really? Did they think he was an idiot, that he couldn't guess what all this nudge, nudge, wink, wink business was?

Abigail blew Mel a kiss and left the room.

The moment they heard her tread on the stairs, Mel announced, "She's met someone." Obviously, she was keen to tell Ben all about this development in Abi's love life. He didn't care enough to listen. He yawned, kept looking at the TV, did his best to make it clear that he was not interested. Unperturbed, Mel spilt details that Abi had apparently shared at lunchtime. "So, what do you think?" Mel probed as she came to the end of her story.

He thought he'd like his wife back, he thought he'd like his home back.

"What do you want me to say? Hold the front page. She had sex with some guy."

"Aren't you pleased for her?"

"Ecstatic," he said sarcastically, clearly showing he was anything but.

"This is great news."

"The only great thing about it as far as I'm concerned is that the upshot is that she's clearly knackered after her activities and so we've finally got some time to ourselves." He reached for Mel's foot and squeezed it. They were sat curled up on the sofa.

"That's it?" asked Mel. He shrugged. "I think this is going to be such fun."

"It's *her* that's dating. Not you."

"Yes, obviously, I know that," Mel said, a little huffily. "I'm just saying it will be fun. Picking out outfits, dissecting the dates."

"Grow up, Mel. You're not kids anymore." Ben surprised himself at how aggressive he seemed. It was crazy to be churlish because he felt left out tonight, and had for weeks now, but he couldn't help it. "What do you want her to tell you about this date? The length and width of his dick?" Ben stared at his wife, challenging her.

"No, of course not, don't be smutty," she snapped back, blushing. He knew from the indignation behind the blush that was the sort of thing Mel hoped Abi might tell her, or at least hint at. He knew women swapped info of that nature. "I'm not some sort of perv wanting to know those particular details, but…" She didn't finish the sentence.

Yeah, of course, she was keen to know whether he was good in bed. Did he do anything special? Did he hold open doors for her? Was he funny? What did they talk about? Ben felt uncomfortable with the idea. He knew that if Abi was talking about her new man in this way, Mel would be talking about her old one, aka, him. It was an unsettling thought. Mel stared at Ben; suddenly she didn't look as playful or excited.

"Ben, there's something else I need to talk to you about," she said. "Last night—"

He interrupted her, he didn't want to know. It would be some ridiculous detail about Abi, what sushi she liked, what underwear she wore. "You're obsessed with her," he accused.

Mel looked shocked. "No, I'm not. That's a crazy thing to say."

"She's all you talk and think about."

"That's not true. I was just about to tell you about something completely different."

"Oh yeah, like what?"

She glared at him, angrily. "You are not in the mood to hear it."

He tutted. "You have nothing to talk about other than her."

"No, that's not true." She sighed. "Look, it's exciting having a friend to stay. She makes me feel…"

"What?"

"Young." Mel looked surprised that she'd spat that out. She'd probably never planned to do so; she must have been tired after all.

Ben's expression froze, turned rigid. "Don't I make you feel young?"

"Sometimes." She stopped herself from elaborating. Even though she wasn't speaking, Ben could hear the truth of the matter. Rarely. He rarely made her feel young. She just wouldn't say so because she didn't want to hurt him. He knew he was right when she added, "It's just, Abi and I knew each other when I was really young and being with her somehow takes me back there."

"Well, we were hardly pensioners when we met," he pointed out. "You were only twenty-five."

"Yes, but I had Liam by then. I was never young again after giving birth." She rushed on, "Eating tea at a restaurant or café occasionally, rather than preparing endless meals, is fun. Drinking cocktails and getting cabs feels reckless. She makes me feel young, Ben. I never had that before."

She must have instantly realised she'd said the wrong thing, because she clamped her mouth shut. Ben thought it was sad, because until recently, he hadn't believed it was possible for them to say the wrong thing to one another. He thought they could tell each other anything, and no matter how clumsy or difficult, they both always had the confidence that they never intended to hurt one another. Where had that certainty gone?

"Oh, I see. You revel in the good old days. Before Liam, or me, or the girls," Ben snapped.

"Don't be like that. I don't mean that. How can you resent my attempts to recapture something everyone is entitled to?"

"And what's that exactly?"

"Unbridled optimism. Youthfulness. Intense friendships."

Ben looked to the floor. He didn't know what to say. Hadn't she felt that with him? Didn't she still? She was his best friend, he felt youthful, unbridled, intense things about her. Maybe not all the time but certainly some of the time, a good proportion. He didn't want her to see how much she'd hurt him. He had his pride. "You know, I think I might go for a run now," he said.

"At this time?"

"It's only nine thirty. I feel I need to get some air. I've been cooped up all weekend."

He didn't mean it as a criticism of her, but she took the comment to have a licking of martyrdom. Irritated, she pointed out, "Well, I haven't exactly been gadding about. I was at my parents' cleaning puke, and then at work all day today."

"I know. I wasn't having a go. I just need some air."

Ben sprang to his feet, keen to be out of the door before either of them said anything else that they'd regret. Mel seemed to be stuck to the sofa. She didn't follow him upstairs and continue the conversation as he changed into his running kit but that was a relief— it would only have led to a row.

Instead she turned to the TV and aimlessly flicked through channels until she found a rerun of *The Simpsons*. Ben heard the signature theme tune as he pulled the front door closed behind him.

CHAPTER TWENTY-SEVEN

MELANIE

Wednesday, 4 April

If it wasn't for Abi, I don't know quite how I'd be managing to raise a smile right now. She is the only positive person in my life. Everyone else is in such a mood. Easter weekend has been and gone, offering none of the renewal and promise that it represents; even the glut of chocolate failed to cheer. The girls are tired and testy. I admit, their routines have been somewhat upended—that happens in the school holidays.

Abigail is being a veritable saint covering childcare when I'm at work and Ben can't work from home. I'm trying not to ask too much of Liam because I want him to focus on revising for his A-levels.

The girls love spending time with Abi but it seems the novelty of meals out at cafés may be wearing a little thin. They've started to say that they miss my cooking, which is hilarious—they never appreciated it before. It was unfortunate that last week's ballet lesson completely slipped my mind, but there are lessons to be learnt outside of classes. I'm teaching them about taking chances, enjoying life.

Abi is a great role model for them. I want them to have careers and ambitions; she shows them what's possible. Ben is just being ridiculous to say that their opportunities are being damaged because their regular 7:00 p.m. bedtime has been a bit disrupted. It doesn't kill a child to be put to bed at 10:00 p.m. every now and again, although now the school holidays are over I should probably make an effort to get back to the 7:00 p.m. thing.

At the moment, Ben is finding fault in absolutely everything I do. It's annoying. He's not confrontational or antagonistic by nature but he's walking around like a bear with a sore head. I mean, it was never written in stone that I'm the one who irons his work shirts; if he finds himself without one, that's his own fault.

And OK, in an ideal world I would find a way to go to the movies with him when he's bought tickets, but the night he picked Abi happened to be in London, Liam ended up going out at the last minute and I couldn't get a babysitter at late notice. It was awkward that he never received my text cancelling the date night; I honestly thought I'd pressed Send. I only discovered my mistake when we were arguing about it that night and I grabbed my phone to show him that I absolutely had let him know I'd be a no-show, and I hadn't deliberately left him standing in the foyer like an idiot. Only, that's exactly what I'd done.

"Oh. I'm sorry, love. I'm just so tired right now and so busy. I was rushing about, trying to get the house sorted, I was late in from work because I had a late start, taking Abi to the station, and—"

"Whatever." He left the room, didn't let me finish. There's a lot going unsaid. As Ben is in such a prickly mood, I haven't found the right moment to tell him about Liam's outburst over his biological father the other week. Liam hasn't said anything more on the matter and so I'm beginning to think it's probably best to just let sleeping dogs lie. If I pull at that thread, then the whole thing might unravel.

I haven't seen much of Liam since. He's working hard on his A-levels, always at the library or at some college revision clinic and, if he's not doing that, then he's at Tanya's house. I'm not stupid, I know he's avoiding me. The only time he seems to be able to stay in a room with me is if there is someone else there, Abi or Ben.

I'm so sad about this. I know I must reach out to him, find a way of reconnecting and getting back some of the closeness we've always shared. But on the other hand, maybe I should just ride this out. Accept that teen years mean that it's usual, and necessary, for a child to demand a little space from parents as they become adults. And it's his A-level year, he's bound to be feeling the pressure. I fully intend to sit down and talk to him at some point. It's wrong to just pretend the scene didn't pass between us, but what more can I say about his biological father?

I accept family life is sometimes just like this; things don't always gel or flow, sometimes things are a little grittier and sticky. Abi is back from London today and she'll have lots to tell about her progress there. She'll have met her agent, her would-be investors, her producers and her lover. There will be so much to discuss.

I am not working today, which is handy because it gives me time to tidy up a bit. I pop into the kids' rooms, picking up loads of dirty washing. I put two loads through the wash and have some left over. It crosses my mind that I could do some washing for Abi. It's a waste to run the machine for a half load. I'd be doing her a favour.

I push open the door to her tiny room. I'm not snooping. I just want to help out. She lives like a teenager. A total slattern, even by my standards. Makeup spilling out on every surface, empty tins of Diet Coke and clothes scattered all over the floor—it is obviously going to be impossible to tell what is clean and what isn't. I pick up the odd blouse and T-shirt and sniff gingerly, the way I do with my family. I know our smells. Our sweat, our perfumes, our mud and blood.

Abi's clothes smell different. They smell of smoke and sex. I think of the man she is sleeping with; I wonder what he's like. He's obviously making her happy.

Because her underwear belongs to a happy woman.

I didn't touch her underwear, obviously, I'm not a weirdo, but I can't fail to see it. Lacy, pretty bras, silky, strappy panties. She wears thongs. Thongs.

Who does that? It's like flossing your bum and besides all your cellulite is on show. I guess she can't have that problem. The room is crowded with silky scarlets, provocative purples, tempting turquoises. I really need to think about buying something other than flesh-coloured sports bras.

Suddenly, I lose confidence in the idea of washing her clothes. Most of the labels say dry clean only and I daren't risk it, but it's not just that, it's the underwear. Even if I haven't touched it, she'll know I've seen it if I pop her blouses in the wash. I back out of the room, hoping that I haven't disturbed anything. Hoping she'll never know.

I prepare a nice lunch for Abi. I'm sure that she won't have had much time to eat well, if she's been dashing around London, hurrying from one meeting to the next. I offered to pick her up at the station but she said she'd hop in a cab. I excitedly watch the clock drag around to one fifteen and then she walks through the door. I fling my arms around her.

"So how did it go?" I ask eagerly.

"Fantastically well." Abi unwraps a beautiful pale-blue cotton scarf from around her neck, accepts the coffee I'm offering and collapses into a chair at the kitchen table. I follow her every movement, drink them up because she's refreshing and addictive.

She tells me a little bit about meeting up with some "really lit guys" who are sure there are opportunities for her, who "love her ideas, just adore them." It's simply a matter of finance or "the grubby dollar" as she describes it with a slightly self-conscious giggle. I think she's a little pained to talk about cash.

It's understandable. She's the talent, she's famous. In America, she probably had a team of people who talked about the nitty-gritty money matters on her behalf. Thinking about it, that team was probably headed up by Rob. This process can't be easy for her. She briefly tells me about how the financing of the show might potentially be structured. I do not claim to know anything about the glamorous world of TV so I check that I've understood what she's said.

"So, they want you to put money into this show, the one that you're going to present?"

"Yes. It's to demonstrate my confidence in the project."

It sounds to me as though it's more a case of her paying to have a job, paying through the nose, actually. The figure she mentioned makes my eyes water.

Abi buries her head in her handbag. She scrabbles around for her cigarettes, lights one and inhales deeply. I root about for the little ashtray I recently bought her. I keep it hidden at the back of the cereal cupboard because if Ben saw it he would go mad and say I was encouraging her nasty habit.

I carefully ask, "Is it the best time to make such a huge investment?"

For weeks now, Rob and Abi have been wrangling about her settlement. I hear her end of angry, accusatory phone calls, I see her outraged reaction to receiving an email from his lawyers, but she doesn't go into detail and I don't ask. I'm always conscious that if I bring up money, it might seem like I'm hinting that she ought to be putting a bit our way, which Ben absolutely thinks she ought, since she's been with us for six weeks now.

"Well, you have to speculate to accumulate, don't you? I suppose it is going to be horribly tight. I'll probably be living on practically bread and water."

I try my hardest not to glance down at the sleek bags that Abi deposited in the kitchen doorway. Agent Provocateur, Cos and Selfridges. I clearly fail, as Abi laughs.

"OK, maybe not bread and water exactly. More likely fags and Merlot, but I'm serious, I'm going to have to make some big cutbacks. That was my very last splurge. I'm going to have to be far more disciplined."

I nod encouragingly. "So, what are the next steps?" I ask.

"Well, I'll need to be in London for at least a few days a week—that will mean lots of hotel living. I don't feel ready to commit to a London rental. I'm not sure that's right just now. I need an element of flexibility."

I'm not sure why, exactly. There could be a thousand reasons. Maybe something to do with Rob and the divorce settlement, maybe something to do with the project. She doesn't elaborate. I don't probe.

Abi continues. "I was thinking that I should rent up here and commute down."

"Really?"

"Yes. I may eventually buy here."

"Here?" I'm overjoyed; a feeling of pure delight washes through my body. I never expected this.

"Yes." She smiles at me. "I like it around here. It's

an easy commute to London and property prices are so much more reasonable. In fact, I've made an appointment with an estate agent tomorrow. Apparently, she has flats on her books that she wants to show me."

She's going to stay around here! On my doorstep! I won't have to dash to London to see her—she'll be close by forever. I think of having access to her glamour and energy on an ongoing basis. This is amazing! I'd never in a month of Sundays imagined she'd think about living here in Wolvney.

I must be grinning like an idiot because she laughs, reaches out and squeezes my hand.

"You seem surprised, but you shouldn't be. You're my best friend here in the UK. Even if you weren't my only friend, I think you'd be my best friend," she jokes. Then more seriously, she adds, "The way you've welcomed me into your home has been phenomenal. So very generous. I never expected as much and I certainly can't ever pay you back. I have no idea why you've been so good to me—after all, we hadn't even spoken for years. You're just lovely."

I feel another surge of emotion seep through my body but this time, it's a more complicated mix. Joy, guilt, relief, gratitude. Somehow, we have managed it; we have turned back time, we're as close as we were before I conceived Liam. We're fixed. I fixed it.

"There's nothing to pay back," I say breathily. "That's what friends are for. I said you could stay as long as you needed and you can. In fact, you have to promise me that you won't just accept the first flat that is offered for rental." Her hand is still on mine. She squeezes and then pulls back.

"You're the best," she says. "Now that's settled, I think I'll go and have a quick shower. Wash London off, hey? You have had the immersion heater on, haven't you? It was just too funny when I ran a bath last week and it was cold. Remember?"

Yes, I remember, not the hilarity so much as the embarrassment because it was obvious I'd really inconvenienced Abi. "Yes, I've had the immersion on."

"Oh good. Isn't everything working out just perfectly, Mel?" she says, and then she practically skips out of the room.

CHAPTER TWENTY-EIGHT

ABIGAIL

Abigail offered to accompany Melanie to the school gate to pick up Imogen and Lily. Melanie was delighted and surprised because Abi always found an excuse not to do so. While Abi adored the girls and was enthralled by children in general, she found that—often—mums were boring, smug and ungrateful. She preferred not to put herself in the way of them. But today she had an agenda. She knew Melanie had been desperate to show her off; it was a kindness that she could grant.

Melanie waved to a couple of women, who instantly dashed over to talk. It was clear to Abi that these were the sort of women who would have Googled her. She was the most exciting thing that had happened to any of them since they went to the last Take That gig. They couldn't quite hide their interest. Few people ever could, although back in

LA people were at least a little more practised at faking nonchalance. A flicker of something scuttled across everyone's faces as she arrived. Even the deputy head nodded and waved. Mel laughed and commented, "Who knew he was the sort of man that notices women anymore? He doesn't act flirtatious with any of us mums, not even the young and pretty ones—he's too professional. You broke him, Abi."

Abi was different from the mums. A fact she was very aware of. It was simultaneously a source of pride and pain. Glamorous, child-free and dazzling. This, they would visit in a zoo. Once Mel's two friends had dashed to Abigail's side, they suddenly seemed overcome with shyness. They eyed Abi with wariness; it was obvious to her that they were intimidated by her. It was a shame that Mel kept such parochial company. She should have confident friends, not the sort to be daunted by a Burberry trench coat and expensive caramel highlights.

"Gillian, Becky, let me introduce you to my good friend Abigail Curtiz. Abi, meet Gillian Burton and Becky Ingram," gushed Mel.

Abi stretched out her long thin hand, Becky and Gillian self-consciously shook it. No doubt they usually settled for waves or smiles, not formal introductions at the school gate. "Good friend!" Abi sounded outraged. She poked Mel playfully in the ribs. "Oldest and best is a better description."

Mel blushed, obviously pleased that she'd been so publicly claimed.

Abigail then pulled her face into one of horror. "Oh gosh, I hope I'm not stepping on anyone's toes.

I guess she's your best friend, too, am I right, ladies? Melanie has always been very much in demand, a cut above. Always so popular—everyone loves her."

Gillian and Becky laughed and agreed, demonstrating kindness and good manners and the fact that they both had instantly fallen under Abi's spell; they'd have agreed with anything she said just to be on the receiving end of one of her broad beams. Abigail briefly wondered whether they would sacrifice their firstborn, if she asked them to.

"Very pleased to meet you, Abi."

"Mel has told us so much about you."

"You were in London earlier this week, right?"

Naturally, she'd been the subject of their conversations.

"Just got back," Abi said with an agreeable smile, conveying that she was glad to be away from the smoke, happy to be here with them in this small town. She launched into a conversation about a play she'd seen at The Old Vic. Both Becky and Gillian professed to being desperate to see it, too.

"Mel has some big news, haven't you, Mel?" prompted Abi.

"Oh, yes. Abi is thinking of staying here in Wolvney, she's going to be looking at flats to rent, tomorrow," she said.

"No, not that," laughed Abi. "About Liam."

"Liam?" Mel looked confused.

"You are being modest. It's a fantastic thing. Tell your friends, they'll be so pleased for you."

Mel shrugged, confused.

"The internship," Abi prompted. Mel still didn't

pick up the mantle. Turning to Becky and Gillian, Abi announced, "Liam has been accepted into an incredibly prestigious internship in Westminster. He starts just after his exams. A three-month commitment, before he goes to uni. It's huge news. Bound to increase his employment chances in the long term. First step to changing the world, hey, Mel?" Abi elbowed her friend gently.

Mel looked as though she was going to cry. "I didn't know."

"What?"

"I didn't know he'd been accepted."

Abi looked embarrassed. "Yesterday. He called me. I assumed—" She broke off.

Mel shook her head. A small, tight movement.

Becky tried to rescue the moment and flung her arms around Mel. "What great news, congratulations to him and you! You must be so proud."

Gillian tried to rationalise Mel's ignorance and Abi's superior position of knowledge. "Didn't you say Abi helped him prepare for the interview? I bet that's why he thought to call her first. He's got great manners. Probably called to thank you, didn't he, Abi?"

Abi looked aghast. Aware her friend had to be incredibly hurt to have been left out of the loop. Such important news. "I just assumed you'd have been the first person he told," she stuttered. Mel shook her head, but couldn't speak. "But it's great news, isn't it?" Abi added.

"Yes, yes, of course. He's talked about getting this placement for about two years," replied Mel. Her voice was scratchy, broken.

The next moment, Imogen and Lily and various other children were clustered around the women's legs, demanding snacks, attention and to be taken home. Everyone seemed keen to scatter.

"I know," said Abi suddenly. "Let's go out tonight to celebrate—we could get some cocktails."

"Surely Mel will want to celebrate with Liam, Ben and the girls," Becky pointed out.

Abi looked anxious. "I just thought that if Liam had wanted that he'd have said so. I don't think he plans to celebrate with his family." A quick, nervous glance at Mel and then she added, "You know what they're like at that age. It's all about girlfriends. He probably has other plans. I don't want Mel to be completely cheated out of a celebration. I mean, after all, her part in his success is not insubstantial. She's done so much on her own for him. You know, in the early years."

Mel couldn't look at any of them.

Becky clocked her mortification and chipped in, allowing Mel a little more time to compose herself. "Good plan—where will you go?"

"Northampton. There's nowhere around here that serves decent margaritas, is there? And believe me I've looked," replied Abi. "Shall we do it? All four of us? It's not much of a celebration if it's just the two of us."

"Absolutely."

"Yes, please," Becky and Gillian chorused eagerly.

"Great. That's settled. Mel will text times. Right, Mel?"

Mel nodded, her face aflame with embarrassment. Abi squeezed her arm, sympathetically. "Don't worry, *we* want to celebrate with you. It will be fun."

CHAPTER TWENTY-NINE

MELANIE

Liam hands me the letter confirming his place on the internship at Westminster the moment we get home. I glance at Abi and she winks at me conspiratorially and whispers, "See, he was just waiting for the right moment to tell you."

I decide there's nothing to be gained by asking him how long he has had this news and why he's kept it from me. Instead I fling my arms around him. "I'm so pleased!" He accepts my hug. Encouraged, I offer, "Shall we all go out tonight, have a celebration meal?" I know Becky and Gillian would understand if I cancelled the cocktails.

Liam shakes his head. "It's OK. That's not necessary. I've some work to do and then I just fancy chilling." Something in his tone stops me pushing.

I wasn't sure whether Ben would be too happy about me going out for cocktails tonight—he's far from some Neanderthal man who makes sullen grunts if I have a social life, but with me missing his cinema date last week, I thought he might still be a bit off. However, Liam's news is so exciting he is all acquiescence. In fact, he seems quite relieved that Abi and I are going to be out of the way and he comments that having Gillian and Becky along will at least stop me going crazy.

"What if I want to go crazy?" I ask.

He doesn't reply to that. He just says he'll take the opportunity to catch up with Liam. "I feel I haven't had any quality time with him for a while. Maybe we'll sit down and have a game of *COD* on the PlayStation."

Normally I'd point out that playing video games isn't exactly what I'd call quality time but I think better of it. I don't feel on very solid ground around Liam but I'm fairly sure he'll think *COD* is exactly that.

Abi has picked the cocktail bar, inside a trendy hotel called Hashtag. I had no idea such gorgeous places existed in Northampton. When I come here with Ben and the kids, I'm mostly limited to a glass of wine and half a dozen dough balls at Pizza Express. The bar is hidden behind a discreet glass door in a boutique hotel. The place manages to be breathtakingly flash and yet intimate at the same time. The walls are leather clad, there's an antique mirrored ceiling, a copper-topped bar. The seats are a plush purple velvet, the lighting is low, and the cocktails are decadent.

"I love it and never want to leave," I comment, although I hardly dare look at the prices.

I haven't had time to eat anything this evening because once I'd bathed the girls and then pulled myself into something that resembled cocktail-bar-ready, the taxi was waiting to take us to the station. Consequently, the alcohol goes straight to my head. Plus, they're really yummy and easy to sink. Besides, I'm drowning sorrows.

Yeah, we're celebrating but I can't quite put aside the hurt I feel that Liam didn't instantly tell me his phenomenal news. Obviously, this is tied up with the disastrous conversation we had regarding his birth dad. I handled that so badly, and on some level, Liam is punishing me. I can't blame him. Tomorrow, I'm going to sit him down. Talk this all through, before the gap between us widens any more. With that decided, I put the matter out of my head and concentrate on the cocktails. After all, when all is said and done, it really is wonderful news.

Soon, we're swapping confidences and gossip, sharing secrets and lifehacks. Gillian tells us that she always has grapes in the freezer because they chill wine without watering it down the way ice cubes can, and no one ever has enough cold wine. We all agree this is genius. Becky says that if you put a wooden spoon over a pan of boiling vegetables or pasta, the pan will never boil over. It's a useful tip but not especially exciting. Abi gives us loads of tips on applying make-up or looking leggier in photos. We lap it up, even though none of us have ever experienced the paparazzi stalking us, nor are we ever likely to. "And do you know how to avoid getting lipstick on your teeth?" she asks.

"No." We lean in, all ears; she's the font of human knowledge.

"After applying your lipstick, put your finger in your mouth. Close your lips around your finger, then pull your finger out. Slowly. The excess lipstick will get on your finger, and not on your teeth." Abi demonstrates. We three stare at her, transfixed. She obviously isn't aware but it is quite a sexy move. I mean, it's impossible not to think about what else she might clasp her scarlet lips around. Gillian, Becky and I giggle nervously.

"Your turn, Mel," prompts Becky.

"Oh, I've discovered the cure for cellulite. One hundred per cent foolproof."

"Wow." Gillian and Becky's eyes are on me now, keen. Almost desperate.

"Take your glasses off every time you stand in front of the mirror—guaranteed smooth bum," I declare and then laugh at my own joke.

Gillian practically falls off her bar stool she's laughing so hard, although Becky looks a bit cheated. Abi smiles vaguely, humouring me.

We have a lot to drink. Far too much. I don't know how much. So much that I lose count. It's turning into a great night. Brilliant. I already know I'm going to have a hangover from hell tomorrow. One like I've never had before, quite probably. I know that but I can't imagine it, and right now, I certainly don't care about it.

I can, however, imagine singing. Maybe even dancing on a tabletop. If there was a beach nearby, I'd be running barefoot. I'd be skinny-dipping!

That sort of drunk. I try to add them up. Three cocktails, because we all bought a round, other than Abi, so yes then, three. That's about ten units. Wow. We order food. Abi suggests it. She goes out more frequently than the rest of us and says we'll never do the distance unless we eat. We order some really tasty bits. Some tacos and tostadas and potato something or other.

The food comes. It smells fantastic. I plan to pile in but as much as I try, the food just doesn't get to my mouth. I have so much to say. Funny stories. Frankly, I'm being hilarious tonight. Everyone is in stitches. Never been more amusing. I'm only telling stories about awful parents' nights or awkward customers in the shop but somehow, I'm making the stories sassy and entertaining. I'm even doing the retellings with (largely inaccurate) accents. So, there's too much talking, not enough eating. Even when the others talk, I don't manage to eat much because their stories are hilarious as well.

The first taco I tackle is overfilled, and I miss my mouth but hit my top. Even drunk I'm a bit annoyed by this. Becky keeps saying the greasy mark will come out with a bit of Vanish but the stain looks permanent to me, this being my area of expertise. However, I don't want to say so. Who wants to be known for having great knowledge about stain removal from clothes? That's not going to get a laugh. But for the record: grass, ink, mud, you name it, I can remove it. This isn't the moment to share that sort of story. I keep that type of thing for the school gate; I can impress there.

Now, what is Abi saying? She hasn't eaten much either. She's sharing her expertise in removing clothes, far funnier.

"So, Mel said you are dating?" probes Gillian.

"I just mentioned it," I say quickly.

Abi smiles; she doesn't look concerned that I've been divulging details of her private life to my school-gate friends. "It's true to say I'm having a lot of fun," admits Abi. "Rob and I got together when I was quite young. I've never had the chance to, shall we say, experiment."

I start to snigger. It's the drink. "Well, you were pretty wild in your first year," I point out. I'm surprised I made the comment out loud. I thought it was in my head. I glance at Abi, to check I haven't offended her.

"Is that how you remember it?" she asks, still smiling, but even through my drunken haze I sense a bite of curiosity. Most people are fairly interested in how they're remembered by others; Abi has a keener sense of that than most. I think it's because she's on TV and it matters what people think of her or say of her. It's not vanity. It's a professional interest. A necessity.

"There were always loads of boys after you. You had your share of casual dates." I decide dates is the most tactful way to describe what went on. Our rooms were next to each other. We went headboard to headboard with just a thin wall separating us. I didn't get much sleep.

Abigail waves her hand dismissively. She doesn't attach any importance to those hopeless hopefuls, and so they've slipped her memory. "I only ever wanted

Rob," she says firmly. "I just hung out with the other guys to make him jealous."

This is possible. I've never considered it before but it smacks of the sort of game Abi might have felt she needed to play to secure Rob. To capture his attention, she had to ignore him and run around with various other boys. At the time, I'd assumed she just wasn't sure about him or was just not that into him. One minute she would be lavishing him with attention, the next, freezing him out. It was exhausting and confusing.

Turning to Becky and Gillian, Abi explains, "Rob had more than his share of young women falling at his feet. Everyone was mad about him, weren't they, Mel?"

The air is heavy and forlorn; before it had been light and promising. She should be talking about her new man, not Rob. "This is ancient history. Bring us up to date," I insist.

"Oh, yes, tell us all the details. We're happily married. No news to report, nothing to see here," jokes Gillian.

"By which she means we're only having very predictable, comfortable sex, we want to hear about your wildness!" adds Becky. "Tell, tell, tell."

A few couples turn in our direction; the men look uncomfortable, some of the women look envious. We're having more fun. We order another round of cocktails and sip them while Abi tells us she is winking, poking, tweeting, messaging. She's meeting, flirting, kissing, and fucking. That's how she says it.

I'm making a concerted effort and I hope my face

is not looking as shocked as I indeed am. I knew she was having sex with a man she calls Stud. She'd told me that much. Which I thoroughly approved of. She is a newly single woman in her thirties with some time to make up, a score to settle, an ego to reinflate and a heart to glue. There is a lot to be done. Of course, she should be getting busy. But the way she said it. Fucking. The word seems brutal, brave, raw. It confuses me. Shocks and excites me.

It must be the drink. I wonder what it is like to be her. Someone who can say what she likes, dress how she likes, drink, smoke, eat what she likes. I have never been that woman. She can have sex on a whim. I have sex on a Friday. Clockwork. Not complaining, just saying.

"Ahh, starting a new relationship." Becky lets out a fond sigh. "So long ago."

"It is amazing. Everything Stud says and does is fresh and interesting, you know. The way he talks to waiters. The way he wears his clothes. The way he walks into a room." Her eyes are shining wildly. She's giggling, gleaming, glorious.

"Really, Stud?" Gillian's tone is teasing.

"Pet names are a minefield, aren't they? I know it's not that original but he likes it. I have variations. My Stud, Stud Man, Stud Muffin. Stud Boy. He calls me Honey Butt," Abi admits with a slow smile.

"When will we meet him?" I ask.

She immediately looks alarmed. "Oh no, I don't think so, I mean, he's in London."

"We could come to London," I say eagerly. "Actually, Ben and I should get away, have a break." We really could do with spending some time together. "I'd *love* a weekend break in London. Liam would look after the girls," I enthuse. I'm ready to book the tickets this instant.

"No, no. That's far too much trouble to put everyone through. No," she says firmly, shaking her head vehemently. "I'll introduce him to you when I'm ready."

Suddenly I panic. "Oh no, Abi, no. He's not married, is he?"

She looks stunned. Sad. Shocked. All these emotions flash across her face in an instant. "No, no, of course not. I'd never do that to another woman. *I* have more self-respect than that."

"Then why can't I meet him?"

"He's—"

"What?"

"He's younger than I am," she says carefully.

"So?"

"Quite a bit younger."

"I see. Well, what's good for the goose is good for the gander, right?" I'm thinking of Rob here. His PA was years younger than him. No one ever bats an eyelid when some old fella bags a young beauty.

"But the problem is, I lied to him about my age."

"Oh, I see."

"I talk about you all the time. He knows we went to university together but…" She breaks off, shrugs, looks apologetic and embarrassed. She doesn't need to say any more. She can pass for someone maybe a decade younger than she is, if needs be. I can't.

"So how old is he?" I ask.

"Young," she says with a grin that shows she's not completely worried about this.

"How young?"

"I don't want to say." Her fingers grasp her glass. Her knuckles are white. Becky and Gillian are all eyes and ears.

"Come on, tell me. What's the age gap?" I swizzle my glass between my fingers and thumb.

"He's twenty-three."

"Abigail!"

"No, just kidding, twenty-six." She says it in a way that sounds like a question. As though she's not absolutely sure, or maybe not being absolutely truthful. Is she trying to find an age she thinks I'll consider reasonable?

"You go, girl." Gillian holds her hand in the air waiting for Abi to high-five her. Abi leaves her hanging because she's watching me, waiting for my response.

"Oh." I take a big slurp of my cocktail and concentrate on what I should say next. The thoughts running through my head are, *Well, this won't last, she's going to get hurt* and *What do they talk about?* I'm also a bit taken aback that she hasn't told me this thing about the age gap before now, but if I act freaked out I guess she'll stop telling me anything. I don't want that. I like her stories. Some of them make me uncomfortable. Maybe even a little envious. Not jealous, exactly, not that. It's just her world is so exciting and free. She got to be young when she was actually so and now she's behaving like a teen again. Sometimes it seems that I have never been young.

But then, I think of her arriving on my doorstep, drooping, depleted, despairing and I manage to rein in all my negativity. She is owed some fun.

"How fabulous," I state firmly, or perhaps slur firmly. I probably should stop drinking now.

She beams at me, grateful, elated. "You think so?"

"Absolutely. I mean, young men have some obvious advantages, right?" We all giggle like schoolgirls.

Abigail sees this as permission to reveal every last detail about their sex life. I hadn't been aware there was anything else for her to tell us, but apparently there is. There really is. She tells us that he can indeed do it two or three times a night, various positions, various locations.

"I now really know what they mean by a leg trembler," she laughs. She divulges that he's grateful for guidance and very responsive, that he can't get enough of her. "You know, I might be in the shower and he follows me in there." She discloses that she's shaved everything clean away because it's what he prefers; apparently, he's clean-shaven down there, too.

"Noooo," we chorus in unison.

"Is that a thing?" I ask.

"Seems so." She nods.

"I thought that was just gay men," says Becky, trying to sound more worldly-wise than she in fact is.

"Nope. They all do it. It makes their cocks look bigger."

I can't stop myself—my hand goes to cover my mouth, like a cartoon of someone expressing surprise. "But why do they need to make their willies look bigger at that point?" I ask. "I mean, you know, you're there…" I hesitate, unsure how to finish the sentence. "You've already demonstrated that you're into him."

"For photos and films and stuff," Abi replies, casually shrugging.

I dare not meet Gillian's or Becky's eyes. I don't think I want to see them feign sophistication or look shocked or embarrassed or—and this would be the absolute worst—see that they totally *are* into photographing and filming their sex lives.

"I feel so old," groans Gillian.

"Of course, I know this stuff goes on," says Becky, in a way that suggests the opposite.

When Liam was a few years younger, his school ran a course about safety on the internet. I remember having that excruciating talk with him about not sharing photos. I remember some parents just advised their kids never to show their faces and their bits on the same shot. I thought this was defeatist advice. Ben said it was perhaps realist's advice. These things go on. We all talked about it *as parents*; it was theoretical. It was something our children might get mixed up in. It was not for us. But then, Abigail isn't a parent. She might be four months older than I am but since she hasn't given birth three times over, she's somehow managed to time travel or drink from the elixir of youth. I feel a bit envious.

"What would Ben say if you suggested filming yourselves making love?" Abi asks.

"Well, once he stopped laughing, he'd probably be up for it, but I'd never offer," I reply.

"Why not?"

"Why would I want to look at my own wobbly

body? I put a considerable amount of energy into skirting past the mirror to avoid my reflection."

"I can't imagine Abi has any wobbly bits, at least not other than those you are supposed to shake," says Becky.

Abi doesn't contradict her; she has no time for false modesty. Instead she gives us a lot of detail about where they meet up and what they do. What he says to her. We interrupt from time to time but overall, she waxes lyrical. We enjoy the way she's telling their story. He sends her cheeky messages on Snapchat—they contrast with a short-term shyness that always dominates the first few minutes of each of their hookups. She tells us about her hesitation about their age gap, his insistence. His sweetness, his selflessness that convinced her they had a connection. It's passionate and fascinating. She seems really smitten by this guy.

We order more alcohol and it becomes impossible to discern whether she's drunk on cocktails or on lust. It doesn't matter. It feels jubilant and exciting and I'm so happy to be a part of it. Even if I'm just an observer. Right now, I feel amazing. Youthful and brilliant. OK, this isn't my love affair, I wouldn't want it to be, but I am getting an indisputable high just listening to Abi talk about "The Stud." I'll take what I can get.

It's only when we start to realise that there's no one else in the hotel bar, that the waiters are all stood about in the corners of the room looking resentful, that we think to ask for the bill.

Becky punches numbers into the calculator app

on her phone, as none of us seem capable of dividing by four.

"Have you got a picture of him? This Stud?" asks Gillian. She's dealing with quite a severe case of hiccups. It's hilarious. She lunges for Abi's phone, which is face down on the table between us, and starts looking through the pics. "I can't see a bloody thing," she moans. "I've drunk too much. Jeez, this is your porn," she yells suddenly, almost dropping the phone. The bartender looks up sharply. So do Becky and I.

Abi quickly snatches back her phone. "I don't have the sort of photos I can show you," she says with an embarrassed laugh.

"Make sure you get one next time you see him. One of his face," instructs Gillian.

"Will do," she replies lightly. "Come on, let's get a taxi."

I don't want to pour cold water but as we are waiting for the cab I can't stop myself murmuring, "Listen, be careful, hey? You've been through a lot this year."

Abi smiles at me. Her face is bright and open. "You have nothing to worry about. Honestly, take that expression off your face. I want this. I really do. This is what I need."

CHAPTER THIRTY

MELANIE

Abi says she's going to have a fag before she goes to bed so heads out to the back garden. Politeness dictates that I should keep her company but I don't want to. It's late and I'm drunk. I yawn ostentatiously and mumble about having to get up at six forty, as usual, tomorrow. She naturally responds by saying there's no need for me to keep her company and shoos me. As I walk upstairs, I reach out to the wall to steady myself.

Ben is already in bed but not asleep. He's reading a magazine about the economy.

The alcohol has made me feel a bit frisky. That and Abi's talk of her new lover. It was odd hearing Abi go into so much detail about her sex life. I am at the stage in my relationship that I don't talk about sex with anyone, not even Ben. We just get on with it. When I first met Ben, I was so absorbed in a wondrous frenzy of lust that I was a bit like Abi was tonight—I'd have told anyone who'd listen every detail. We took a lot of risks back then. It wasn't that we were thrill-seeking, it was that we couldn't contain ourselves; we seized every opportunity to tear each other's clothes off. As the years have gone by, more kids have come along and things have, naturally, settled down. It's not that we have dull sex. It's intense and incredible sex, but talking about it no longer seems daring and fun, it just seems a bit messy. I get embarrassed by it. I mean, if you think about sex for too long it becomes comical.

I don't want to think about it. I want to do it.

"Boring," I say in a sing-song voice as I snatch the economics magazine from Ben.

He looks a bit irritated. "Hey, you'll rip that."

"Aren't you going to ask me about my night?" I start undressing on the spot. Well, not exactly the spot, I'm swaying ever so slightly, despite my best but doomed intentions to appear sober. Ben glances at my discarded garments with a hint of a rebuke. I don't care, I'll be the one picking them up in the morning, it's not like I'm asking him to do it. "Well, aren't you?" I demand.

"I imagine you're going to tell me," he says pleasantly enough, accepting I'm too hyped to quietly slip into bed.

"She's only gone and got herself a toy boy." I deliver this news triumphantly. The glamour of it.

"Really?"

"A twenty-six-year-old lover." The scandal of it. "She's fucking a twenty-six-year-old." I feel a bit self-conscious because I'm stood in my bra and pants now. Yes, the flesh-coloured ones. That sort of word demands a bit more from underwear. I'm not sure why I even used it. I should have said dating. Only, that wouldn't cover it. "Well?"

"Well, what?"

"Well, what do you think?"

He shrugs. "Nothing much." I stare at him, stunned by his lack of reaction. Becky and Gillian were far more involved and they've only known Abi a matter of hours.

"I'm pleased for her," he adds, yawning.

I punish him, hold back the juicy details and march into the bathroom to clean my teeth. Once done and naked, I slip under the duvet but my friskiness was fleeting. I'm now at the stage of drunk when I feel sleepy, heavy, achey. I put my cold feet on him and he doesn't even flinch. There are about a hundred thousand things about Ben that make me smile— his ability not to flinch when I put icy feet on him is one of them.

"I hope she enjoys it while it lasts," he murmurs.

A flash of irritation shimmies through me. It's the cocktails. I'm never good on spirits. I become unpredictable, unstable. I take offence easily and I'm argumentative. I never remember that when I'm necking them.

"Why won't it last?" I demand hotly, even though I had the exact same thought about the unlikeliness of longevity.

"They'll want different things. If not now, then a

few months down the line. Certainly by a few years down the line. It's a novelty thing."

"Brigitte and Emmanuel Macron seem to have managed."

"I suppose, but they're French. The French have different rules when it comes to sex. No rules at all, actually."

"What about Madonna? She's always dating significantly younger men," I point out.

"Oh yes, she's everyone's role model."

"Well, why not? And Susan Sarandon and Tim Robbins. There was about thirteen years' age difference between them."

"They divorced."

"After twenty-three years. It was a good innings. Anyway, isn't she dating some guy thirty-one years her junior now? I think. Or she certainly was at one point."

"Some people never learn."

"You're being sexist," I accuse crossly. "No one would care in the least if it was the other way around. There's a quarter of a century age gap between Rupert Murdoch and Jerry Hall."

"Unquestionably a love match," he points out dryly. He sighs. Bored of my regurgitation of facts gleaned from my favourite gossip magazines. "I'm not saying I object."

"Then what are you saying?"

"Nothing. It's none of my business." He rolls over and turns off his bedside lamp. Lies with his back to me.

"Nothing?" I mumble grumpily.

I'm unwilling to turn out my lamp, too. I start to think of the things Abi told us about her lover. Three times. They had sex *three* times in one night. Almost a month's worth of sex! I shuffle closer to Ben, my cool body next to his hot one. I want to caress him, arouse him. My hand comes down a little heavily, more of a flop.

Ben slowly rolls over, lies on his back, too, staring at the ceiling. He takes hold of my hand and squeezes it. It's an affectionate gesture but one that says sex is not on the agenda. It's the gentlest of possible turn-downs. I guess he's tired. He has his weekly status meeting with his boss tomorrow; the last thing he needs is a shag-hangover. Sometimes it amuses me how long it takes us to recover from sex nowadays; sometimes it makes me feel melancholic.

"I just think she has to be careful," he says.

Even though I understand his concern is coming from a decent, caring place, I find myself snapping, "That's just it, she doesn't. She can be as wild and bold as she pleases. Age is just a number. You are only as old as you feel."

I think we both simultaneously reach the thought that if the saying is correct, then we're both fifty-plus at the moment. I didn't even get to have a party. We stay silent with our thoughts until I can't keep it in any longer.

"Ben, they record themselves having sex," I whisper.

"Is that wise?" he asks.

"Wise?" I don't understand the adjective. "It's sexy, it's exciting, it's fun," I insist.

"I just mean, she's in the middle of a divorce. That

sort of thing in the wrong hands…" He trails off and I'm glad. He's being boring. "Mel, there was a call from Liam's college today."

"What about?"

"I don't know. I missed it. There was a message on the answering machine. A name and number to call back."

I wonder for a moment what that might be about. I start to fantasise about prizes and plaudits. Liam is a great student. Well-liked by the staff and kids. I guess they've heard about his internship and want to congratulate us.

Ben kisses my forehead. "Early alarm clock tomorrow, plus you'll have a hangover. Should I get you a glass of water?" He gets out of bed and heads towards the door.

My eyes spring open. "Ben. You must put pyjamas on! Abi is downstairs smoking," I hiss.

"Oh, I'm far too old for her," he says with a grin, but I'm relieved that he reaches for his pyjama bottoms.

CHAPTER THIRTY-ONE

MELANIE

Thursday, 5 April

It's a quiet day in the store, for which I am eternally grateful because someone is taking a cleaver to my head and repeatedly smiting it. The agony is so real I expect to see blood splattered all over the rails of clothes. I'm grey, shivery, my back and even eyelids ache. Yes, this is absolutely the hangover I expected. My boss takes pity on me. I don't think, for a moment, that she buys the story that I'm coming down with a flu bug.

She simply replies, "Good night, was it?"

I nod, shamefaced. She laughs and tells me I can go and tidy the stockroom. We all know this is code for "take a couple of aspirin and sit on the stockroom floor with your back up against the wall until the world stops spinning." Most staff members have availed themselves of this facility in the past, at one time or another. The best thing about "tidying the stockroom" is that I have a chance to look at my phone. Ben has sent me a text. How's the head?

I type, Not great.

My phone pings again. This time there is the blushing face emoji. You were pretty well oiled last night.

I know. This morning I discovered I have a bruise on my knee where I tripped as I clambered out of the taxi. Literally legless. I don't need him to remind me. Maybe his tone is supposed to be playful but I feel embarrassed. I don't reply.

A few minutes later another text arrives. Did you speak to Liam's college?

No. Damn, I haven't. Not yet. I got the girls to school wearing clothes; I consider that an accomplishment. I turn off my phone.

Somehow, I manage to struggle through to the end of my shift, which is 2:30 p.m. today. I didn't think I was in a fit state to drive this morning so I caught the bus, so naturally I must do the same again. As I wait at the bus stop, I find my attention being drawn to the young men who walk past me. Men in paint-splattered overalls, men in jeans and hoodies, men in suits. I try to guess their ages. I realise that I haven't got much clue. Most men look "young," then "about my age," then "old." I can't finesse the categories down any further.

I'm good at this game when it comes to children. I can differentiate between a seven- and an eight-year-old just by looking at their teeth. I know if a teenage boy is sixteen or seventeen because of the way he holds himself. There's something about their upper backs—they tend to stand taller at seventeen, broaden at eighteen. But adults? No, I have no clue.

I'm still very curious to know what The Stud looks like. I feel silly referring to him that way. I need to ask Abi what he's really called. My guess is he's called Brad or Dex. Something cool.

I arrive home and push open the front door. I yell hello but no one answers. I think Abi must be out looking at flats this afternoon. I head for the kitchen, needing a big glass of water. I notice two things: one, the home phone is flashing; we have a message. It will be my parents or someone from Liam's college or the girls' school—no one else uses the landline. Two, Abi's phone is on the kitchen table.

Abi never leaves her phone unattended. It's usually surgically attached as she never wants to miss a call from her lawyer or her London contacts or now, presumably, her lover.

Her lover.

I don't think about it. If I think about it, I won't do it. I reach for the phone. Luckily and surprisingly, it's not password protected. There must be a shot of this guy. Why is she being so coy? She must have a photo and I can't imagine he's ugly. I am not planning on looking at the home videos, the ones Gillian stumbled upon last night. I'm just...

Curious.

It's the first thing I see. It pops up on the screen without me even knowing how I've accessed it. It must have just been the last thing she was looking at herself. I've never seen a home sex tape before. My body starts to pulse, my hands are clammy, my heart is beating so fast I think it's going to explode. She is lying on the bed, legs spread, shaven, like she's told us. Her panties are around her ankles, they are black and lacy, they look a little like bindings. Her bra has been pulled up over one breast, she's clasping both her breasts, fingering her own nipples while she stares provocatively at the camera. Her expression is a more extreme version of one I have seen before; she is teasing, then pouting.

It's a beautiful hotel bedroom, the sheets are white and silky. She slides and glides, wiggles. I can almost feel the sheets shimmer down my back. She puts one finger, first in her mouth, and then inside her. I should stop this but I can't. I don't. She's beautiful. Her skin is golden, smooth and then red, raw. Like a wound. Private. I should not be seeing this. I press the button to stop it playing but as the image freezes her expression changes—she is alight.

He has just walked into shot.

My finger hovers over the button that would get the images to play on. My heart is beating so fast and furious, I think my ribcage is going to explode, I think my ear drums are. This is what Gillian saw last night, probably. That's all.

I press Play and her lover walks onto the shot. Toned, smooth, paler skin than hers. I can't see his head as the image is cut at his broad shoulders, but as he crawls onto the bed, arse in the air, head dipped to pleasure her, I see it.

The brown birthmark on his right buttock.

Then I throw up. Over the phone, over the kitchen table and all over my life.

CHAPTER THIRTY-TWO

MELANIE

I want to fling the phone across the kitchen. Smash it into a thousand pieces. Erase the image. Erase the action. But I don't. I airdrop the video onto my phone. I don't know how I manage this when her phone is slick with my vomit and the stench is everywhere, when my hands are shaking and my stomach is still queasy, but I do. It's instinctual. Evidence.

I realise I'm in shock. This happened to me once before when Imogen split her head open falling off a wall in a friend's garden. She was concussed, out cold. I managed to call an ambulance and accompanied her to the hospital, answering the medics' questions, but as I did so I fought the feeling that I was living a second before or after reality, not quite in the moment. I was running through a thousand scenarios where I had intervened just a second before and prevented the accident from occurring and I was also thinking, what next, what? What might happen? What can I do?

I feel the same now.

My throat is parched and painful, I keep gasping at the air but can't get enough oxygen. I'm shaking so much I want to sit down, lie down. Fall down. But I can't, I need to clean up. I nearly run her phone under the tap but stop myself just in time. I quickly reach for the paper towels and wipe away what I can. I set to work cleaning up the sick, but I know I can't. This sickness can't be eradicated.

The landline rings. I pick it up, even though I am not sure I'll find a voice to speak.

"Mrs. Harrison?"

"Yes."

"It's Mark Edwards here. Principal of Wolvney Sixth Form College. I've left you a few messages." He sounds a bit irritated, all business.

"Yes. Sorry. Erm, yes. I know." I should tell him that I've been planning on calling him back. I should have called him back. Whatever, I can't find the words and it's too late now. The unwanted images keep assaulting my consciousness. The birthmark. I know. I know it is him.

The principal was perhaps expecting more, but no doubt used to dealing with tricky parents, he clears his throat and launches in, keen to stick to his agenda. "I'm ringing because Liam's attendance has been extremely irregular over the past five weeks. I know there was the Easter break, but even before then. I wondered whether that was something you were aware of?"

"No," I whisper. No, I know nothing about my son. Or at least knew nothing. Now, I know more than any mother ever should.

"Well, I'm sure you can appreciate this is a critical time. A-levels are just around the corner. He really needs to be in school." He pauses, waits for me to comment, to agree. I have no voice. "With most of our pupils, if truanting occurs in upper sixth, there's little or nothing the parents can legally do. But as Liam is not eighteen until June, I thought we might be able to work together on this. Assuming, that is, Liam still lives at home."

"Yes, yes, of course he does," I mutter finally. Liam is a child, my child. Yet. "What are we talking about, exactly?" I ask in what I hope is a normal voice.

"Three or four days of absenteeism a week. Very little homework handed in."

"I didn't know," I whisper.

"I was wondering whether there was a problem at home that we're not aware of. Liam has a good academic record. When he arrived at our sixth form, we were very excited, we thought great things were in store."

"Yes, yes," I agree eagerly. I think I sound manic. "He's just secured an impressive internship. He's going to UCL."

Mr. Edwards pauses. I bite my lip. Anything I say will be wrong. "Well, the internship will be subject to references, I assume, and UCL is a conditional offer. This level of truancy is certainly going to have an impact. He's in danger of dropping two or even three grades below our predicted ones, as it stands now."

"Oh."

"So, is there?"

"What?"

"Anything going on at home or within his friendship groups, maybe girlfriend troubles?" Mr. Edwards laughs self-consciously at this suggestion, almost as though he'd rather not hear if it is the latter. I want to scream. Maybe I do, because Mr. Edwards adds, "Have I caught you at a difficult time, Mrs. Harrison?"

"Yes, yes, actually you have."

"Perhaps it would be best if we made an appointment for you and Mr. Harrison to come and speak to me. To sort this out."

"You can sort this out?" I grasp at straws. I'm not thinking clearly.

Mark Edwards tries to sound upbeat and confident. "Well, most likely. We need to have a conversation and then we need to engage with Liam. If he wants to turn things around, then we can work together to do so. We just need to get to the bottom of what's going on in the young man's mind. All is not lost, Mrs. Harrison."

But it is lost. I know what's going on.

My son is having sex with my best friend. My son is having sex with Abigail Curtiz, wife of Rob Larsen. I don't know how we can turn that around. I suspect that will be outside the principal's area of expertise.

I put down the phone and then curl into a ball on the floor, in the corner of the room. The smell of vomit lingers.

Liam hasn't been going to school.

For five weeks, he has been lying to me, to be with her.

I think back over the past weeks. Have there been signs? Clues that I've missed? When did it start? During the Easter holidays, when I took extra shifts and Abi and Liam were mostly here, with no company other than the girls? I thought he was revising. Was it before then? Did they share looks, codes, messages that I've been oblivious to? How could this affair have been raging under my very roof?

I thought I knew him. I thought I knew him better than anyone.

And her? I thought she was my friend.

The feeling of hazy shock vanishes as I'm seized with livid fury. A ball of angry fire swirls around my stomach. He's throwing away his career on that bitch, that interloper, that manipulative slut. I hate myself for falling on the hackneyed phrases that hurt women; I'm a feminist and don't call women names. I'm ashamed that my response is so basic, so lacking and backward. But I don't know how to be better.

I think of the things she told us last night. How her lover was obsessed with her, couldn't get enough of her. He followed her into the shower. Liam. I don't want to think these thoughts but I do. I think of her, hands flat against the wet tiles. His hands on her hips. Or maybe her breasts. Have they done it here in our home? Well, they must have. In his childhood bed? Maybe in mine and Ben's bed? The kitchen table? Anything is possible.

I need Ben. I have to speak to him. Him first. He'll

know what to do, what to say. I text Gillian and ask if she'll collect the girls and keep them for me, then I grab my car keys and head for the door.

"Oh hello, you're home. I didn't hear you come in."

I hear her voice behind me. It's like a knife being plunged between my shoulder blades. Slowly, I turn around. She's stood on the stairs, wearing not much, no surprise there. Her short silky robe, the one she wears to come to breakfast. I've often marvelled how she can climb out of bed and look so gorgeous and together; now I consider it isn't as effortless or artless as I had thought. She's dangerous.

"Were you in bed?" I ask, my voice scratching.

"I've been painting my nails."

This is her explanation for being half-dressed in my home at three thirty in the afternoon, an excuse she's given me before when I've found her here semiclad. Other times she's said that she was having a lie-down. I'd always imagined her having a dreadful afternoon, needing to retreat, to reminisce and recover, time to grieve for her marriage. I sympathised. I treated her with kindness. Now I understand. She's been spending the afternoons in bed with my son when I thought he was at school learning about great philosophers and political theory.

"Is he up there?"

She doesn't even deny it. "Yes, he's taking a shower."

I don't know how she expected me to respond but I scream, it's loud and primitive and I can't stop it. All my frustration is pouring out of my mouth. This is not what I want for my boy. This is not what any mother could want.

Liam comes running out of the bathroom, a towel around his hips.

Abi orders him back into his bedroom. "I have this," she says calmly.

And he goes. Like the obedient boy he is, he backs into his room, glancing at me just briefly. His face colours but I know my son: that blush isn't for his embarrassment or his shame; it's because he feels pity. Pity for me.

Abi slaps me. I feel the sting before my brain can register what she has done. She steps smartly away from me, in case I retaliate. I wouldn't have. I don't want to touch her. The slap, short and sharp, does the trick she wanted. I stop screaming. I stare at her, stunned, waiting to see how else she will choose to hurt and humiliate me.

"Shall I make us both a cup of tea?" she asks.

"No."

She walks through to the kitchen anyway. I see her sniff the air but she doesn't say anything. I notice she glances at her phone. I realise that she's played me. The phone was there for a reason. How lucky that it was unlocked and the porn was on the screen. She knew I would pick it up. She knew I was curious about her and her boyfriend, that I'd want to find a photo. She'd told me just enough to pique my interest. "I didn't know how to tell you," she comments, shrugging.

She has her back to me, looking out onto the garden. The girls have a swing, there is a deflated football under a rose bush. A boy's toy. Does she notice?

"You didn't know how to tell me because you know it is wrong," I mutter.

"It doesn't feel wrong," she says simply. "It feels absolutely perfect." She turns to me and smiles.

I hold up my hand, wanting to silence her. My retinas are scarred; I don't need my ears to bleed, too.

"I didn't expect that OTT reaction." She moves her head in the direction of the hallway. "A little extreme, even for you."

I stare at her. I can see her but she's a stranger, a monster.

"I mean, last night, you thought my dating a younger man was a fabulous idea. Quite titillating."

"You said he was twenty-six."

"Well, if I'd said he was seventeen you might have guessed straight away. I wanted to help you get used to the idea. To embrace it."

Her complete lack of embarrassment, regret or even rancour almost floors me. Surely, she ought to be more frantic. I'm shaking still, wondering when my usual fluency will return. I'm articulate as a rule, verbose when irritated; I have a torrent of things to say but I daren't let it out, I must control it. "What you are doing is unnatural," I say. "Sick. Immoral."

"That's just your view."

"You could have given birth to him."

"But I didn't. You did."

"Exactly. Me. I'm his mother and I'm your best friend. Doesn't that mean anything to you? Aren't I owed any loyalty?"

"For being my best friend? Ha!" She laughs. "That's really funny."

Why am I using phrases like *best friend* on this bitch? This woman who has come into my home, seduced my son. I start to sob. I'm as surprised as she is. I'm not a crier. Under pressure I'm a fighter, a screamer, but nonetheless, huge ugly sobs are erupting from deep inside me.

Her expression changes; she's not moved so much as irritated. "Look, I'm not trying to be his mother," she snaps. "Don't worry, I'm not going to take your place." She laughs in a way that's sickening. As though being his mother is somehow less, somehow embarrassing, compared to what she is to him.

I let out a guttural roar. I can't think about what she is to him. What she does with him, it is all too much. "You're not thinking straight, after your breakup," I cry desperately.

"On the contrary, I am very clear-sighted and focused."

I stare at her, confused. "You're exploiting him. He's naive."

"I don't think so." She rolls her eyes into the back of her head, accessing a memory. A dirty one. I hate it. I can't bear the idea.

"Why him?" I ask. "You could have any man you want."

"I want Liam."

"I said *man*. He's a boy."

"No, he isn't. Just to you. That's not how the world sees it. And Melanie, as his mother, you must know and appreciate his fabulousness more than most." I stare at her, stupefied. She waits and then eventually says, "Think of it as a compliment. You know you can't choose who you fall in love with."

In love with him? She's talking about being in love

with him? I slump into a chair, put my head in my hands. "Abi, you have everything, why did you have to have Liam, too?"

"Everything?" She looks surprised, amused.

"The looks, the figure, the hair, the career, the freedom. For fuck's sake." I shout this. I'm glad I'm finding my voice until she stares at me, cool and calm. I just look idiotic, aggressive, uncontrolled, a loser. I want to go upstairs and see Liam. I want to talk to him but I don't know what I'd say. Where to start. Plus, I couldn't stand it if I knocked on his door and he told me to go away. He might. She is Liam's gatekeeper now. I see that.

"You've got it all wrong, Melanie. You're the one with everything to envy. You're an adored mother and wife."

"Don't patronise me."

"I'm not."

"I'm not an especially adored mother right now, I don't imagine."

"Liam will come around. He'll forgive you."

Since when has she become the expert? I want to slap her now. What is she doing, telling me about my child? My son. Forgive me? For what? I should be the one doing the forgiving. Or not. Shouldn't I?

I can't stay in the room with her for a moment longer. I need Ben.

CHAPTER THIRTY-THREE

BEN

Ben waited for Mel in a café just five minutes from his office. His face creased with concern. He had already ordered a black Americano for Mel; the most functional, grave coffee on offer. She'd texted him that she'd spoken to Liam's principal and that they had something very serious to discuss immediately. He'd dropped everything for her. For Liam. Naturally.

They sometimes did child-handovers in this café, if one of the kids needed taking to a club or a party and another needed to be elsewhere, because neither Ben nor Mel had developed superhuman powers, and try as they might, they couldn't be in two places at once.

Today, Mel charged into the café, frantic and sweating. There were no pleasantries about whether they should get cookies or cupcakes to take home for a treat, no appreciation of the rich smell of coffee beans and no time to chat with the friendly barista.

The stuff they usually did. From the look on Mel's face it seemed that sort of thing belonged to another world, another life. A life that no longer existed. Ben felt dread surge through his body. What could the principal have said to cause her this much panic?

She sat down opposite him. Suddenly, she seemed at a loss for words. With a huge sigh, she dredged them up. "Liam has been missing school."

"I don't understand," he said, confused. "Liam likes school. He has plans. He knows how important this year is." Plans that Ben and Mel were proud of. Neither of them could ever really get their heads around how smart their son had turned out: smart, kind, funny. Ben thought it was admirable that his son wanted to go into government and try to change things for the better in this world; he liked his son's optimism and work ethic. He was not the sort to skive off school. If this was true, there had to be a big reason for it. Bullying, gangs, drugs?

"Why?"

"I know why," Mel muttered, darkly.

"Then tell me."

It was clearly difficult for her but she admitted to picking up Abi's phone. To snooping about. Mel looked ashamed, awkward. "I can't quite explain why I thought doing so was OK," she mumbled. "I guess the boundaries have got blurred for me."

He understood more than his wife imagined. He knew Mel thought Abi's life seemed thrilling and exhilarating, and recently Mel had started to think hers was dreary, a bit humdrum. Abi's life was full of famous personalities, TV types and sexy dates, Mel's was packed with picky customers, ironing and sock-pairing. Ben had watched, over these past six weeks, as his wife had tried to cling on to Abi's coat-tails; obviously, she had wanted to be dragged somewhere fabulous. He'd stood by, confounded, helpless.

Mel confirmed that he did at least know her well when she admitted, "I just wanted to be near her. To be a very tiny part of all that is going on for her. I didn't want to watch her porn, just to find a photo of her new man."

"Why am I no longer enough for you?" Ben asked.

Mel's head shot up. She'd been staring into her coffee; now she met his gaze, she looked startled, surprised perhaps that he'd read her so clearly, or maybe she thought his question was left field—they were here to talk about Liam's truancy, after all. But Ben wanted to seize the moment; they had so little time together nowadays, face-to-face, out of the house, he had to ask. "Me, our three kids, our home, our ordinariness, it used to make you happy. You were content."

"Content," she muttered, shaking her head. He couldn't decide whether she was snarling at the thought of having once been so or the impossibility of being so ever again. "I'd give anything, anything at all to be just normal and ordinary. Anything, to be worrying about what to serve for tea rather than—" She broke off.

"Rather than what?"

"Rather than be the mother of a boy who is having an affair with a woman more than twice his age."

"What?" Ben was lost.

"It was Liam."

"What do you mean?"

"In the video."

Ben's face slowly morphed from confusion, to incredulity, to surprise and then, finally—treacherously—it rested on something that looked a little like pride.

"Wow. Go Liam," he said, letting out a deep breath. "I was not expecting that. When you told me about him bunking out of college, I thought it was going to be something really awful, like an illness or drugs or that he'd got mixed up in a gang."

Mel threw Ben a look that was clearly intended to strike him down dead. It certainly stopped him in his tracks.

"You have to take this seriously," she said.

"Yes, of course, but—"

"If you don't take this seriously, I won't be able to survive. *We* won't be able to survive."

Ben thought Mel was being a bit overly dramatic, but he was not an idiot. He'd been her best friend, lover and husband for years; he could see the cold fury in every molecule of her strained expression. Ben immediately adjusted his face again. "I'm sorry," he muttered. "Right, this is serious, of course. I'm just saying it's not drugs."

"It's an abomination!" she yelled, slamming her fist onto the table. Her cup jumped, the coffee spilt into the saucer, some slopped on her sleeve.

Ben reached out and rested his hand on her arm. "Mel, calm down. He's had sex with her. They're not getting married," he pointed out quietly. He watched his wife, who seemed to be battling with the idea of throwing her coffee cup at the wall.

ADELE PARKS

"Marriage? Marriage?" She rubbed her chest—it looked like she was struggling to breathe. "You know I drove here at quite a speed, just desperate to see you, to hear some calming words of wisdom, to hear you promise that you'd make everything all right and now you are talking *marriage*."

"I said it's not like they are getting married."

"Just shut up." She clamped her own mouth closed; he was glad. He knew that in their rare but intense rows she said things she didn't mean, things she regretted.

He felt sorry for her; he tried to comfort her. "Look, this is definitely a bit odd. Certainly tricky, not ideal, but it's not the worst thing in the world." He reached across the table and squeezed her arm.

"You are not taking this seriously because you fancy her, too," Mel accused angrily.

"What? No, I don't." He snatched his hand away, as though her words had burned him.

"Yes, you do," she insisted.

"I don't, but if I did, I had my ch—" He stopped himself.

"What? You had your what?" she demanded.

He shook his head. "It's not important."

"Yes, it is. You were going to say you had your chance, weren't you?"

He looked about; this café was often frequented by his colleagues. It was a relief that he didn't recognise anyone. He leaned towards her and quietly admitted, "There was one evening that I thought she was coming onto me."

"Why didn't you say something at the time?"

"I handled it. I wasn't sure. What if I was wrong

270

and she was just being friendly? Anyway, you probably wouldn't have listened," he added grumpily. "You've admitted that you've been in Abi's thrall."

"I would have listened," Mel insisted.

"Maybe." He doubted it. "Or maybe you wouldn't have wanted to know. Maybe you'd have said I was imagining it."

Mel stared at him but didn't argue the point. Ben shrugged; he wasn't interested in this battle. "It's not what's important now, though, is it? All I'm saying is that it is understandable that he's done this. She's attractive, she's living in his home. He's young and undisciplined."

"So that makes it all right, does it?" Mel snapped.

Ben knew she was not really angry with him, but he was sat in front of her; neither Abi nor Liam were within firing distance. He patiently tried again.

"What's the big deal? I can think of worse things than being broken in by Abi."

"We're not living in the 1840s Wild West, where young men are taken upstairs at the saloon to visit a lady of negotiable affection. We're not even living in the 1960s when Mrs. Robinson was seen as iconic. We're a couple of decades into the twenty-first century and this is not acceptable."

"OK, OK." Ben really wanted her to stop shouting. The café wasn't busy but the staff would be able to hear. Quietly, he added, "Anyway, I'm joking. We both know that Liam wasn't a virgin. He'd slept with Tanya. You had no problem with that. You've taken mugs of tea into them in the morning."

"Obviously I had no problem with that. They were

a similarly aged couple and in love. Oh my God, poor Tanya."

"They split up a few weeks ago," said Ben calmly.

"What? How do you know that?"

"He told me last night, when we were playing *Call of Duty.*"

"A few weeks ago?" It was obvious that she could hardly process it. "How many, exactly?"

He shrugged. "Not sure. Didn't you wonder why she hadn't been for Sunday lunch?"

"Well, yes, but I've been busy, what with my parents picking up that stomach bug and having to do extra shifts at the shop and entertaining Abi—I hadn't thought to ask him about it." Defensively, Mel added, "Didn't you wonder?"

"No," admitted Ben. Mel tutted. His life was easier than hers because he wouldn't beat himself up for not wondering about his son's girlfriend's lunch attendance.

"Why hasn't he mentioned it before?" Mel wondered aloud. Ben raised his eyebrows. The answer was obvious. "He finished with Tanya for Abigail," she surmised, disappointed.

"I imagine there was some overlap."

Mel shuddered. "Lovely little Tanya. Young, fiery, hopeful. I can see them now, two young people studying together at our kitchen table, heads bowed, hopes high."

Ben knew that Mel would be feeling dreadful that her son had finished his first serious relationship and she'd had no idea. If she'd known, she would have guided him, comforted Tanya. It was hard to take on board. Naturally, they wanted Liam to be a good guy. It seemed unlikely. They'd always drilled into him the importance of respect and fidelity. Yet, here they were. "Imagine how Tanya will feel when she hears about Abi," groaned Mel. "She'll be crushed."

"Why should she hear about it?"

"You think we're going to be able to keep this to ourselves? You think something like this can be kept a secret? This will be choice gossip, it will fly through the corridors and classrooms, tear around the town, linger in the local pub."

Ben sighed; he thought Mel was making hard work of it. "Maybe for a week or so but then people will talk about something different."

"I'm astonished at your naivety," Mel snapped.

"Isn't it just sex, just a fling? Not a thing," argued Ben. "Look, the only important thing here is he's not going to college. That worries me. But I'd say regarding the Abi issue, it's best not to make a fuss. Let it play out. If you don't offer any resistance, Liam won't feel the need to cling to her, to play the rebel. This smacks to me as some sort of protest."

"Protest?"

"To get your attention."

"He has my attention!" she shouted.

"Mel, he's growing up, and bunking college is a mistake that we need to guide him through but whatever he decides to do with his sex life is up to him. Do you remember when he had that phase of short, unsatisfactory relationships?"

"After Austin died."

"Yes, and I said he was just trying to find a way

to have fun and you thought his inability to form a long-term relationship with a girl was going to be a forever thing. That he was going to turn into some sort of cruel commitment-phobe."

"Well, now I wish he was commitment-phobe or gay. Gay would be good. Then he—" She couldn't finish the sentence. She was in danger of crying.

"Then he wouldn't leave you? Wouldn't replace you?" Ben's eyes were soft, gentle, because he knew his words were killing her. "At least that way you'd stay his number one woman?"

"I can't talk to you," Mel muttered sulkily because he'd nailed it and she was not ready to rationalise this betrayal yet. A whorl of her hair had fallen into her coffee; she hadn't even noticed. "I feel betrayed, excluded, by both of them," she said sadly. "My son and my best friend. I thought I had special links and relationships with each of them but they had this enormous secret that they were keeping from me. They've probably been laughing at me."

"You know, if he were gay he might still date someone older," pointed out Ben reasonably.

"Then I'd have a sexy forty-something man in my house who had an interest in home decor. That wouldn't be a bad thing."

"That's such a cliché, Liam would be outraged."

She almost smiled. They both remembered Liam's pomposity at Sunday lunch the first weekend Abi had arrived. At the time Ben had thought Liam was maybe showing off to Tanya. Now, he couldn't help but wonder if he had been trying to impress Abi.

Sensing a thaw, Ben carefully pointed out, "You said age was just a number."

"I did."

"Then that must apply in the fact, as much as the abstract."

"I suppose."

"And you wouldn't mind him having an older lover if he was gay?"

"Well." She shrugged; she'd just said so.

"Then why does this bother you so much?"

"She's known him since he was a baby. It's weird. Wrong." Mel's hand contracted convulsively around the paper napkin she'd screwed into a ball.

"She barely knew him. They'd only met once, was it?" Ben pointed out calmly.

Mel shook her head. "I can't explain." She looked desperate. They sat in silence for a few minutes—it felt like weeks to Ben. Eventually, Mel asked, "So what should we do?"

"Go home, cook tea. Carry on as normal," he advised.

"That's it? You're happy with this?"

"No, but I don't think we should get worked up. If we go to war, throw her out and insist he stops seeing her, it will just draw them together."

"Our seventeen-year-old boy is having sex with a thirty-eight-year-old woman and you don't think we should get worked up?"

"What can we do?" He held his hands wide.

"I don't know," muttered Mel darkly. "But something."

CHAPTER THIRTY-FOUR

MELANIE

Ben insists I go home, start tea. Act normally. Carry on. I do as he tells me. Not because I think it's such a great plan, but because I don't have any ideas of my own. None at all. He says if we don't offer any resistance, the relationship will burn out swiftly. Liam will come to his senses, get bored. Ben says we have to carry on as though Abi was any other girlfriend Liam had introduced, that I must appear to be accepting if I can't manage friendly, which I absolutely cannot.

Ben volunteers to collect the girls and we agree to meet back at the house. I think he knows I'm still in shock and he probably doesn't trust me driving with them. I appreciate that he's not going back to the office; it shows that while he doesn't think this is the disaster it clearly is, he understands I need him.

When I get home, there is no sign of Abi but Liam is sat in the kitchen. Just sat there. Not doing homework or playing on a video game, not eating, not even pretending to be busy. Waiting, I suppose. For me, for Ben. For the fallout.

"Hi." I drop my handbag on the floor and stand in the doorway.

"Hi," he replies. He looks up. His face is a mix between defiance and terror. The last time I remember him wearing this expression was when he was fourteen and he'd sneaked into town to have his nose pierced.

I try to look at him objectively. Is he a boy or a man? It's almost an impossible call. But I try. He's six foot two. Three inches taller than Ben. He has a broad back and relatively muscled arms, for his age. I don't imagine he'll get any taller but I know he'll fill out some more; he's not done growing. He's good-looking. Others no doubt can see a man, almost a man. I can only see the boy.

I think of the times I've sat on the edge of his bed reading stories, listening to his excitement after a good day when he's scored a goal or aced a test, and on a bad night when he's been woken in fear after a scary dream about *Doctor Who*. I try not to think of the things Abi told me last night, when I thought she was describing an anonymous twenty-something.

"Your principal called today. He says you've been missing college." I start with this because it's my territory: education, rules, procedures, guidelines. For seventeen years, I've checked temperatures of baths, food and bodies, I've checked start and end times of clubs, parties, exams, I've checked contents of bags, pockets and rucksacks. I've checked attendance of school. It's firm ground. Asking him about this is carrying on as normal.

Liam shrugs. "I've been going to London with Abi."

I'd worked that much out. I shrink, praying he won't give me any details. Abi gave me details. She told me how she and her lover had taken a swanky hotel, how she'd fleetingly demurred about the age gap, how he'd said it was unimportant—if she is to be believed, I don't know what to believe—how he couldn't get enough of her. Now, I must bury those memories, silence the words rattling around my head.

Liam says, "We did a tour of the Houses of Parliament once."

I don't know whether to laugh or cry. He's telling me this news as though that will excuse his affair, his bunking off. Does he think I'm going to be pleased and ask what he thought of Westminster Hall and the Queen's Robing Room? I wonder if a small part of him still wants my approval. Or maybe it's just habit, he's just telling me his news because that's what he's always done. I somehow manage to resist the urge to shout that he's clearly been getting quite the education and force myself to stay on track.

"You need to go to college. Your A-levels start in June, less than two months."

"For fuck's sake, Mum, is this all you want to talk about?"

"What would you like to talk about?" I ask coolly.

"I thought you'd have something to say about Abi and stuff."

I try to remember Ben's advice. "I think the age

gap might be difficult to negotiate," I say carefully. My throat is dry, tight. I'm trying so hard not to say the wrong thing and alienate him, so it's almost impossible to say anything at all.

He folds his arms across his chest, his stance challenging. His smile is cold. He's a stranger. "What was it you said to Abi last night? 'What's good for the goose is good for the gander.' That was it."

She's told him. They spoke about me. I imagine them laughing at my antiquated turn of phrase, maybe my pathetic willingness to ingratiate myself with her by trying not to appear shocked by her news. I glare at Liam, furious with him, with her, with the whole disgusting thing. I don't know why I spouted that crap. To please her? I hate her. I want to do serious damage to her. I take deep breaths and hope my son can't read my mind.

He carries on, "And I agree with you, Mother. It's just sexist. No one passed judgement, or even so much as passed comment, when Rob started sleeping with his PA and the age gap was almost the same as it is between Abi and me."

"That was different."

"Why?"

"I didn't give birth to Rob's PA. If I had, I'd have had plenty to say."

Liam looks bored, embarrassed for me. "You're so suburban, Mum," he says with a slow, sarcastic roll of the eyes.

"Well, yes, that's true. I was born in the suburbs and have chosen to live my adult life in suburbia. I like having a garden. It doesn't mean I'm stupid."

Against my better judgement, because I'm riled, I add, "This isn't going to work, Liam."

"Yeah, it is."

"What do you even talk about?"

He grins, slowly, secretly. He thinks I don't know what is going on in his mind but I do. I read the smile just as clearly as if he'd said the words: *they don't do much talking.*

"But she's so old," I yell, frustrated, abandoning my plan to play it cool, bite my tongue, carry on as if nothing had happened. It was a stupid plan, anyway. Not mine, Ben's.

"Thirty-eight isn't old."

"Liam, I've been seventeen and I'm almost thirty-eight. I'm not exaggerating when I say there is no common ground. I was a completely different person at seventeen compared to the person I am now."

"She's nothing like you," he snaps. "She doesn't fawn and grovel at the world, she grabs it by the throat. Shakes it, makes it her own. She's exciting, and I like being with her. There's nothing you can do about that."

We stare at one another, both of our chests moving up and down rapidly.

Do I? Do I fawn and grovel at the world?

"I'm going to move Abi's things into my room." He's not asking me, he's telling me.

I nod and seize the only advantage I can. "OK, but you go to school."

Liam's face breaks into a wide beam; he's my boy again, but only for a moment. He doesn't hug me, he leaves the room. I'm about to ask him what he wants for tea but I stop myself. That's a question for children.

We all six sit together to eat the roast chicken, sweet potato chips and broccoli that I've made. This dish is Imogen's favourite, so she is happy, at least. We've all sat together and shared meals for weeks now, meals that I've enjoyed immensely; chatty, funny, loud occasions. Tonight is completely different. The conversation is stilted, no one is laughing, I can't bring myself to look at Abi or Liam. I keep my attention focused on my food, only just managing to meet the gaze of the girls or Ben. Not that it would matter if I was trying to make eye-contact with either Abi or Liam—they only see each other; they seem to be oblivious to the fact that the rest of us are in the room.

The sexual chemistry between them is obvious. How could I have missed it? Or is it a case that because I now know and the genie is out of the bottle, they're being extreme and no longer wary or careful? Instead they are flagrant. Blatant, immodest, brazen. They reach for one another's hands, she squeezes his leg under the table, he throws his arm around the back of her chair and caresses her shoulders. Ben tries to talk about—oh, I don't know, his work, I suppose, or the traffic. It doesn't matter, there's no way in. They're a unit and we are consigned to the role of spectators. There's no place for us in their private world. I can't follow Ben's attempts at conversation. I can't even hear it. I feel like I'm submerged underwater. I can't hear, see, speak, move or think at my usual pace. Everything has been turned off inside me. Maybe it's the only way I can function.

Watching Liam and Abi together is like watching a catastrophe on the news unfold behind the glass wall of a TV screen. You can see it being reported but you can't do anything. You can't change it. You'll probably watch the same footage several times. Each time you see the footage, you're horrified, shocked that the events have not turned out differently, that it's always the same horrible thing.

I can't touch them or reach them. I can't change things, but I know it is coming.

A tsunami is rolling in. The earth's crust is cleaving apart, a volcano spluttering, and then there will be a deluge. People will drown, scream, wail, flee. I wonder which people.

I feel the earth tremble.

CHAPTER THIRTY-FIVE

MELANIE

"You did well, tonight," says Ben. As if I am a child. "It wasn't so awful, was it?"

I'm already in bed. I came up with the girls. After they were tucked up, I didn't bother going back downstairs. No one came to check on me. I didn't offer any excuse. No one seemed to expect it. I heard Ben making conversation with them, I even heard the occasional shot of laughter. I know my son's and husband's usual laughs and what I heard didn't sound natural; they sounded forced. Even so, it feels like a stab in the back that Ben is trying to make jokes with them. I am flopped on the bed; I've taken off my trousers but I'm still wearing all my other clothes. I haven't bothered to clean my teeth. I don't answer Ben's question because it was awful. It was the worst night of my life. He doesn't want to hear that.

He comes to bed and tries to snuggle into me. I edge away from him. Throw him an infuriated glare.

"I wasn't suggesting sex, Mel," he says, offended. "I thought you might appreciate a cuddle."

I would but now can't bring myself to admit as much. Instead, I say, "Oh my God, to think that when she talked about The Stud, I was actually turned on. It's disgusting. I was turned on and she was having sex with my son."

"Look, Mel, you didn't know it was Liam. You had no clue."

She'd made the relationship sound so romantic and yet at the same time erotic. I remember her telling me how beautiful it was. He was. She described his beautiful body in detail. She talked about taking his cock into her mouth. It is too much. Why? Why? If she planned on me finding out his identity one day, why would she tell me those things? Did she get off on it? Before, I felt like an intruder, but I admit, I was curious. Now, I feel I am in a headlock forced to look when I want to turn away; my eyes are prised open when I just wish I could shut them tight.

"The cradle-snatching bitch whore," I mutter.

"Mel, you need to calm down. Stay cool."

"She failed to mention it was *my son* she was shagging, presumably in *my house*. I think you have to admit that omitting that particular fact colours our relationship."

"Our son. Our house," he corrects.

My stomach clenches with anxiety. I don't respond to his comment. I have no time to mollycoddle his feelings with careful words. I am devastated. I feel physically weak when I think of the times I have changed the sheets in Liam's bedroom. Their sheets.

We lie still, listening to the sounds of the house. The TV has been switched off, they have put on some music. It drifts up the stairs, a mellow, slow tune. I don't recognise it; it might be his choice, it might be hers. It's the sort of music people have in the background when they—I stop the thought. I can't allow it in my head. I know they are going to go to bed at some point, together. I don't imagine it will be the first time they've done so in this house, but it's the first time I've known, and it's hard.

"How can you bring yourself to be nice to her? You do fancy her, don't you?" I ask. I've been mulling over what he told me. She came on to him, too.

"No, not at all." Ben sighs. "I've thought she was hard work for some time now, I've only put up with her for you, but I can see that Liam would think she's smoking hot. Absolutely shaggable."

So, what was she doing when she flirted with Ben? Was she just flexing her muscles or maybe throwing me off the scent? Or maybe if he'd taken her up on her offer, she wouldn't have moved on to Liam? Why did she have to have one of mine? Was it proximity alone or was it something else? Something more worrying? I'm so mixed up I can't work this out.

"Maybe you should have taken her up on her offer."

"What?"

"Taken one for the team, kept her away from Liam." I don't mean this. It's another bad joke but this time Ben stares at me horrified, hurt. He thinks if I had to choose, I'd sacrifice him. I'd sacrifice Us.

"I thought for a while there that you were a little bit in love with her yourself," he counters.

"I hate her."

"No, you don't."

"I do."

"That makes me pretty certain you must have loved her fiercely, once."

It's true. I was under her spell, too. I know these past few months I've been prioritising her, pandering to her needs, giving her my attention.

"Why did you invite her into our lives, Mel?"

I shake my head. Why indeed? Gratitude? An old debt? Those things seem irrelevant now. We fall silent again, which means we can't help but hear Liam's and Abi's voices drift up from the kitchen. They must be clearing away the drink glasses; Liam never does this without being reminded to. The small domestic act irritates me, because they're doing it together.

"The Cougar Who Came to Tea," whispers Ben.

"What did you say?"

"You know, a twist on the book we used to read to—"

"Liam. We used to read that book to Liam. For fuck's sake, Ben. This isn't funny."

"Come on, Mel. He's a grown man. At least you got him to agree to go back to college. That's the important thing."

We listen to them come up the stairs; they're giggling, murmuring, speaking in low, exclusive voices.

Abi suddenly calls out, "Goodnight, Mel, night, Ben."

I clamp my hand over Ben's mouth to prevent him calling back; I don't want her to think we heard, I'd rather she assumes we are fast asleep. I hear her and

Liam collapse into giggles. Then I hear his bedroom door open and close behind them.

"Oh my God," I whisper. "She doesn't seem to be accepting any responsibility for this...this wrongness." I want to say "this evil" but I just stop myself.

"It won't last," Ben says, firmly.

"What if it does?"

"This is a short-term thing."

"If he stays with her, they won't be able to have kids."

"Well, Liam might not want kids."

"But he does! He's always said he does."

"Well, they might be able to have kids—she's thirty-eight, not fifty-eight."

"Aghhh. I don't want them to have kids! I don't want him to be a father before he's twenty!"

Ben hisses, "Stop being overdramatic, Mel, this isn't helping."

But what would help? We are beyond help. I turn away from him. I've nothing to say.

CHAPTER THIRTY-SIX

ABIGAIL

Thursday, 12 April

Abi hated the way Melanie was behaving as though she was some innocent, passive victim here. As if everything that had happened to her was so unfair and unreasonable, when the truth was that Melanie was the architect of her own destruction.

People remembered things differently but always wanted to know how others remembered them. Was it vanity? Or insecurity? It depended on the person. Maybe, it was incredulity that two people could go through something together but still see it so differently. Abi didn't know. It was awful thinking about how alone everyone was.

Abi and Liam had lived at Mel's, as a couple, for a week now. Liam seemed to be taking the situation in his stride. He flaunted their togetherness with an amused casualness that Abi believed to be sincere and not simply designed to irritate his parents; he seemed to give their feelings no thought at all. His selfishness was so natural for a teenager—it was also incredibly convenient.

Abi had watched as Mel had shrunk in front of her. She looked loose skinned, baggy, boneless. Spineless. She had lost substance.

Abigail had always thought of Melanie as a sturdy, capable person. She remembered when they first met one another in the student union bar twenty years ago. Most students had been standing around looking nervous and overwhelmed; Melanie had struck up a conversation with a couple of botanists or biologists or whatever. She seemed jolly and open, somehow pure. Abigail had thought she'd make a wonderful wingman and had made a beeline for her, disentangled her from the embryonic friendships she was making, claimed her for herself. Even when Melanie had announced she was just nineteen and pregnant, she hadn't seemed cowed. She'd been sure of what she wanted. "I'm keeping my baby." Abigail had admired her confidence, her grit. But then she didn't know everything at that stage.

When Abigail had arrived on Melanie's doorstep back at the end of February, she'd been struck by how much Mel had grown. Abi didn't mean her waistline and thighs (although they had), she meant something a little grander. Melanie looked beyond substantial, she'd looked complete. Her devoted, handsome husband, her tall, beautiful man-boy son and sweet, impish girls completed her. Abigail had felt such rage surge through her body; Mel had so much and Abi had nothing. It wasn't fair.

Now, the tables had turned. Now, Melanie looked like a refugee, lost, disorientated. Reduced.

It was obvious that she wanted to ask Abi to leave, but she couldn't. Abi had to hand it to her, Mel was playing a clever game; not throwing her toys out of the cot was wisest. Abi had not anticipated any sort of self-control from her. She was so unreasonably wrapped up in Liam, Abi had thought she would instantly explode; it looked like it might be a delayed implosion instead. Abi had expected to be thrown out immediately after she left her phone lying around, knowing full well that Mel would not be able to resist prying. Ben must be working miracles, continually talking her down from the roof.

Mel had maintained a cool politeness in front of Liam, managing to stay a breath away from rude, although a long way from friendly. Naturally, Liam was surprised, too, but he was pleased that his parents had been so accepting of their status as lovers. He'd kept his end of the bargain; this week he'd attended college every day. He pointed out that they no longer had to sneak off to London to be together, so he had time to study.

Abi knew Mel was hoping that by taking away the secrecy, not objecting too much, too often, too vocally to their affair, then the passion would be dulled. Or maybe she was hoping that, eventually, the tedious domesticity of living in the small house with his parents and sisters would make Abi bored or squeamish, possibly even repentant, and that she would leave of her own accord. Mel was hoping that the great raging blaze of their lust would cool to smouldering embers and that it would ultimately be stamped out altogether now they were surrounded by the ordinary clutter of day-to-day living. If Abi left the house, then Melanie could exercise her influence on Liam more.

When Liam was at college, Melanie did not speak to Abi at all. Abi didn't care about that; it was a relief not to be subjected to any more of Melanie's self-indulgent, sanctimonious incredulity. She did small spiteful acts that were designed to irritate and incense Abi, such as making just enough tea in the pot for one person or hiding the remote control so that Abi couldn't watch TV. Mel no longer stocked hummus, soya milk or William Chase gin (which was Abi's preferred brand). These things had all been abundant until Mel found out about the affair. She banged on the bathroom door almost the moment Abi went into it, instead of patiently lingering outside. There was never a warm, fluffy towel waiting. Obviously, she was hoping to make things uncomfortable, drive Abi away with petty acts of spite.

Abi was not going to be riled, she was not going to storm out. To maintain Liam's sympathy, maybe even love, she needed Melanie to throw her out. If she was thrown out, Liam would come with her. If she walked out, after his parents had been so seemingly reasonable, he might not.

Then they could move to that smart hotel in Northampton, the one with the cocktail bar she'd visited with those schoolmum friends. That would do, until an apartment became available. That wouldn't take long now. It was all falling into place with satisfying ease. A couple of days in a hotel would be the perfect transition for Liam, from childhood to manhood.

Abi liked hotels. Decent ones. Ones with discreet and polite doormen, dramatic lobbies and rooms with dim lighting and plush furnishings. She liked the neat, clean sparse bathrooms and a fully stocked minibar. She could afford it. Contrary to what she'd hinted to Mel, there had never been cash-flow problems. Rob was too guilt-stricken to be tight.

There was a certain satisfaction to living openly with Liam, right under Mel's nose, as she could see the distress it caused, the turmoil, but Abi had had enough now. Liam's bedroom had his football trophies on one shelf, a poster aging and categorising dinosaurs hung on the back of the door. Obviously it had been there for years, so long that others had stopped noticing it. Abi didn't like it—she took it down and put it in the bin. It was time to set aside childish things. It was time to move things on a bit.

Melanie was ironing in the sitting room, in front of the TV. She always did that on a Thursday morning, just before she started work. It amused Abi how Mel had clung to her routines. It somehow underlined how very ordinary and limited she was. Dreary, really. Melanie looked surprised when Abi walked into the room with a tray, loaded with biscuits and tea.

"I thought you might fancy a cuppa," Abi offered, smiling her most ingratiating smile. Mel didn't reply. "Do you?" Abi challenged. It would be an act of such childishness if she point-blank refused to answer that simple question.

"No, thank you," Melanie replied.

Abi sighed and sat down, although she had not been invited to. She set about pouring two cups of tea, despite what Mel had just said.

"You know, Mel, I didn't want things to turn out like this. I didn't do this to hurt you," she lied.

Mel glanced up from her ironing and glared at Abi. "What did you do it for then?"

"I fell in love. *We* fell in love."

Mel let out a small sound, somewhere between infuriation and disbelief.

"You know, I just found him irresistible." Abi watched the colour creep around Mel's neck and chest, up her cheeks into the roots of her hair. "I tried to explain that to you before you knew who he was. I thought if you could understand and accept how I felt about my young lover before you knew it was Liam, then things would be easier."

"You said your lover was twenty-six. Liam's a teenager," Mel insisted.

She was boring, she sounded like a stuck record. "He's eighteen in June, just a couple of months away."

"Yes. A teenager."

"A man. How long are you going to extend his childhood for? Why do you insist on infantilising him?"

Mel bit down on her lip. Turned it white. Abi wondered whether she'd draw blood. She hoped so. She chose her words carefully, for maximum impact. "Honestly? I do see your point. I suppose it was a concern to me, too, at first. I told you that. I thought I'd want to do it with the lights out because in the darkness, I could lose the sense of my age. Forget exactly who I was and how I was tethered by thirty-eight years. I could float into any age I wanted. I could be twenty-seven, when I was in the prime of my career or better yet seventeen, like him."

Mel stared at her, mouth slack and wide now, gawping.

"But *he* insisted age didn't matter. It was him, Melanie, you must understand that," Abigail stated with intensity, as though it was important to her that Mel believed her. It wasn't. Then she added, "We do it with the lights on, Mel. He makes me feel *that* good."

Melanie gasped satisfyingly. She'd stopped ironing. She didn't pack up and leave the room, though. Abigail's words pinned her to the spot like a morbid spell.

Abi continued, "The way he looks at me, Mel. No one has ever looked at me that way before." She gently shook her head from side to side in wonderment. "He sees me as no one has ever seen me. It's so different with him. It's difficult to appreciate what it feels like, after nearly twenty years of being faithful to one man, to be kissed by someone other than that one man. To feel the different technique, the variance in pressure. To smell his hair and skin rather than Rob's. To be on the receiving end of attention."

A fat tear ran down Melanie's cheek. She wiped it away with the back of her hand. "It can't be him," she muttered.

"But it is," Abi insisted.

"It mustn't be."

"Why not, Mel? Why not him?"

Mel shook her head.

"The thing is, you see a kid, maybe even a gawky, awkward kid."

"Because he is!"

"No, he isn't. He's a sensitive, interesting, mature, beautiful young man." Abigail held Melanie's gaze. "I want to gobble him up. Consume him."

Melanie kicked the plastic basket that held the clothes that needed to be ironed and yelled, "Fuck you! Get out of my house. Just get the fuck out of my house."

CHAPTER THIRTY-SEVEN

MELANIE

It was not my finest moment.

What I wanted to say is that I know he is a sensitive, interesting, mature, beautiful young man. I know this better than anyone. I've been there every step of the way. Every mum thinks that their child is a marvel, exceptional. Certainly, I do. But it was the way she said *beautiful*. With something near reverence. It made me feel dirty and furious and helpless and hopeless. She filled the word with lust. She made it sound so sensuous.

I've been calling him beautiful all my life. A beautiful bouncing baby, later he'd draw me a beautiful picture, then in his teens, on occasion, I'd be moved to say he'd done a beautiful thing. Sometimes, I said this with a heavy sense of irony (he might have put his plate in the dishwasher) or I might have meant it for real—like that time he visited Austin's parents for the weekend in Liverpool, after they moved away from here. I knew he didn't want to go but he did, because they needed to see a friend of Austin's, found it comforting.

Now, she's taken the word and ruined it. She's put sex all over it and it is disgusting. Her words bounce around my head. *I want to gobble him up. Consume him.*

When he was a baby, I used to kiss and kiss and kiss his belly and I'd say, "I could eat you, you're so delicious." It was sweet, innocent. Her claims of passion have echoes of my love and yet it's entirely different. One was wholesome and good. The other unnatural, unhealthy.

I am surprised to find I can still be shocked by what life throws at a person. I thought I pretty much had it covered. A one-time fling leading to an unexpected pregnancy ironically leaves you feeling oddly smug, at least on one level. You think you can't be any more surprised or shocked. But I was wrong.

I am broken.

It has been an impossibly hard week living with the pair of them, under this roof, pretending not to mind. I've barely managed to carry on, but both at work and at home, I've had to act as though nothing is wrong when absolutely everything is. I've felt constantly queasy; it's been hard to eat. To sleep. The reality horrifies me so much, I've had no alternative but to live in my head. I've spent the week disassociated from everyone and everything else around me, everything other than Liam and Abigail. I think about them all the time. I wonder if they hold hands on public transport. Do they stop in the street to kiss one another lustfully? What must people think?

Simple conversations with Ben or the girls, or in the shop, when I'm serving someone, have become impossible. I lose the thread of my thoughts, forget how to swipe a customer's debit card, I can't remember where I've parked my car. Everything is falling apart.

I didn't owe her this much.

He is my baby.

I know, I know. He's almost eighteen. He has a lover. But. After my outburst, Abi goes upstairs and packs her bags with remarkable efficiency. She calls a taxi. Together, we wait for it, in silence. I think of her as perfect, at least to look at but she's not, not quite. I notice that when the light catches her top lip there are small beads of sweat nestled in between fine hairs. There are lines around her mouth. I guess she hasn't found anyone to do her Botox here. I wonder when Liam will notice these things about her—if he already has.

Does he mind?

"I'm going to stay in that hotel we went to for cocktails, in Northampton, Hashtag. Will you explain this to Liam?" When I don't reply, she shrugs. "Never mind, I can always text him."

"Why stick around at all?" I ask. "Why not go back to London? Or America?"

"Liam's here," she replies simply, unapologetically, as though it should be obvious to me. A half jeer. Heavy-lidded eyes. Knowing.

"Leave your key," I say flatly.

* * *

I arrive at work an hour late because I wanted to make sure Abi left the house before I did, so I promise to work through my lunch break to make up the time. Now I know she's not in my home, I am somewhat more focused. I manage to make decent sales and the day moves along quickly. I never thought coming home from work and making tea for the girls, anticipating Ben's—and hopefully Liam's—return, would be such a welcome simplicity, but it is.

I make shepherd's pie and serve the girls first. I plan to eat later with Ben—and, again, hopefully Liam. Always hoping. Nothing is certain anymore. I realise that he may not come home for supper. He may not come home again. It depends if she's been in touch yet and what she says when she is. Part of me regrets throwing her out, another part of me thinks it's the most honest thing I've ever done.

The girls and I sit around the table together, talking about the hamster, ballet class and *SpongeBob SquarePants*. I stay in the moment and delight in their carelessness, in the fact Lily puts her feet on the table to demonstrate pointy toes; I make a big fuss of Imogen who has been awarded certificates for spelling and for being kind in class this week. I have spent some evenings with just the girls since Abi arrived, when she was in London, but I realise now that it's been a long time since I've been settled with them, listened to them and given them all my attention. I'm still desperately concerned about Liam and Abigail's relationship but maybe, now that she's out of immediate proximity, Liam will find some perspective.

Maybe we'll be able to talk some sense with him and perhaps he'll simply feel less infatuated. I have not have been granted a pardon but I have at least secured a stay of execution.

"Where is Abi tonight?" Imogen asks.

"She's staying at a hotel."

"Is Abi Liam's girlfriend now?"

"Yes, yes, she is," I admit, with a hard, bright smile on my face that is unlikely to convince anyone, even an eight-year-old.

"But she's not your friend anymore, is she?" chips in Lily.

"What makes you ask that?" I'm nothing if not polished at sidestepping tricky questions.

"You don't laugh together anymore. Or drink wine together. She's always with Liam now. Kissy kissing." Lily makes kissing sounds in the air, wraps her arms around herself and wiggles on the spot. I'm glad I told Abi to leave. What effect must all this be having on the girls?

"Is Tanya sad or does she have a new boyfriend now?" asks Imogen thoughtfully.

"I don't know," I reply honestly. "I imagine she's a bit sad."

"She must miss me," declares Lily.

I kiss her forehead. "I'm sure she does."

Liam comes home from football practice at six thirty; he bursts through the door, excited, expectant. "Where's Abi?" he asks.

She obviously hasn't texted him yet. It's too much to hope that she's losing interest. I suppose she's testing me to see if I tell him where she's gone. If I don't, she can say I was trying to separate them and that will widen the rift between Liam and me; if I do, he'll probably run to her and I'll have to live with that.

"She decided she'd be better in a hotel," I reply carefully.

"What? Which hotel?"

"One in Northampton. Hashtag. I've been there," I say brightly, although that's hardly likely to impress him right now.

"What's gone on?" he demands, immediately suspicious.

"Nothing," I lie. I know lying is bad but the girls are still up and I don't want to go into details in front of them. I don't want to go into details at all.

Liam looks at me as though I disgust him. "Why am I asking you? You never tell me the truth about anything."

"That's the pot calling the kettle, isn't it?"

He pulls his face into a sneer that makes me feel old and foolish. Why do I resort to my mother's antiquated sayings when I'm under stress?

"You haven't been especially truthful with me, of late," I point out.

"What do you want to know?" He turns to me, arms wide, the picture of a reasonable man.

I daren't take time to shoo the girls, because this may be a one-off opportunity to make some progress, to reconnect. I'd like to persuade him to sit down, I'd like to get him to eat shepherd's pie and then we could talk things through properly, but I daren't offer it in case he thinks I'm stalling and leaves the kitchen, runs out on me, as he has done so many times of late. I want to know when it started. I want to know if he's serious about her. I want to know if he thinks they have a future.

Before I get a word out, Liam's phone pings. His face lights up—it's obviously a text from Abi. Or maybe a WhatsApp or Snapchat; she's far too cool to send a good old-fashioned text message. Liam reads the message and then glares at me. "Abi has told me what a total bitch you were to her this morning."

The girls gasp. They've possibly heard the word before but never out of Liam's mouth and never aimed at me.

"Watch your language." I nod towards his sisters.

"You are such a hypocrite," he comments. "She told me what you said to her. That you made her leave here. She'd brought you tea and biscuits, Mum. What is wrong with you?" He turns on his heel and leaves the kitchen.

He stays in his room all night, only emerging to answer the door to the pizza delivery guy. Ben tries to engage him but doesn't get much back so he gives up. We all get an early night.

"Have I lost him?" I ask Ben, as we lie in bed. My heart is breaking, bleeding all over my world.

"Give it time, Mel. Let's see."

I don't find this much comfort at all.

CHAPTER THIRTY-EIGHT

BEN

Friday, 13 April

Ben's phone vibrated on his desk. He sighed. Mel. What this time? Another problem, or more accurately, the same one. Liam and Abigail. Another *development*, as Mel would call it. He said, she said. It wasn't that he was unsympathetic, as Mel had accused him of being, or even unaware of the seriousness of the issue—he got it, his family was in turmoil.

The thing was, he was in the middle of a big audit and early signs were that the business wasn't going quite as well as his bosses would like. He couldn't afford to make any errors. He had to check and re-check everything he did, working twice as hard just to stay still; these constant distractions weren't helpful. Yes, his family was in turmoil but matters would only get worse if he messed up at work, lost his job.

Not that he was saying he was at that stage, but things were hairy.

"Hi," he said, hoping his wife would understand the inference of his tone. *I'm at work, I can't chat.*

No preamble, she rarely bothered with such niceties anymore. "Liam has moved out."

"What? When?"

"I don't know exactly. This morning I banged on his bedroom door and yelled at him to get out of bed. I could hear the shower as I hurried the girls out of the house."

"You didn't wait to give him a lift to the bus stop?"

"I was pretty confident he wouldn't want that after last night. Neither of us was ready to face the other yet. I finished work at five, as usual, and came home but Liam hadn't collected the girls. No one was here."

"What, he just left them at after-school club?" Normally Liam picked up the girls from after-school club on a Friday—he got paid to do this and to make their tea. It was an arrangement that suited everyone. Liam made some money and the girls loved it.

"There was a message on the home phone voicemail from their headmistress. She was not impressed. I didn't get there until six fifteen. You know the club finishes at five. They looked like little lost orphans, standing waiting for me. I could kill him. They were really upset. They'd got it into their heads Liam had been in an accident."

"Oh no, the poor things."

"It's so inconsiderate of him."

"So, wild guess you think he's visiting Abi at her hotel."

"Not visiting. His room has been emptied."

"Emptied?"

"Nearly all his clothes, his college books, his laptop. I suppose he must have moved in with her. In the hotel."

Ben sighed. "Right, well, it's not completely unexpected, is it? Have you called him?"

"Yes, and texted several times. He hasn't responded."

"Have you called her?"

"Oh Ben, I don't want to."

"You might have to." Ben believed the important thing was keeping a relationship with Liam and that might mean accepting Abi; Mel was light years away from agreeing to that.

"I have called Tanya."

"Tanya? Why?"

"I thought he might be there."

Ben sighed again. It was unlike Mel to fight the facts, fight reality in this way. He'd always thought she was quite a rational, practical person. "You're grasping at straws."

"She's coming over."

"Why? How will that help?"

"I don't know but I need to see her. I need to see someone who finds this situation as hard as I do."

His wife hung up.

CHAPTER THIRTY-NINE

TANYA

Liam's mum called me today, finally. I'd thought she might have called me before now. I mean, I thought we were quite close—in fact I thought that all the Harrisons liked me, not just Liam. But I guess I was wrong about that, too, because she hadn't been in touch once in these past weeks. I wanted to hear from her because I thought maybe she'd have some idea as to what is really going on with Liam. I do not buy his crap about exam pressure, concentrating on his grades and it being best to end it now because long-distance relationships never work and I didn't get into the RVC in London.

My friends just think he's being a dick, they keep saying I can do better and I should just move on and not think about him anymore. But that's ridiculous, insane, because for one, when I was going out with him, they all loved him. They were always going on about how hot and yet considerate he was. Called me a lucky bitch. And for two, I just can't. I mean people say put him out of your mind, but how? He is all I think about.

I know what I'm supposed to do. I'm supposed to act all bright and bubbly, busy, unconcerned. But I can't. I keep going over and over our last few times together and trying to work out what went wrong, what I did wrong. But I don't know. I just don't know. I asked him but he shrugged, kept to his story about the impossibility of long-distance relationships, the unfeasibility of us managing to sustain what we currently had. Those didn't sound like his words. I wondered if his mum had come up with the excuse for him or something. It sounded like an adult's excuse. Something a parent might say. It sounded rehearsed.

So, my friends, who used to say he was cute and built and sweet, are now saying he's a total emotional retard as he's unable to give me a proper, *truthful* explanation as to why he finished us after nine months. They all think he's met someone else because ninety-nine times out of a hundred that is what happens. But no way do I believe that.

I'm thinking he's having a breakdown, like maybe A-levels *are* too much work. Not that he's been doing much work—he's been skipping college, which is so not like him, but maybe that's just to avoid me. I don't know. He isn't seeing much of his other friends either, I asked around.

I miss him. I love him. I hate him, too.

When Liam's mum called, I could tell immediately something was very wrong. She wanted to know if

Liam was round at mine, like *as if*, or if I'd seen him at all today. I guess she's finally caught on to the fact he's bagging college a lot now.

"I didn't see him in maths."

"Could you have missed him?"

"There are only eight of us in the group." I looked for him at lunch, too, but there's no way I'm going to admit to that and sound desperate.

"Oh God."

"What is it, Mrs. Harrison?" She was always telling me to call her Mel, but I never got in the habit; most often I just avoided calling her anything at all. Saying Mel now would seem doubly weird.

"I think he may have run away from home."

All the anger I felt, that she hadn't contacted me before, had just dropped me after months of me hanging at her house, dissolved. She sounded gutted. It was probably wrong of me but I felt relieved, justified. I knew something was properly off with Liam. A breakdown rather than a break-up. I could help then. Change things.

"I'm coming around to yours, right now."

Oh my God, I hardly recognise Mrs. Harrison. She seems like she's lost loads of weight since I saw her a few weeks ago and it does not suit her. She looks like she has cancer or something. As she leads me into their sitting room, I start preparing myself for her telling me that; maybe that's why Liam has freaked out and run away. It would have been awful, a horrible, horrible thing but what she tells me is somehow worse. Look, I know it's not. Not really. No one is dying. But it is. It's worse.

"What, hang on. You saw a porn video belonging to your friend, Abigail, and Liam was in it." I don't get it. It makes no sense.

"Starring role," she quips. I have no idea why—there is no humour in this situation.

"You're sure?"

"I recognised his birthmark," she says.

I know it. It's on his right buttock. It's distinctive. It looks like a rabbit's head. I guess his mum won't have seen it for a while but she'd know it, too. I feel dizzy. Faint. She describes, in excruciating detail, her response to finding the film. Puking over it but then copying it.

"Why did you do that?" I ask, horrified.

"To check I hadn't made a mistake. I thought I'd have to watch it again to confirm things but I didn't, because at that point, Abi just sauntered down the stairs. In her robe."

I suppose Mrs. Harrison must be too upset to think how her words are affecting me. They are blows. Or maybe she is aware but doesn't care because she knows there's nothing she can say to comfort me.

"When do you think it began?" I ask carefully.

"I imagine it's been going on for a while, the movie doesn't strike me as a first-date production but I could be wrong. What do I know? Nothing, apparently. I know nothing about my son or my best friend." She shrugs. "I've been wondering whether it was before or after his trip to Edinburgh."

"What trip to Edinburgh?" I ask.

"He went to see the Scottish Parliament, with the sixth form."

I shake my head. There was no trip.

Mrs. Harrison looks startled. I guess she's counting up the lies. I certainly am. "He said he wanted to cool things off because he wanted to concentrate on his grades. The bastard."

"Well, I know his A-levels are important to him," she mumbles. She's in the habit of defending him and it's pathetic. I glare at her. Stupid woman. Stupid, stupid woman. How did she let this happen? Under her fucking nose.

"Been doing a lot of studying recently, has he?" I snap, unable to tame my bitterness.

"No," she admits.

She tells me they've been going to London together, staying in fancy hotels, that they spent most of the Easter holidays together here, alone, while Mr. and Mrs. Harrison worked. She spews up the story, holds nothing back. I think part of her wants someone else to be as shocked and hurt as she is. She wants her pain validated. Apparently, Mr. Harrison is behaving as though it is the most normal thing in the world that her oldest friend is having sex with her son.

"Agggh."

The sound explodes, surprising me as much as Mrs. Harrison, no doubt. I don't recognise the sound, I've never made it before. Like a cat in pain. I feel terrible, frustrated, vulnerable. He preferred that old woman to me. It's embarrassing. He's crawled all over her. It's gross. He's lied to me. It's unforgivable. I didn't see this coming. I should have, but why would I? She's old. Who would have thought?

He was a bit obsessed with her. He Googled her as soon as she moved in with them. He watched every You-Tube clip of her, and there are hundreds. He read everything about her. I thought he was just curious about their house guest. I didn't see his curiosity tip into desire.

"I'm so sorry, Tanya. I'm sorry for what my son has done. Can you stay for a cup of tea? Shall I make you a cup of tea? Sweet, I think. You've had a shock."

She leaves the room to put the kettle on and I immediately reach for her phone. It's not difficult to crack her code, 1.2.3.4.5.6. Hardly Bletchley Park-level encryption. I search about until I find the video. I press Play. I can't not. I know I don't want to see it, that I'll regret it but I can't stop myself.

It's so degrading, seeing him like that. With her. Some of the moves he pulls on her are the same as the ones he did with me. That hurts. But what hurts the most is seeing the new things he did with her. Does with her, I suppose. He seems so much more confident, more passionate. That old woman. I don't get it. She's just not right, it's weird and sick.

Parents look at us and see children, young adults at best. That slightly patronising halfway house. Honestly, I have never felt like a young adult. I am a kid. I live with my parents. I don't pay bills. The only work I do is a bit of babysitting now and then. I am a kid. Or I was.

Now I feel very adult. My heart is crumbling and nothing makes a girl grow up quite as swiftly as having her heart broken.

CHAPTER FORTY

ABIGAIL

Friday, 20 April

Abigail ignored Rob's calls. He rang four times but she knew there was value in letting him fester, fume. Besides, she wanted to take this call in front of Liam; it was important that he understood how Rob treated her. If anything came out, further along the line, she had to be sure that she'd coloured his view of Rob sufficiently. It wouldn't be difficult. Rob was vain, selfish and predictable. He would posture, he would rave.

She had told Liam that the most recent offer Rob's lawyers had made was laughable. Insulting, ludicrous.

"He's reduced it? Why?" Liam asked, confused.

"I'm not sure. He didn't say. I suppose I'll have to talk to him. I can't accept it."

Liam was full of frustration. "Why is this dragging on?"

"I know it's a complete pain, my love. I just want to be free of him."

Liam had returned to the hotel at about 6:00 p.m., having been visiting one of his friends. Abigail was lying on the bed. Hot, apathetic. The air conditioning was playing up. She'd rung housekeeping but nobody had come up to fix it yet. She hadn't done much while Liam had been out. Made some calls, had a manicure. It was surprising how exhausting doing little could be.

The charm of the hotel room was wearing thin. A few days in the hotel had been fun, but they'd lived like this for a week now; when she had work to do it was untenable, he couldn't so much as put on the TV. It didn't matter. This was their last night here. Tomorrow they would move to their apartment. Their new chapter as a couple would begin. Liam clearly loved the place she'd picked out. A rooftop apartment in the centre of town, a balcony, a view across all of Northampton. He thought it was the height of sophistication. It hadn't been difficult persuading him to leave the hotel for the more permanent arrangement. She'd had to pay a premium to get in so quickly but that was life.

Time was money.

Time was of the essence. No time to lose.

The most certain way to succeed was to try just one more time.

Abigail didn't know how long she'd need. Her goal might take months, a year. Still, she was prepared to wait. The difficulty would be keeping him around for the duration. So far there was no indication that his ardour was flagging but youth didn't tend to be the friend of patience. Creating the rift between him and his family was a help; isolated, he would naturally cling to her. The trendy apartment was a lure and she had other things up her sleeve. Rob's reduced settlement offer, for example. She would make that work for her.

Liam flopped onto the bed the moment he walked through the door, well, more like launched himself. It made her smile. His youthful enthusiasm, his energy. He instantly started to kiss her, his hand went up her top, she could feel his hardness through his jeans, pushing on her thigh.

When her mobile rang, he mumbled, "Ignore it."

Not breaking from the kiss, she scrambled about on the bedside table, found the phone, behind his head she checked the screen. Then, pulling apart, she said, "I must take it, it's Rob. He'll just keep calling. I know. He can be bullish that way. Sorry."

"You've received my email, I take it?" Rob demanded. He sounded smug, in control. It was a change in tone.

Since she'd walked in on him screwing his PA, he'd made an effort to sound contrite and if not reconciliatory, then at least reasonable. Now, all his dissembling had gone.

"I did, yes. What is it? Your idea of a joke?" she asked.

"It's my final offer. That's the settlement. Take it or leave it."

Rob was loud and Liam was lying close to her so she was pretty sure he could hear every word, but to be certain, she put Rob on speaker phone. She'd always told Liam she'd treat him as an equal; this was his business, too.

"It's less than half your opening offer. That's not how things work, Rob. You're the offending party. I get to take you to the cleaners. It's called justice." She smiled at Liam, flirty, conspiratorial.

"I have your latest showreel," Rob said. "The pornographic one."

"What?" Her expression changed instantly, as though someone had drawn the curtains. She sat up straight in bed and looked puzzled, confused, scared. "I don't understand," she stuttered. Her eyes met Liam's in panic and horror now. Yet, she did understand, she knew exactly what had happened. "How did you get it?" she asked.

"Someone emailed it to me."

"Who?"

"I don't know. It was a weird, made-up email. Jane Doe zero zero at something or other. This changes everything. You won't get anywhere near the original settlement I offered. You put on quite the show, Abi. He's a clever guy, his face isn't ever in shot. You weren't clever though, were you? Your face is clearly visible, that and every other part of your body. Fuck, Abi, those close ups."

"She didn't tell you who he is?" Abi asked hurriedly. She threw a look of reassurance at Liam; he returned one of pure panic.

"You say 'she.' You know who sent the video?" Rob asked, sharp as ever.

"No, I'm guessing it's a she. You said the email address is Jane Doe, not John Doe."

"You don't think it was the guy in the video then? A setup?"

"No! I don't think that for a moment." Abi squeezed Liam's arm as he frantically shook his head in denial.

Rob paused. Suspicious. "He looks young. Very young."

"That's none of your business."

"How old is he?"

"Old enough. British law."

"Fuck, Abi, do you mean sixteen? Seventeen?"

"I'm not going to discuss this with you."

"If he's under eighteen, you're in muddy water according to US law. What the fuck are you doing, Abi? It's disgusting. You disgust me."

Outraged, Liam reached to snatch the phone, but Abi didn't want him to cut Rob off. She needed to hear what he had to say. She shook her head gently, mouthed, "It's OK, I can handle this."

Liam couldn't, he scrambled to the edge of the bed, sat hunched, head in hands. She rubbed his back, kissed his shoulder. Took a gamble that she should continue letting him listen.

Rob always showed his pain through anger. He'd been reminded of what he was missing, what he had thrown away.

Internally, Abigail smiled. She was glad about that at least. No matter what the cost, she wanted him furious and in pain. She wondered what thoughts had gone through his mind when he watched the film. She looked good on it, she knew she did. Hot and happy. No, more than happy, ecstatic. She'd made sure of it. She hoped it had hurt him, wounded him. She was realistic. The blow would be to his pride, not his heart, but even so. She hoped he'd been humiliated, demeaned as he watched his wife frolic with a younger, fitter, better-looking man. At least that.

She felt a crazy clash of emotions, euphoric and victorious yet aching that it had come to this. Twenty years of loving had come to this. She told herself it wasn't disgusting, what she'd done was fair and right. All is fair in love and war, right? She had wanted revenge and here it was. She needed to stay focused on what would happen next. She had to stay calm and cool, a step ahead. It wasn't the moment to let her emotions overwhelm her.

"Well, I hope you enjoyed the peep show but the film can have no effect on the divorce settlement. I only had sex with him after I'd moved out of the marital home. The blame for the breakdown of our marriage is still with you."

"OK," Rob drawled. "You know what? I think you're right, that's what the courts would say. If we went to court. You'd still get your pound of flesh and a chunk of my empire." Rob paused, allowing his words to settle and his full meaning to be understood. "So, I'm going to have to be more creative."

"What do you mean?"

"Well, there are lots of sites for this sort of film on the internet. You must be aware of that, Abigail. I think, with your name attached to it, we'd have an internet sensation on our hands. It would go viral within hours, I should imagine. Your private little party wouldn't be quite so private anymore," he sneered. "Your career would be well and truly over. No one would hire you as an anchor of any serious programme if you become known as the star of a cougar porn film. Can you imagine thousands, maybe hundreds of thousands, of grubby little perverts looking at the film, getting off on your secretive, beautiful moments?"

"You're bluffing. Even you wouldn't be so cruel."

"You know me, Abi, a hard and ruthless businessman. You've watched me over the years outwit, outthink, outmanoeuvre anyone from cameramen to CEOs. You used to think it was sexy."

"You're just a bully, prepared to screw over anyone who stands in your way."

Rob laughed.

She had to stay firm, not show her fear or panic. "If you air the film, you'll end up looking like a dick. I'll tell the world you weren't satisfying me and I had to turn to a younger lover. I'll brazen it out."

"Maybe you would, Abi. But then I don't suppose it would take me long to find out the name of your younger lover. He has a very distinct birthmark on his ass. I'm sure someone will recognise that. Plus, I can get my IT guys to do some digging on the email address. Get a private detective to follow you for a while. It's my guess that I'd have a name within forty-eight hours. Will he want to become famous for this?"

"You bastard."

"I'll have my lawyers send over the papers for you

to sign. Don't shilly-shally, Abigail. I'm not in a particularly patient mood. By the way, I'm moving this divorce petition to Alaska—we can finish up in just thirty days. Do you understand?"

Abigail hung up the phone and slowly inched towards Liam. He was still sat on the end of the bed, quivering. Abi didn't know if it was shock or anger.

"Who do you think sent the video to him?" he asked. "You know I didn't, right?" He turned to her. His brow, usually so smooth, was creased with concern.

"It was your mother," Abi said confidently.

Liam's mouth and eyes were wide with shock. Three big noughts on his face. "My mum?"

"Obviously. It's my fault. I underestimated her. I never imagined Mel would have the presence of mind to copy the film. I could kick myself. I am not someone who usually miscalculates a threat or a foe."

"It's private. She shouldn't have even looked at it." Liam's outrage mounted. "Will he do as he threatens, Rob?"

"Yes."

"Fuck."

"I know, baby." Abi kneeled on her haunches behind Liam, her legs spread wide around him, wrapping her arms around his chest. Pushing her hot body into his. "I know you want to go into politics. There's your internship at Westminster to consider. Your offer from UCL…" She trailed off.

The implications hit him. "That would all be ruined."

Abi nodded sadly.

"How could she? How could she do this to me?" he demanded.

"She's angry. She's hurt," Abigail said with false sympathy.

Liam stood up and then turned to her. His fury and frustration burned; he almost looked like he wanted to cry. It moved her, he was so unguarded and open. Transparent. "How can you be so understanding when she's been such a bitch? I hate her. I'll never forgive her," he spat.

CHAPTER FORTY-ONE

BEN

What now? What now? The hammering on the front door was insistent and angry. Ben couldn't think who would be making that sort of racket. He rushed to answer it before the rumpus woke the girls, whom he'd only just got to bed. They were not as easy to settle at bedtime since Liam had moved out. They missed him. This past week they'd been tricky, sometimes tearful, insisting only their brother reading a bedtime story would do. He immediately recognised Liam's form through the sandblasted glass panelling and sprang the door open. "Why didn't you use your key?" he asked.

"I don't have a key anymore, I left it here," Liam replied as he pushed past his dad. The sadness of this sentence hadn't quite sunk in before Liam demanded, "Where is she? Where is the bitch?"

"Liam, watch it." Ben and Mel didn't agree on

what was the correct response to this situation but there was no way Ben was going to allow his son to refer to his wife like that. They'd never been that sort of family.

Mel heard the commotion and came out of the kitchen wearing rubber gloves. Somehow this softened something inside of Ben; she was a mother, a wife, doing her best, trying to pick her way through this awful time. They had just been clearing away the pots from supper, Ben had hoped that they might open a bottle of wine and if not relax exactly, then at least spend some quality time with one another. That looked as though it was off the agenda now.

"How could you do that?" Liam yelled as he charged through to the kitchen. Ben hurried after him and carefully closed the door behind them, in the hope the shouting wouldn't make its way upstairs and into the girls' bedroom. "How could you?" Liam looked furious, his face split into shards of something that looked frighteningly like hatred.

Ben was becoming used to seeing pain, anger, fear in the faces of those he loved most in the world. It was so sad. He'd started to be able to read the nuances of the expressions. Liam's anger was mixed with confusion, disbelief. He looked like a man who had been betrayed.

"I know you aren't happy that Abigail and I are together now but how could you stoop so low?" he demanded.

"What?" asked Mel. Her expression was harder to read. She looked cautious, caught out.

"What have you done, Mel?" Ben demanded.

She shot him a look that could kill. "Nothing."

"She's sent the film to Rob."

"What?" Ben couldn't believe it. Would Melanie be that stupid, that vindictive? He thought of her visceral objection to Liam and Abigail's relationship, he thought of her despair and distraction over these past two weeks as they lived together, Liam and Abi a couple in this house, and when they moved out. He thought of Mel's threats to do something and he feared the answer was yes, she would.

Mel shook her head. "No," she muttered.

"He's going to post it on the internet!" Liam yelled. Mel did not respond. "He's going to name her. She'll never work again. You've destroyed her."

Now, Mel shrugged. Unmoved.

Liam looked as though he wanted to hit something or someone. His mother's passivity was only serving to incense him further. Liam's adult anger suddenly diffused; he was drowning in more youthful emotions. He looked panicked, afraid. He didn't take his eyes off his mother, never once glanced at Ben. It was almost as though he believed his mother—who had caused this problem—might still fix it, too, because that was what he'd always been able to depend on her to do. Fix things. The colour rose in his face as he realised that was never going to happen.

"He's going to find out it's me and tag me, Mum. Do you understand? Your nasty, spiteful little act will affect me, too. I can't imagine I'll keep that internship if this film goes viral. Can you? What about when I go to uni? I'll be a laughing stock."

"No, you won't," Ben reassured, trying to defuse

things. "It won't come to that and even if it does, you aren't the first victim of revenge porn—it will blow over. People really aren't that interested in other people's sex lives, at least not for long."

But he wasn't sure. Maybe his son would become a laughing stock. What if the media got hold of this story? She was famous enough to attract scandal. Rob was wealthy and important—the connection to him would, Ben feared, guarantee coverage. Plus, the tabloids would object to Abigail's audacity; women laughing in the face of cultural norms were always hung, drawn and quartered. Liam was very likely to be collateral damage in this story. Hadn't Mel realised as much?

"Rob won't tag you. He won't post the video," said Mel. It sounded like wishful thinking to Ben. How did Mel know what Rob would or would not do? She peeled off her rubber gloves, carefully put them aside. Ben noticed that her hands were quivering.

Liam made a sound like a bark, sarcastic and infuriated. "He says he's going to. Unless Abi accepts an insultingly small divorce settlement."

"Well, she'll have to accept it then. He can't expose you that way," stuttered Mel.

"Fuck, Mum, have you heard yourself? It's *you* that has exposed me by sending him the film. Otherwise he couldn't blackmail us." Mel flinched. It was probably the word *us*. Liam shook his head. Despair? Disgust?

"That's not true, Liam."

"Don't worry, she's going to accept the deal. She doesn't want to ruin my life before it's even got started. *She* loves me." Mel blinked, once, twice but didn't say anything more. "Your spiteful trick has cost her millions. Do you understand, Mother? Millions." He towered over her. His words were spat out. Mel flinched, practically cowered. "I will never forgive you."

With that, he turned and stomped out of the house, slamming the front door, leaving his parents gawping after him.

Ben slowly turned back to his wife. Her whole body was quivering now, as though it was doing a little involuntary dance. She reached for the wine on the table and poured herself a big glass. She glugged it down and only then thought to offer him one.

"Do you want one?"

Ben shook his head. He didn't want to pull out a kitchen chair, sit down and drink with her. They'd gone through a lot these past few months, he'd put up with her unexpected guest and all the giddiness and carelessness that resulted, he'd got used to being shoved down the pecking order, he'd shouldered a bigger percentage of childcare while she was distracted and infatuated, he'd supported her when she discovered Liam and Abi were having a relationship, even though he thought she'd blown the entire thing out of proportion—it was just sex—but this? He was unsure how to reconcile this. Melanie had hurt Liam. Compromised his future. Why, after seventeen years of nurturing, prioritising, sacrificing, would she do that?

"What have you done?" Ben asked.

"So that's it? I'm tried and convicted."

"Well, you're not denying it. What were you thinking?"

"You tell me, Ben, what was I thinking?" she snapped sarcastically.

His voice was steel. "You should have left them alone. This is their business. It's not our business."

Mel poured herself a second glass and quickly started to drink it. She looked loose, slack. "Easy for you to say."

That annoyed him. It wasn't easy for him to say. He knew she wouldn't want to hear it. He knew saying what he thought might lead to another row and no one wanted that, but he had to say what he believed. None of this had been easy. He didn't like to see his wife and son fight. He hated the fact that Liam had moved out of their home, that all this turmoil would very likely be detrimental to his A-level results and future chances, even before factoring in the release of the porn film. He hated the fact that the girls were unsettled and Lily was wetting the bed again. It was so selfish of Mel to say it was easy for him. Selfish and inaccurate. He decided to challenge her. "Why do you say that it's easy for me?" he asked carefully.

"Well, it's different for you," Mel replied. "None of this has bothered you the way it has bothered me. You don't care that he's sleeping with her. A woman old enough to be his mother." She wasn't looking at him. She was looking at the pictures hung on the fridge. Paintings and drawings that the girls had done at school, certificates for spelling and swimming, bus timetables, Liam's fantasy football league table. "And do you know why that is?" she demanded.

"Why? Because I'm a man?"

"No," she snarled. She should have said yes. She was not thinking straight—what she splurged next was careless, not thought through in any way. Her words were bound to hurt, were perhaps designed to do so. Maybe, subconsciously, she wanted to hurt him for no other reason than because she was in agony. That's how horrible she felt. Frustrated. Exposed. "It's different for you because I did six years as his parent before you even knew his name. You are not responsible for him in the same way."

Ben stared at her. Silent. Horrified. His nostrils flared, ever so fractionally. He tried to stay calm. He had admirable self-control. When Mel was hot and fiery about something, she didn't think through consequences, she said things she didn't mean. He took a deep breath, gave her the opportunity to retract her words, soothe his pain.

"He is my son," he said firmly. That was what they'd always agreed. They'd pitied smallminded, idiotic people who sometimes challenged him and said he must feel differently about Liam than he did about the girls, that he must feel less. They'd often laughed at these people's rude, ignorant, stupid comments. They'd always believed that presence and caring, not biology, made a parent. They'd said it a million times, to one another, to other people. He knew she didn't mean what she'd just said. He waited for her to take it back, to apologise.

Melanie threw back the second glass of wine. She was incensed. In pain. Confused. She said, "Then why aren't you angrier? I think you should care more."

"What did you just say?" Ben whispered the words. He was beyond hurt. He was hollow. She had just scooped him out. He wished she'd shut up but she wouldn't. Ben knew she wouldn't because she never could when she was humiliated or agitated and she was both.

"You don't feel as protective of him as I do."

"That's not true."

"I want to rip her head from her shoulders. Why don't you?"

"And so that's why you sent her ex-husband the film?"

"That's what you think?"

"Well, nice job. So much for protecting him. You've made things worse. He's right. How is he supposed to go into politics now?"

"I didn't make the film!"

"That's your defence?" Ben turned his back on her; he couldn't look at her. He wondered if she would, even now, wrap her arms around him, like a blanket. Whether they could work this through. He waited. She didn't move.

"I think I'll sleep in the spare room tonight," he said.

It was a test. She'd tell him not to be daft. She'd run to him and kiss him, apologise, promise she'd sort things out, that they could do so together.

"Fine," she said. "Abi's not using it."

CHAPTER FORTY-TWO

MELANIE

Saturday, 21 April

I don't get much sleep, not surprisingly since I don't have Ben to cuddle up to, but I do have the threat of Rob posting the film on the internet hanging like a sword over my head. I lie surrounded by shadows and suspicions, pain and regret. I started the night angry, telling myself time and again that it's not fair that I've been blamed for this latest mess. Vexing myself further by recalling that nothing about this situation is especially fair. I remind myself of what I tell the kids: no one says life is going to be fair, it's going to be wonderful, dreadful, heart lifting, heartbreaking, a learning curve.

I did not send the video to Rob, I would never do that. How can my family think that of me?

However, I fear I am responsible. I wrack my

brain, trying to recall whether I left Tanya alone with my phone when I made tea. I think I did. I'm the one that told her about Abi and Liam. I shouldn't have done that, she's just a kid, too. She's bound to be jealous, demeaned, frantic and she won't know where to put all those emotions. I gave her the weapon to lash out. I don't want Liam to know Tanya is to blame. They had nine months together—it may be crazy of me but I'm nursing a slim hope that he might come to his senses and get back with Tanya. If he knows she sent the video to Rob, the minuscule chance of that happening gets reduced to no chance at all.

I'm glad Abi will have to accept the reduced settlement. She deserves to be punished. I don't hold out any hope that as she's in straitened circumstances some of her glamour will fade for Liam; he's not a gold-digger. In fact, I fear a consequence of Tanya's impetuousness will be that Liam and Abi will be drawn closer. I certainly can't let the video come to light. I know Rob said he wouldn't seek revenge if Abi took the reduced settlement, but I can't risk him changing his mind at any point. I need to contact him, explain it's my son in the video. What a mess.

Despite the rage Liam poured on me last night, I miss him. Of course I do. I love him. This is not what I wanted for my son. Is it a crime to desire specific things for your children? Maybe. Ben would say so, he thinks projection veers dangerously into controlling. I don't know how much say I'm entitled to, now that my son is seventeen, but I do know it's wrong that he's not living under our roof. In the middle of the night I panicked, imagined them moving back to America. I dashed downstairs to check that we still had his passport; I was relieved to see it in the kitchen drawer, nestled between the other four. He didn't think to pack it, that's something.

I miss Ben, too. The lonely, sleepless night has allowed me to think about next steps, what I can do to put things right. Or if not right exactly, then to make things better, a little more bearable. As the birds started to chirp, their happy chorus incongruous to my mood, I realised that while I'm angry with Ben for thinking the worst of me, I do understand why he might. I have not been presenting myself in the best light of late. Far from it. That needs to change.

The moment I hear the girls stir, I jump out of bed and shepherd them downstairs. I don't want them coming into our bedroom and seeing that Ben is not here; it would upset them. I'm hoping he'll get up this morning and, like me, feel calmer; that a cooked breakfast will go some way towards getting him to forgive me. I am so utterly ashamed of what I said last night. I have no idea how the words escaped from my mouth, bad enough that they somehow temporarily formed in my mind. It was the drink and the stress talking, not me. It's ironic that I blurted out the wrong thing—something I don't believe or mean—but I haven't told him what he really needs to know.

I have a secret buried, like a stone in my shoe, not visible to the eye but always causing me discomfort.

A deep, old secret and it's time I told him. Way past time, actually.

I think maybe I'll call into work and say I can't work this weekend. We really need to spend some time together. I'm determined we all have a good time and that can only happen if I clear the air with Ben and assure him that I can get Rob to promise not to post the film, no matter what Abi does. I usher the girls downstairs, luxuriating in their easily bestowed cuddles and sweet simplicity. I chatter to them with a false brightness, then encourage them to put on the TV; as the sound of cartoons fills the house, I start to make breakfast.

As I hoped, the smell of bacon and eggs swiftly lures Ben from his bed. I hear his tread on the stairs. Little butterflies of anticipation flutter in my stomach. Confessing everything will be horrible, but I'm anticipating his forgiveness, his understanding. If I stay focused on that, I'll be strong enough to say what I must. What I should have said a long time ago. Ben comes through the door and I'm surprised because he's fully dressed—I'd expected bed shorts and T-shirt. He looks a little formal for a cooked breakfast but I plough on regardless.

"How do you want your eggs? Poached, fried?"

It's our way to get over our occasional rows; we offer an olive branch, pretend the row hasn't happened for a sentence or two and then whoever is at fault will apologise. We'll laugh, put it behind us.

"No, thank you," he says stiffly. He puts his head around the door to where the girls are sprawled on the sofa, absorbed by some brightly clad, unfeasibly smiley children's TV presenter. "Come on, girls, eat your breakfast quickly. We've got plans today."

"Plans?" I ask.

"I'm taking the girls to my mother's." He doesn't

meet my eye, but starts to pour orange juice. Two glasses, one for Imogen, one for Lily. He doesn't pour one for me, although I have orange juice every morning.

"Your mother's? For how long?"

"The weekend, at least. Maybe longer. I think I'll take the girls out of school next week."

"You can't just take the girls out of school."

"Yes, I can. I'm sure their headmistress will understand when I explain everything."

"But what about work?"

"I'll explain to them that I have personal issues. I'll work remotely."

I'm stunned. Ben has been going on about how busy work is at the moment; he never takes time away from the office. He'd have to feel desperate to do that.

I point out, "But you can't even get Wi-Fi at your mother's. You hate trying to work from there."

"I'd rather be there than here."

The words slap me, as they are designed to. "I don't understand, are you—?" I stutter, "Are you leaving me?" The thought is absurd.

"We need some time apart, we both need some time alone to think."

This is the last thing I need. I've done my thinking, last night. Now I want to tell him all about it. I need to cling to him. We all need to cleave to one another, stick together. Not dissipate.

The girls choose this moment to trail into the kitchen with demands to be fed, so I'm unable to plead my case. I try to concentrate on making the breakfast but I burn the toast and the eggs stick to the bottom of the pan, they split as I scrape them onto the waiting plates. Lily lets out short, sharp yells of disappointment and Imogen tuts, as though this is all she can expect of me. The breakfast is consumed without any joy. Lily asks if I'm coming with them to Nana Ellie's but before I can answer, Ben jumps in.

"Mummy has to stay here and work."

The girls know we can only manage a summer holiday all together by sharing childcare cover throughout all the other school holidays, which means that Ben and I usually take most of our holiday allowance separately, so they accept this. The moment they've finished, Ben ushers them upstairs, tells them to get dressed and brush their teeth. I see suitcases in the hallway. I open them up and a quick poke about confirms that he's packed for himself and the girls, enough for a week at least.

"Don't do this," I plead.

Ben still won't look at me but tells his shoes, "I have to. I don't know you right now. I don't understand you." He sighs. It's a weighty, clouded sigh, as though all hope is leaving him. "If I stay here, we'll just row. I don't want the girls to hear any more of that. They've been through enough recently."

"I understand, nor do I want to put them through anything more," I insist, putting my hand on his arm. His skin feels warm and familiar, I long for him to pull me into a hug. "Stay, we won't row. I promise."

He shakes his head, moves away from my reach. He doesn't believe anything I say anymore. I can hear the girls upstairs, chatting while the tap water is running. They're excited to be going to see Nana

Ellie in Newcastle. She'll spoil them. They're likely to dress in a hurry. I know that I only have about ten minutes to explain myself.

"I'm so sorry about what I said last night—you know I don't mean it." The apology isn't up to much. It's spiked with embarrassment. Words are sometimes so inadequate.

Ben is underwhelmed; he shrugs. "How could you have sent that film to Rob? You've made things worse."

"Look, forget about that," I say impatiently. I haven't got time to explain all that right now. Instead I say, "You don't need to worry about that."

"How are you sure of such a thing?"

"Once I call Rob and tell him it's Liam in the film, he won't release it."

"Why not?"

"Because Rob is Liam's father. Biological father." The words tumble out, messy and unapologetic. This isn't how I wanted to explain. Seventeen years of holding this secret tight from anyone, ten years of lying to Ben, specifically. I thought I'd find a way of announcing this more carefully. But I'm short on time and options.

Ben's mouth drops wide open. "Rob is?"

"Yes." I nod.

"Abigail's husband?"

"Yes."

"But you said—" He doesn't finish the sentence; we both know what I said. I said I didn't know who the father was, that he was an anonymous Ian who had swooped, scored and then been swallowed back into the south, never to be seen or heard of again.

"Does Liam know?"

"No."

"Abi?"

"No. Nobody knows, except Rob."

We're interrupted by the sound of the girls' footsteps clattering down the stairs. They've been even swifter than I anticipated. I turn around to note that they are both in strange get-ups; Imogen is wearing striped leggings with a spotty top and her party shoes, Lily is wearing her Disney pyjamas overlaid with a tutu, and she's put on every piece of dress-up jewellery she owns. Normally, on a more usual morning, I wouldn't let them out of the house like this, and certainly not to go and visit my mother-in-law, but I have so much more to worry about now so I let it slide.

Ben glares at me. Distrust slithers between us, I feel it like a physical barrier. He opens the front door, points his keys at the car and clicks.

"Get in the car, girls," he instructs, sharply.

I want to bar their way to the door but instead I swoop down for kisses as they rush past me. I can't think what to do to stop this tragedy. I have no choice other than to pretend I'm OK with the plans, rather than cause a distressing scene. Hiss-whispering, I urge, "Please, Ben, don't do this. You can't take the girls. We need to talk." The girls are on the driveway, dancing about near the car like little butterflies, fluttering and pulsating. Imogen opens the door—they're climbing into the car now. Out of my grasp.

"We've had ten years to talk," he says simply and

picks up the suitcases, strides out of the door. His bulky strength, which I've always admired, now seems intimidating, unstoppable.

"But don't you see? This is good news. Rob isn't going to post a porn video of his own son." I rush to explain but immediately want to swallow my tongue, bite it right off.

Ben turns to me and glares. After longing for him to look me in the eye, I now wish he hadn't bothered. His expression turns me to stone. "Really? If you think Rob Larsen is such a good bloke, what a shame you didn't choose to let Liam know his dad all along." He throws the cases in the boot and violently slams it closed.

"You're his dad," I shout, but he doesn't hear me. The car door bangs closed, the engine starts up and swallows my words.

The girls wave to me. Their little hands like starfish through the window. I hold my poise until the car is out of sight, then I close the door behind me. I slide to the floor, curling my legs up to my chest. I slam the palms of my hands against my head in frustration. What have I done? What have I lost? The house seems to sigh along with me. Eerie. Empty.

I've never felt so alone.

CHAPTER FORTY-THREE

MELANIE

Sunday, 22 April

Saturday and Sunday smudge into one dark blob.
After Ben and the girls left, I sat in the draughty hallway for so long that my body turned stiff. I didn't care.
I didn't have the energy to move, to stretch. What was
the point? The cats mooched around me, probably
wondering why I wasn't feeding them. I wondered if
this was how the cliché starts, the one about a single
woman being found dead, eaten by her cats.

Eventually, I called work and told them I had a
stomach bug, then I dragged myself upstairs and lay
on my bed. Not quite sleeping, certainly not awake.
Numb. The only time I hauled myself downstairs
again was to make a slice of toast, get a glass of water.
It struck me as correct that a penitent such as I am
should exist on bread and water.

I called Ben three times. He didn't pick up and I didn't leave any messages. I don't need to; he knows I want to talk, it's just that he doesn't. On Saturday night, he sent me an email asking me to respect his need for a bit of space and time. He said he had a lot to think about. He sent the email well after midnight. I imagined him putting put the girls to bed and then chatting to his own mother in her kitchen. I wonder what he's told her. Has he confided all our woes? Has he told her about Abi? The sex recording? Rob? Or has he kept his problems to himself? Proud? Ashamed? I don't mind what he's saying to Ellie. Whatever Ben needs.

The enormity of my confession seeps into my bones and soul. I can't believe that someone else finally knows who Liam's biological father is. The someone else being Ben is perfectly reasonable and yet I've held that secret so close forever, it seems unreal that it's no longer a secret.

I can't believe he just left, that he didn't want to talk about it.

But then again, I can. I didn't want to talk about it for years.

I still don't really, but I know I must. I slept with my friend's boyfriend. Not an easy thing to talk about. Even after all this time. I know he asked for space but I must reply. I have to tell him everything I should have told him years ago, everything I wanted to tell him the morning he left but couldn't get out among the shock and disappointment. I decide to write a letter. It's somehow more sincere than an email, it has more import. Writing a letter will force me to consider every word before I commit to them as I don't want this to be a page of crossings-out. You can't cross things out in life, cancel or erase. I know that to my cost.

I start slowly.

My darling Ben,

This is not an excuse, it's just the explanation you are owed. I know you are reeling right now and I'm so sorry for that. I really am. Obviously, I haven't handled any of this at all well. OK, so now you know. I slept with my best friend's boyfriend.

They were an on-off couple. Abigail was always flirting with other boys, Rob had other women. They were not exclusive. This was the justification I made to myself at the time. I've cowered behind it since but I don't want to be slippery, defensive. The fact is, I knew she loved him and I betrayed her.

When it happened, he was not in love with her, or at least if he was, he didn't show it in any conventional way, not through fidelity, compliments or even time investment. He did send her poems. Not his own, a cryptic line or two from someone else's from the canon. He turned up at her door after the pubs had cleared out. I argued it was a booty call, she argued it was a deep connection. Then, one night, she wasn't in, so he knocked at the next door. My door.

She was out with another guy, actually, let's not pretend she was ever a saint. She may have

*been sleeping with the other guy or she may not
have been, I don't know for sure. I do know that
she wanted Rob to believe she was, she wanted
to keep him on his toes. So, it was what I allowed Rob to think, too.*

I break off. My writing is neat but a fat tear
splashes down onto the paper. Causes a puddle over
the words *it was*. I remember it so clearly. How come
I sometimes can't remember what I've walked upstairs to do, but I remember that night as though I'm
living it right now?

I opened the door to him and Rob leaned against
the post, territorial, entitled. He was unshaven, his
hair was a mess but artfully so. He stared at me from
underneath his floppy fringe. "Is she out with that
goon who played Banquo in *Macbeth*?" he asked.

"Jed is not a goon. Who even says goon? Jed is
hot. Everyone thinks so," I replied.

"Do they now?" He smiled, almost amused.

"Yes."

"Does everyone include Abi?"

"Almost certainly."

At this point in the conversation, I thought it was
still about her. I thought I was doing what she wanted
and then he asked, "And what about you? Do you
think Jed is hot?"

"He's OK." I did in fact think Jed was gorgeous
but I found myself colouring, adding, "He can be a
bit immature."

We locked eyes. He understood. It was a particular criticism to hurl at poor Jed; in fact it was a particular invite to fling at Rob.

"Can I come in?" he asked.

"To wait for Abi?" I knew it was unlikely she'd be home that night. She didn't like getting the night bus alone and she'd taken her toothbrush.

"Yeah, to wait for Abi," he said with another slow smile. We weren't alone in the house but my housemates were already in bed. We drank red wine and whisky in the kitchen.

Then we lit candles in my bedroom.

I can't bring myself to give Ben this level of detail. It wouldn't help in any way. But I must be truthful. Pain is so often inextricably linked with truth, people forget that. I continue with the letter.

I wanted him. I have never looked too closely at why exactly I wanted him. Because he was beautiful, because he was a tutor, sophisticated, different—all the same reasons as Abi wanted him? Or, simply, because he was hers? I don't know.

I do know that I didn't want to take him away from her. I never had ambitions in that direction. I adored Abi. It sounds crazy saying that in the middle of this story, but I did. I thought she was vivacious, confident and impressive. Even then I knew she was going places.

I think the truth of it is, I wanted to be her. Just for one night. I don't know. I can't honestly remember. It's such a long time ago.

The sex was good. The sort of good that allows you to tell yourself that you are not doing anything wrong, the sort of good that makes you want to do it three times in one night, the sort of good that means you sneak him out of the house at the crack of dawn and when your best friend comes home and asks you how you spent your night, you reply, "Early night, quite dull really."

It was just that one night. That doesn't excuse anything I know, but you must believe me when I say it wasn't an affair. The next morning, sick with guilt, I almost convinced myself it hadn't happened at all. It was something dreamlike and peculiar. Unreal. I couldn't believe I'd done what I knew I had done. I thought it was best to just forget it. Pretend it had never happened.

He never tried to get in contact with me nor did I try to reach out to him. The odd thing was, Abi didn't see him for over a week either and then, when he did arrive at our door, he turned up with a bunch of sunflowers and asked her to go exclusive with him. They came out as a couple, so to speak. She was incredibly happy. Delirious. Apparently, he'd finally had a change of heart. Finally felt he'd sewn enough wild oats.

I guess I was the last one. And the most fertile, as it happened.

By the time I found out I was pregnant, two months had passed. They were in love, the talk of the uni. More gossip-worthy than ever. It was too late to say anything to Abi. Even if I had

wanted to, what would I have said? How could
I ever have explained my betrayal to her? How
could I have told her about Rob's treachery? I
had no choice but to keep my mouth shut.

Yes, Rob knows he is Liam's biological fa-
ther. I told him I was pregnant because I
thought that was the right thing to do. What-
ever the circumstances, we had made a baby
together. I thought he had a right to know. Al-
though in such a sludge of wrong things, it was
almost impossible to tell.

He wasn't what anyone could describe as
overjoyed.

I fall into my habit of being ironic and playful
here because it kills me. Rob's reaction kills me and
I know it would kill Ben, too, if I say how absolute
the rejection was.

Rob said, "I'm really sorry to hear that. I'll pay for
an abortion, of course. Or at least go halves. Private
will be faster, more pleasant for you."

Pleasant? "I'm not going to abort," I replied,
sounding stronger than I felt.

He sighed. "Well, that's your decision, I suppose.
Although a stupid one. But to be clear, this has nothing further to do with me. How can I even be sure
it's mine? I've only your word for it."

I left his office without saying another thing.

His rejection of my baby was brutal but I
didn't believe I deserved any particular cour-
tesy. I knew then that I'd have to leave uni and

Abi and all my other friends. As you know, I've always been quite tough and determined but I couldn't cope with daily encounters, I didn't have the skills to dissemble on an ongoing basis. Staying would cause trouble, risk exposure. Abi would have guessed there was something wrong.

I wasn't afraid of exposure for myself. Maybe I deserved it but despite everything and how it must seem, I didn't want to cause Abi any more upset. Most important, with exposure came rejection, rejection of my baby. If Liam ever knew that his father had wanted him aborted, wanted nothing to do with him, it would break his heart. I had to protect my baby and put him first. That's why I made up Ian.

Ben, I've never thought of Liam as anyone's other than mine, and then mine and yours. I didn't think Rob mattered. I still don't.

Oh Ben. My heart aches when I think of how confused and angry you are right now because of what I've done. I suppose you realise now that I invited Abi into our home because I owed her, not just because she was kind when she found out I was pregnant, but because I got pregnant to her then boyfriend. The man she married.

If I could go back in time, I would do things differently. Not with Liam, I wouldn't do anything differently there. To be clear, having him has demanded sacrifices, prematurely aged me, thrown untold responsibility my way—respon-

sibility that at times seemed debilitating—but I have never regretted the decision to keep him, not for a moment. Even though he can't bring himself to speak to me right now, let alone live under the same roof.

If I had a time machine, I'd go back just a few months. I wouldn't invite Abi to stay with us. I wouldn't even reply to her email. I'd let sleeping dogs lie. But I can't go back in time. Yet I don't know how to go forward, I need you and the girls at home by my side.

I'm sorry, my love. Sorry, sorry a hundred times over. Sorry about what I said last night about you not caring about Liam the way I do. I'm sorry that I never told you about Rob and that I invited Abi into our lives and that Liam thinks he's in love with her.

The one thing I didn't do is send Rob the video. I'd never gamble with Liam's future, I'd never put him or any of our children in jeopardy. Since the moment he was born, I've done everything I could to look after him. You know that.

I love you. Mel

I carefully fold the letter into three and slide it into an envelope. I address it and find a stamp. Even though it's 1:00 a.m., I pull on a coat over my pyjamas and walk around the corner to put the letter in the post. I do so without rereading it or thinking about it further. I've hesitated for long enough.

CHAPTER FORTY-FOUR

MELANIE

Monday, 23 April

It takes me until Monday, at around the time others would recognise as lunchtime, to force myself out of bed and into the shower. I smell bad enough to bother myself. I'm just lathering shampoo into my hair when I hear a beep from my phone announcing the arrival of a text message.

Ben! Liam! I almost slip as I scramble out of the shower. My wet footprints make a Hansel and Gretel trail as I dash, naked, to my bedside table. My legs nearly buckle beneath me as I have been so slow and inert all weekend. I reach for my phone. Ben can't have received my letter yet but still I wish for it to be him, texting to say he's coming home to me so we can talk. I hope so, or I hope it's from Liam, telling me the same.

The name Gillian Burton flashes on to my screen. Normally I'm delighted to get a message from her, today frustration shimmies through my body. I start to second-guess why she might be messaging; maybe she wants to suggest an afternoon in the park with the girls. What will I tell her?

The text reads Congratulations?!

It's a bit cryptic for me. What in the world can she be congratulating me on? Did Imogen do something impressive at school last week that I ought to be aware of? I can't be bothered to fake it. I text back.

?!?

Her reply is instant. Facebook now. Liam's page. Call me!

Oh shit. Obviously, the cat is out of the bag. Liam has probably done something absolutely stupid like changed his status to "In a relationship" and tagged Abi. I haven't mentioned any of this mess to Gillian or Becky yet. I don't know where to start, it is all too embarrassing.

Liam is not very into Facebook; he says it's old-fashioned and for my generation, not his, but it is useful for keeping up to speed with his football club's training schedule. Gillian is addicted to Facebook and posts five or six times a day; she constantly combs friends of friends for new contacts. I know she sent Liam a friend request last year and he accepted it, just to be polite. If she had a teenager of her own, she'd realise how deeply uncool it was to send him the request. She does on occasion snoop around his page.

With soap still in my hair, I reach for my robe. I stumble downstairs into the kitchen and sit in front of the family computer. I fire it up, go to my Facebook page and then to Liam's. I feel so done in, beaten. It's inevitable that this news about Abi will ooze out like a bad smell. Although, if he's posted his acting debut, that would be beyond awful.

I notice the stream of comments that read, Congratulations! and Wow? and Good luck with that mate!?!

Many messages have question marks or exclamation marks, which is unsettling. It's never easy to interpret the intended tone of messages on Facebook, especially those left by teens, they're so often heavily laden with sharp irony or heavy sarcasm. There are dozens and dozens of them. I recognise some of the people who have posted comments. Liam's friends, Tanya's friends.

Tanya's best friend, Marsha, has written: Seriously?! What can I say? Congrats?!

I start to wonder whether maybe Liam and Tanya might be back together. That would account for Marsha's tone. Supportive but a touch reluctant, sceptical, concerned for her recently wounded bestie. Is it too much to hope? Has he come to his senses? A ray of optimism worms its way into my heavy heart when I read, So you two are back together? And then, What did her mother say?

I scroll to see what Liam has written to prompt

such an outpouring, and then I see it. Posted just an hour ago.

My girlfriend has just told me she's having a baby. Apparently, I'm going to be a daddy.

CHAPTER FORTY-FIVE

MELANIE

Tanya is pregnant. I can hardly take it in. One shock after the next. This. This of all things. I feel like I've somehow conjured it after spending so much time recently thinking about my own teenage pregnancy, although, of course, that's ridiculous. I do know that's not how babies are made.

Liam's number is stored at the top of my phone. My number one favourite. Ben teases me about this all the time, says his number should be first, but Liam was the one who did the storing of numbers and so naturally he put his own in the premier position. I only have to press Favourites, then 1. Two buttons, but I'm shaking so much that I jab at the phone four, five times before I'm connected.

I go straight through to his voicemail—it's what I expected. He'll have seen it's me calling and be blanking me. I call him again, then a third, fourth, fifth time. On the sixth occasion, I leave a message because I'm afraid he'll switch his phone off soon and I'll altogether lose my chance to speak to him.

"Liam, sweetheart, I know you are angry with me right now." I want to say I'm angry with him, too, but it's not the moment. I can't risk scaring him away. He needs to know he has a friend and ally in me. I take a deep breath and be the parent. "Please, please can you call me? I've seen your Facebook page. Please."

My voice breaks on the final please. I no doubt sound shattered, pathetic. Maybe that's what finally tugs on his conscience because after just thirty minutes of me sat staring at the phone, he sends a text saying we can meet if I want.

I text back and say of course I want, where?

He suggests the café at the local park, the one where I used to take him to play as a child, the one where he plays football now. I nearly run out of the door there and then but remember just in time that I'm not wearing anything more than my robe and I still have soap in my hair. I haven't brushed my teeth. I dash up the stairs and quickly prepare myself.

Although, how can I prepare myself?

He is sat on a bench outside the café, waiting for me. I glance about but can't spot Abi and I'm relieved and pleased. Could I be right? Has this news of Tanya's pregnancy changed everything? Well, it must have. This is an added complication, no one would have wished for it, yet—and this is low of me to admit—I can see an advantage to this latest turn of events. No matter what Tanya and Liam decide they want to do about this pregnancy, they have to decide together. This will remind Liam that Tanya is his focus; she has been his girlfriend for months now, almost a year. That's forever if you are a teen.

Abi is simply a distraction. A heady, irresistible flirtation that has got out of hand. Not a relationship that can have any sort of future. Tanya and Liam are a suited, legitimate couple. A challenged couple, at this exact moment in time, I admit, but they are not the first young couple to find themselves in this position. I can and will help them through this. I'll be at his side again, where a mother should be.

There are countless mothers buzzing about with their small children, repeatedly walking a tottering toddler up the steps of the slide or holding them tenderly, tightly as they bounce on a seesaw. I recall the hours I spent pushing Liam on the swing, catching him as he sped down the slide. Basic parenting, the easy bit. Some of the parents look involved and delighted, most look a little bored. This isn't a reflection on the depth of their love for their children, it's just that the familiarity of the action can mean it becomes automatic; the mothers will be thinking about shopping lists, work problems, orthodontic appointments, what to serve for tea. I don't know exactly, it could be a myriad of things, but they will be thinking about their children.

I hurry towards Liam, drawn to him, as though he is a magnet and I'm just a shaving. Despite his angry accusations on Friday night, I want to throw my arms around him, hold him close. Kiss his forehead. He doesn't notice me approach because he is sat forward on the bench, also looking at the children playing on the swings. I guess he's contemplating fatherhood. So soon, so soon. I was nineteen when I found out I was going to be a mother, young. That seems like a grand old age compared to seventeen—at least I had my A-levels under my belt.

I sit down beside him and he starts, surprised. For a flash of a second he looks pleased to see me, relieved. Then he remembers where we are and pulls his face into something more guarded and apart.

I don't suggest we move inside for a coffee—I doubt I could swallow and I don't want our conversation further inhibited by the proximity of other people, sitting at densely packed tables. I don't waste time with a preamble. I pile in. "So, Tanya is pregnant. It's OK, Liam. I'm the last person to judge."

"What the—?"

I interrupt him. "Obviously, a teenage pregnancy is a serious matter but I feel I can help. Me more than most."

He looks disbelieving, which is hurtful. I know we are going through a bad patch but surely, he understands he can count on me, especially in this particular situation.

I push on. "I remember as if it was yesterday, how scared I was when I discovered I was pregnant with you. I don't want you or Tanya to feel as alone. I promise I won't push an agenda. I just want to help," I add.

Liam stares at me, his expression now fat with disdain. He sighs. It's weighty, dark. "No, Mum, you've got it all wrong as usual. You only see what you want to see and from your own blinkered perspective."

Mentally, I recoil from his words but I try not to physically flinch. I mustn't show him how much he's hurting me. He's just a kid. I know that, even if he's old enough to get his girlfriend pregnant, he's still a kid and he needs me. "Your dad and I will support you and Tanya. No matter just what you decide."

I'm heartened by his post—at least he's not going to repeat history and do as Rob did, he's not going to shirk his responsibilities—but they need to take a breath. The Facebook announcement was possibly a little premature. A little immature. I smile at him, encouragingly.

"Is that right?" he asks.

"Of course. I mean, I know you said you're going to be a daddy but there are other options. You need to think those through, too. Both of you. We can talk about it. She doesn't have to do what I did. She could—"

"Oh, thanks, Mum, thanks a bundle. You wish you'd aborted me. Is that what you are saying?" His face is twisted, insulted, wounded.

"No, no, absolutely not. I didn't mean it like that. I'm glad I decided to have you. It was the right decision for me. I'm just saying that it might not be the right decision for Tanya. She doesn't have to feel it's the only way, just because it was my way. Being a young mum is hard."

"Well, cheers, Mum, this little chat has been really enlightening," he says sarcastically. "So good to know how you really feel about everything, but you don't need to worry. Tanya isn't going to be a young mum." He stands up, towers above me.

Confused, I stutter, "I saw your Facebook status. You said, *My girlfriend is having a baby. I'm going to be a daddy.* Is it a joke?"

Liam sighs, shakes his head. "Abi is my girlfriend. She is pregnant. She is going to be a mum."

I can't take this in, it's unimaginable. "But people were congratulating you, asking if you'd got back together, asking what her mum thought of it. They were referring to Tanya."

"Well, not everyone is up to speed with the Abi and me situation. They just assumed." He shrugs. "But you are up to speed, Mum, so what were you thinking?"

I guess I wasn't thinking. I guess I was hoping. Lack of sleep combined with severe emotional turmoil, I leapt onto the scenario I most wanted to believe.

Liam continues, "Why did you even come here?" His tone is accusatory; I've disappointed him.

"To support you," I mutter.

"But I guess that was conditional support, right? Now that Abi is my baby's mummy, you are going to turn into a nightmare again."

I don't know what to say. There's nothing I can say that he wants to hear. I clamp my mouth closed and stare at my feet.

"I don't understand why you won't give her a chance. The age thing is not such a big deal."

I still can't find any words.

He shakes his head, sad. "I shouldn't have come

here. I thought you were going to be more reasonable. You know she's incredible. She was your best friend. Why are you surprised that I find her incredible?" He makes it sound reasonable. I'm almost lulled into the belief that it is. He goes on. "You know, she really gets me. Gets me in a way that no one ever has."

"Why do you say that?" The words squeeze their way out of my mouth, clawing at my throat.

"We were talking about Austin and she said something that showed so much perception and heart. You know." For the first time in this conversation, he looks hopeful. He's hoping I'll understand. His eyes are gleaming. Bright, alive. When he thinks of her, he is hopeful.

"What did she say?" I ask.

He looks shy, a child again. "You won't get it," he mumbles.

I'm hurt, he's pushing me away again, but I pursue him. "Try me."

"I still feel so guilty about Austin. Guilty and just so fucking sad." His eyes flash with sorrow and aching. I nod. "I miss him. And it's my fault he's dead."

"Because you asked him to go to the party?" I murmur. We have talked about this before. I've told Liam again and again that he wasn't to blame for inviting Austin along.

"Yes, that but also—" He breaks off. Looks about him. The afternoon is still warm, children are shouting and laughing as they play, I can hear an ice cream van's bell announcing its arrival. It's a good day to be alive. "You know Austin was gay, right? But struggling to come out."

"Yes."

"Abi said something that I've always sort of thought, feared. Something I've never wanted to face."

"What did she say?"

He smiles, regretfully, modestly. He's a beautiful boy. "She said it was me Austin was in love with. That's why he came along to the party, to be around me, and that's why he couldn't come out, because he was worried how it would affect me and our friendship."

"Abi said that, did she?" My words. She used my words to reach Liam.

"Yes, insightful, huh? And she told me that I'm not to blame."

"You're not."

"You thought I was over Austin's death. Everyone did, but I'll never completely get over it. She gets that. She sort of goes deeper than anyone else. She really knows me."

I hear his criticism of me, of Ben. We did not think he was over Austin's death but somehow, we have allowed a gap to open up in his world and we haven't been able to plug it. Did we give up too easily? Did we stop talking to him too early? I was the one who mooted this theory to Abi. Her articulating it to Liam has thrown her into such a flattering light: perceptive, compassionate, understanding. I should have dared to talk to him about it but I was treading carefully, trying not to burden him; instead I abandoned him. I cannot believe she's used Austin's death as part of her seduction of my son.

"She's a really beautiful person, Mum. Selfless. Why can't you see it?"

I shake my head. He waits for me to say something but I don't have words.

"She's having my baby. You need to get used to the idea and if you can't, then we're done."

Before I can say anything more, he stands up and strides away. I watch his back as he disappears into the crowds.

CHAPTER FORTY-SIX

ABIGAIL

Abigail floated around the apartment. Their new home. From the moment the estate agent had shown her around, she had hoped for great things from this place. She'd imagined it would be a fun love nest, a place where she made love with Liam and war with Mel. She had not dared to dream that everything would be so changed, so wonderful, so perfect and so soon! She had anticipated it would take a lot more time, but she'd been given a gift early. Early, and yet late. Unexpected, although much anticipated. How could something she'd longed for take her by surprise? At last! At last! The life she deserved. The life she was owed had begun.

It was a high-spec flat, Abi wouldn't think of anything other; even with Rob's ridiculous threat of exposure and a reduced settlement hanging over her head, she was not prepared to compromise. The truth was she was a wealthy woman either way. If she had accepted the first settlement he'd offered, she'd have been extremely rich. She'd only ever argued about it to annoy him, to stay in his life. That wasn't a necessary strategy anymore. She had something much more concrete now. Much more important.

Rob's new proposal, while severely reduced, was still generous enough; she'd be more than comfortable. It certainly wasn't the car crash she'd allowed Liam to believe. She'd ranted to him about what a bastard Rob was, how paltry his offer was, how much she would have to sacrifice to supress the sex video, although she always took care to reassure him that he was so worth it. Liam thought he owed her now, which was no bad thing. It was a good idea to keep him in her debt.

People ought to be more honest about what relationships were. A set of scales. She had thought it would take months to get pregnant, perhaps even years. While she looked significantly younger than thirty-eight years (at least she did after she had put on make-up and blow-dried her hair), she was fully aware of the biological reality of her age. The papers and magazines were always spouting doom and gloom, implying that it was impossible to expect a quick, easy, trouble-free conception and that any clear-thinking woman froze her eggs the moment she hit thirty, but it wasn't so. At least not in her case. Just another example of sexist, controlling society trying to guilt-trip women who dared have a career and delay motherhood.

It was a miracle. The little blue cross on the test,

like a kiss, that said yes, yes! She was having a baby. A baby! Her baby! The joy was blinding.

Liam had been adorable. Despite everything she had done to secure his support, she still hadn't dared to count on it. Not absolutely. After Rob, she didn't have a very high opinion of men—she didn't expect any loyalty. But Liam was being a delight. He'd cast aside his family with seemingly relative ease. Since they'd known of her pregnancy, he'd rarely left her side. He was smothering her in kindness and consideration—offering to get her drinks and snacks, rubbing her back when she vomited, nipping to the shops to buy ginger nut biscuits, because they read on the internet that they eased morning sickness. From the moment she'd told him, he'd been so excited. Within an hour, he'd posted on Facebook that he was going to be a father. Not especially considered, but endearingly impulsive. Youthful. Wasn't that what she had wanted? Needed? His youth.

Liam was a joy, really. He marvelled at everything. Took pleasure in everything, especially in her which was flattering, pleasant. He was like a puppy: eager, playful, devoted. She was in a position of power, his mistress; she could let him off his leash but she could also bring him to heel any time she liked.

Before they kissed, he held the power, then afterwards she did. Decisively.

Abigail was the sort of woman who was used to being in control. On the whole men wanted to please her, with the notable exception of Rob; he only pleased himself. But she had wondered whether Liam's youth might be a weapon that he could and would use against her. He could have looked at younger women with longing or admiration—that would have driven her wild with jealousy—but he only saw her. He could have embarrassed her by drawing attention to her outdated cultural references; instead he told her nineties music was cool. Everything she introduced him to he was grateful for, excited about: the restaurants they visited in London, the sex toys she kept in her suitcase, the famous names in her address book. He seemed to find her thrilling. They had few possessions—just some clothes, no furniture so she had rented a fully furnished place. Liam had been all goggle-eyed with wonderment.

"I didn't know you could do such a thing," he'd marvelled. "This stuff is so cool."

He'd taken endless photos of the Eames lounge chair, Kartell Bourgie lights, the king-size sleigh bed. Then he sent Snapchats to his mates. They'd messaged back with variations on the theme of "you lucky bastard."

They had been given the keys on Saturday morning. Liam had insisted on carrying her over the threshold. It was crazy. She'd laughed and said that was only for brides.

"I don't care," he'd insisted, picking her up with a show of obvious strength. She'd allowed it. Liked it. He'd flung her on the bed and they'd stayed there for the next forty-eight hours. Even food seemed unimportant: they had one another to devour.

It was only on Monday morning, when Abi woke up with the symptoms of cystitis, that she finally pulled on a T-shirt and some joggers to nip to the pharmacy which was just a few minutes' walk down the road; that was the joy of a central location. She didn't bother to shower. She didn't care if the chemist could smell sex on her, if her dishevelled appearance shouted that she had just tumbled out of bed. She wanted to be there and back as quickly as she could be. Liam said he'd make breakfast in her absence. She knew this meant nothing more than him pouring cereal into a couple of bowls but she appreciated the effort.

There was a queue in the pharmacy. So dull. She'd bounced up and down on the balls of her feet, waiting to get served, longing to get back to bed, back to Liam. She'd simply been glancing around the shop, to kill a moment or two. It was far from interesting: hair dyes, cough syrup, sanitary towels and pregnancy tests. Hardly Selfridges. Nothing that she might be tempted to buy on impulse. Although she eyed the pregnancy tests with keen interest, the way a young boy might gleefully eye packets of sweeties or fireworks, something akin to the way an eight-year-old girl regards her mother's high heels. *Could that be for me? Could that ever be my life?*

She had never had the need to buy one. She and Rob had obviously never tried for a baby and her periods had always been clockwork—you could set Big Ben by them; there had never been a scare that meant she needed to check. But standing in the chemist's, the sun streaming through the grubby windows, she pondered. Suddenly, hoped.

She had not had a period since, when? She tried

to recall. She was on the first week she arrived in the UK, but, no, nothing since. Could that be true? She approached the counter, ready to pay for her cystitis treatment when the chemist said, "These sachets shouldn't be taken if you're pregnant."

Abi speculated whether the woman had just seen her staring longingly at the pregnancy kits, or did she somehow have a gift that meant she knew more than Abi knew herself? It was farcical to imagine such things, but Abi swiftly snatched up a kit and paid for that, too.

On the short walk back to her flat, she'd laughed at herself. Quite remarkable upselling by the chemist, she thought cynically, because it just couldn't be true. Could it? Yet she went straight to the bathroom. She'd better check before she dissolved the sachets in water, just in case. A precaution. Not a likelihood. Not a chance. Not really.

But there it was. The blue cross that said, yes, she was pregnant. Then Abi wished she'd bought two kits, three maybe. Just to be certain. She didn't want to get her hopes up, only for them to be dashed in the cruellest way. But there it was. A blue cross. A kiss.

And thinking about it, the past few weeks, she had been feeling slightly nauseous in the mornings. She'd thought it was the excitement of sneaking around with Liam behind Mel's back or the late nights, the drinking and smoking—oh God, the drinking, the smoking. Had she damaged her baby?

The thought made her tremble. That had to stop immediately. She should have been preparing her body for this. She should have been swallowing vitamins, not shots.

She'd stumbled out of the bathroom. Liam had not fulfilled his promise to make breakfast—he was still in bed, sprawled like a Greek god after a night of feasting and debauchery, which was a pretty accurate analogy. She went to crawl back into bed, planning to curl up with her arms wrapped tightly around her secret but she must have been smiling because Liam teased her.

"So, you seem pretty pleased with yourself? What are you thinking about?" He then kissed her nipple, drew on it hard.

She couldn't keep it in. Couldn't help but blurt, "I'm going to be a mummy."

She'd waited, unsure how he'd respond. Her young man. Then his face slowly cracked into a broad smile. "And I'm going to be a daddy."

Abigail was surprised by Liam's loyalty to her; it seemed fierce and absolute. She'd forgotten how intense a young man's devotion could be. It had been so long since Rob had been devoted. If he had ever been so at all. She was glad Liam had posted on Facebook. It wasn't just the fact that doing so showed his commitment to her, but also, she knew that Melanie would be alerted. Alerted, then horrified. Devastated.

"Yes, darling. If that's what you want. Why the hell not?"

When Liam got back from his meeting with his mother, he didn't give Abi any details as to what was said, but he looked miserable. Squashed. When probed, he mentioned that his mum looked skinny.

"Skinny, really? I can't imagine that." Abi couldn't resist the dig. Even though she was happy, even though she'd won.

"Yeah, she was in this thin top." He looked concerned and also annoyed. Annoyed at himself maybe, for being concerned. Then he bit his lip as though he was swallowing back whatever it was he felt. "When she leaned forward I could see the bumps of her spine. It was freaky. Gross."

They went to bed. It was always Abi's answer. As usual, the sex was distracting, all-consuming. Afterwards, as they curled into one another, Abi found she couldn't fall to sleep as easily as she usually did; instead her mind started to whirl. They'd taken a six-month lease on this place but did she want her baby born in Britain? An American passport would be advantageous. Frankly, she was no longer particularly interested in any of her potential projects here in the UK. They would all require so much time and energy. Time and energy she now wanted to lavish on her baby.

"Would you like to be a daddy in America?" she asked, just mooting the idea, not sure if she was serious yet, but he leapt at the suggestion.

"I've never been to Los Angeles. I've always wanted to."

She wasn't clear as to how it might work. There were practicalities to consider. His green card for a start.

And then he said it. Shyly. "We could get married."

The room smelt salty, syrupy, a little raw. He traced his finger over her body, across her hip bone, her stomach, her clean-shaven mound. She looked at his hands and thought they were beautiful—he should have played an instrument, Mel should have ensured that; Abi's baby would have piano lessons as soon as he or she turned four. She also thought she needed to shave and then she wondered, did pregnant women bother? Was there a reason for pubic hair? Did it protect the vagina in some way that was more necessary now she was pregnant? More necessary than aesthetics. She'd Google it.

He was staring at her, waiting for a response. What was he saying? "I mean, you're nationalised, right? As you're an American citizen, if we married, I'd be allowed to stay there, too."

Married? She'd never thought of taking it that far.

"We can't get married until you turn eighteen," she said with a smile in her voice.

He was adorable. So willing, so pliable. She vaguely wondered whether the taste of such absolute power would ever become cloying. Wasn't that why Rob had held her interest above all others, all these years? She never really believed he was hers. She pushed the thought out of her head. It was a downer. She feasted her eyes on Liam instead. His smooth, taut skin, his young, strong muscles. She laced her fingers through his hair and studied his beautiful features. He had a graceful nose, good eyebrows. He was a pleasure to look at. Everything was perfect.

"That's not long now. Just two months," he insisted.

"And I'd need to be divorced," she reminded him.

"Well, yes, obviously." Liam's cheeks flared with colour. He didn't like to think about Rob, her husband. He was jealous. It was sweet. "But after then? Accept his settlement, get a quickie divorce and marry me."

He flipped her onto her back and climbed on top of her. He began to kiss her neck, her throat, her breasts. He was impossible to resist.

CHAPTER FORTY-SEVEN

BEN

Tuesday, 24 April

Today was the third day that Ben had woken up in his boyhood bedroom; it was a faintly depressing thing. He didn't want to regress in life but he felt staying in his boyhood bedroom was exactly that. It was early, just after seven. He'd only fallen asleep at about two.

His mother hadn't changed things much since he moved out to go to university. There was no need—she never had anyone stay over, other than family, and they'd got used to the skinny, hard bed pushed up to the wall under the window and the tatty furniture that was so out of date it was having a revival. It could probably be sold in London somewhere, to someone who identified as a hipster and would call it ironic. There had been posters of *Bill and Ted's Ex-*

cellent Adventure on the walls until Mel had taken them down and suggested they could be sold on eBay.

The girls were in his sister's room—they delighted in waking up to her posters of the *Little Mermaid*.

This morning when he'd woken up, he'd listened to his girls' voices seep through the thin walls of the house and just lain there. Still unable to galvanise the energy to get out of bed. Greet another day. At home, Ben rushed at days, couldn't wait to get started; now he dragged himself through them, faking interest and joy for the sake of the girls, who skipped around the museums while he lumbered.

So far, they'd visited the Life Science Centre and Beamish Museum. He'd done this mostly for their entertainment, but also because he knew that when Mel called them, she'd be impressed. He hadn't been able to bring himself to speak to her yet, but she'd spoken to the girls twice a day. Each time they did so, he pretended not to be listening in, but he'd heard them tell their mummy that they'd spotted the Angel of the North, one of their favourite things to spy; Lily said the Life Science Centre was "brilliant" but would have been better if her mummy was there. In the Beamish gift shop, Imogen had asked him whether she should buy a purple or a green skipping rope, and he'd said both were cool. She'd deliberated for ages but in the end, didn't make the purchase. When he'd asked her why not, she'd sighed. "I couldn't decide. Mummy would have known which one was best." He'd felt dreadful.

Since they'd been staying at his mother's, Ben had run the gauntlet of emotions. Initially, he'd felt full to the brim with anger and hurt. His wife had lied to him for their entire marriage. She had always known who Liam's father was and she'd refused to tell anyone. Refused to tell *him*. He thought they knew each other inside out. That's what he counted on, the belief that they were on the same team had been unequivocal. But she'd lied. Why? He understood that she might have wanted to conceal his identity when she was very young and first pregnant, because her parents were threatening shotgun marriages and such, but why conceal something so monumental from him? From Liam? Didn't they have a right to know?

He'd continued to count her crimes.

She had invited Abi into their life, to assuage her guilt, he supposed. She'd prioritised this long-lost friend while neglecting him and the girls, taking them for granted as she fell under Abi's glittering spell. And the way in which she was behaving towards Liam, for doing exactly the same, was ludicrous. Ranting and raving wasn't going to help matters. Plus, she had sent the damaging sex recording to that man, somehow allying herself with him, somehow rejecting Ben.

He couldn't quite straighten out in his head exactly why he felt that way, but he did; her actions were a slight, a betrayal. Yes, he'd felt furious. But then, he'd started to feel something different. Sadness. It was all ruined. Their marriage had been as beautiful as a snow-covered field first thing in a pink-sky winter morning, but now it was turning slushy, wet, grey, trampled upon. Disappearing altogether. They'd been so happy. Other people used to comment on what a fun, easy-going family they were. Where had all that contentment, gratitude, joy slipped to? Now, they felt knotted, tangled.

Their happiness had been paper thin, the past had ripped through, the present was torn to shreds.

This morning he'd woken up and felt deep longing. He missed her. He missed the smell of her hair, her skin, her breath. He missed the way her body rolled into his, hot, solid. He felt weary with being angry at her—it took too much energy being furious, incredulous, frustrated. It had started to feel like an act. He just wanted to hold her. He didn't care what she'd done or said or failed to say. He wanted to see his wife, to fix things. He was sure they could, couldn't they? If they both wanted it enough? They had that in them, didn't they? Ben leapt out of bed, invigorated, certain.

He walked into the kitchen and his mother smiled brightly at him; she immediately saw that he'd thrown off something, seized something once again. He kissed the top of the girls' heads; they carried on chatting to one another, barely acknowledging him, drowning in a glut of chocolate milk and bread and Nutella, a breakfast that Mel would only consider on their birthdays. He hadn't had much of an appetite recently but now he felt hungry. He popped a couple of slices of bread in the toaster and put three Weetabixes in a bowl.

His mother mooched about, dishcloth in hand, wiping surfaces and chatting to him about the neighbours creosoting the boundary fence. She asked his advice—ought she to do the same on her side?

Ben picked up on the hint and wondered whether

he should offer to do that before they set off back to Wolvney. He had been planning on hitting the road ASAP but he could do so this afternoon, after painting the fence. His mum had been great these past few days: listening and asking just enough questions, walking the thin line between being concerned and prying. It was the least he could do.

"There's a letter for you," said his mother, handing him the long white envelope.

Naturally, he recognised the handwriting immediately. His mother's house was small; there wasn't anywhere to go that interested eyes couldn't follow him, other than the loo. So, he read her words in there.

Her words were a salve. Humble. Honest. Hurtful. Healing. He read her letter carefully, allowing each word into his head and his heart.

Not an excuse, it's just the explanation you are owed. I wanted him.

I wanted to be her.

It was something dreamlike and peculiar.

If Liam ever knew…it would break his heart.

Ben, I've never thought of Liam as anyone's other than mine, and then mine and yours.

I need you and the girls at home by my side.

I'm sorry, my love. Sorry, sorry a hundred times over. Since the moment he was born I've done everything I could to look after him.

I love you.

As soon as he'd finished reading the letter, he rushed downstairs to search for his phone. It had run out of battery yesterday and he'd left it on charge overnight in the sitting room. He wanted to call Mel. Tell her he had read her letter. Tell her he was coming home, that he had been on his way anyhow. They were going to sort out this craziness together.

As he switched on his phone it started to beep, signalling the arrival of texts. There were three messages from Mel and one from Liam. Pleased, because he hadn't heard from him since he stormed out of the house last Friday, Ben opened Liam's first.

Dad, I've proposed to Abi. She's said yes. Be happy for us.

Ben froze. His insides turned to liquid. All the joy he'd felt just a moment ago slid out of his body. Ben reread the message twice, three times.

For fuck's sake. The stupid boy. Was this for real? He stared at the message, seeing if the words would change in front of his eyes because they couldn't be right. Ben didn't hear Imogen trying to get his attention, or rather he heard—she was asking whether they could go to the park—but he couldn't form a response. Liam had proposed? He was seventeen. No way. This was just a fling. That's what he'd thought. That's what he'd told Mel. He'd promised her it was nothing to worry about.

"What is it?" asked Imogen, but before he could form an answer, she grabbed his phone off him and read the text. She stared at him, wide-eyed with astonishment and trembling with excitement. "Is this true, Daddy?"

Ben couldn't think how to respond. He stretched to retrieve the phone but Imogen had swiftly passed it to her Nana.

His mother adored Liam; she looked up from reading the text and shook her head, clicked her tongue on the roof of her mouth. "I think you should be getting home, son," she advised. "Your holiday is over."

CHAPTER FORTY-EIGHT

MELANIE

I don't know how to fix things for Liam or for myself. Abi is pregnant. She's having my son's baby. My grandchild. I haven't given any serious thought to being a grandparent, I thought it was a while off, but if I had ever imagined the moment, I wouldn't have thought it would be like this.

I'm over a barrel; she thinks that I'll accept things for what they are. I guess she imagines I'll be so desperate to reconcile with Liam that I'll willingly play the happy granny, I'll pop round and babysit whenever they ask me to, I'll invite them for Christmas and smile gratefully when they agree to come—not for lunch but for an hour in the afternoon because they have other plans. Maybe it will come to this. I don't know.

I don't have the answers. I long for Ben. I wonder whether he might have any answers and if he does, when I will get to hear them. I called him the moment I left the park and several times since but his phone is off or dead. It's so frustrating. I need him. When will he stop being angry at me? I send him a text message. Call me. Then, I think about it for a moment and send him another. Please. I realise that's still not what I want to say so I send a third. Come home. I need him here. It's where he belongs.

Online, I book a train ticket to Newcastle for later this afternoon. The first seat I can get that doesn't break the bank. It's a five-hour journey with a change, but I don't care. I shouldn't have waited this long. I should have followed Ben and the girls the minute they drove away. I nip next door and ask the neighbours if they will feed the cats.

There is one more thing I must do before I can go to Ben and the girls. I can't do anything to help Liam right now—he doesn't even think he needs my help, let alone want it—but I know there is someone else I must help, if I can. I called Tanya as I left the park but her phone was switched off, too. I despaired and wondered how we managed before mobiles and why everyone I know seemed not to want to talk to me. I texted her asking her to come around ASAP. I hope she sees it soon.

The doorbell rings at noon on Tuesday. I charge down the stairs, not sure whether it will be Ben and the girls, Liam or Tanya. I'd be delighted to see any of them. The house seems large for the first time ever. I'm lost and alone.

It's Tanya. She looks young and vulnerable, a stark contrast from Abi, who I last saw striding down my path into a waiting taxi, competent and in control. I hold the door wide, and there's an awkward moment. I want to hug Tanya—she looks in need of a hug and I certainly am. I put my arms around her, pull her close. She's slight, flexible, fluid. She smells of strawberries, a shampoo I imagine; I'm assaulted by the fact of her youth.

"Come on in, I'll put the kettle on."

I make tea and put biscuits on a plate, although neither of us appears to be particularly interested in eating or drinking, it just gives us something to do with our hands. Tanya wraps her fingers around the mug, as though she finds the warmth comforting, even though it's not a cold day, quite the reverse. It's stuffy and close. I notice she's started to bite her nails.

"I have to ask, Tanya, did you make a copy of the film? Abi and Liam's film?"

Tanya stares at me, defiant and angry, yet I see some shame in her face, too. She's a lovely young woman. Underhand tactics are not her modus operandi, or at least not normally. She's been driven to this spiteful act through desperation.

She nods. "I wish I hadn't. I can't stop looking at it."

I pity her inability to resist that compulsion. It was horrific enough the first time around. I guess she was looking for something, trying to understand something; something that seems remote and out of her grasp because she's seventeen, not thirty-seven, which must frustrate her, confuse her. "The way he goes at her..." She shakes her head.

I hold up my hand. I really don't want to hear—I

already know far too much about my son's sex life as it is.

But Tanya is oblivious to my sensitivities. "Like an animal. It's revolting. That sordid, filthy woman repulses me." All her anger is directed at Abi, even though it is Liam who has betrayed her. Blaming him is impossible. I understand.

We both love him too much.

"I know it's awful, Tanya. I understand that completely but it hasn't helped, you sending the video to Rob. It's just caused more trouble," I point out, carefully.

"What?" Her head shoots up, she glares at me.

"Rob has reduced Abigail's settlement offer."

"Oh, my heart bleeds for her."

I smile. "I'm no fan, I agree with you, but Liam is outraged. It's brought them closer together and they think I sent it. In a way I am responsible. If I hadn't copied it from Abi, then you couldn't have copied it from me."

I don't tell her Ben's left me because he's so furious over the matter. She shouldn't have to shoulder that level of responsibility. Besides, it isn't her fault. That's between Ben and me. It's hurtful that my husband and my son thought I was capable of petty revenge and that I'd inflict hurt on Liam. I wish they'd trusted me more.

Tanya is staring at me, her expression confused, even offended. "I didn't send the recording to her husband."

"It's OK, sweetheart. I'm not angry with you. I only called you round here and brought it up because

I have had to tell Ben it was you and maybe I'll need to tell Liam. I'm sorry."

"But it wasn't me." She's adamant.

"We're the only ones with a copy. I didn't send it."

"Nor did I." Tanya shrugs and her denial is flat, emotionless and therefore convincing.

"Then who?" I only have to think about it for a moment. "Abi."

"Abi? She sent her own husband her scandalous sex video? Had her settlement reduced as a consequence. Why would she do that?"

"To destroy me."

"Fuck, Mrs. Harrison, that's so messed up. You have to tell Liam. She's batshit crazy."

I'm almost amused at the juxtaposition of her expletive bang up against her formality in addressing me. It somehow signifies where she is in life. Straddling adulthood and childhood. Her naivety is highlighted when she thinks telling the truth is the answer, that it is even possible, that it will solve things.

"He won't believe me if I do. He'll just think one of us is responsible and either you or I are lying. He's too in her thrall to doubt her." Tanya doesn't bother to contradict me. "Tanya, there's something else I need to tell you before you hear it from anyone else."

"What?" she asks fearfully.

"I take it you haven't been on Facebook for a while, or I presume any social media."

"No, I haven't bothered with it for a day or two. It's too easy to start stalking Liam and I don't want to find myself doing that at two in the morning. Why?"

There's no easy way to say it. "Abigail is pregnant."

"Abigail is having a baby!" The excited exclamation doesn't come from Tanya, who is sitting in shock, mouth gaping, colour drained so that she looks somehow present and yet invisible—the excited cry came from Lily.

I turn and to my horror see Lily, Imogen and Ben stood in the kitchen.

"We sneaked in, we wanted to surprise you," says Ben lamely. He looks horrified.

The girls meanwhile are dancing about the kitchen, exclaiming, "A baby! A baby! We're going to be aunties."

"And bridesmaids," adds Imogen.

"Bridesmaids?" I ask, confused.

"Abigail and Liam are getting married, aren't they, Daddy?"

The girls are skipping about the room, skirts twirling as they spin and dance, high on the excitement of being bridesmaids, giddy with the romance of it. I feel like I'm in a trance, the room is swaying. My body is contracting. Every molecule is tight and then loose. I feel like I've just been punched.

"I knew about the baby, but not the wedding," I stutter.

"I knew about the wedding, but not the baby," says Ben.

He rushes to me and folds me in a hug. I surrender to it. My legs feel weak; they might collapse under me.

Tanya grabs her bag and pushes past Ben and me, crying, running for the front door.

CHAPTER FORTY-NINE

MELANIE

Saturday, 2 June

It surprises me what a person accepts. What I have accepted. It has been six weeks since I last saw my son, since that sad conversation on the park bench. I haven't even spoken to him or received a text from him—he's blocked me on all his social media channels. It's June, approaching summer, normally my favourite part of the year, where the days are hot and long, children play in gardens while sausages sizzle on barbecues; this year I hide from the sun and the march of time.

I called him frequently and sent several texts until I discovered he'd changed his phone, which I only understood when we got our monthly statement. He hasn't let us know his new number. Previously, we had paid for his phone, under our contract; I assume

Abi is paying now. I don't know where he is living. It's come to this—he's going to be a father, he's going to be married and I don't even know where he's living.

It appears he quickly reneged on his promise to return to college. I guess he prefers to lounge in her arms. I went to his sixth-form college, spoke to Mr. Edwards—he told me that Liam hasn't attended for weeks, and he doesn't hold much hope of him even turning up to his exams, let alone passing them. Mr. Edwards seemed harassed, distracted, but not especially surprised. It's coming up to exam period, he has four hundred pupils to watch over. He's not a babysitter or a policeman.

We've been to the police. But a missing love-struck teen, just weeks away from his eighteenth birthday, who has announced he's leaving to live with his girlfriend, isn't a missing person of any concern, apparently. No one can force Liam to school.

The fury that seized me and held me hostage has abated; now I feel uselessly spent, empty. I'm drowning in a sense of powerlessness. If she loves him, why wouldn't she want him to continue with his studies, pursue his career? Although I know the answer. I guess she doesn't want him going away to university, broadening his horizons, meeting other women. I guess he doesn't want this either. Not anymore.

I search for him on the streets. I scan the groups of teenagers that huddle outside the kebab shop, that spill out of pubs and clubs. Occasionally, I even chase lone figures up the street, desperate to catch up with him, only to discover it's not him at all. Never him.

It's not football season; if it was, I'm sure I'd catch him playing a game at his club—he wouldn't give that up, would he? But his team have disbanded for the season and I don't know where they live. We're long past the age when I had a handy list of addresses of classmates; it's been a long while since I arranged play dates for Liam. Naturally, I've been to the houses of his school and college friends that I do know, two or three of them have been familiar faces since childhood.

If any of them know where he is, they are not saying. They look uncomfortable, stare at their feet, tell me they don't have an address or new telephone number, say they're staying in touch via Facebook. I doubt they're telling me the truth. I ask them if they can at least let me know if he's safe, if he's happy. That causes them to smile slyly, as though I'm crazy to worry.

"Oh, very happy," they assure me. Their grins are slick, secretive. They're the sort of grins that slide on and off faces with remarkable speed.

I know I won't find him on the streets. I know he is in a king-size bed somewhere, tangled sheets and limbs. Unthinkable.

"Do you think he's seduced by her celebrity?" I ask Ben. It's Ben I chew everything over with. My parents and some close friends know the facts but hardly anyone has the stomach to dissect our situation as regularly as I feel the need to.

"Well, she's not that famous."

"Then her wealth?" I stop myself from saying anything more. I almost asked whether Liam might have been attracted to her experience but I'm afraid that Ben will say yes, I'm afraid my husband will confirm that my son has been seduced by her age. The very thing that repulses me must attract him. Where I see fault, he sees novelty, advantage.

Or maybe it's simpler than that: maybe he doesn't see her age. I recall that when I first met Abi and indeed when she arrived in our home in February, I was instantly beguiled by her. She had such self-belief and charm. I had flutters in my stomach, a spark. She is somehow wildly charismatic, compulsive even. Not to me, not now, but to whomever she shines her light on.

I try to concentrate on what I have. The old-fashioned Band-Aid of counting my blessings. Ben and I are good. We hunker down and watch boxsets of shows that everyone else was talking about three years ago, but we always felt too busy to devote ourselves to. Now time seems to stretch, bend. Even though it's a glorious summer and the evenings are long, I feel safest, calmest curled up on the sofa at home. I hold Ben carefully, close. I have a feeling that if I move suddenly, we will shatter into a thousand tiny pieces. He has, I think, forgiven me for not telling him about Rob being Liam's biological father. We've talked about it at length. It was challenging, there were tears, but I think he understands that my shame and desire for it to be other than it was meant I blanked out the fact of Liam's parentage and stuck to my fiction instead.

"Do you think you should tell Liam now, about Rob?" he asks.

"I can't tell Liam anything. I don't know where he is."

"Good point. But I mean, do you plan on telling him when we do eventually find him? When we're all speaking again."

I'm touched by Ben's confidence that this day will come, but I don't share it. "I don't know, Ben," I answer honestly. "A lot depends on what's going on between him and Abi. If they're a couple, then will telling him help? Rob is Abi's ex-husband. How can we tell them that he's also Liam's father?"

"It's tricky."

"It's impossible."

"But don't you think it will be better that it comes from you? After all we've been through, there are far worse things than having to sit him down and admit that you had sex with a man who was having an on-off thing with your best friend."

"That's no longer the big confession, though, is it? I hid Rob's identity from Liam for his entire life. I think that's the bit he'll find unforgivable. And I'll have to tell him that Rob knew of him. Has always known and didn't want anything to do with him. That will break his heart."

Ben looks uncomfortable. "But if we don't tell them the truth, Rob may. If Abi mentions the name of her young boyfriend, Rob is bound to put two and two together straight away, don't you think?"

"I don't know."

"I mean, how much does Rob know about Liam?" Ben turns away from me but I know him well enough to know that the particular curve in his shoulders, the angle of his neck, means he is trying not to show me his pain. "Have you been sending him updates and such?"

"No, no, of course not." I run to Ben and wrap my arms around him.

"I'd understand," he says stiffly.

"You're his dad," I tell him because it's true and because it's what he needs to hear. We kiss. A long kiss. A kiss that says sorry. Sorry over and over.

When we break apart, Ben says, "It's a mess."

"It is."

"Do you really think she sent Rob the sex tape?"

"Well, I certainly didn't," I point out hotly.

"I know that. I believe you. But Tanya?"

"I believe *her*."

"I don't know, the more I think about it, the stranger it seems. Why would Abi risk Rob getting hold of something so dangerous? He can hold it against them forever."

"But they're divorced now." I saw the announcement online. I'd been searching for it. It made the papers in the States.

"Yeah, but even so."

"She must have wanted to make Rob jealous."

"If he ever finds out who it is in that video…" Ben shakes his head, concerned.

"I know, I know." I can't bear thinking about it.

Ben is being amazing. He hasn't said *I told you so*. He hasn't said that I drove Liam away because I couldn't be calm and temperate. He doesn't have to, because I beat myself up every day.

Nor do I say *I told you so* to him. He thought this

was a fling, just sex, nothing to worry about. This is the beginning of the next generation of our family. It's real and not going away.

We concentrate on giving the girls the most stable, steady environment we can. Naturally, they miss Liam. They are bewildered that they haven't seen him for what feels like forever to them.

"Doesn't he miss us?" Lily asks one day. It is hot and sticky; even ice lollies can't distract or cool sufficiently.

"I'm sure he does," I reply.

"Then why doesn't he come to see us?" Imogen asks grumpily. "He's not actually tied up, is he? Like a hostage. He could come if he wanted."

I miss and love Liam but I'm also angry with him because Imogen is right. He is not being physically restrained by Abi, and no matter how furious he is with me right now, I'd have thought he wanted to see his sisters. He must know that his sudden absence is baffling for them. We had been preparing them for him going to university in the autumn, that they understood, but his sudden and total absence is agonising for them. For us all.

I try to explain the situation. "You know at school when you might fall out with one of your friends?"

"Yes." Imogen nods, very familiar with this situation. Lily shrugs—she doesn't tend to row with people, she's the sort of person people fight for.

"And then, sometimes, people take sides. Even if they weren't part of the row in the first place. Like when Clara fell out with Denni and you didn't want to be Denni's friend anymore either."

"Yes, I remember."

"Well, it's a little bit like that. Abigail and I aren't friends anymore and Liam is Abigail's boyfriend now, so he doesn't think he can be my friend either."

"But you said that falling out with your friends is silly."

"Yes, I did."

"And you said taking sides with Clara was silly, because it wasn't my fight and it wasn't nice," points out Imogen.

"Yes, I did." It's tricky when your kids quote your good sense back to you and you have nothing to offer them.

"Can't you make friends with Abigail, Mummy? So that Liam visits us again." Imogen's voice is full of longing and need. She puts her ice lolly down on the garden wall, uninterested, and sighs. I watched the sticky red juice drip and splatter on the patio. It looks like blood.

"I would, darling, if I could."

And that's the truth of it. I don't want my teenage son to be marrying a thirty-eight-year-old woman because she's having his baby, but he is. So yes, I would do anything to be "friends" again, given a chance. I don't want to be locked out. But I don't think there is going to be a chance. I don't know how to reach him.

Tanya visits me one afternoon. She isn't wearing make-up and has her hair scraped back into a pony tail; she looks fresh but also exposed. She tells me that her A-level exams have started, that she sat her first maths paper the day before.

"I don't suppose he…"

"Turned up? No."

"Oh, Liam."

I still can't believe my son has jacked in his studies. I can hardly comprehend that the world has continued to turn. I feel I am living in some alternative universe. I want to live in the world where Liam sweated over the paper and came out of the exam with a cautious sense of optimism. He's been so conscientious for so many years.

I think of the small boy who stayed up late to finish making an abacus out of dried pasta. I think of the time he dashed home, flushed with excitement, because he'd been chosen to be on the Junior Mathematical Olympiad team. They didn't do too well, and I had to resort to the well-worn phrase that it was the taking part not the winning that counted. And do you know what? He believed me. He was just so excited to see what was possible, where he might go, what he might do. I think of his absolute triumph just two years ago, when he collected his GCSE results.

"Well, I hope you do really well in the rest of your exams, Tanya."

She has been offered a place at Liverpool University but the grades she needs to secure are high. She'll make a wonderful vet. She's shyly confided that she now thinks she wants a country practice somewhere. Maybe in a Yorkshire village. I can imagine her striding around the countryside in muddy wellies, her no-nonsense manner a comfort to the farmers. If she'd stayed with Liam maybe she'd have tailored her ambitions—maybe she'd have limited herself to a city practice, looking after pooches that spend too much time in handbags and not enough time in fields. Tanya and I have become something like friends. I guess we're a cross between comrades in arms and survivors. We are both devastated by the loss of Liam. We are both clouded and concussed by it.

"Try to put all of this out of your mind."

"How am I supposed to do that, Mrs. Harrison?" She stares at me with such blunt defencelessness that I ache for her.

"I don't know, but if you can."

"That's what my mother says, too. 'He's not worth your head space.' Like I have a choice in what I think about." I guess her mother says a lot more about Liam and I imagine it's vitriolic. I know I would have plenty to say if the shoe was on the other foot. "Have you heard from him?" Tanya looks hopeful, shy.

I shake my head. "You?"

"No." She sighs.

I squeeze her shoulder. "Just try to stay focused, if you can. You know. You owe it to yourself."

"I don't care about myself."

"Then do it for me." I couldn't bear it if Abi robbed another young person of their future.

CHAPTER FIFTY

BEN

Thursday, 7 June

The thick silver envelope arrived on Ben's desk at work; it was in among a batch of direct mail approaches. He almost missed it but as he threw the unsolicited marketing in the bin, he recognised Liam's handwriting—large, loopy, with a tendency to slant upwards. He carefully tore open the envelope and pulled out the card.

It was far from understated or traditional. The card was a lime green and the crazy writing was silver, embossed. The invite looked like a kid's party invite—he'd have thought Abigail would have opted for something more classic. He wondered whether she was deliberately trying to appear more youthful, avoid looking at all staid, or perhaps the pregnancy hormones were affecting her decisions.

As he read the invite, Ben thought the wording was likely to infuriate Mel. He considered that it was perhaps designed to do so.

Liam and Abigail joyfully invite you to join as they celebrate their wedding day. They're in love and they want everyone to know it!
At Hashtag Hotel, Northampton
on Friday 22, June 2018
12 noon

He hadn't believed it was really happening. He thought perhaps they would change their minds, but whatever the typography choice, the fact was his son was getting married in two weeks' time. Sooner than ideal perhaps, by about a decade in his opinion, especially as Liam had only known Abigail for fifteen weeks—Ben had checked in his diary.

But it was as it was. Ben was determined to go to the wedding; he hoped Mel would go, too. The wedding of their son—how could they not go now they had been asked?

There was another, smaller envelope inside the first addressed to Imogen and Lily. Ben didn't feel too awful easing that open and reading the note. He loved Liam but no longer trusted his judgement; he didn't want there to be anything that might distress the girls further. It was an invite for them to be bridesmaids. Hardly likely to distress them. Indeed, it was what they wanted more than anything on earth.

Dear Imogen and Lily,

I'm sorry I haven't seen so much of you both recently. I've been thinking about you. The thing is I'm really busy getting things ready for our wedding and baby. Busy times!

Ben tutted at that. What exactly was a seventeen-year-old boy's role in arranging his wedding? How long precisely did it take to paint a nursery, if that was what he was doing?

Abigail and I are getting married in a hotel in Northampton. It's not going to be a big wedding but it's going to be very cool. We'd love it if you were both there. Abigail is hoping you'll be bridesmaids for her. She's seen some gorgeous dresses. You'll get to carry bouquets, get new shoes and maybe wear a flower in your hair, I guess. You'd need to talk about this with Abi. She's asked me to include these pictures from a bridal magazine she's read. She thinks this is the sort of dress you'd both suit.

What do you say? Fancy it?

Love you both,
Liam and Abi

He'd signed it from them both; even though it was Liam's handwriting, Ben felt it was clear that Abi had exercised some influence and input. Ben wondered what Mel's reaction to this would be. He had a fair idea.

That evening, Ben helped bathe the girls, then popped them in front of the TV. They were watching "*Beauty and the Beast* with Hermione," as they'd explained it. He poured a glass of wine for him and Mel before he slid the invite and the letter across the kitchen table.

He watched as she read it. Her face a dance. She was not able to hide her emotions: her frustration, her sorrow, her disappointment, her relief.

"Is this really happening?" she asked.

"It seems so."

"'Getting things ready for our wedding and baby,'" she quoted the letter. "I can't imagine it. Somewhere there is a cot, a changing mat, maybe a mobile waiting for this baby."

"For our grandchild."

Mel nodded and asked, "What can we do?"

"Nothing."

"Then we must go."

He let out a sigh of relief. Mel didn't sound what anyone might call enthusiastic but he'd settle for resigned. "Yes. We must."

"It's something. A way back to him."

"Yes, I guess we have to find a way of accepting her into our lives. She's older than him but she doesn't know why you are objecting so viciously. She doesn't know he's Rob's son."

Mel nodded. "I need him in my life. That above anything else."

"I know you do. We all do."

"What do you make of the separate note to the girls?" Mel ran her fingers across the words of the letter. The words Liam had written. It was obvious she wanted to feel close to him.

"Well, they're going to be delighted," Ben pointed out.

"Yes, I can't decide if he's an idiot or manipulative."

"I wouldn't want to deny them the opportunity. I mean, if he's going to go ahead with this, then they might as well support him and fulfil their dreams of being bridesmaids."

"Yes. I still say he's too young."

"And I absolutely agree."

"I feel so helpless." Mel sighed.

He was turning eighteen tomorrow. A man. He could and would make his own decisions, and however dreadful his parents thought those decisions were, they didn't have much sway.

"He's alive and well, at least the invite tells us that," added Ben.

Mel nodded. She squared her shoulders, seemed to make a decision. "It's enough. I know that having the responsibility of parenthood thrust upon you at such a young age is not a walk in the park, but he'll cope. We all will. I don't like Abi. I believe she's trapped him but I am not the first mother-in-law to disapprove of her son's choice. I must stay quiet. If I want to stay in his life, I have to stay silent. She must love him, right? I need to believe that."

Ben stood up, moved around the table and crouched

by Mel's chair. He pulled her into his arms. "Well done, Mel. I'm proud of you. You know I love you."

"I do know that and I love you, too."

They stayed like that for a while. Allowing the heat of one another's bodies to merge and comfort. Until Ben broke away and asked, "Now, do you want the fun of telling the girls they've been invited to be bridesmaids?"

Mel shook her head. "No, you do it."

CHAPTER FIFTY-ONE

ABIGAIL

Friday, 8 June

Liam's eighteenth birthday was of course a cause for celebration. He was now legally allowed to do as he liked. Leave school, visit a pub, vote, marry Abigail. However, Abi did not know how to approach the day. It surprised her to discover that she felt a tiny bit uneasy, almost prim about this official marker that said Liam was now quite definitely a man. It highlighted the fact that up until that point there had been some ambiguity, just as Mel claimed.

Abigail asked him what his friends had done to celebrate the milestone. While he was one of the biggest in the year, he was one of the youngest, so he had seen many friends cross this threshold.

"Varied," he replied vaguely, stretching his arms above his head. His T-shirt rose a fraction. She saw his flat stomach that she found so attractive, but this time, the twinge of lust was countered by a more overpowering sense of nausea.

The strangest thing had happened in the last week or so: whenever she felt aroused, her morning sickness seemed to intensify. She'd looked it up in all the pregnancy books but couldn't see reference to other women complaining of similar. She was thirteen weeks pregnant now and really thought that she'd be through the morning-sickness stage; wasn't that supposed to be the first trimester?

Morning sickness was a crazy name for it anyway—she felt sick at any time of the day, most times of the day, except when she was eating. She didn't mind really, it was a small price to pay for such a blessing. She had got into the habit of carrying around a packet of crackers to nibble on. She delighted in sliding them out of her bag and eating them while she stood in a queue at the local artisan bakery, in the coffee shop or sat in the back of a cab, because then she'd have to grin and explain, "I'm pregnant. I find eating is the only thing that eases the sickness." Then she'd smile bravely. Adorably. Wait for people to congratulate her, praise her, reassure her. Make her feel special.

She loved saying those words: "I'm pregnant." She said them in her head and out loud whenever she could. "I'm having a baby." "I'm expecting a child." She stopped just short of "I'm with child," because that sounded totally crazy. She loved the fact of it and the response it caused. People were always so delighted and solicitous. They'd offer her a seat, ask when the baby was due, told her she had an extremely neat bump, as though she'd done something wonderful, which of course she had.

Once or twice, well, maybe more regularly than that, she had pulled out the crackers even when she wasn't feeling nauseous, just for the thrill of being able to announce her fecund state.

"Well, how do people celebrate their eighteenth birthdays nowadays? Give me a scale?"

She hated it when she used the term *nowadays*; it was a mistake. Normally, she managed to avoid it. Nor would she be caught dead saying, "in my day" or "when I was younger." She wasn't fully on her game or she'd never have made that slip. The truth was, no matter what she'd said to Mel, Abigail rarely managed to forget how young Liam was. Often, she delighted in his youth; occasionally, she found it a little inconvenient. Liam's age was glaringly apparent to her when he communicated poorly. Or maybe that was just a man thing.

"Like I said, varies."

"How does it vary? Give me an idea. Are we talking anything from lavish parties to a beer in the pub?" She sounded prickly, naggy. She knew she did and that just irritated her further. It was a hot summer and heat always made her snappy. Abigail was infuriated that decent summers still seemed to take the British by surprise. Although she was British, she'd lived in America for long enough to have forgotten that the UK was not equipped to deal with mercury rising; no air conditioning in shops or restaurants, no clue how to dress. People slouched about, hot and sticky. Herself included. She couldn't wait to get back to the States.

"Yup, that's about right, parties, beer garden." Liam smiled. If he'd noticed her tetchiness, it didn't seem to bother him. He was settled in front of the TV, playing some sort of racing-car game. She didn't know which one; she was just glad it wasn't *COD*. She couldn't stand the sounds of gunshots echoing around the apartment. In fact, she'd bought him a high-end pair of Beats headphones to use while he was playing the more violent or noisy games. He'd loved the gift; she loved it more.

"What would you like to do? Do you want a party?"

"No, don't think so. There's a lot of hassle and we've enough on, planning the wedding and stuff."

She was relieved. She didn't want to throw a party either. He was a mature guy for his age but not all his friends were similarly disposed. She remembered when she was living at Mel's that Liam had gone to a party and she'd heard Mel discussing the party prep with the hosting parents. The discussion did not centre around streamers and music choice; they'd talked about supplying white spirits only, "because the vomit was easier to deal with than red wine or darker spirit vomit," and they'd bought six plastic buckets and strategically placed them around the house; it was all very basic.

"We could go out for dinner. Somewhere special. Maybe in London?" Abi suggested.

"Sounds good."

"Where might you like to try?"

"I don't know, you decide."

Until Liam and Abi had got together, Liam had only eaten in horribly touristy restaurants in London; the Hard Rock Cafe and the Rainforest Cafe. He explained it was because his trips had been with his sisters. But really, they could have done better than that. London was the perfect city for lovers. The place was chock-full with charming bookshops and interesting galleries. They wandered around hand in hand and sometimes fell upon pretty fountains or unexpected squares with trees and benches, where they might briefly pause to passionately kiss.

Liam had been impressed with the places she took him—Little Venice to see the narrow boats, Richmond Park to see the stags and Shoreditch for the street art and street food—but they hadn't been to a restaurant together. Not a formal one. It just wasn't something they did, preferring instead to grab a sandwich on the run. Mostly they'd spent their time in hotels and ordered room service that they fed to each other, sometimes ate off one another's bodies.

In public, Abi liked to keep on the move because they attracted less attention that way. Not that she was hiding from anyone, but if she had been, London would be the perfect place to do so. The wine bars they went to were dimly lit and no one ever asked for ID. It was easy to be anonymous there because it was a hedonistic city and nobody cared what anybody else was up to.

It was time for them to go public. He wasn't gauche, he'd know how to behave in a decent restaurant, he wouldn't need advice on which cutlery to use, she wouldn't have to tell him to put his napkin on his lap, rather than tuck it into his shirt. This wasn't a Pygmalion story. But the fact was, they were not in a position where he might suggest they visit a restaurant that a colleague of his had dined at or one he'd read about in a Sunday supplement. She didn't mind.

Well, not much. Sometimes she felt the responsibility of him weighing a little heavily. She had to make the money, the choices, the decisions. It seemed like a lot to shoulder. But that was probably her hormones making her feel a touch more vulnerable, a lot more exhausted. She wondered whether she should have encouraged Liam to stay on at college instead of doing the opposite. But there were risks involved. She'd always encouraged Rob to reach for his dreams and goals and that hadn't worked out too well for her. Ultimately, he'd reached for a sexy younger woman with smouldering eyes and sashaying hips.

"How about The Shard?" suggested Abi.

Liam kept his eyes trained on the video game. The cars zoomed around the track, throbbing, roaring. "I thought The Shard was like apartments, with a viewing platform. There's a restaurant?"

"Multiple, actually."

"Cool, yeah, cool."

"You can't wear trainers."

"Oh."

"Do we need to go shoe shopping?"

"I guess."

Abi booked the Aqua Shard because it served British cuisine which she thought would appeal most to Liam; he hadn't seemed too sure about the concept of Asian fusion. The restaurant was on the thirty-first floor and offered spectacular views of London. She expected it would be romantic to watch the blue sky turn blush pink, then vibrant orange and finally blue-black. She imagined them watching the lights of London glitter beneath.

Her bag was scanned and they had to go through an airport-style sensor before they could get to the restaurant. Abigail wondered whether the sensor might affect the baby. She thought it was silly to ask, to make a fuss, because of course there would be warnings if it was unsafe, but she couldn't stop herself. There was no point in taking a risk. She'd already rung ahead to ask about the menu—she needed to avoid soft cheeses, oysters, pâté, raw eggs. The woman on the phone had been very accommodating, very patient.

"I'm pregnant, is it safe to pass through?" Abigail demanded of the security guard, even though she'd just told herself it was an unnecessary question.

"Metal-detector scanners use a low-frequency electromagnetic field to look for metal objects or anything that generates or uses electricity—you don't have to worry unless your baby has superpowers like Blanka, Black Lightning or Electro."

Abi stared at the smiley, chubby man but didn't understand.

Liam laughed. "They're superheroes, Abi. Ones that use electricity. Come on, let's go eat."

Sometimes that sort of thing happened; he didn't know what Asian fusion food was, she didn't have an encyclopaedic knowledge of superheroes.

In the lift, Liam hit the button three or four times. "I think it's automatic," commented Abi. He stared at her doubtfully until a voice piped through a sound system confirmed as much.

Up they sped. He grinned, "My ears have just popped. Yours, too?" It was charming, the things he took delight in.

Abi noticed that the hostess that greeted them and asked if they had a reservation was all flashy-eyed and flirtatious with Liam. It was her job to be pleasant and he was delicious but it was a bit annoying. Abi wanted to wave her Visa card and yell, "Hey, I'm paying. I'm your customer."

Liam didn't respond; he kept his eyes on the view of London. This should have been a relief, but Abi couldn't help but think his non-noticing of the attractive hostess was a little too purposeful, almost an effort. She felt a slither of irritation run up and down her spine. She was being unreasonable. Liam had shown her nothing other than devotion and loyalty, yet she couldn't help but occasionally be whipped by the panic of how long that commitment would last. She was not unrealistic; she realised that Liam might lose interest at any point, despite the baby, because of the baby. The fact was, she was more than twice his age. The trick was to get him into a position whereby when he did lose interest, he had no alternative but to stay anyway.

"This is incredible," he gushed. Turning to her with a wide, broad grin.

She smiled back at him. Allowed herself to relax. Why was she looking for problems? They were blissful right now. It was her hormones ambushing her reason. "Shall we have a cocktail first? Or go straight to our table?"

"Cocktails, definitely."

He bounced towards a small table for two, close to the window. His keenness to bag the seat outweighed his usual display of good manners. She trailed behind him. There was an extensive cocktail list; Liam read over it carefully and then selected the one called C'est La Vie, lime juice shaken with Cîroc vodka and French pear brandy. Abi was secretly grateful, relieved, that the waiter didn't card Liam but simply nodded discreetly. She had doubted that they would be questioned for ID but there had been the risk, and while he could now legally drink, no one wanted the embarrassment of attention being drawn to his age. Or, more accurately, the age gap.

Abi less enthusiastically selected a mocktail. She didn't resent giving up alcohol for her baby, she didn't resent anything that the baby needed, it was just hard to be excited about a drink that was basically an expensive fruit juice. She had enjoyed getting drunk and irresponsible with Liam these past few months. She missed it. Abi had found that since she discovered she was pregnant, she was less and less interested in going out; why bother when she had everything she wanted at home? Part of her would rather have been curled up in front of the TV right now—she'd only made the effort because it was Liam's birthday and naturally that had to be celebrated.

They sipped the beautiful cocktails that Abi had to admit were works of art: colourful, fruity and in

Liam's case, potent. If Liam would have preferred a simple, thirst-quenching lager on this hot evening, he didn't say. He simply beamed at her, gazed around the room, made the right noises about the views. There was music playing, gentle murmuring of polite chatter and the clink of glass against glass and from the restaurant cutlery against crockery.

Abigail began to relax as they talked about places they might want to go on honeymoon. Once married, they were returning to America so it made sense to honeymoon there. Abi was relieved that Liam didn't suggest Vegas but seemed interested in going to Chicago or Boston. They ordered a second drink. This time Abigail agreed to have a glass of champagne.

"French women do it all the time," said Liam. He reached across the table and squeezed her hand reassuringly.

She wore a new glistening diamond on her left hand now. It was large and pure. She'd chosen and paid for it herself but that didn't matter, Liam had come along with her. Abigail had wanted to be in control.

Abigail felt eyes upon them; she wasn't unused to this experience, far from it. She smiled, generally, rather than specifically. They no doubt made a striking couple. Liam looked good in the blue Boss suit she'd chosen for him. It wasn't necessary to wear a suit to dine here; some people were dressed less formally but Abi had wanted to know what Liam would look like in a suit. He looked good. Very good. Older. She'd also bought him a shirt from Jermyn Street, a Paul Smith belt and shoes, and a Tag Heuer watch.

His face as he opened each package had been a study. Overwhelmed, excited, animated. Although she'd noticed that he'd been almost equally exuberant about the birthday gifts his mates had bought: a pair of underpants that had the word Vintage emblazoned on the butt, an inflatable giant football and a magnetic dartboard. Still, that just went to show how appreciative he was by nature.

In his new gear, he could pass for twenty-one, maybe even twenty-three.

By the time someone came over and said their table was ready, Abigail was floating in a general sense of well-being, of bliss. She put her left hand on her belly and spoke to her baby. She did this often. She told her baby everything was all right, it had all been worth it, she'd made the right choices. That she was justified.

They took their seats. It was a relief Liam didn't do any of that hovering-around-her-chair-until-she-sat-down-before-he-would-sit business. It was antiquated. The waiter pulled out Abigail's chair and then he handed her the wine and cocktails menu. Momentarily she thought that she'd have preferred it if he'd at least made a gesture of passing the list to Liam, but then she reminded herself that assuming the alcohol choice was the male prerogative was dated and sexist, too. It was much cooler and more equal if that sort of assumption was not made.

"What is rainbow chard?" Liam asked.

"It's a leafy vegetable. The stalks are often red or orange."

He pulled a face; generally, he was not impressed

with vegetables. "How is cornmeal porridge a main meal?"

"I bet it's delicious."

"What do you think I should have?" He looked at her, his eyes bright and beautiful but maybe not as cheeky and confident as they were when they lay in bed together, dizzy, heady, lusty. Now, he looked unsure.

"I'm having the sea bream."

"I'll have that then, too."

"Do you want a starter?"

"I thought maybe dessert." He had a sweet tooth.

"We can have all three," she said, although she knew she wouldn't, she'd have a coffee. She hadn't eaten pudding since before Liam was born.

Liam grinned. "Excellent. OK, so I should have the duck salad, right? Do you think I'd like that? Even though it's a salad, there will be plenty of meat, yeah?"

She smiled and nodded and tried not to wonder whether she should have taken him to Bill's for a burger instead.

The waiter came back for their wine order. "You pick for me," Liam urged.

"Duck, then bream," Abi mused, glancing down the impressive array of wines.

"Yeah, tricky because red with duck, white with fish," Liam commented with a smile, clearly quite proud of his knowledge.

"Or do you want another cocktail?" asked Abi, snapping the wine menu closed.

"Good idea. I think I want to work my way through them."

Abi doubted the prudence behind this decision but didn't want to say so.

"Special occasion, is it?" the waiter asked.

"My eighteenth," confirmed Liam.

"Congratulations, mate." The waiter smiled at Abi. Casually, confidently. "Great treat, Mum."

Abigail froze. The moment was stamped onto their history. Staining. The joy of the evening snapped. Abi felt it being wrenched out of her; it snagged around her throat, temporarily stopping her from forming words or even breathing evenly.

Liam saw her shock and pain. "We'll just have what we had before," he said quickly.

The waiter left them alone. "I look old enough to be your mum?" Abi asked, stunned.

"I have a really young mum," Liam pointed out.

"But I thought you looked about twenty-three tonight, and me maybe around thirty, thirty-one." She'd always thought she could pass for twenty-nine, but it was too embarrassing saying so. She was clearly very much mistaken. Abigail's head was assaulted by a memory of Mel complaining that when she took Liam to playgroups when he was a baby, people didn't think she was his mother because she looked too young, and now, here Abi was, Liam's lover being mistaken for his mother.

Mel was such a bitch. She had all the luck.

The waiter returned with the drinks. Liam nervously downed his cocktail in one, then leaned across the table and kissed her passionately. The kiss was all tongues, teeth and hormones. It was all hurt pride and a desperate attempt to educate the waiter.

It was sweet of him. It was humiliating.

She let it happen and, when he finally pulled away, she smiled and told herself that his eyes were still glazed with lust; it wasn't the fact that he'd drunk too much too quickly and couldn't quite focus.

CHAPTER FIFTY-TWO

MELANIE

Sunday, 17 June

"Hello, it's me."

I instantly recognise her voice, although I'd like to pretend I don't know who "me" is. She's called on a Sunday evening. It is the most irritating time she could have rung, that's why she's chosen it. People are never sharp on a Sunday evening—we are at our most vulnerable and defenceless, dreading Monday.

"Hello, Abi." I try not to sound breathless, even though I feel there is a lorry parked on my chest. I don't want her to hear the panic, agitation, stress.

"I thought it was time we talked."

I don't want to talk to Abi. I wish I never had to hear her voice or even her name again. I would ideally like her to disappear altogether but I know that's not going to happen. I force myself to mutter, "About what, specifically?"

"The wedding!" She sounds gleeful, joyful. The way brides are supposed to sound. I hate her for it. "I am so glad the girls are going to be bridesmaids. They'll look adorable."

"Yes." They will. It's strange that there is this unalterable fact among all this mess. No matter what the circumstances are of this wedding, Abi can and will make it a beautiful-looking event; my adorable girls will be part of that.

"I have had the dresses sent directly to you. You'll get them tomorrow."

"Right." Obviously, I've had very little to do with the preparation for the day. Liam sent Ben a text saying that Abi wanted to take the girls dress shopping. I knew they would have loved that but I also knew I'd have to go along, too, and I just couldn't bring myself to do that. I couldn't stand in a bridal shop and simper and smile, hear the compliments that would inevitably be showered upon Abigail—what a wonderful friend to have asked my daughters to be bridesmaids—or worse still, listen while she explained to the assistant that I was the mother of the groom.

Maybe that's selfish of me, but I made an excuse. End of term, sports days, concerts, special assemblies and school trips, there wasn't time. I couldn't resist pointing out that the engagement had been so particularly short. I half-heartedly suggested they wait a while, postpone the wedding, everyone take a breath. If Ben even texted back my message in its entirety— which I doubt—then my suggestion fell on deaf ears.

I knew it would. Liam (which meant Abi) simply sent a text back asking for the girls' shoe and dress sizes.

I wonder what sort of wedding this is going to be. I imagine it will be stylish, no expense spared, the catering will be impressive, the bride will look beautiful, the heady scent of flowers will be intoxicating. Exactly the sort of wedding I would normally love. Indeed, I love any sort of wedding; a knees-up in a barn would usually have me jumping for joy.

I'll hate this wedding.

I know I must go; how can I not see my son married? But I'm dreading every moment. He's too young, she's too old, she was once married to his father and although she doesn't know this, I do. The whole thing is weird from start to finish. And now there's a baby involved.

I wonder who she will invite. She'll have had to vet the guest list carefully. Avoiding the squeamish and judgemental. There must be so many people stomping in on their relationship, which up until now she's managed to keep private. What do the registrar, the florist, the band members, the hotel chef think of the age gap, of the groom's youth, of her pregnancy? Is she used to seeing eyebrows raised, snickering behind hands? Or am I being silly? These people probably couldn't care less, if they are being paid.

But her American friends, her relatives, her colleagues and contacts, his school, college and football friends—those people must have a view. Will things change when they see each other through their guests' eyes? People barge in on fragile new relationships, asking questions and offering opinions. Will their voices shrilly tear at this tissue of the romance?

I hope so. I know that's terrible of me. I'm mean and bitter. I'm frustrated. I don't like myself at the moment.

But I like her even less.

I can't imagine the conversation when she introduced my son to her mother. Mrs. Curtiz must have been shocked, disappointed, she probably said something like, "Well, I'm glad your father isn't alive to see this." It's dreadful to think that my beautiful son is the cause of distress and dissatisfaction. I've always imagined that he'd be the sort of boy that would make a potential mother-in-law proud and relaxed. That she'd be pleased her daughter would be safe and happy.

"How are you? The girls? Ben?" asks Abi, as though we are simply two old friends catching up after a few of weeks of not seeing one another, nothing more harrowing or traumatic.

"Fine," I mutter, in a manner that clearly means the opposite.

She doesn't care anyway. "Good, good."

There's a beat and I'm compelled to ask, "And how are you?" I aim to be crisp, efficient and civil, or at least not outright rude, but I don't really want to know anything about her life.

"We're getting used to each other. I'm learning all about his little quirks."

I feel momentarily jubilant. Quirks? Something she finds distasteful, irritating, a deal-breaker in the making. "Like?"

She laughs, girlishly. Girlishly! It's as though he's making her younger. "Oh, you know, like the way he absolutely piles his toast with jam, inches of it. Adorable."

Adorable then. Not irritating. I do know of Liam's jam habit. The other day I opened the cupboard and noticed I had three jars of strawberry jam in there. I've continued to automatically pop a jar in my trolley every week. I hadn't realised that consumption had slowed so significantly now Liam isn't living with us.

"He's so very excited about becoming a father. He loved going to the scan. He insisted on coming along. What a tender, wondrous moment that was." I don't know what to say. It's obvious she's trying to goad me. "Anyway, I'm ringing to make some plans for the actual day. Just five days to go now. I can't believe it."

"Nor can I," I mumble.

"Oh, come on, Mel. Don't be a sore loser." She's enjoying this. "I want the girls to come to the hotel before the ceremony."

"That's not necessary. We can meet you there, five minutes before the start." I don't want the experience to stretch on any longer than it must. But then I remember it's going to stretch on forever. She'll be his wife. She's having his baby.

"It's traditional to take some photos before the service. I want the girls in the photos," she says with the determined certainty of a monarch.

"Fine," I mutter, resentfully resigning myself.

"Are you knitting yet?" Abi quips. "I know it's all a little back to front but so many couples do it this way, nowadays, don't they?" I refuse to answer her question, refuse to indulge her. "Aren't you excited about becoming a grandmother?" Her voice is gloating. She's won. The battle, the war. Of course she has. She was arming up when I hadn't even realised we were enemies.

"What time do you want us?" I ask.

"About ten. We've taken over the entire hotel—lots of our guests have rooms because they've travelled a distance. We'll be serving champagne in the reception bar all morning. Do you remember the bar, Mel? It's sumptuous."

Every word is like a blow. I do remember visiting the bar, when I was under her spell. Has she chosen that hotel to rub salt in my wounds? I mean, there are other hotels in Northampton. Why get married up here at all? Why not in London? I'd have thought that would suit her media friends more. "OK. Ten."

I'm about to ring off when she asks, "Do you have a view about what flowers the girls should carry?"

"Aren't they ordered yet?" It's late in the day to still be finalising details such as flowers for the bridal party, but I quash the impulse to care.

"Oh, I've ordered both baskets of petals and bouquets of small roses. I just wondered which you thought might work best. I mean, I consider you a quasi-maiden of honour."

I'm clasping the phone so tightly my knuckles are white; through clenched teeth, I say, "I'm sure whatever you pick will be great. You have good taste."

"Don't I just," she says, her tone entirely nudge, nudge, wink, wink.

"I didn't mean—" Obviously, I didn't intend any innuendo about her having good taste in men. It cost me to pay her a compliment, and I want to bash my head against the wall in disgust that what I said might be taken to have a deeper meaning. I'm nervous. Not thinking clearly.

"I ordered the flowers from that lovely little florist in Wolvney's garden centre," says Abigail. "You know the one. It's called Bloomin' Lovely."

I know it. I also know the woman who owns it; she has a son in Lily's class. I'm certain I mentioned that to Abi when we visited once, so I doubt her choice is arbitrary; she probably knows the proximity will cause me some embarrassment. "You're getting your flowers there? I thought you might use somewhere in Northampton."

"I'm really trying to make this celebration as local as possible, you know, for Liam."

This doesn't make any real sense. Traditionally brides try to celebrate ties to their local area, not the groom's, and anyway, why would Liam care where the flowers are ordered from? I can imagine Abi sniggering to herself. The name Bloomin' Lovely seems potent, with inferences of fertility, fruitfulness, fecundity.

"Can you pick up the flowers on the morning and bring them over to me? I mean, it makes sense if you're bringing the girls over to the hotel."

I see she's locking me in, ensuring I don't change my mind on the day. She doesn't wait for me to respond but takes my agreement as given. She has me over a barrel.

Mothers rush towards tsunamis to save their children. They find the strength to lift cars. They run back into burning buildings. I know, because I've spent a lot of time Googling acts of heroism that mothers have performed for their children. In each case the mothers say it's not heroism, it's more basic than that. It's instinctual. There was one Canadian mother I read about who threw herself between an eighty-eight-pound cougar and her child. She took a mauling but they both survived.

The irony isn't lost on me. I feel thwarted. It's a stark reality but the only way I can show my son how much I love him is by doing nothing, saying nothing, appearing to accept what he's chosen. It's strange to know this and yet to want to kill her. I mean, not for real but, well, almost. For the first time, I understand what people mean when they talk of crimes of passion. When things just get out of control, when you can't stop yourself. You're not planning it. You just can't *not* do it. You can't do the right thing. You no longer know what that even is.

I imagine her being gone. Not pushing her under a bus exactly. Just her gone.

"Yeah, I'll pick up the flowers."

"Excellent. That's settled then. Look, I haven't got time to chat any longer. I should go. I'm meeting Liam for dinner. See you on the big day. Do text if there are any problems with the dresses."

Then she hangs up.

I throw the phone at the hall wall. It makes a satisfying dent. I can't believe I once painted that especially for her arrival. More sensible preparation would have been barricading the door, heating tar, sharpening knives.

CHAPTER FIFTY-THREE

LIAM

Friday, 22 June

Dan is snoring and farting. I know it's tradition that the best man stay over the night before the wedding but I'm seriously regretting sharing the hotel room with him. It's not just that he's considerably less fragrant than Abi, it's just… I dunno. I wish he was awake and talking, instead of sleeping. Normally he talks a lot. Non-stop. That's why I asked him to be BM. Subject matters of choice: football, drinking and shagging. He does two of those things a lot, the third, not so much. A lot of wishful thinking, artful bullshitting.

Abi has been really worried about his speech. She made him write down what he was planning on saying and show her it, then she edited it like an English teacher. Well, to be precise, she paid some professional to rewrite it completely. I think Dan was a bit put out—he'd really worked on his speech—but Abi says his chatter redefines banal. I guess he can talk a lot of nothing. It's what I like about him. He's not heavy.

Everything seems heavy in my life right now.

I check my phone. Snapchat is full of messages from mates. Most are just memes taking the piss out of marriage. You know, pictures of hot brides with think bubbles: "Now I can get fat," or words of wisdom like, "Marriage—a deck of cards: starts with hearts and diamonds, ends with you wanting a club and a spade." I've been receiving similar since we sent out the invites. They normally make me laugh.

Today, they sort of piss me off. I'm not sure why.

Abi has sent a Snap of her tits. They're great. They cheer me up. Not that I'm uncheerful. Nervous, I guess. That's it. It's to be expected, right? We only ever Snap now, after the whole thing with that twat Rob threatening to post the video Mum sent him. It bothers me that he has that. I know he's promised not to release it now they're divorced, but as Abi says, he could change his mind at any point. It's a good thing I don't want to go into politics anymore; he could hold it over us forever. He's obviously a total bastard.

Dan wakes himself up snoring too aggressively, then turns over and goes back to sleep again. It's 5:00 a.m. I can't expect him to be up—we were still drinking just four hours ago. Austin would have been up with me, though.

I check my texts. Mostly it's usually just Mum and Dad who text me, so I'm not really expecting anything at all. It's not likely that they'll suddenly start sending ecstatic parental advice and greetings. But. Well. I'm just checking.

Then I look at Facebook. There's a message from Marsha, Tanya's bezzie. I like Marsha. Well, I used to. We got on well enough for a boyfriend and a best friend. Obviously, we're not exactly harmonious right about now. Her message, posted at 2:00 a.m., reads: You are a fucking wanker. Do you know what you have done? Tanya is destroyed.

I bet she was drunk. I delete the message but I still hear the words. They're true enough to hit home. The thing is, Tanya and I were good together. I did really care for her. At the time, I thought I loved her. I never meant to hurt her. But then Abi came along. It wasn't as though I was comparing like for like. Abi was on a different stratosphere. The sex, London, the hotels and now the baby. It's a wild ride. I do sort of miss Tanya, though. She's cute. We used to have a laugh.

I send Abi a Snap but she doesn't respond. I guess she's asleep.

The room's stifling. Dan switched off the air con last night, says it gives him a bad throat.

I turn over my pillow to find a patch of coolness. Mum always tells me to do that. I close my eyes and try to go back to sleep. It's like I can hear her voice saying stuff: *You have a long day ahead of you, try to get some sleep, you'll enjoy it more then.*

My mum's voice. How weird is that? It's not like I've heard her actually speaking to me for ages and even when I did, she said nothing but vile stuff that I didn't even want to listen to. Abi is a saint to have forgiven her over the sex video and all the other bitchy things she's done. Abi just has me front-of-mind all the time. She's always saying that she only ever wants what will make me happy. That's why she was so against me inviting Mum to the wedding. She said, of course she knew it was the right thing to do, because I was worried that one day I'd regret not inviting her, but she tried to stop me because she didn't want to see me hurt if Mum turned down the invite.

Abi's right. That would have hurt like hell. She didn't, though. She's said she'll come. Abi keeps warning me not to get my hopes up. She says even if Mum does come, it doesn't necessarily mean we'll find our way through this. Abi treats me like an adult. She admits some things can't be fixed.

I dunno if Mum will come or not. She just can't get her head around us being a couple. Abi told me they always had a peculiar relationship. She said Mum was always jealous of her. That they were continuously fighting over boys when they were younger. That messes with my head. Can't go there. Abi says Mum sees me as the last one in a line of boys they fought over. That's just fucking weird.

But. Well, I sort of hope she does come. I know Dad will and the girls, but I'd like Mum to be here, too.

She's nuts and annoying and totally controlling but she's my mum.

CHAPTER FIFTY-FOUR

MELANIE

The first thing I do when I wake up on the big day is check my phone. I'm hoping there's a text from Liam saying he wants to call the whole thing off. There isn't.

Ben stirs, turns to me and sees me holding my phone. "At least you have his new number now."

"Yes." Although in fact he texted Ben, not me, so he didn't exactly give it to me, Ben did. But yes, yes, I have it. A means to contact my son. A lifeline.

It's a hot morning. Not a breath of a breeze. The sun is flooding through the curtains, making the still air stale and showing the dust on every surface. The phrase "Happy is the bride that the sun shines on" pops into my head. Maybe so. But in my view, today is far too hot for a wedding. Eyelids and flowers will droop, hair will tend to frizz rather than curl, people's throats will be dry and they'll drink more champagne than is sensible. Tempers will be a little shorter. It is a day to be at the beach. Bright blue skies buttressed against the curl of waves; it is not a day to be in a city. I wish I could run away.

I get out of bed and fling open a window. I breathe deeply but feel I'm suffocating.

"Do you remember his *Ben 10* phase?" I ask Ben. "He had a *Ben 10* bucket and spade. Do you remember, we bought it at Frinton on Sea?" I'd give anything to be a normal family, piling towels and deckchairs into the back of the car, squabbling about who is sitting in which seat, moaning that the traffic is too slow, anticipating ice creams.

Ben is lying with his hands behind his head. He looks handsome and capable. I can't remember why I thought my family wasn't enough, why I thought I needed to have Abi stay with us to make our lives more interesting. "Absolutely, I do," Ben replies with a wide, gentle grin. "He had a *Ben 10* lunchbox and bath towel, too."

I smile at the memory. "Underpants, cap, tent."

"Beanbag."

"He loved him because he had your name."

"Or maybe he loved me because I had *Ben 10*'s name," laughs Ben.

"Do you remember how we'd be going about our business when suddenly he'd stand dead still and then start hitting his wrist?"

"His Omnitrix," Ben corrects. "And he'd yell, 'I am Heatblast. I am Diamondhead.'"

I laugh, impressed. "How do you remember their names?"

"Easily, it seems like yesterday."

And it does. That's the problem. I can still see his little body quivering with excitement. I can still feel the weight of him on my lap, lips pursed as he mouths the words of his reading books.

Ben must be having similar thoughts because he asks, "Do you remember how he liked to sit on my shoulders when we were walking down the street?"

"He did that for far longer than he should have."

"Yes, probably."

"I thought you were going to develop disc problems!"

"'Dad, Dad, make me the king of the castle,'" Ben repeats the phrase that Liam used to yell.

"Yes! That's what he'd say. And you could never refuse him. I had to have Imogen just so you would make him walk," I add laughingly. We both fall silent. Lost in the memories. Safe there. I sit back down on the bed. Not ready to start the day. Not sure I'll ever be ready.

Ben kisses my forehead, tenderly. "You should text him."

"What would I say?"

"Something good."

I wonder whether Liam is feeling nervous, excited, lonely even? Have they observed tradition and slept apart last night? If so, where did Liam sleep? Who is he with now? I hope he's at one of his friends', maybe Dan, he's a funny, easy-going lad. He'd be good company. I hope he has someone.

My phone rings. I grab it without even checking who is calling. Hoping that I've somehow conjured Liam by thinking about him, longing for him. "Liam," I say anxiously.

"Erm, no, it's Jennifer." For a moment, I have no idea who Jennifer is. I can't place the voice. The caller obviously realises this and helps me out. "Austin's mum."

"Jen, of course. Sorry, I wasn't thinking straight."

Ben jumps out of bed and takes the opportunity to nip into the shower. We're going to need to be efficient this morning, if we're to get the girls prepped and at the hotel by ten.

"Busy day?" asks Jen, as though she is in the room and witness to Ben's speedy retreat.

"Well, yes. I suppose."

"I won't keep you. I was just wondering if you knew anything about the policy on confetti."

"Confetti?"

"I didn't want to call the hotel because they are bound to say it's not allowed at all if I ask, and I really don't want to hear no. Sometimes there are questions that are best not asked. I love confetti, don't you?"

"Well, I suppose." I can't quite catch up with the conversation.

"But I thought maybe the bride might prefer petals or even rice. Some girls don't like confetti nowadays, do they? The dye gets on their dresses. I'm in Paperchase, at the station, right now. They have a great range. I was wondering petals, pink or white? Or satin hearts? I mean, is it a full-on themed and coordinated wedding or can I just take a punt?" Jen sounds excited. Happy. It's been so long since I heard either emotion in her voice that I hardly know how to respond. Since Austin was killed, her voice has been thick with grief. Sore. Flat.

"You're coming to the wedding?" I ask.

"Well, yes. We were invited." Jen immediately sounds less happy, less certain and I realise her confidence is tissue thin. I feel dreadful.

"Absolutely, of course. I'm so glad he invited you. So glad." And I am. Because there's something about this gesture that shows Liam is still Liam. Kind, thoughtful and, importantly, connected to his old life. "It's just I haven't had much to do with the wedding planning. I didn't know," I confess. "It will be lovely to see you and Matthew. Really lovely."

Jen immediately realises something is a bit off but tries to quickly gloss over any possible problems. "Wedding planning tends to be the bride's domain, doesn't it? I guess her mother has been quite hands-on, has she? Since they're so young, they'll need some guidance, I should imagine."

If only that was what I was dealing with here—a competitive in-law. "It's a bit complicated," I admit.

"How so?" Jen asks this calmly. Her manner suggests nothing can surprise or shock her. I suppose it can't, not anymore.

"He's marrying a friend of mine, someone I've known since university, actually. A woman my age. She's pregnant," I blurt.

"Oh, I see."

"It's not what I imagined for him."

"No, I don't suppose it is." Her voice is soothing, accepting.

"We've rowed about it. He's dropped out of college. He won't be going to university."

"I'm sorry to hear that."

She's so tranquil and composed that I find myself adding, "Abi, the woman he's marrying, was married to his father."

"I'm sorry, you've lost me now."

"His biological father. Liam doesn't know."

"Does she?"

"No. I don't know what to do. If I tell Liam now, he'll think I've chosen this moment in the hope of stopping the wedding, but if I don't tell him and it comes out later, there will be more trouble and he'll never forgive me."

"That's very difficult," admits Jen. She is the only person, other than Ben, that I have confided this much in. We've known each other since our boys were five years old; I know that she won't gossip or gloat, she will resist being scandalised or sanctimonious. She'll just want the best thing for Liam.

"What should I do?" I beg.

Jen sighs. It's a long, slow sigh that acknowledges she's unsure, confirms there are no easy answers. Eventually, she says, "That's up to you, Mel. I'm afraid I can't make the decision for you."

"No, I know," I mutter despondently.

"But if I can offer you some advice…"

"Yes, yes, please." I'm desperate for some direction.

"Don't lose him." She hangs up.

I sit on the edge of the bed, phone in hand, shaking, and do the thing that we all have to do from time to time: I take a deep breath in and then let it slowly out. Once more. In and out. *Don't lose him.*

Since I saw that video of Abigail and Liam doing… well, you know… I have felt such grief. Because I did lose him. My boy vanished from in front of my eyes. I've even felt that I've crashed through some of the stages of grief.

First denial—no, no. Not my boy. My sweet, hard-working, well-intentioned son wouldn't do something so irresponsible, so stupid. He wouldn't throw away all his chances. Then anger. I have never considered myself an angry person; I didn't know I had such depths of fury to spew up at Liam, Abigail, Ben, Rob and myself. Mostly myself. I lingered and wallowed in that stage for longer than was healthy.

But I see now that there is no time for bargaining or depression—I need to fast-forward to acceptance. Things are not ideal but they could be a lot worse. They could be irredeemable. I know Jen would do anything to swap places with me. She wouldn't care whom her son was marrying if only he was alive. My son is alive.

And there's going to be a baby.

New life. A new soul. Someone who will need all the love and support possible to find their way through. Because the world is tough. Bad things happen. Family, friends, they are there to compensate, to comfort. And Liam is young, that's my whole objection, the source of my fear and disappointment. He is young. He still needs me. Us. I can't change where we are at. I can just stand with him. My son. My unexpected baby. The being who changed me from a carefree student to a Boudica. I promised to look after him, no matter what came hurtling our way.

Now Abi has her own unexpected baby. I think of her telling me about her longing for a child and now she is going to have one. I concentrate on what is important. Abi must love Liam. He certainly thinks he loves her. I don't approve, I don't like it, but it is what it is. They may be OK, if they love each other and if they are braced and buoyed by us. If they don't waste any energy or lose focus, for example through arguing with me, then maybe they'll have a chance. Suddenly, I'm overwhelmed with an intense need to tell Liam that I love him. That I will always love him. No matter what. I send a text.

Beautiful weather! Mum x. It's so horribly British. Next, I'll be offering him a cup of tea. I wait just a beat. Then I send a second one. I love you. Because that's it. That covers everything. I wait.

And wait. Breathe.

Wait.

My phone pings. Good to know. See you later.

Good to know! Good to know! Liam's standard "all is right with the world" response. My shoulders seem to cave towards my chest in relief. We're OK. It's going to be OK.

"Come on, girls," I yell through the bedroom wall. "You need to get up." I hear them screech and giggle. They don't have to be asked twice.

CHAPTER FIFTY-FIVE

ABIGAIL

So, Mel had forgiven Liam. The emotion of the big day had got to her and she'd dug deep, found the resources to forgive him, and he in turn had melted. Instantly.

The thought infuriated Abigail. That was not part of her plan. Despite what she had led Liam to believe, she had no intention of being part of one big happy family. That was not what she'd come to the UK to do.

Liam had called her the moment he'd received the text from his mother. He'd tried to pretend the call was about finding a YouTube video on how to tie a Windsor knot but she could hear it in his voice, he was almost giddy with excitement.

"Oh yeah, and Mum texted. I think we're all OK there now."

"Really? Why? What did she say?"

"That she loves me." He sounded relieved, shy, as

though he'd doubted it. Abigail had never doubted it. She'd depended on it.

"I'm so happy for you," Abigail lied. "How did you respond?" She needed to know everything. Luckily, Liam was in the habit of sharing. Until she'd come along, he'd told his mother more or less every detail of his life. He wasn't the secretive sort by nature— she'd had to foster that skill. Abi wasn't saying she had replaced his mother—that would be creepy—but she had to admit, he probably shared more than a man in his forties would ever deem necessary.

"I texted back 'Good to know.'"

Abi was pleased. He hadn't given Mel the reassurance she must be craving; he hadn't said, "I love you, too."

But then he added, "'Good to know' is our thing. Like a code."

Abi seethed. She didn't want them to have "things," "codes." "Well, I'm glad. It's going to make our day so much more comfortable and enjoyable if your mum isn't still being nasty," she pointed out.

"Right." Liam laughed, a little uneasily. "I think it's going to be fine."

"I'm sure you're right. I love you."

"I love you, too," Liam replied. They didn't have a thing. They just said what everyone said.

Abi rang off.

CHAPTER FIFTY-SIX

MELANIE

We arrive at the hotel at five to ten. Ben goes to park the car but Imogen, Lily and I hop out and linger in the reception, holding the huge box of wedding flowers. The girls are hyper, skipping, jumping, hopping, twirling, chatting, giggling. It's lovely to watch. I'm not sure what's exciting them the most: the thought of being bridesmaids or the thought of seeing Liam.

The hotel is in the centre of town and even though it's early the heat is intense. All the doors and windows are open, someone is dashing about looking for electric fans. There's a small courtyard that has clearly had the benefit of a clever gardener. We wander out there, hoping to find some shade or a breeze. I breathe in the sweet-smelling flowers and listen to the whisper of the rough, rustling grasses. They've been watering recently and the scent of damp woodchips and plant leaves lingers in the air. I allow the fragrant whiff of lavender and eucalyptus to calm and soothe me—progress, because yesterday I thought I'd need a heavy-duty cocktail of Valium and alcohol to see me through this ordeal.

Ben appears and says he's going to track down Liam, who apparently is somewhere in the hotel with his friends, the best man and groomsmen. I ask at reception for Abi and I'm told that she's in the suite on the fifth floor.

Abi opens the door; she looks dazzling, luminous. She's already wearing her wedding dress. My eyes sweep from top to toe. An elegant empire-line dress that only the very svelte ever really suit. She's all softness, a waterfall of chiffon and lace. The girls take their excitement to a new level. They leap about, shrieking; she swoops down to them, gives them kisses, tells them they look glorious. It gets us over the threshold.

"Come in, come in."

I enter with good intentions. "You look lovely." She looks stunning, gorgeous, beautiful. I'm only up to lovely. She touches her stomach. Subconsciously, I think, or maybe a reminder to me of her state, as if I could forget for a moment. I try harder. "You look beautiful."

"Thank you." Her response is a little cool. I thought she'd melt at the first sign of my warming to her, to the situation, but apparently not.

The hotel suite is enormous—it stretches across the entire top floor. More like an apartment than a hotel room, really. It's tastefully decorated in pale greys, whites and silvers. The girls bounce about, twirling, giggling, repeatedly drawn to the full-length mirror, enchanted by their own reflections.

The dresses Abi chose for Immie and Lily are undeniably wonderful. They're a pure brilliant white—kids with paler skins would struggle to carry off that colour but they look sensational on my girls. The simple, sleeveless bodices are embroidered and give way to enormous calf-length tulle skirts; the satin sashes are lime green and tie in the most enormous bows at the back.

Abi looks me up and down. I know my outfit falls short. I had no enthusiasm for shopping for anything new, and at the last minute, I pulled out the first thing that came to hand from my wardrobe, a navy shift dress. Now I wish I'd made more of an effort, partially to appease Liam when he sees me and partially to avoid falling so woefully short in comparison to Abi's level of glamour. Not that it's reasonable to compare a bride and a guest, but maybe as mother of the groom more was expected of me.

This isn't going to be easy.

I think of Jennifer and Austin. I count my blessings and smile, determined. "I didn't know if it was a hat sort of wedding," I say, apologetically.

"You could have called to ask," replies Abi, but she doesn't confirm whether it is or it isn't, so I've no idea how underdressed I am. She obviously isn't planning on making this easy. I follow her through to the sitting room. Her veil is laid out over the sofa, delicate, beautiful. I am still carrying the huge box of flowers containing her bouquet, headdresses, posies and rose petal baskets for the girls.

"I'll put these in the bathroom. They'll stay cooler and fresher in there," I offer.

In the bathroom, I quickly put my wrists under cold running water; it's a tip my mother taught me to keep temperatures down. I emerge and instruct the girls to calm down. I give them each a glass of water and ask them to sit quietly in front of the TV in the bedroom while I talk to Abi. They don't look keen but they agree. They've been bribed and threatened with everything under the sun and know that today it is paramount that they behave impeccably.

Once I walk back into the living room, I launch into my prepared speech. "Look, Abi. I've had some time to think about everything. And what with the developments—" I nod towards her stomach. It's just slightly swollen. Some women start to plump out immediately, but I knew Abi would not be that sort. No doubt, she'll have a basketball bump at nine months and no other signs of pregnancy; no swollen ankles, no saggy bum or sign of multiple chins. I push that out of my mind. I should stay on brief. "—I think I owe you an…" The words stick in my throat.

"An apology?" She sashays towards a console table that has an ice bucket on it, inside of which there is a bottle of champagne chilling in ice.

"Yes, perhaps." I'm not sure I'm ready for an all-out apology, I mean she's the one who— I stop my train of thought. "I'd certainly like to press the start-over button. I want this to work."

"Do you now?" She looks sceptical. I can hardly

blame her. I don't entirely believe myself. "Is this Ben's idea?"

"No, but it's certainly what he wants and I know it is what Liam wants, too."

"Has he spoken to you about it?" she demands sharply.

I shake my head sadly. "No, we haven't spoken yet, but I do know it's what he must want, so…" I shrug. I can't lie. It's not exactly what I want. It's the next best thing. It's what will work in the world I find myself in. It's a compromise.

"So, we're going to turn the page. A clean sheet?" she asks.

"I'd like that."

"And you honestly think we can live happily-ever-after?" She stands in front of me, a bride in all her finery. Beautiful, but her gently blooming radiance has been replaced now with a new, charged expression. She looks more alive than anyone I've ever seen before. There's a biting sharpness to her that unnerves me. Despite my goal to be friendly, I find I'm thinking of vampires in horror movies, after they have fed on someone's blood. She picks up the champagne bottle and then efficiently eases out the cork. The pop sound makes me jump.

"I honestly don't know, but I think we should try, for Liam's sake," I reply.

"*Honestly.* Mel and honesty. Now there's a conundrum. Do I mean conundrum or do I mean oxymoron?" She laughs and shakes her head as she starts to pour a glass of champagne. "So, tell me, *honestly,* does Ben know?"

I'm confused. "Know what?"

"About Rob being Liam's father?" she says calmly.

"You *know*?" I stop dead. Caught and wrong-footed, it's horrifying, but suddenly, it makes sense. It's the opposite of seeing the light. I've walked into a dark shadow, cold and bleak.

CHAPTER FIFTY-SEVEN

ABIGAIL

"Of course, I know. That is why I'm here. In your life." Abigail didn't add *ruining things* but the implication hung in the air. "Would you like a glass of champagne? You look as though you could use a drink."

Abigail took delight in watching Mel blink repeatedly. Shock or battling tears? Either response was a result. Mel trembled. Stumbled backwards and slumped into a chair. Abigail thought of one of those pool toys when it was punctured. Shrivelled, deflated, wrinkled and useless.

"How did you find out? I never wanted you to know," Mel stuttered, stunned.

"Really?" Abigail was sceptical.

"Never," Mel insisted. "As soon as I realised I was pregnant, my first reaction was shock that it had happened, and my second was fear that you would find out."

"Find out what a bitch you are, you mean?"

"That you'd find out and be hurt. That's why I left uni, lost all those chances, sacrificed all my friendships. Sacrificed my friendship with *you*. I didn't want to cause any trouble."

Abigail wanted to throw the champagne at her. She gripped the stem so tightly she thought it might snap in her hands. "You slept with my boyfriend. I'd say that constitutes causing trouble." Mel hung her head, the very picture of shame, but Abi didn't buy it. Not for a minute. Mel was simply regretting that the past had finally risen to meet her. "Tell me—not that it matters, but just out of interest—how long did your affair last?"

"It wasn't an affair. It was a one-off. A dreadful mistake." Abi tutted, disbelieving. Mel pushed on, "I didn't want to steal Rob away from you. That was never my plan."

Abi scoffed. "Yes, you did. You just couldn't."

"What's the matter, Mummy?" Lily asked. Both girls had emerged from the bedroom, uninterested in cartoons when there was a real-life bust-up right here, right now. They hung on the door frame. Their smiles faltered for the first time in their magical day.

"Go back in the bedroom, Lily, and close the door." Lily didn't move. Abi liked the girls well enough but she had often noted that Mel really didn't have a grip on discipline. "Now!" Mel shouted, which caused Lily and Imogen to scurry away.

Abigail stroked her stomach. When she was a

mother, she would never resort to shouting. She'd reason.

Mel stretched out her hand for the champagne glass. Abi handed it over with a cold smile. "If you didn't want to cause trouble, why did you send Rob a photo of Liam?"

"Sorry?" Mel froze. She looked like someone had thumped her. Although no one had. Not yet.

"The photo of Liam clutching the list of GCSE results. I found it."

Mel looked as though she was going to pass out. She probably wanted to. Pass out. Block it all out. All her nasty betrayals. "It was an impulse. A stupid, ill-thought-through impulse. Just one photo in seventeen years," she gasped, panicked.

"Really?" Abigail was relatively confident that there hadn't been an ongoing correspondence between Mel and Rob because she had searched their homes, his office, his computer and phone with forensic precision and she hadn't found any evidence that he'd been sending money to Mel or supporting Liam in any way. She didn't discover any other pictures, emails or texts. Just the one.

But Abi didn't believe Mel that the sending of the photo was an impulse. Not for a second. She'd probably been plotting and planning on how to win Rob's attention forever. Of course she had. Rob was magnificent. Handsome, powerful, intelligent, obscenely rich. Abigail couldn't believe Mel wouldn't want him.

The email had been entitled *The boy done good, if you've been wondering*. There was nothing written in the body copy. Awful grammar. Quite shocking. No doubt Mel thought she was hitting a jocular, pally note but she just showed her ignorance of Rob's mindset and sensibilities. He couldn't stand that sort of idiom. He thought they were common.

To start with, Abigail hadn't understood what she was looking at. She often snooped around his computer, just to keep an eye on him. What wife didn't mooch about from time to time? The name on the email—Melanie Harrison—wasn't immediately recognisable to her. For some time, she'd stared at the picture of the handsome boy—square jawed, tall, laughing—he was somehow familiar. She'd thought he must be an intern and this was perhaps a mother thanking Rob for placing him, giving him an opportunity. Even that was enough to make her suspicious; Rob wasn't known for his acts of altruism.

She'd Googled the woman's name. Images popped onto the screen, an array of Melanie Harrisons on Facebook. Then she recognised her. Melanie Harrison was Melanie Field—they were Facebook friends, as it happened, but Abi had over twenty thousand Facebook friends; she couldn't be expected to recall every name. Melanie Field was someone she had been friends with thousands of moons back, someone she hadn't thought about for years. A silly girl who had fallen pregnant and had to leave university.

And then Abigail had understood. The bitch.

Abi employed a private detective, who hired an IT specialist—they could be more thorough than she could ever hope to be when searching for evidence of a relationship. They didn't find anything more. Just the one photo and his altered will.

The bastard.

It wasn't the money. There was more than enough to go around—a few hundred thousand left to this boy wouldn't materially have altered her lifestyle—but putting two and two together made Abigail understand quite completely what Melanie Field had stolen from her.

"I never wanted to hurt you," Mel said again. She sounded like a stuck fucking record. Of course she'd wanted to hurt her. That was why she sent the photo. Melanie must have realised how rich and influential Rob had become, and she'd decided to cash in her chips through a spot of blackmail, perhaps. Or maybe her jealousy had ultimately got the better of her. Maybe Melanie could no longer stand the idea of Abi living happily with Rob; she'd probably turned bitter after pining for him for seventeen years! So, she sent the photo hoping Abi would find it. She sent it to destroy Abi's peace of mind.

To destroy her mind altogether.

And it had worked. Sometimes Abi thought she was losing the plot. That she'd taken things too far. Other times she felt justified, vindicated. Her view changed almost daily. That could be her hormones. It could be desperation.

Melanie's expression slowly began to morph from contrition to outrage. She really could be quite horribly dim. It was so obvious that Liam got his brains from his father. "You came here, knowing who Liam was?"

"Yes," Abi admitted with a casual shrug. "You fucked the love of my life. And now I'm fucking your son. Tell me you can't see the poetic justice." There was a knock at the door. "That must be the photographer. Time to get this show on the road."

CHAPTER FIFTY-EIGHT

MELANIE

I can't move. I'm pinioned to the chair, overwhelmed with shock and disbelief. I'm vaguely aware that the hotel suite is filling up with different people. Someone from housekeeping has arrived; she's plumping pillows, refreshing glasses, managing to be in ten places at once. I imagine that Abi has spent a lot on this wedding and is an important client to the hotel.

The photographer and her assistant arrive; I keep my back to them as I don't want to have to make pleasant conversation. I'm not up to it. I think there's also another woman checking Abi's make-up and hair. These people are buzzing, chatting happily about the day ahead as though this is a normal wedding, as though Abi is not blind with a desire to dish out reprisals and retaliation.

It's so peculiar being here with her. Knowing what I do. From the outside, she looks like every other bride might look. Beautiful, excited, happy, normal. But inside, she's crazy, cruel, deranged. She has plotted to hurt me and has embroiled my son in her Greek revenge tragedy. Other people don't know and I can't tell them.

Lily and Imogen are called from the bedroom. They eye me warily. I force myself to throw a reassuring smile in their direction and I note their bodies relax. They grin and accept the compliments that everyone is showering their way; someone pins flowers in their hair and then they start to scrupulously follow the photographer's instructions. They sit at Abi's feet, skirts spread, they hold their posies in front of their chests. I watch all of this as though I am behind a glass. As though I can't reach them. I need to take them by the hand and march them out of here. I need to find Ben and Liam and tell them everything I know.

I think of the photograph of Liam holding his fantastic results. No. No. No. I feel it like a physical pain. I caused this. This is all my fault. If I hadn't sent the photo to Rob, Abi would never have come into our lives, none of this would have happened. What was I thinking? I had never been in touch, hadn't so much as uttered Rob Larsen's name aloud to anyone, ever, in seventeen years. If he drifted into my mind, I always violently pushed him out of it. I didn't romanticise the man. I didn't demonise him either. All my efforts went into pretending he didn't exist at all.

And then the day Liam got his GCSE exam results, Rob liked my Facebook post.

It was unbelievable. Such a disconcerting, unexpected act. I hadn't even posted the picture that every other parent felt entitled to post. All morning, other people's pictures had choked my feed. A beaming child, gripping the slip of paper that amounts to the culmination of years of school work, proud parents standing by or tightly hugging their teens. But I didn't allow myself to post our version. While I had no reason to think Rob had ever looked at my Facebook, had ever given me another thought in his life—why would he?—I had always been cautious about the information I posted about Liam. I never dared post pictures of him. I didn't want to attract attention. I really didn't.

However, I couldn't quite resist celebrating him that day. Not after all his work, not after all he had achieved. Celebrating? Bragging I suppose, that's how Abi sees parental posts. Bragging, taunting, tormenting.

Naturally, interested friends and family were writing on my timeline asking how he had fared, so I wrote: We're so proud of Liam. His results are just what he deserves after all his hard work and preparation! It was low-key. I didn't write what I wanted, which was Ha! That's one in the eye for you doomsayers that swore a teen mother would make a crummy job of raising a child and that the state would be burdened with a delinquent. He's a bloody genius!

Quite controlled of me, actually.

Obviously, old friends and acquaintances pressed Like, alongside the parents of kids in Liam's class. People are generous on results day. We're all happy for each other. Relieved. The Like count grew and grew. Thirty, forty. Fifty. Some smiley faces and many congratulatory comments were added. I guess Rob Larsen and I must have had enough mutual friends—Abi for a start—my Facebook setting was too lax. Set on Visible, friends of friends caught the post; I hadn't thought of that. Or maybe he looked us up. It's possible that he worked out that Liam would be taking his exams and Rob may have been curious. Who knows. Anyway, he liked the post.

And it threw me.

His Like, there among all the others. A poke. A question. A nod. It seemed significant. The first interaction we'd had since the night I told him I was pregnant.

It wasn't tricky to track down an email address for him. I sent the photo I'd taken of Liam, grinning from ear to ear, gratified, jubilant. The one I'd decided not to post because I never wanted to give Rob the satisfaction of seeing him grow. It makes no sense. I don't know why I did it. Maybe it was to do with the fact that we'd opened a bottle of champagne at breakfast, just as soon as Liam had picked up his results online. I'd had two, maybe three glasses by that point. I was feeling carefree. Emotional. Victorious.

Generous.

That's the irony. It came from a good place. That may be hard to believe and understand now but all I wanted was to share Liam's fabulousness. I wanted, on some level, to acknowledge that Rob had a part in it. Even though he hadn't, not really.

Ben.

Oh my God, what will Ben think of this news? He asked me if I'd kept Rob updated on Liam and I lied. I said I never had. I should have told him about the photo when I had the chance, but I just didn't have it in me to come clean. I wasn't courageous enough, I suppose. We were just getting back on an even keel when the subject came up, and I couldn't face any more trouble. Although we've trouble enough now.

In the subject box, I wrote *The boy done good, if you've been wondering.* What an idiot I am. After I pressed Send, I regretted it immediately. First, I didn't know if Rob would understand that I was trying to be funny; maybe he'd just think that because I didn't finish my university career, I struggled with basic grammar—he really could be an intellectual snob. But mostly I regretted it because Liam belonged to us, to Ben and me, and I felt I'd betrayed our unit.

Ben was the one who had pored over Google and textbooks when Liam had a problem with some homework, Ben was the one who came to parents' evenings, option-choice talks and career-information seminars, Ben dashed to the shops to buy a protractor at the last minute the night before a maths exam. It was nothing to do with Rob. Sending the email spoilt my day; my mood shifted. I remember feeling a sense of despair, impending doom even. I was right about that much.

I've ruined everything.

I stand up. My legs are shaking but I manage to walk across to Abi—she's sat at her dressing table. The make-up artist is lightly brushing powder on her nose and the photographer is checking light levels, flash bulbs keep popping. The girls are in the corner of the room now, being entertained by the photographer's assistant. I know all these people are with us, I'm aware of them, but I don't care about them. I feel as though it's just the two of us. We're like boxers in a ring; we must slug it out.

"You used Liam to get back at me?"

She's calm and cool. "Who better to use?"

"How could you?" I'm incredulous; such cruelty.

"I wanted to hurt you. I wanted to make things even," she replies, matter-of-fact. "Not that I could ever do that. I could never get back the seventeen years you stole from me."

"What are you talking about? I didn't steal anything from you. What I did was wrong, and I'm sorry for it, but I tried to get out of your way."

Abi looks disdainful, not believing a word I say. She stands up and imperiously indicates to the woman helping her with her make-up that she wants her veil fastening onto her headdress now.

"I made a mistake," I admit. When she doesn't acknowledge me, I add with infuriation, "Abi, do I have to remind you that I wasn't the only one Rob slept with at the time? He had others. You know he did. So did you. Your relationship hadn't reached the exclusive stage—it was very on-off."

"None of his other flirtations were my best friend, none of the others got pregnant," she insists stonily. "You stole from me, Melanie."

The photographer glares at me. Besides judging me as the devil incarnate, I'm obviously hindering her work. Although, somehow, Abi still manages to move about the room, turning her head and her smile towards the camera when necessary. Gathering I'm preoccupied, the photographer's assistant corrals the girls and the bridal party sets off towards the door. There's talk about going downstairs and getting photos in the impressive wood-panelled hallway and stunning reception, by the fountain in the courtyard, too. It seems nothing must get in the way of the preparation for this wedding, least of all conscience, truth or morality.

On the landing, Abi suddenly stops dead in her tracks. Lily stumbles on Abi's dress hem—indeed we all nearly tumble into a pile. Abi turns to me and glares. She leans close. "Don't you get it, Melanie? He knew he had a son. That's why he never needed to have one with me! You stole my chance of a child." She says this with absolute conviction, but her logic is so flawed that it is breathtaking to me.

"That's not true. He didn't want his son. When I told him I was pregnant, he said he'd pay for a private abortion. When I refused, he said that was up to me but he didn't ever want to have another conversation with me again."

It was brutal. The man she's loved for twenty years, the man I conceived a child with, was—and no doubt still is—a selfish monster.

"Can you lower your bouquet, please? You're hiding the detail of your dress." The request comes from the photographer. Abi obliges. Turns to the camera, flashes her kilowatt smile once again. I wish all these people would just go away. This is madness. Abi moves towards the stairway and leans against the ornate iron railings. The photographer tells her to stretch her arm to the left to better show off her engagement ring. The pose looks unnatural although I'm sure it will make a lovely shot.

"Liam is in his will. Do you know that?" Abi hisses to me through clenched teeth.

"No, I didn't. No." I shake my head. It doesn't fit with what I know of Rob. He's never contributed financially, and I've never asked for a penny. Why would he bequeath anything to Liam? Although, who else? He's constructed his life in a way that means there is no one else. Not even Abi. "I don't want his money. This has never been about his money," I state firmly.

"Whatever." She holds up her hand, uninterested, unbelieving. "Well, you may have stopped me having a baby with Rob, but now I have the next best thing."

And then the full horror of this situation settles into my bones. I move close to Abi and tug on her arm, turning her so our backs are to the others. "You *planned* all of this. You meant to get pregnant by Liam. This wasn't an accident," I whisper.

"Give the woman a prize," she sniggers. She glides towards the top of the stairs.

I feel unbalanced. Out of kilter. My senses are not behaving properly. I can taste metal in my mouth. "Do you love him at all?" I demand, hardly caring who hears us, just needing answers.

It makes no sense. I don't want this woman anywhere near my son—she's mad with vengeance and incapable of clear thinking, but she's pregnant with his baby and he is in love with her. It will destroy him if he learns that he was just a pawn in her messy, nasty game. I want to hear she loves him. Only that might keep him safe.

"He's a sweet boy. I thought he'd be too young for me at first, that I might get squeamish about it, but he's well built, isn't he? Very able in the sack, as we discussed, and virile, which was the most important thing."

I gawp at her, devastated. Each word she utters cuts like a knife.

"He looks quite a lot like Rob, don't you think? That will be nice for my baby. It will look like I've always imagined it would."

I shake my head, stunned, bemused. Unsure of what I can say.

She takes my gesture as a denial and this makes her angry. "I know why you never posted pictures of your children on social media—it's not because you are nervous of paedos, the thoughtful, evolved custodian of their privacy—"

"I never said that." It's pointless trying to interject with any reasoning. She steamrolls on.

"It's because Liam has more than a passing resemblance to his father, isn't it? You must have known I'd notice it straight away. I saw Rob in him the moment I walked through the door. How could you have invited me to your home? You knew I would. You must have wanted to hurt me again."

"No, no, it wasn't like that. I invited you here because I thought that maybe with Rob out of the way, we could have a friendship again. I thought you needed me." She glares at me. I carry on, "Liam doesn't look much like Rob. He's blonde, yes, tall, yes, blue-eyed, but his chin, his jaw, those are mine." I know I sound crazy. It's not clear whether I want to deny being arrogant or hurting her or the fact Liam looks like Rob. All of it. I want to deny all of it. "I didn't post pictures because I didn't want Rob to see him grow. I felt he didn't deserve that. I never considered that you'd see a resemblance because I've never seen it."

Abi turns to the make-up artist, who is wide-eyed, agog with the drama, and demands, "Hand me my bag." She is given a small, silky clutch bag that she obviously intends to hold once she's put down her flowers. I imagine it contains a lipstick for reapplication, maybe her phone. Abi opens her bag and pulls out a packet of old photographs. She starts to scrabble through them.

"Look," she demands. I don't move. She tuts impatiently and then scatters picture after picture onto the floor at my feet.

Rob, a student in jeans at a barbecue, smoking a joint; Rob in what looks like his first suit, nervously stood behind a lectern, probably about to give an early lecture; Rob with her parents walking dogs in a park; Rob on a beach, no more than twenty-eight or-nine years old. In these photos, he looks nothing like the big bold man I've recently seen in gossip magazines or online. There is a resemblance between him and Liam, even considering the vagaries of fashion. I had forgotten. They're not identical, but there are enough similarities to make a comparison. I had never seen it. I hadn't wanted to. I suppose she wants nothing more.

Eventually, she stops throwing photos at me. Slowly, she bends and tenderly picks them up, seeming surprised to see them scattered. She carefully secretes them away, as though they are worth a thousand pounds each. The photographer has stopped clicking, the make-up artist is no longer fussing. We all stand in silence.

Finally, I understand with absolute clarity: she still loves Rob. She has only ever loved Rob. Poor Liam. What will she do next? Will she keep him dangling or will she cut him loose? I lean close to her and quietly ask, "How could you use Liam like this?" I am bewildered. "None of this mess is his fault. He thinks you love him. You told him you loved him." My blood freezes. "You want to ruin his life, please don't," I beg.

"I'm not ruining anything. I'm having a baby. He can be involved as much or as little as he wants. I'm not unrealistic—I realise that Liam might lose interest anyway, sooner or later. And then he'll move on, but I don't mind. I'll have a baby, *my* baby. Rob's grandchild." She throws out a slow smile that's closer to a sneer.

"I'll tell him all of this."

"He'd never believe you or anyone else over me." The truth of this punches and paralyses me. Abi carries on, her tone is almost sing-song. As though this is a game to her. "You know, he might not lose interest. He's devoted to me now. Hangs on my every word. Holds me so close. He's given up his education for me and next he'll give up his country. We're going to America, Melanie, I bet you didn't know that?"

Naturally, I didn't. She's seen to it that we haven't been speaking. America, so far away.

"Yes, there's every chance that I might lose interest first. I sometimes think I'm already getting bored. Then what will he have left? No home, no education to fall back on. He'll be a divorcee, the baby daddy to another woman. He won't be such a catch anymore. Still, you don't have to worry about that just yet. At the moment, I like having him around. It suits me. So, let's get on with this wedding, should we?"

And it is instinct. Not a thought-through action. Not premeditated or considered at all. A sudden push, a violent shove. Just something to get her to stop going on and on. Something to shut her up.

But suddenly she is falling, limbs and skirt tangled as she plummets down the stairs. It's a long, endless moment that is simultaneously over in a second. I see her bouquet rise into the air, her legs, too. Like she's a puppet and the puppeteer has jerked her strings upwards. Thud, thud, thud, thud. One after another, over and over again. Until she is still. Nothing. The puppeteer has thrown her down. Her limbs are all strange, poked out at sickening angles.

Everything stops. There's silence and no movement. Until Imogen screams.

Then I run down the stairs to where Abi is lying dead still and a brown-red stain is already flowering on her white gown. "Call an ambulance, someone call an ambulance."

CHAPTER FIFTY-NINE

TANYA

It was easy to get into the wedding party. I'd dressed up a bit, not full-on fascinator and floral print dress—I didn't want to draw attention—but I made some effort: a skirt, heels, sunglasses. I needed to blend in but look different enough from my usual jean-wearing-self to bob under the radar somewhat. I walked into the hotel lobby with a group who were clutching invites (lime green, totally naff). I didn't recognise any of them; they all looked as though they were in their thirties—Abigail Curtiz's friends, I suppose.

It's not a massive wedding, there aren't like a hundred old relies tottering about, plus a hundred more hot young things—a rough count puts it at about fifty, I'd say. No expense has been spared though; the first thing I'm offered is a glass of champagne, served in those shallow glasses, from a silver tray. Very posh. I take one and neck it as fast as I can. Fortification.

I spot a few of Liam's casual mates who I vaguely recognise, people we know through social media and parties, but none of his real mates from college or footie, which is a relief.

The social media mates are grinning stupidly, laughing too loudly and taking selfies. So overly excited by the drama of it all, not aware of the consequences. Happy to be getting drunk at someone else's expense. I don't blame them. This is the normal reaction of eighteen-year-olds. This is what Liam and I would be doing together if we were invited to a wedding where some dork had got his girlfriend pregnant and then thought the best idea was to marry her— don't even get me started on the age-gap thing.

I see that people have brought cards and gifts; there's a table stacked with beautifully wrapped boxes. I didn't, obviously. People are clinking glasses, small sleek packets of confetti are tightly gripped, someone is probably running a bet on how long the speeches will last. This is what people do at weddings. I am the only one judging.

I can't see Mr. and Mrs. Harrison or Imogen and Lily but I do spot both of Liam's nanas and his grandad. Mrs. Harrison's mother looks weepy, her father looks stony. Mr. Harrison's mother is wearing a big hat and she's smiling bravely; the very model of a woman who is trying to make the best of it. They all look awkward and don't seem to have much to say to each other or anyone else for that matter. I'm sorry to see their distress, yet I'm glad that they are not behaving as though this is normal, as though this is a cause for celebration.

I notice the photographer unloading the car. She looks hassled. I think she must be late. She's parked illegally, right outside the hotel, and is negotiating with the man on reception for a spot in the car park, at the same time as she's pulling all her gear out of the car and ditching it at his desk. He tells her the car park is full and that she should have rung ahead, that they could have booked her a space if she'd done so. I see my chance. I sidle up to her and offer my help.

"You're here for the Curtiz-Harrison wedding, right?"

She nods, her face flushed with stress and she looks a bit sweaty. Abigail won't be thrilled.

"I can look after your stuff while you move the car."

She is obviously torn: worried I'll nick her expensive cameras but not wanting to risk her car getting towed if she leaves it where it is.

I look honest and reliable and I don't overdo it. I shrug and start to walk away. "Well, if you can manage without me, then—"

"No, no. Sorry. Please stay with my stuff, that will be a big help."

By the time she returns, nearly fifteen minutes later, I've already stacked her gear by the lifts. "The bride is on the fifth floor," I say helpfully. When the lift arrives, I just start to pick up some of her things and get in the lift with her. I think she assumes I'm with the hotel or the wedding party; she doesn't ask, she just seems grateful for the help now.

I haven't got a plan. I don't really know why I'm here at all. I'm not planning on throwing myself at

Liam's feet and crying, "Don't marry her, marry me." I'm not planning on waiting for the bit in the service when they ask, "If any persons here present can show just reason why these two people may not be joined in matrimony, let them now declare or else for ever-more keep their peace." I'm not here to cause trouble exactly, although if I could stop this farce, I would.

The truth of the matter is, I just couldn't be any-where else today. I just couldn't stay away. I've thought of nothing else for days now. I've wondered what she'll wear. What he'll wear. Who was invited and who will come? What will they eat? Will Imo-gen and Lily be bridesmaids? I couldn't have spent more time thinking about this wedding if I was the one getting married. I just needed to be near.

Him. Or her.

Near the wedding, I suppose.

It's like going to a funeral. It's important to say goodbye, to find closure. If I don't see this wedding with my own eyes, I'll never believe it has happened because it shouldn't be happening. It's madness. I can't believe he's going to do this. It seems the most extraordinary and ridiculous thing. He should be starting his internship next week. We should be going to prom together tomorrow. That's what we planned, ages ago. We've talked about prom since last Sep-tember. It's extraordinary to me that, one minute, a person's life can be going in a certain direction, with meaning and purpose, and then suddenly it isn't. It's just not. We were on a track. Liam has changed all that. He asked me to prom, we were going to do Jäger-bombs, I was wearing red, and now he's marrying an old woman instead and he's going to be a dad. I can't get my head around it.

I did not expect to find Mrs. Harrison in Abigail's room but I am not surprised that when I do, they are arguing. Imogen spots me immediately and runs straight into my arms. Lily quickly follows suit. They look adorable. I put my finger on my lips and whisk them into the corner of the room.

"You look so beautiful, girls," I say with a big beam.

"Don't we just," confirms Lily, pleased with my compliment, pleased with herself. "Do you like my hair flowers?"

"I do."

"And do you like my shoes?"

"Yes, very much."

"And do you like my dress?"

"Yes."

"What about my bracelet?"

"Everything is gorgeous. You look entirely gorgeous," I say, cutting her off.

"Mummy has hardly noticed us," comments Imogen sulkily. "She's too busy fighting with Aunty Abi."

I won't lie, the Aunty bit hurts. "Well, I don't think I'll say hello to your mummy just yet, she does look busy. I tell you what, let's just stay over here quietly, and let them get on with it."

"I didn't think you'd come to the wedding," states Immie. "I didn't know you'd be invited. But I'm glad you are."

I pull out my phone and we start playing on my Hair Salon app to keep them from messing about and drawing any attention. I'm not sure what Mrs. Harrison will say if she sees me here, but I can't imagine Abigail will let me stay.

I don't even have to strain to listen into their row. Abigail Curtiz has that posh, entitled thing going on, whereby she doesn't think staff—like me, the photographer, the maid and the make-up artist—are real people. She doesn't care what she says in front of us, she barely knows we are here, except to do her bidding. It's different for Mrs. Harrison, though, she's normally hyper-aware of being polite and normally she makes sure the girls only hear suitable conversations; she never curses in front of them. I can only assume she is literally too worked up to give a toss what we hear.

"You used Liam to get back at me?"

"Who better to use?"

I don't understand what they are going on about. Mrs. Harrison stole something from Abigail Curtiz. No, hang on, she had sex with her boyfriend! OMG, Rob Larsen is Liam's father!

While they're arguing, Abigail manages to flounce around the room; she flings out orders about her veil and make-up and everyone just jumps to it. It's genuinely surreal. The girls look totally confused and only happy when they're called to be in a shot. I throw smiles and winks their way. I pull funny faces to make them laugh.

Next, the row spills out into the landing as we all leave the bedroom. Abigail is saying more and more wild things. She shouldn't be saying stuff like that in front of Imogen and Lily. In front of me. She should

shut up now. She's done enough damage. She's seduced Liam to hurt Mrs. Harrison, she's having his
baby to tie herself to her ex-husband. Abigail used
him simply as a substitute for Rob Larsen. He'll be
demolished if he ever works that out. It's totally fucking mental.

Mrs. Harrison looks devastated. Wrecked. I've
never seen anyone turn invisible before, but that sort
of happens—she disappears in front of my eyes like
someone's just cast a bloody Harry Potter spell.

"Well, you may have stopped me having a baby
with Rob, but now I have the next best thing."

"You *planned* all of this. You meant to get pregnant by Liam. This wasn't an accident."

"Give the woman a prize."

"Do you love him at all?"

"He's a sweet boy. I thought he'd be too young for
me at first, that I might get squeamish about it but
he's well built, isn't he?"

Oh God.

"Very able in the sack."

Shut up.

"And virile, which was the most important thing.
He looks quite a lot like Rob, don't you think? That
will be nice for my baby. It will look like I've always
imagined it would."

Just shut up.

No, no, it's too sick. Abigail Curtiz has pictures
of her husband in her bag. She's about to marry *my*
boyfriend. The boyfriend she stole from me. And she
is carrying pictures of another man in her bag on her
wedding day.

She doesn't even love him.

She came to the UK planning to steal him. She meant to cause trouble.

She won't disappear, penitent and ashamed. She's right here, ruining my life.

"He's devoted to me... Hangs on my every word... Given up his education for me and next he'll give up his country... I'm already getting bored... So let's get on with this wedding, should we?"

And it is instinct. Not thought through. Not pre-meditated or considered. A push, a shove. Just something to get her to stop going on and on. Something to shut her up.

CHAPTER SIXTY

BEN

Ben was sat in his son's hotel room—which smelt of stale male bodies and last night's alcohol—making small talk with Dan about movies and music. Liam was in the shower. They were behind schedule. It wasn't ideal. Despite Mel's recent commitment to making things work, the day was likely to be fraught; tardy timekeeping could only exasperate.

Ben had repeatedly knocked on the door before Liam stirred this morning. He explained he'd woken up early and had then fallen back to sleep at 8:00 a.m., the time he should have been getting up; he looked done in. Dan was buoyant enough, but he'd had his headphones on and hadn't heard Ben knocking.

"As best man, aren't you supposed to keep an eye on timekeeping?" Ben muttered grumpily.

Dan shrugged and said he'd done his Duke of Edinburgh expedition just last week and had been lousy on timekeeping then, too. "I honestly thought we were going to fail. It was a total bitching nightmare."

Ben felt a pang. The gap between Dan's and Liam's life experiences now was vast. Ben wished the most Liam had to worry about was whether he passed his gold DofE or not. Dan switched on MTV and asked if anyone had any paracetamol, he had a hangover. He made no concessions to the fact that it was Liam's big day. He suggested they flip a coin for use of the bathroom. "Heads I win, tails you lose."

Liam just rolled his eyes and let his mate go first. "Have we missed breakfast?" he asked his dad.

"Probably not. I imagine they serve until ten thirty, maybe eleven at a weekend, but your guests are already congregating in reception, quaffing champagne."

"Already?"

"Yeah, so you possibly shouldn't go down looking like you are. I can order room service."

Ben ordered three full English breakfasts while Liam was in the shower. He'd already eaten toast with the girls but his son was getting married. He wanted to try to observe the rituals, although when it came to it, Liam barely touched his.

"Are you not eating that sausage?" asked Dan. He was showered and dressed but he didn't seem concerned when he dripped egg down his tie.

"No," said Liam.

"Then don't mind if I do." Dan reached to Liam's plate, picked up the sausage with his fingers and gobbled it down in two bites. He then looked hopefully at Ben's plate.

"Help yourself." Ben had been planning on eating the sausage himself but had such respect for Dan's appetite that he didn't want to stand in his way. Boys this age could eat anything and everything. Twice. Usually. "Are you nervous, buddy?" Ben asked Liam, looking at his barely touched breakfast.

Liam quickly shook his head. "Just not hungry."

Ben mentally kicked himself. Stupid question; of course Liam wasn't going to admit to nerves in front of Dan.

Dan punched Liam's arm playfully. "You big girl. Eat something. You'll need your energy later." He laughed, vigorously chewed and swallowed, then headed to the door. "Anyway, I'm going downstairs to introduce myself to the bridesmaids. I'll leave you to it, yeah?"

"The bridesmaids are my sisters, and they're eight and six," Liam pointed out.

"Oh, mate. Shit planning." Dan looked dejected. "Well, the guests then. Has Abi got any fit mates, like her, or do they all look like my mum?"

"Piss off, Dan," said Liam affectionately.

"I'll go and find out for myself." Dan closed the door behind him, unconcerned about his best man duties of seeing Liam suited and booted, ready for the ceremony.

"Just us two then," said Ben. It was a relief, in truth.

"Yeah," Liam smiled half-heartedly. He started to pull on his shirt.

Ben asked, "Are you OK, son?"

"Just tired."

Just not hungry. Just tired. They were reasonable enough excuses, but Ben felt they were exactly that, excuses. Liam seemed overwhelmed, sad. Had the enormity of what he was about to do finally hit him? Wasn't he supposed to be jubilant, upbeat on his wedding day? Yeah, he was, but Ben thought that was an unlikely expectation under the circumstances. He'd settle for quietly confident or even comfortable.

Ben stood up, looked for the TV remote, turned down the volume of MTV. He didn't risk turning it off. The silence would have been too loud. He wondered what to do next. Should he offer his son a drink? That would steady his nerves, see him through. Or he could chat about the weather, the ceremony and pretend nothing was wrong because teenagers often didn't want to talk to their parents—it was excruciating. Or he could do what he knew was right. He could tackle the elephant in the room. Man to man. Father to son. He picked up Liam's tie and robotically threaded it through his fingers. The slip of the silk was somehow hypnotic. Soothing.

"You know, you don't have to go through with this, Liam. If you are having any second thoughts, this is the time to say so. We, your mum and I, will help you out, mate. We can sort it all out." Liam said nothing in response. Ben found himself repeating his point. "You really don't have to do this."

"You know I do." Liam took the tie from his dad. He put it round his neck.

"You could at least slow things down, take a breather."

"The baby has its own timetable. I can't slow down

a baby," pointed out Liam. "Even if I wanted to and I'm not saying I do want to."

"This is because your mum was on her own with you in the beginning, isn't it?"

Liam sighed and then slowly nodded. "I don't want Abi to feel alone. I don't want the baby to feel alone."

Ben slumped into the armchair at the end of the bed. "Do you feel alone, son? Even now? I thought I'd—" Ben's voice cracked a little. "I thought I'd fixed that."

"You did. You have. That's just it. You've been an amazing dad. You still are. The best. And I want to be like you. Not like the man who made me, then fucked off, careless of his responsibilities. Careless of consequences."

"But that was different."

"Not really."

"Abi is older than your mum was when she got pregnant, and she has resources."

Liam nodded. "Right, Abi can go out to work and I'll be a stay-at-home dad. That's why we agreed I don't need to carry on with my education."

"But you wanted to go to university."

"Yeah, I did, but things change."

"That doesn't have to. You could still do a degree."

"Abi thinks it would be better for the baby if I focus on him or her."

"Abi does?"

"We *both* do." Liam turned away from his dad and studied his own reflection; he carefully started to knot his tie. "Look, Dad, haven't you always taught me to do the right thing?"

"I have, but that's just it. I'm not sure this is the right thing."

"The way I see it, it's simple. If I'm old enough to make a baby, I'm old enough to look after that kid."

But it wasn't that simple and Ben, a man, knew as much. Liam, a glorious, well-intentioned, earnest boy-man, didn't. Ben realised that Liam would prefer to let the matter drop now but he couldn't. He had to ask, "Liam, do you love Abi? You've said before that you did, but have things changed now you've lived together?"

"Dad." Liam looked pained.

"Come on, son, answer me. Because whether you love Abi or not, and whether she loves you, that's all that counts."

"Of course she loves me. She's, like, obsessed with me." Liam glanced at his phone. "Shit, look at the time. I need a shave. We're going to be late." He strode into the bathroom and locked the door behind him.

Ben was inwardly rolling his eyes. The boy had just put his shirt and tie on, now he was getting a shave. He wasn't anywhere near ready to look after a baby, he couldn't quite look after himself.

That's when Ben heard the ambulance sirens outside the hotel. He looked out the window and could see a crowd of wedding guests gathering. Had someone overdone it with the champagne already? It was such a hot day. Or maybe something was wrong with his mother, or Mel's parents.

"Liam, I'm just going to see what the commotion is. I'll be back in a few minutes," he called through the bathroom door and then sped out the room.

CHAPTER SIXTY-ONE

MELANIE

I froze; for one shameful, dreadful moment, I did nothing. I just watched her lying there—her limbs tangled and twisted, her body unnaturally still. And do you know what I thought? I thought she was dead. And I was relieved.

I look at the policewoman, who has been talking to me for over ten minutes now, and I wonder whether I've just said that out loud. Maybe, from the uneasy look on her face.

She has a no-nonsense face, the sort that never looks young but therefore ages well. She'll be the woman who, on her fiftieth birthday, people will sincerely compliment and swear she hasn't changed a bit. She's wearing a little black bowler hat with black and white checks on it. It's flattering. I almost tell her she suits a hat. Not many people do. It's the sort of compliment that I readily give in the shop but I stop myself as I realise how inappropriate I'd sound. She's also wearing a belt, off which hang handcuffs, a baton, something that looks like a pepper spray and a host of other office equipment. She's twice spoken into a radio. Her accessories are horrendously sobering.

I think I'm in shock. Tanya has been led away by some medic because she was shaking so violently. You didn't need to be a trained professional to see what a mess she was, but no one has offered me a sugary drink. I wish they would. They've taken Abi away, too. Bleeding, battered, shattered Abi.

"You are not being charged at this point. We're just inviting you in to give a statement," the policewoman tells me.

"I need to go with my friend. I need to follow the ambulance," I insist.

"I'm afraid that's not possible."

"Is she conscious?"

"Someone said she did say something."

"What did she say?" I ask eagerly.

The policewoman flips over her notepad to read her own notes. I get the feeling this is an unnecessary gesture, some sort of show, for my benefit. She knows the answer to my question. "The patient in the ambulance was mumbling, drifting in and out of a fully conscious state, but it appears she said, 'Keep that woman away from me.'"

"That woman being me?" I ask.

"It appears so. What is your relationship to the injured party?"

"I'm her friend." I don't know if this is true. I don't

want to lie to a police officer so I add, "Well, I was her friend. Once. I was about to become her mother-in-law." The policewoman wrinkles her forehead a fraction. "She was supposed to be marrying my son today. He's just turned eighteen," I add, but I realise that doesn't offer any clarity, or maybe it offers too much.

The policewoman says, "I see."

"Has anyone told my son about Abigail? He'll want to go with her to the hospital."

"You don't need to worry about that right now." But I do. "You need to come with us." Oh, I see.

The girls watch me being led away by two police officers; that, just after they've seen Abi plummet down the stairs. It is horrifying. They're both sobbing, confused and scared. I'm relieved to see that my mum has appeared from nowhere. Thank goodness. She keeps saying to me, "It's OK, honey. I'm with the girls. I have your babies. I'll find Ben. Go with the policewoman now."

Her voice is soothing and her eyes plead with me. *Go quietly. Be polite. Don't make a fuss*. She thinks I've pushed Abi down the stairs. My own mother.

Someone puts their hand on my head and eases me into the back of the patrol car. I am aware of guests still hanging about, mouths open in shock or to pass on gossip. The hotel staff are running around, panicked, trying to get the guests off the street. I look for Ben and Liam but can't see either of them. I can only hope they are together.

The back of the car smells of sweat and fear. I wonder whether it is my own. I'm not cuffed because I haven't been charged, I've come voluntarily, just to give a statement of events.

However, I heard the photographer scream repeatedly, "She did it. I saw her. They were fighting and that woman shoved the bride." She was pointing at me. I heard this and so did the policewoman who was talking to me. The one who is sat in the passenger seat in front of the car right now. I know I'm in trouble.

I pray for Abi in the back of the police car. For Abi and for her baby. I'm not big on prayer. God must think I'm a lousy bet; I only ever appear when I want something: safe deliveries of my babies, happy friendship groups for the girls, a promotion for Ben, good results for Liam and now for Abi to live. For Abi and her baby to make it, because she doesn't deserve to die. The crazy, angry, misguided woman doesn't deserve to die. I hope maybe he'll answer my prayer because he'll know I really want to pray for myself, pray that I'll be going home to my family tonight, pray that I'm not going to be blamed and punished, but I'm holding back. I'm trying to be a good person. A better person. I'm trying to make amends.

At the police station, I'm led into a small, airless room with a grubby Formica table and three uncomfortable-looking plastic chairs; one is at the side of the room, the other two are at the table in a face-off. The unadorned room is set up to be daunting, comfortless. Naturally, it's a place where criminals are interviewed.

There is a policeman waiting to take my statement. The policewoman who brought me here hands me over and then says she has to be elsewhere. I stare after her, much the way a toddler might stare after her mother on the first day at nursery school. I miss her sensible face that suits hats. It is ridiculous to have formed any sort of attachment but I feel even worse than I did on the hotel stairs; I feel lonelier. The policeman with the pen and notebook, who is waiting to take my statement, is in his forties. He's carrying a few extra pounds as well as the weight of dealing with all that is wrong with the world. I sense his disappointment in me. I feel ashamed.

I tell him what I can. I didn't push or shove Abigail Curtiz. I didn't touch her at all.

He writes that down. His passive face does not betray whether he believes me or doubts me, but he observes (almost gently), "We have a witness statement to the contrary."

"The photographer?"

"Yes." The policeman sits up an inch straighter and makes another note. He looks quite pleased with himself, as though what I've just said is akin to a confession.

To clarify, I add, "Yes, I heard her say that—well, yell it—but it's not true."

"Then why would she say it?"

"She's mistaken. She was taking photos."

"Let's go over your statement one more time, shall we?" It isn't a question. "See if there's anything you've left out."

And so I tell them. Yes, I was rowing with Abi. Yes, I know her. Yes, we were having a dispute. I suppose you could call it a family dispute. Yes, I can give details if they think it's really necessary.

He does.

The tale sounds sorry and sordid. It is. The police clearly think I have a motive for pushing Abi. I do. Liam. Liam. What must he be thinking now? Who is he with? I've watched enough cop shows to know I am in trouble. I wonder about asking for a lawyer but would asking for one make me look guilty? I don't know and I'm struggling to be logical. I'm too law-abiding for this to be my life.

"What do you think Abigail Curtiz will say when she can make a statement?" the police officer asks.

"I have no idea," I say with a sigh. It's not like she can be relied upon to tell the truth and she's no friend to me. "Is she well enough to make a statement? Is she even conscious?" I am concerned for her but I fear my question sounds self-motivated, as though I'm hoping she can't make a statement. "How's Tanya?" I ask.

"Tanya?"

"The photographer's assistant." I shouldn't have mentioned her. "She seemed very upset. Almost hysterical."

"We ask the questions around here," says the policeman stonily.

After an hour and a half, most of which I spend alone, like a child on some incredibly serious naughty step, I am brought a cup of tea by another police officer. "When can I go home?" I ask.

"Whenever you like," she confirms. "You're here voluntarily." I wonder if it's a trick but she smiles at me. "We have your statement now. Plus, I think they have everyone else's who was at the scene, too, so really there's no need for you to be here. Go home to your family."

I immediately pick up my jacket and leave the tea. I realise that I didn't bring my bag with me, so I have no money or phone. I suppose it must be in Abi's suite at the hotel; that's the last time I remember having it. I'm too embarrassed to mention this to the police— it's hardly their problem. I don't want to ask to borrow their phone to ring Ben, I just want to get out of here. I'll find a taxi driver and pay them when I get home. The important thing is just to get out.

As I walk back into the reception, I see Gillian Burton waiting for me. She spreads her arms wide and I collapse into her bosomy hug, only just holding back tears of relief.

"Ben is with Liam at the hospital. Your parents wanted to come but I persuaded them to stay with the girls."

I appreciate that she's given me the exact information I need. Where my family is. Who is looking after my children. "Thank you, Gillian. So much." Polite concern compels me to ask, "Have you been hanging around long?"

"Ben called me the moment you were led away by the police. He knew you'd want him to stay with Liam."

"You've been here almost two hours?"

"Don't mention it. What are friends for?"

Gillian drives me home calmly and efficiently. She extends the favour and further proves the depth of her friendship by not asking any questions other than, "I bet you could do with a cup of tea?" I'm so utterly grateful to have her sensible, solid presence by my side. How could I have ever undervalued this friendship, one that is centred around ballet classes and childcare arrangements? Suddenly that seems like the most wonderful foundation for a relationship imaginable.

When I get home, the house is full; my parents, Ellie, the girls, Gillian and Becky and their kids and husbands are all dashing about. I'm offered tea about a hundred times. It's painfully obvious that the adults want to ask for details of my ordeal but can't do so in front of the children. Gillian and Becky swiftly and discreetly say they'll leave us to it and usher their families out of the door. My mum and Ellie slip into the garden with Lily and Imogen. My dad says, "We're here, when you're ready to talk about it."

"Have you heard from Liam and Ben?" I don't want to talk to anyone until I have spoken to them.

"They rang from the hospital. I don't think they know anything about Abigail. No one will talk to them. Liam's status as her fiancé isn't being taken particularly seriously, I'm afraid."

"I'm going to have a shower. I feel…unclean."

Ben and Liam get home just after 8:00 p.m. Surprisingly, the girls are already in bed. I'd thought we'd never get them to sleep because they'd be hyper or alarmed by the events of the day, but in fact the shocks have taken their toll and they were both sound asleep by seven. My parents wanted to stay with me but I practically pushed them out the door and I insisted that Ellie take up their offer to stay with them so that Liam, Ben and I could have some time alone together. They only agreed to leave when I promised that if Ben and Liam didn't make it home within the hour I'd call, then one of them would come back so I wouldn't be alone.

I'm glad of the backup plan but I'm delighted I don't have to use it. When I see our car pull onto the drive, I jump up, buzzing with relief, excitement but also trepidation and concern, a cocktail of dizzying emotions. I don't know what reception to expect. I hear Ben's key in the lock, I see my men in the hallway, and then I feel my son in my arms.

I run to him, fling my arms around him, not knowing whether he'll push me away, not even worrying about it. I just need to hold him. Then Ben folds himself over us like a blanket and we all cling to one another for a long time, like survivors picked from a stormy sea.

"How's Abi?" I ask the moment we break from the hug.

Ben answers my question. "We just don't know. No one is telling us anything. One nurse let slip that she has a concussion and some broken ribs. I think she's probably going to be OK but we don't know anything about the baby." Ben shakes his head sadly.

Abi was bleeding when they lifted her onto the stretcher. A dark stain on her beautiful dress. I turn to Liam once again. "I'm so sorry, my darling." He shrugs—it's not a careless shrug, it's a helpless one. "Can't you get any information as the father of the baby?"

"They are being very circumspect. They said they only have my word for it that I am the father of the baby."

"So, she can't be conscious then because she'd have told them," I comment.

"I just don't know," says Liam.

He doesn't know what to say or do. I don't even know what to hope for. I throw my arms around him again and then it strikes me, I am not hugging him, he is hugging me. My head rests on his chest and he's patting my back. My man son.

It's been such a hot day that the air is still warm. Normally, in temperatures such as these, we'd sit in the garden, perhaps with a glass of wine. Instead, we settle around the kitchen table as we can't risk the neighbours overhearing us. I pour us each a glass of lemonade. We need the sugar and we don't need to be woozy.

I start to tell them about my day. About how I went to Abi with high-minded plans, how those quickly deteriorated, how we started to argue.

"Why? Over what specifically?" Liam asks.

I don't know how to reply. I know if I tell him everything, he will be utterly devastated. Abi is lying in a hospital, we don't know if she'll hold to his baby; I can't choose this moment to tell him she doesn't love him, that she only used him to get pregnant, specifically to forge a connection between her and her ex, his father. I can't tell him that much of her reasoning to do this was to punish me. It's too much, too dreadful. Today in particular, it would be an impossible thing to hear. The day he thought he was getting married. However, I know I can't tell him any more lies. It's because I've told lies that we are all in this position. Liam must read from my expression that I'm struggling with deciding what to tell him.

"Come on, Mum, I'm a big boy. All grown up."

And he is. Well, almost. "We were rowing about your father. Your biological father," I admit.

"That makes no sense."

"Liam, I'm so sorry, my darling, this is going to be a huge shock." Ben takes hold of my hand and squeezes it to encourage me. "I should have told you a long time ago. You had every right to know." I nervously glance at the table—taking in the salt and pepper shakers, the tall glasses, a smudge of tomato sauce left over from the girls' tea—hating having to look into my son's eyes.

"Go on."

I finally meet his gaze. "Rob Larsen is your father."

Liam lets out a snort of disbelief. "Rob, as in Abi's bastard ex-husband?" he asks. I nod. "Shit, that's literally like being told Darth Vader is your father. I'm bloody Luke Skywalker."

I almost laugh because his response is so youthful, so uncontainable. It's impossible to know what the right response could be to this news, but I think in this situation, which is awash with impossibilities, his response is perfect.

"Well, now at least I understand a little more about why you were so against me and Abi getting together. I guess it felt a bit claustrophobic. 'Of all the bars in all the towns.'"

It feels so good to hear Liam tease me again. Even

if his humour is something close to gallows humour. I have missed his cheeky irreverence, his irrepressible spirit and I'd forgotten about his resilience. He's a gentle soul but he's also tough. I'm glad. When Abi moved in with us, he changed. No doubt because he fancied her, and then because he was having an affair with her, he became more restrained and severe, at least towards me. I guess it was an attempt to impress her, a desperate effort to appear more adult.

"So, you had an affair with Abi's boyfriend at university?" Liam asked.

"More of a fling. I told you, it was a one-night thing."

If Liam still feels inclined to judge me, Ben heads it off because he adds, "Your mum was nineteen, just a year older than you are now."

"I get it, immaturity leads to mistakes."

"You were never a mistake," I assure him swiftly.

"No, I'm bloody marvellous, but sleeping with your best friend's boyfriend is a mistake," points out Liam.

"Sleeping with your mother's best friend isn't exactly a well-thought-out move," adds Ben.

"Touché," says Liam with a laugh. Then more seriously, he asks, "So did Rob Larsen always know he was a father?"

"Yes," I admit.

Liam looks sad but not surprised. "And did Abi know it, before today? Or did you tell her today? Was that why you rowed?"

"She knew it before she came to the UK."

"Really?" Ben's eyebrows shoot up to meet his hairline because this is news to him.

"Yeah, she told me so today. *That's* why we rowed."

Liam nodded and observed, "I guess me being his biological son didn't bother her as much as it bothered you, or else we'd never have become a thing."

In that moment, I am so grateful for his uncomplicated, innocent, almost self-centred view of life. Liam has not considered that Abi might have had darker reasons for seducing him and his naivety will protect him, at least for a while. At least for tonight.

Then Ben asks, "What happened at the police station?"

"It was surreal. I can't believe I've been questioned in a police station about an actual crime. Me."

"Did they press charges?" asks Ben gently.

"No." I don't add *not yet*, although that is my feeling, they might. This isn't over.

"Did they cuff you?" asks Liam, with a hint of alarm.

"No."

"Or put you in a cell?"

"No, no, nothing like that." I want to reassure him. "They gave me a cup of tea but it was a bit frightening. An ordeal. It's all a big mix-up. The photographer apparently thinks she saw me push Abi down the stairs."

Suddenly, Liam stands up. "Look, I'm going to go up to bed. I want to have another go at getting through to Abi at the hospital, at least see if they'll tell me anything more. And then I need to crash."

I get it, he needs to be alone. He needs some space from me and even Ben. I'm scared that I've said too much, that I've upset him. "Are you OK, darling? Look, don't worry about me. It will all sort out."

"Yeah, I know." Weariness has swallowed him. I can see it in his every movement. He looks as though he's carrying a tank around on his back. We say goodnight.

I resist jumping up and holding him again. Even though I want to sponge up as many hugs as possible following the dearth of them over the past months, I understand that he needs his space. Ben and I listen as Liam drags his feet upstairs. We hear the bathroom door open and close behind him. It sounds so reassuringly normal to hear him go about his ablutions.

"So, he didn't want to go back to his flat tonight?" I ask.

"No, I asked him. He said he wanted to come home."

"Did he say 'home'?"

"Yeah, he did." Ben smiles at me and we both sink into the moment, one of relief and gratitude. "Do you fancy a glass of wine now?"

"I do, but I'm going to resist. I need to keep a clear head."

"In that case, Ribena or elderflower cordial?"

"Elderflower cordial, please."

Ben stands up, and while he has his back to me, he says, "Your experience at the police station sounds awful."

"Well, it wasn't a picnic and I don't think it's over yet." I accept the glass he's handed me. "Did you notice that in all the questions Liam asked, there was one he didn't bother with?"

"Which was what?"

"He didn't ask me whether I pushed her."

"He'd never think that of you," says Ben reassuringly. Then after a beat, he adds, "Did you push her?"

"Ben! No." I'm not offended that Ben has asked this. I feel he's entitled for the avoidance of doubt. His question is a consequence of me feeding him information on a need-to-know basis for over a decade.

"Don't get me wrong, I didn't think you'd maliciously set out to hurt her, but I couldn't rule out the possibility that she somehow had provoked you. I know you've been under a lot of strain and I know you'll do anything for Liam, for any of our children."

"Well, she did provoke. She said she came here to get pregnant by Liam, as a sort of proxy to Rob. She said she was owed as much because I stole her opportunities to become a parent with Rob when I fell pregnant."

"What? That makes no sense."

"She said that she just wanted to steal him away from me and to destroy his opportunities, to get him to give up college and even leave the country. To punish me."

"Fuck. Are you sure you didn't push her? I might have if I'd been there."

"No, I didn't." I sigh. "But Tanya did."

Ben is shocked, stunned. "Tanya?"

"I hadn't even realised she was there. I was too caught up with rowing with Abi, but she was there. She was the photographer's assistant. Well, not really, but that's who everyone thought she was, and I think the photographer assumed she was with the hotel."

"I'm not following."

"She sneaked in to Abi's room. I'm not sure why, exactly. I imagine it was for some sort of showdown. I didn't notice her, there was too much going on, but she heard everything Abi was saying to me. All the taunts and threats and accusations. She pushed Abi. I saw her do it. She was right next to me."

"You've told the police this, Mel?"

"No, no, I haven't."

"But you are going to." Ben is a picture of concern. I think he knows me well enough to correctly anticipate, and therefore dread, my answer.

"I don't know. I'm not sure I can let Abi draw another young person into this mess. Our mess. If I point the finger and they believe me, they'll charge Tanya. She'll have a criminal record. Her life will be over before it's begun. Ben, she wants to be a vet, with a practice in the country. That's not going to happen if she gets charged with assault."

"But if they don't charge her, then they'll charge you."

"Maybe, but they have no evidence I did it, because I didn't do it, so a charge won't stick."

"I'm not sure that will be the case, Mel. Things don't always work out that way. And anyway, you said the photographer made a statement declaring that she saw you do it."

"Through her lens, yes, but she made a mistake."

"Then you'll have to refute that."

I shake my head. "I don't know what to do."

Ben weighs it up. "And you think the charge will be assault?"

"I do, but there are varying degrees of assault. A lot depends on Abi."

"Abi?"

"How serious her injuries turn out to be and to what extent she wants to pursue the matter. I heard a lot of confusing things at the police station. Common assault, actual bodily harm. If—" I break off. It's too sad.

"If what?"

"If things go really badly for Abi and the baby, then the charge will be grievous bodily harm."

Ben shakes his head, at a loss. "What can we do?"

"We can hope. That's all. Just hope."

CHAPTER SIXTY-TWO

ABIGAIL

Monday, 25 June

It hurt, everything hurt. Her ankle, her ribs, her head. Those parts of her body throbbed, admittedly with an intensity that she hadn't felt before, but at least the sensation was familiar. The pain between her legs was different. She felt tender, precarious.

She had told them that she didn't want visitors, they were not to admit anyone. She had medical insurance and a private room. She didn't want to speak to or see a single soul. They were not to discuss details of her condition, no matter who asked.

The nurses looked concerned when she issued this instruction. They believed visitors could be cheering, valuable. "People want to know you are conscious and comfortable. Your friend Melanie has called about half a dozen times."

"Tell her nothing, or I'll sue you," snapped Abi. The nurses rolled their eyes, used to empty threats and worse.

Later, Abi was told, "There's a young man here to see you. He says he's your fiancé."

"He's a fantasist. Don't let him in," she commanded, then she turned her head away from the door, looked towards the wall. She didn't move her body. Not an inch.

On the second day, Abi had called the estate agents who managed the apartment she was renting. She'd explained her circumstances, and for a fee, she secured their cooperation. Other people no doubt would ask friends to help out, but Abi had no friends here in the UK—there had only ever been Mel. The estate agent could delegate to professional removal people. They would pack everything up. Her clothes and possessions in one case, his in another. They had to clear the baby's room. She told them what to bring to her, what to leave in the apartment. "You can do as you please with everything else."

On the third day, when Abi was checking out, she decided she was ready to take Mel's call; it came at 10:00 a.m. Abi had just signed all the necessary papers for her release and was tentatively walking down the hospital corridor. She felt like her body was made of delicate glass.

"What do you want, Melanie?" she asked.

"How are you, Abi?" Mel's voice was full of concern. It was peculiar, confusing. She had no right to be concerned. "We've been trying to get some news. No one would tell us a thing. Liam has been going out of his mind with worry." And yet, Abi noted wearily, it was his mother calling. Persisting. Abi sighed. Her fiancé was a boy, after all. "So, how are you?" asked Melanie, again; breathless, anxious.

"Hollow."

Mel gasped, taking the meaning of Abi's response just as Abi intended. "The baby?" she asked fearfully.

"Gone."

"Abi, I am so—"

"Don't say it. Just don't fucking say it, Melanie. You are not sorry." Abigail could hear Melanie's breathing down the phone; it was jagged, ripped, but she didn't say a word. Abi kept walking. "This is what you wanted." Her tone was accusatory, angry.

"No, it isn't. I didn't want any of this and I am sorry for you." Mel sounded almost calm, certainly controlled. It was infuriating, insulting.

"The police have been here, questioning me about what I remember. I get the feeling they think my fall down the stairs wasn't accidental. Your name came up."

"Really."

Abi had expected Melanie to sound more desperate, to deny it more vehemently. She was usually so panicked, so apologetic and therefore easy to manipulate. Abi was disappointed by Mel's reaction, strangely hurt by it. She tried to goad her. "They seemed very interested in the fact that we were rowing and they wanted to know where you were standing when I fell."

"You can't remember, can you?" Mel asked.

Abigail wondered how to answer. She could lie.

Finish this. Finish Mel. Blame someone for her hurt, for her pain. However, the truth was, no, she couldn't remember. The last thing she remembered was kneeling down to pick up her photos of Rob. She'd had a concussion. People often lost a few moments of their life after a concussion, especially those leading up to the injury. Maybe it was the body's way of dealing with trauma; it blanked out the horror, to enable healing.

Still, there would be nothing easier than saying she could remember the feel of someone's hands on the base of her back. No one could prove otherwise. If she closed her eyes and concentrated, she could imagine the feeling of being shoved. Hands giving her a jolt, leaving an imprint that scorched her, as though she was branded. Yes, she could easily imagine that. Almost remember it. She didn't know if Mel had pushed her, but she wasn't an idiot, she had gathered from the police officers' questions that they thought maybe someone had. Mel deserved to be blamed and Abi had never been overly attached to the truth if it wasn't expedient for her.

But then, if she told the police that, there would be a court case. She'd have to stay around here. She didn't want that. She wanted to get away. Far away, as quickly as possible.

"Liam wants to see you, Abi."

Abi strode down the corridor, pressed the button for the lift. "I don't want to see him. You have to tell him about the baby."

"Oh, Abi, I will if that's what you want, but the two of you need to work through this loss together."

"No, that's not what I need. I'm leaving."

"You're leaving?"

"I want to get away from here."

"What do you mean? Where will you go?"

"I might go back to the States, I might go to Australia. I just need some space. Will you tell Liam?"

"You must to talk to him. He should hear it from you."

Abi was surprised. She'd thought that Mel would do anything to stand between Abi and her precious boy. She had not expected Mel to dignify their relationship, not even the end of it. She'd expected to be able to ring the death knell without any resistance. Impatiently Abi said, "For fuck's sake, Melanie. It's not much to ask, is it? It's what you wanted. I'm going away. I'm not taking your son with me. Isn't this all your Christmases at once?"

"But why go?"

"I don't want him anymore." She hung up.

CHAPTER SIXTY-THREE

MELANIE

"Liam, get your coat," I scream up the stairs.

The urgency of my voice grabs his attention immediately—he knows I'm not going to ask him to pop out for a carton of milk. He shoots his head out of his bedroom door, concern making his brow furrow. "What is it?"

"We need to get to the hospital, now. Abi needs you."

I drive as fast as I possibly can; Liam keeps asking me what is going on. "I spoke with Abi."

"What did she say?" He looks apprehensive. "How is she?"

"You need to see her. I'll explain when you see her. Or she will." I can't say anything more. I screech my car to a halt outside the hospital doors and tell Liam to get out. "I'll move the car and catch you up."

I park the car as quickly as I can, cursing each second that's ticking by as I queue for a parking ticket, scrabble in my purse for the right coins and then run to the hospital reception. I don't know if this is the right call; maybe I should have simply passed on Abi's message, let her disappear from our lives, just melt away, but I feel my son is owed more than that. He ought to have the chance to say goodbye to Abi and to their baby. It's his right, and while Abi might not want to give him that level of respect, I do.

At the hospital reception, I give Abi's name but before the receptionist can tell me which ward she is on, I feel someone tap me on the arm. I turn and see Liam standing next to me. "She's checked out," he says. "I've already asked about her. They said she checked out."

"We'll try your apartment." I grab his arm and start pulling him back towards the car. "You'll regret it if you don't try to find her," I insist.

We drive to their apartment. Liam has to give me directions as I've obviously never visited. He still has his key and so we don't knock but let ourselves in. The minute I enter the flat, I know all I need to know. It is beautifully furnished, tasteful and plush, yet it feels empty, deserted. There is a suitcase parked in the middle of the hall. Liam opens it. I can see over his shoulder; I recognise the T-shirts. He stands up, shakes his head with incomprehension.

I move into the sitting room. It's immaculate and impersonal. A show home. I don't spot a single personal possession or any sign that anyone lives here. There are no stray trainers, no discarded video games spilling out of their boxes as I might imagine, no headphones, books or magazines. It seems that all Liam's clothes and possessions have been packed.

He now walks into the bedroom. I watch as he opens the wardrobe; it's empty except for coat hangers. Perhaps I imagine it, but I think they are still moving. Most likely a breeze, but it feels like we've only just missed her. I shiver, although I don't believe in ghosts.

Liam walks back into the hall and then heads into another room. I follow him. The walls are painted mint and white. There are silver stars painted on the ceiling and walls, clustering in one corner where there is also a moon. On one wall, written in gold paint, the words *Loved to the moon and back*. There is nothing else in the room.

"The cot? The changing mat? There was a mobile hanging here. It's all gone," he says.

I realise that Abi could not have had time to pack everything away since she called me. She must have had help or possibly checked out of the hospital before she rang me today. For all I know, she was calling from the airport. She might be on a flight now. A flight to goodness knows where. Once again, she had everything planned. Once again, she is a step ahead of me. I can't lie. I'm glad to see the back of her. I won't miss her. But Liam?

"She's gone?" he asks. I nod. "My baby? Gone, too?"

"The fall." My voice cracks.

Liam turns to me and we drop into each other's arms. I hold tight to my baby as he mourns the loss of his. We cling to each other until my arms begin to ache, until my tears make his T-shirt damp.

Liam pulls back. Nods his head as he takes one last look around. "Let's go home." He picks up his suitcase and then he slams the apartment door shut behind him.

CHAPTER SIXTY-FOUR

TANYA

Saturday, 30 June

My mum wants me to stay in bed. She thinks I'm having a breakdown. Maybe I am. I certainly do not feel anything near normal. Whatever that is. I suppose it is what I used to feel when I worried about exams or whether I could afford a pair of shoes I didn't need, whether I should or should not have eaten a second piece of cake. I can't imagine being concerned about anything so mundane anymore. Those everyday matters were forgotten when Liam split up from me and they were obliterated on his wedding day.

My doctor says I'm suffering from nervous exhaustion. A break-up and sitting important exams like A-levels can cause that; witnessing a traumatic accident triggers the sort of shock that may very well exacerbate a nervous condition. That's what my doctor thinks. She's recommended rest, quiet for a few days.

My diagnosis is that committing a crime can send you nuts.

I killed a baby. I didn't mean to, but it's my fault the baby is dead. I told my mum as much and she says I'm confused.

I'm not confused. I'm disgusting.

My mum tried to keep the news of Abigail Curtiz losing the baby from me but it's all over social media. Of course it is. Some people have been sending their condolences to Liam—sad-faced emojis and things like that—others have just been gossiping about the whole mess behind his back.

Mum does not want me to call Mrs. Harrison—she's said so three or four times, in fact she says so every time I suggest that I should. Mum does not want me to speak to anyone connected with what she calls the "whole terrible business." Not even the police. Especially not the police. Even though they've asked for me to go into the station to make a statement about what I recall of the events. Mum told them I would, once I was up to it. I've told her I am up to it and she's told me that she knows best and she'll decide when I'm up to it.

Then yesterday, a week after the awful wedding that never was, Mum got another call from the police station saying that there was no need for me to make a statement after all, that they had all the information they needed on the matter now.

"What does that mean?" I demand.

My mum looks tired, tired of the whole business. "It means you can put it out of your head," she replies.

"But does that mean Mrs. Harrison has been charged with pushing Abigail Curtiz down the stairs?"

"I don't know." She says this in a way that means she doesn't care. My mum can hardly bear to hear the name Harrison in our house.

"I need to ring her," I say, sitting up in bed, scrabbling around for my phone.

"No, you don't," says my mum firmly.

"I do," I insist. "Mrs. Harrison didn't do it!"

"No one is saying she did."

But Mum has to go to work and can't babysit me forever; the moment she leaves the house, I call Mrs. Harrison. I have to call their home phone because I don't have her mobile number. As it rings, I panic, dreading the possibility that Liam will pick up. I heard he moved back there. To my great relief, it's Mrs. Harrison who answers. "Melanie speaking."

"Mrs. Harrison, it's Tanya here."

"Tanya, sweetheart, how are you?" Her voice oozes concern, which immediately makes me want to cry. My eyes sting and I scrunch them up.

"It's my fault the baby is dead," I gush. "I pushed Abi." The words tumble out, I can no more keep them in than I can keep the tears in.

"No, you didn't," she says carefully.

"I did. I hate myself. I killed that baby." I start to sob now because it's too awful. I hated Abigail Curtiz for what she did to me and Liam, I might even hate her still, but I never planned on hurting her and I'd never have deliberately hurt an innocent baby. Never.

"You are not to blame." Mrs. Harrison sounds firm. "You aren't remembering events clearly. You were overwrought when it happened and shocked since. You're confused. Abigail tripped."

"No." My tears are coming thick and fast now. Shame and sorrow flood from me, compounded by Mrs. Harrison's obvious desire to protect me, rather than punish me, which is what I deserve.

"Yes, she said she tripped."

"Abigail did?"

"Yes. She sent an email to the police station yesterday saying that she's regained full memory of the events and she remembers her heel getting caught in her dress and losing her footing."

"Seriously?"

"Yes."

While I think Mrs. Harrison would say anything to make me feel better, I can't imagine Abigail Curtiz doing me any favours. It must be true. I must have remembered things falsely. This news doesn't bring the baby back, it doesn't fix everything, but it does assuage my guilt.

"How's Liam?" I ask. My voice is small. I'm humiliated that I care still, but you can't switch feelings on and off like a tap, even if you want to, even if it would be wise or convenient.

"He's sad," admits Mrs. Harrison. "But he'll be OK."

"I'm so very sorry," I whisper.

"I know you are. We all are."

"What can I do?" I ask.

"What you need to do now, Tanya, is to go to Liverpool, study hard, become a vet and put all this behind you. You deserve to be happy and you must decide to be so."

CHAPTER SIXTY-FIVE

MELANIE

Tuesday, 3 July

"Rob, it's Melanie Harrison here." I pause and then for clarity add, "Melanie Field." The words seem strange on my lips. Melanie Field was a lifetime ago.

"Yes." He sounds polite but cautious. I know he does at least recognise my name because he coughs and asks, "What can I do for you?" He thinks I'm bringing trouble to his door. That's what he believes I've always done. I sigh and refuse to care what he thinks of me.

"Are you alone? Can you speak for a few minutes?" I've never felt entitled to his time. The brief hours we spent together that resulted in Liam were stolen; the time I visited him to tell him I was pregnant and he offered me money to abort felt sneaky, pilfered. Now I take my time and his. He owes me. I'm entitled, or at least, Liam is.

I tell him everything I can. Embarrassed, I recall how I flung open my doors to Abi; he doesn't ask why. Maybe he doesn't care or maybe he cares enough to understand that I felt I owed her. I'd betrayed her long ago and I needed to make it up; it's just possible that he has enough about him to understand that. I tell him that she had an affair with Liam.

"Your Liam? Your son?" he demands with incredulity. I hear how he is careful not to claim Liam and I don't know what that means. Is he being elegant and generous? Does he understand that Liam is mine and Ben's child, that he has no right to him? Or is it that he has no interest in him? I don't know and I don't know which I need it to be.

"Yes."

"The crazy bitch." I quickly tell him that their affair is over now. "You're sure about that?"

"Certain."

"How do you know they won't get back together?"

"I can't tell you everything. It's private between the two of them, but I can give you my word, it's over." I hope he can't hear the fear and pain in my voice. I hope he believes me. I've a favour to ask him. I never wanted to owe him a thing. I never wanted to prostrate myself in front of this man but I will for Liam. I'll do anything for Liam.

"He's the bloke in the video? That's why you're ringing me?" guesses Rob. There's a hint of bewilderment, possibly disgust in his voice.

My heart contracts. This is a risk. I don't know Rob well enough or at all. I made a child with him but I don't know him. It was biology, nothing more. I feel a flash of dread and panic. I should never have called. He could destroy Liam. He might do so to spite Abi or me or simply for the hell of it. I have no idea.

"Yes," I confess. "I'm ringing you to ask you to destroy the video. You got your quickie divorce. You are rid of Abi. You don't need the video anymore and I don't want Liam to have to start his adult life with this hanging over him."

"I see."

I think I can hear the cogs of his mind. He's weighing it up. I imagine he's wondering what would happen if he exposed Abi and Liam. He'd become the sympathetic party in their celebrity divorce. No doubt the opinions of their friends and colleagues have been swaying like a pendulum. He did, after all, have an affair—rumours will be emerging, women will be coming forward with stories of their own encounters, keen to claim their fifteen minutes of fame. It can't be good for his career or his ego to be badly thought of. This video scandal would take the spotlight of shame away from him and shine it on her.

What have I done? I should never have called. I should have left well alone. You'd think I'd know by now not to get embroiled in Rob's and Abi's messy lives.

"What the fuck did she do that for?" he mutters.

"She knew who Liam's father was and in some sort of twisted way used Liam to get closer to you," I say cautiously. I don't give him any more details. The pregnancy, the loss of the baby, is still too difficult to talk about. Her plan didn't work so Rob doesn't need to know quite how desperate and damaged Abi was.

I risk adding, "I suppose she loved you very much, in a crazy, obsessive way."

He sighs. "You say she targeted Liam for this video because she knew who his father was?"

"Yes."

"Well, Melanie, I know who his father is, too. I'll destroy the video. I'll never let it see the light of day. You have my word on that."

The relief is enormous. A tidal wave that nearly washes me off my feet. I breathe out and feel the tension leave my body, my shoulders, my head; my heartbeat regulates. I mutter, "Thank you."

"Of course. It's the right thing to do."

I admire his word choice. He didn't fall into the platitude of "it's the least I can do" or "it's nothing." He found words accurate and fitting. He's recognising something but demanding nothing. I imagine he's as relieved as I am to be closing the door on this. "Well, if there's nothing else?"

"No, nothing else," I assure him. "Goodbye."

He hangs up.

I don't imagine we'll be in contact again. I listen to the sound of a dead line. It sounds strangely soothing in its finality.

I turn to Ben, who has been nervously standing by my side, listening to my half of the conversation, supporting me and hoping, praying for the best outcome. His eyes are wide with concern, his eyebrows raised in anticipation. I smile and nod. He smiles back as I fall into his arms.

CHAPTER SIXTY-SIX

LIAM

Friday, 20 July

It's Mum's idea to do something to say goodbye to the baby. At first, I didn't know if I could bring myself to make a thing of it, but after a few weeks of walking around feeling lost, I admitted I probably needed to. I don't miss Abi. It surprises and shames me to realise as much, but I just don't. Those last couple of weeks that we lived together had started to get weird. I knew she was hormonal because of the pregnancy and stressed because of the wedding, but things changed between us. If it wasn't for the baby, I'd probably have called it a day, but I just couldn't. It wasn't an option.

Today is not about Abi, though, it's about the baby. We buy a pink balloon.

"Pink?" asks Mum.

"Yeah, I always had the feeling it was a baby girl."

"Did you?" She smiles.

I nod. "And even if it wasn't a girl, I'd have had the sort of son who was comfortable enough with his masculinity to be OK with pink. You know… I was terrified about becoming a dad," I admit to my mum.

She nods. "Understandable. Nearly everyone is terrified about becoming a parent."

"But I was also determined to make a good job of it. To be a good dad."

"And you will be, one day. You have time."

We let the balloon go at the children's play park. I picked somewhere noisy and vibrant. Not sad at all. Dad asks if I want to say anything. I don't. I don't want them to say anything either. It's enough that they are here, by my side, looking grim but supportive. A few of the kids in the park spot the balloon as it floats away. They leap up and try to catch the trailing ribbon, although there's no chance; it's out of reach. We watch it bob and drift until it floats right out of sight. I take a deep breath and whisper goodbye.

Then we walk to Wolvney Sixth Form College to enrol in upper sixth again. I'm going to have to repeat the year but I'm OK with that and luckily Mr. Edwards, the principal, is, too.

EPILOGUE

One year later

Abigail Curtiz was in love. She had not been certain that she'd ever fall in love again, but she had—more deeply, more profoundly and more assuredly in love than ever before. She realised now that being in love was not about subduing her own needs and desires, as she had with Rob for so many years, and it certainly was not about manipulating or controlling to get her own way, as she had with Liam. Thinking about both relationships was uncomfortable for Abigail. She'd made mistakes. Some dreadful ones. She's been extreme and even cruel.

Sometimes, she couldn't believe her luck. Sometimes, she didn't believe she deserved this little baby, with her sparkly flashy eyes which were so very beautiful although they were not blue like Liam's or Rob's, but brown, almost black, like her own.

Abigail's daughter, Mila, was safely delivered six months after her mother and father had been due to marry and now she was six months old. When she recognised this, Abi found herself thinking, *Time flies when you're having fun.* As the slightly banal cliché scuttled through her head, she thought of Mel, with her endless platitudes and faintly hackneyed truisms, and she found that she had a sudden affection for them, an understanding of them. Maybe it was motherhood, maybe it allowed for a softening or commonality.

Abigail and Mila lived together in southern Italy, in a small, white, dry-stonewalled house with a conical roof, called a trullo. When she had initially been hunting for somewhere simple and remote to escape to, she had stumbled across these pretty dwellings. She read that they were initially constructed as temporary shelters for agricultural labourers, in a particular historical period when the construction of stable dwellings was highly taxed. As a consequence, the clever inhabitants of the region boasted a great capacity to adapt. The trulli were now much sought after and had successfully transitioned from precariousness to stability. They somehow symbolised recovery and endurance. The limestone walls, cool in the summer, warmed by open fire in the winter, called to her.

Mila lay in the centre of the trullo, kicking on a rug as Abi collected together the things that they would need to spend the day at the beach. She stopped to stoop and kiss her baby's stomach, letting her lips melt into her delicious skin, which was as soft and velvety as fresh cream. Abigail drew in her daughter's smell, lovelier than recently cut grass or cakes baking in an oven and sweeter, purer, clearer than mint or lavender.

Mila started to grumble. Abi recognised the particular tone of the gripe. She was hungry. If she was not fed soon, she would start to scream, an unforgiving, piercing scream that would draw their lovely Italian neighbour out of her house with enquires of whether she could offer assistance. It was true, what was said about Italians: they loved babies. Abi had never felt alone here, with a constant stream of kind and interested people offering to hold the baby, play with the baby, feed the baby. Mila might not have a father, but she had a village. Abi felt no stigma about being a single mother in Italy; all mamas were beloved warriors here.

Abigail picked up Mila and pacified her with cuddles while she unfastened the buttons on her simple summer dress. This dress was one of Abi's favourites, not because it was especially flattering or fashionable, but because it offered easy and reasonably discreet access to her breasts. The baby started to feed, content. Abigail sighed, gratified. It still surprised her that she was good at this mothering business. A natural. That's what her own mother had said when she came to visit in the spring. Abigail had made some mistakes in life, but Mila wasn't one of them.

Abigail had left the wedding in an ambulance, bleeding, sure she was losing her baby. The one she'd tricked and schemed to secure. The one she had longed for and would love with all her heart. She'd never been a religious woman or even a superstitious one but suddenly she found herself making pleas, pacts and bargains. She promised whoever— God, fate, herself?—that she'd let Mel keep Liam if only she could keep her baby. That was all she'd ever really wanted him for anyway.

Her plan had been a selfish, merciless one, she saw that now. She had been driven by fury and pain to seek revenge and retribution. It was only when she thought she might lose her baby that she began to develop some understanding of what she had subjected Mel to. How Mel must have thought about losing Liam.

Abigail had thought she was owed; she'd believed Mel had cheated her and that she was justifiably equalling an old score. But lying in the ambulance, in physical and emotional agony, she had wondered for the first time whether perhaps she'd got it wrong. The hospital could bind up her foot and give her painkillers to ease the ache in her ribs, but all they could do about her baby was instruct her to lie still and to hope. At that point she was still bleeding, but the doctors said there was a viable heartbeat, a possibility. Her baby was a fighter.

Tanya had pushed her down the stairs. She knew that because a few days after the fall, she remembered it quite clearly. Abigail realised that Mel was under suspicion for the shove. The photographer had proven to be a slightly hysterical and very insistent individual. She said she was sure but in fact her view was obscured, through a lens. Her brain made the connection that Mel—an argumentative, angry woman—was the most likely suspect, while the helpful teen who had carried her bags of equipment seemed blameless. The photographer swore it was Mel who had committed the crime and the police had no reason to disbelieve her.

Abi could so easily have added fuel to the fire. Abi had a feeling that if she incriminated Mel, then Mel would do little or nothing to clear her own name, as she would not implicate Tanya—she would protect the teenager at all costs. She was obsessed with teenagers getting to live their youthful lives to the full, having the chance to unfurl and develop into adults, not to be forced, pushed, shoved into unexpected maturity. Abigail supposed it came from Melanie's own experience. Her time as a young adult had been curtailed; she had not been able to immerse herself in all that was gifted at that period of life: optimism, incredulity, naivety, innocence, fun.

Abigail supposed it was because Mel was selfless.

She could see it now. Mel had moved away from the university because she believed it would be the least damaging thing. The least hurtful thing for Abigail. Yes, she had slept with Abi's boyfriend, which was horrendous, but after that she had tried to make amends. Mel had wanted to minimise the disruption and pain for Abi, even if it cost her the chance of finishing her degree.

Abigail had lain in the hospital bed and considered the possibility that perhaps Mel had simply sent the photo of Liam to Rob on a whim, because she was proud of him, grateful even to Rob for helping create him, even though he'd never nurtured him. Maybe she was grateful that Rob hadn't been involved, that he'd let her forge a new life with Ben. Undeniably, things had worked out well for them. At least they had until Abigail had turned up.

Abigail admitted to herself that Mel had left her alone to enjoy her student years with Rob. Other young women might have decided that they didn't care that Abigail would be hurt; they might have stuck around, even tried to win Rob from her. Not that he was a prize. Abigail could see that now. After a lifetime of loving him, adoring him, worshipping him, she could finally see him for what he was: selfish, callous, pitiless. They'd managed very well together for a long time because Abi was also selfish. And callous. But not, it appeared, pitiless.

She emailed the police and said she remembered putting her heel through the hem of her wedding dress. She remembered tripping herself up.

She had moved away with her baby, because it was the least disruptive and painful route.

Abigail had been blinded with a furious sense of revenge, retaliation and retribution. Her mind had been temporarily clouded with rage, lust and want. She had tricked Liam, used him. But then she had set him free.

* * * * *

ACKNOWLEDGEMENTS

A heartfelt thank-you to my editor, Kate Mills, who is fabulously enthusiastic, dedicated and all-round brilliant! I'm so lucky to have you! Also, to Lisa Milton for the most wonderful warm welcome to HQ, Harper Collins.

I'm so delighted to be working with such incredible teams in the UK and across the globe. I am thoroughly grateful for and appreciative of the talent and commitment of every last person involved in this book's launch. I've been in this business for long enough to know that if a book is lucky enough to be successful, then that's because there's an enormous team of people doing their jobs incredibly well. Some of those people are JP Hunting, Georgina Green, Eleanor Goymer, Darren Shoffren, Sophie Calder, Claire Brett, Celia Lomas, Jack Chalmer and Louise McGrory. Thank you *all* very much.

Also I want to send a massive thank-you across the seas to James Kellow, Loriana Sacilotto, Margaret Marbury, Leo McDonald, Carina Nunstedt, Celine Hamilton, Pauline Riccius, Anna Hoffmann, Birgit Salzmann, Eugene Ashton, Olinka Nell, Rahul Dixit and many others whom I have yet to meet. Thank you for taking my novel from my desk in Surrey, England, to incredible places far and wide throughout the world. That's so ridiculously exciting. I'm incredibly grateful. Thank you, Jonny Geller, for eighteen years of support, encouragement and friendship. Eighteen years! We are quite simply an awesome team, right?!

Thank you to all my readers, bloggers, reviewers, retailers, librarians and fellow authors who have supported this book.

Thank you, Jimmy and Conrad, for everything. Always.

Finally, I'd like to warmly acknowledge Gillian Burton for her generous support of National Literacy Trust, an independent charity working with schools and communities to give disadvantaged children the literacy skills to succeed in life. It was a pleasure slipping your name onto one of my big-hearted characters.

Keep reading for a special sneak peek at
Lies, Lies, Lies
The next exhilarating novel from Adele Parks and
MIRA Books

2016

CHAPTER ONE

DAISY

Thursday, 9th June 2016

I don't think it is a good idea to bring Millie here to the clinic. I've said as much to Simon on half a dozen occasions. Besides the fact that she's missing her after-school ballet class and she'll be bored out of her mind, it isn't the sort of place children should be. There's the issue of being sensitive to the other patients for a start. It's too easy to imagine that people who are trying for a child adore every kid they encounter; it's not always the case, sometimes they outright dislike them, even adorable ones like Millie. It's too painful. Millie's tinkling chatter in the waiting room might inadvertently irritate, cause upset. It sounds extreme, but infertility is a raw and painful matter. Plus, I'm worried about what to do with her when we go into the consultancy room for a chat with the doctor. This is *only* a chat. That's all I've agreed to. Yet, I can't very well have her sit through a conversation about sperm and ovulation, the possibility (because it's not a probability) of her having a sibling. But nor am I comfortable with the idea of leaving her with the receptionist; she's just six.

We hadn't initially planned to bring her with us but at the last moment our childminding arrangements fell through, as child-minding arrangements are wont to do. We had little choice. I wanted to postpone the meeting. For ever, actually, but Simon was eager to get talking about the options and said postponing was out of the question.

"The sooner we know what's wrong, the sooner we can get it fixed," he said optimistically, his face alive with a big, hopeful grin.

"There's nothing wrong, we're just old," I pointed out.

"Older. Not old. Not too old. Lots of women give birth at forty-five years of age," he insisted. "Some of those are first-time mothers. The fact that we've already had Millie means you're in a better position than those women."

I think the fact that we already have Millie means we should leave the matter alone. Be content with one child. I think contentment is an extremely underrated life goal. Simon isn't interested in contentment. He likes to be deliriously happy or miserable. He'd never admit as much but we've been together seventeen years and I know him better than he knows himself. It seems to me that we have spent far too much of our married life in clinics such as this one.

Places with beige walls and tempered expectations, places that take your cash and hope but can't guarantee anything in return. When we had Millie—our miracle!—I thought all this aggravation, frustration and discontent was behind us for good. One is enough for me. I had thought, hoped, it would be enough for Simon.

Millie is perfect.

We shouldn't push our luck. I've always been a count your blessings sort of person. I don't want an embarrassment of riches, I prefer to scrape under the radar with a sufficiency. Simon and I do not think alike on this. Obviously, he agrees Millie is perfect. For him, it's her very perfection that's driving him want to make more babies.

For the last couple of years, more or less since Millie started pre-school, Simon has been saying we ought to try again. I've nodded, smiled, acknowledged his suggestion without entering into any sort of real discussion. I mean, in a way we are trying, at least we're not avoiding the possibility—we don't use contraception. However, at our age, with our history, that's not trying hard enough. We'd have to get some help if we want a second child. I know that. Recently, Simon has significantly upped the ante in terms of his persistence with this idea. He can't seem to just enjoy what we have.

Half term is a good example. We took a cottage in Devon because British families have been doing so for generations and, evidently, we lack the necessary imagination to buck the trend. This year we took a chance, selecting a new part of Devon that we hadn't previously visited. The cottage was dated but well-scrubbed, and whilst the water pressure made showering a slow and disappointing process, there was a fireplace, a beautiful kitchen and a shelf of puzzles and board games, so we thought the place was perfect. The garden opened to a footpath that led directly to the beach. I'm always surprised by beaches. They're never as restful or ideal for contemplation as I imagine. British beaches are noisy places: waves crash, seagulls squawk, the wind scrapes the sand, and children laugh, cry and shriek. It's best to accept this, embrace it. We're keen to offer Millie every opportunity that might be presented in an Enid Blyton novel so despite the sometimes iffy weather, we took long walks and endured breezy picnics without admitting to the chill. We went crabbing and scoured rock pools for mini creatures that delighted Millie. We were just a short drive away from a petting farm and a small village packed with pastel-colored buildings, where every second shop sold fish and chips. Yes, perfect.

It was hardly a retreat though. The place was too picturesque to remain a secret. Indeed, we'd discovered it because it was featured in a glossy Sunday newspaper supplement. Yet despite the identikit families trailing plastic buckets and shovels, we managed to carve out some privacy, some time to ourselves. We ignored the crowds and the queues, and we drew a magic circle around us. Naturally, Millie made friends with other children on the beach. She's confident, open and pretty, just the sort of kid other kids like to befriend, but when the parents of her new acquaintances invited us to join them for a scone at the café or a barbecue in their rental, we declined. We made up excuses, told small lies about already having plans and commitments. I'm not at all like Millie, I'm not confident about making new friends, I never have been. I was never what anyone would have considered a pretty girl. It's not the worst thing in the world, although some people seem to think it is. As a child, I concentrated on being kind and funny, well informed, with aspirations of being thought of as reasonably clever. It was enough. I got by. I have great friends now but I'm not a fan of making casual, transient relationships on holiday. Why bother? Besides, we were so blissful, just the three of us, we didn't want or need anyone else. Three is the perfect number. Fun facts: the Pythagoreans thought that the number three was the first true number. Three is the first number that forms a geometrical figure, the triangle. Three is considered the number of harmony, wisdom and understanding. I've always thought that three is particularly significant as it's the number that is most often associated with time: past, present, future; beginning, middle, end; birth, life, death.

I sigh, glancing around the fertility clinic reception, I really don't think we need to be here, trying for another baby. It's like we're pushing our luck. Being greedy. Asking for trouble. We're happy as we are.

Simon squeezes my hand. I think of the last night in the cottage. Millie was exhausted after a week of fresh air and long walks, she almost nodded off at the kitchen table over supper. We got her to bed by 7 p.m. and she was asleep the moment her head hit the pillow. Simon suggested we have a glass of wine in the back garden, make the most of our last night and the privacy that our cottage offered. There was a gas heater, one of those that's bad for the environment so I demurred, but Simon persuaded me, "Just once. Go with it."

Let's just say, the wine (not a glass but two bottles in the end) and the sound of the sea crashing on the beach, the novelty of spending time alone together without other people or even Netflix, had an effect. We made love under the stars and a blanket. It was exciting, daring. The last time we did anything as risky was so long ago I can't remember when it was exactly. Years and years ago. Afterwards, we lay snuggled up under the slightly scratchy picnic blanket, clinging to one another for warmth, and just allowed ourselves to be. Be relaxed. Be satisfied. Be enough. It was blissful. Until Simon kissed the top of my head and said, "Do you know the one and only thing that could make this moment more perfect?"

"A post-coital cigarette?" I joked. I've never been a smoker and Simon gave up when we first started dating. I know he still misses it, even after all this time he craves the nicotine hit. Simon likes hits and highs. I don't get it at all. I'm not the sort of person who values kicks above health.

"Well, that would be good, but no. I was thinking a baby, asleep in the other room."

"We have a baby asleep in the other room."

"We have a little girl," he said gently, not unkindly.

"Well, they can't stay babies forever."

"That's not my point."

I felt the warmth of his body along the length of mine and yet I still shivered. "You're serious?"

"I love Millie so much. And you," he added swiftly. "I can't bear to think that we're not giving her everything."

"We do give her everything we can," I pointed out.

"Other than a sibling," he countered.

"Yeah but it's not as though we tried to deny her that, it just hasn't happened. It's unlikely ever to because neither of us are getting any younger." And conceiving was never something we were good at. I don't add that. We don't talk about the horrors we went through to get Millie. It's generally agreed that the pain of childbirth is forgotten once you hold the baby in your arms. In my case it was also the pain of years of trying to conceive.

"We should make it happen. She's so gregarious and loving. I can't bear the idea of her missing out on having a sibling."

"Having a sibling isn't always a bonus," I argued. "You're not at all close to your sister."

"No, but you adore yours. I want Millie to have what you and Rose share." He turned to me and I saw fire in his eyes. I should have understood then that he wasn't going to let the matter drop. He's a very determined man when he wants to be.

Stubborn, my mum says.

CHAPTER TWO

SIMON

The waiting room was chilly. The air-conditioning was a little too vigorous. It was bright outside so people had risked T-shirts and sun dresses, except for Daisy, she always felt the cold so she was sitting in her jacket. It looked like she was ready to make a dash for the door at any moment. It looked like a protest. Simon knew Daisy didn't want to be there. He understood. He remembered the heartache associated with these sorts of places, certainly he did. And she was right, they were perfectly happy as they were, but his point was that maybe they could be happier still. Why not? Why settle?

When bored, or nervous, or stressed, Simon had a habit of repeatedly tapping the heel of his foot on the floor. This had the effect of causing his whole leg to continually jerk in violent shudders. He never noticed he was doing it until Daisy reached out and put her hand on his thigh, calming him, silently asking him to stop. She did that now. He stopped, picked up a newspaper and quickly flicked through it. There was nothing to hold his attention. Just reports of financial crises and politicians caught with their pants down, nothing new there. He put down the paper and started to whistle. He wasn't aware that he was doing so until Millie giggled and began dancing to his tune, probably saving him from a swift reprimand from Daisy. Daisy always forgave his restlessness, his quirkiness, if it entertained Millie. Despite the vicious air-conditioning he felt clammy. He could feel sweat prickle under his arms. God, he could do with a drink.

He had persuaded Daisy to visit the clinic on the understanding that they were just going to have a chat with Dr. Martell, one of the country's best fertility doctors. They were simply going to ask about their options, explore possibilities. That's what he'd told her. But he'd lied. He'd already visited Martell ten days ago for a general health check, as well as a specific test of the health and fitness of his sperm. He wanted to get things moving. Many years ago, he had been told that his sperm was slow but in the end that hadn't been a problem. It had been a case of the tortoise and the hare, Millie was proof of that. However, Daisy made a good point, he was aware that he was seven years older now than when they had conceived Millie, they both were, obviously. That didn't necessarily mean they were out of the game though, did it? Simon was keen to know if there had been any scientific advancements since then, something that could give his boys a bit of an advantage—or at least something that might level the playing field again. He was forever reading articles about the increase in the number of women having babies in later life. He thought that by taking the initiative and putting himself through the tests first, Daisy would be encouraged. He knew it was a lot to ask. The tests and possible subsequent treatments Daisy might require were significantly more arduous than anything he'd have to endure. IVF had been a slog. But it would be worth it.

He stopped whistling, but Millie didn't stop dancing. She was in a world of her own, clearly the music continued in her head. Maybe she was listening to a full orchestra. Maybe she was on stage at the Paris Opera House. She was a marvel! Millie had an incredible, exceptional talent. She danced beautifully. She was the sort of child who naturally bounced, flew and glided through her day. Daisy often commented that she was in awe of her daughter, as she hadn't been the sort of girl that anyone ever suggested ought to take dancing lessons: her nickname as a child—as bestowed on her by her family—was Fairy Elephant. She lolloped and lumbered, rather clumsily. As a boy, Simon had never been taken to dance lessons either, his family were far too conventional to consider that, but he liked to think he had been pretty good at throwing shapes on the dance floor (a phrase he used self-satirically); certainly, he was good at sport in general. He'd always thought that Millie had inherited her natural ability to dance from his side of the family, his sister had been a great gymnast and was quite good at tap as a child. She was certainly good at doing flits, thought Simon with a sigh. His sister had announced she was emigrating to Canada about a month after their mother was diagnosed with Alzheimer's. He kept telling himself it was a coincidence, but he didn't know for sure. It was certainly an inconvenience.

Millie adored all things frilly, pretty, floaty and twirling. Daisy had started her at dance classes just before she turned three. It's not that Daisy was a particularly annoying, overly-ambitious mother, it was simply that Millie needed to channel her energy and desire to coil and whirl somewhere. It turned out she was very good, quite extraordinarily so. Her dance instructor said that in her nineteen years of teaching, she had never seen equivalent talent, focus and drive in a child so young. Daisy was a teacher—not a dance teacher but a Year Six teacher at a state primary school—and she was aware of the value of that observation. She'd excitedly told Simon that teachers had to be very careful about what they said to parents, as parents all tended to get a little carried away. Everyone believed they'd produced a spectacular little miracle, when in fact most kids were within a normal range.

Although, evidently Millie *was* a spectacular little miracle.

Simon's eyes followed her around the waiting room; she was on her tiptoes scampering, arms aloft, like ribbons, chin jutting at an elegant angle. An adorable mix of childish abandonment and earnest concentration. Everyone in the room stared at her with an intensity almost equal to his, it was impossible not to.

The emotions she triggered varied: amusement, delight, longing. Daisy looked torn, somewhere between jubilant and embarrassed. She'd said she thought it was tactless bringing a child to a fertility clinic, as though they were showing off.

"We don't need to rub their noses in it," she'd warned. Simon thought her turn of phrase was amusing, quaint. He thought Millie's presence in the waiting room had to be inspiring. Other parents would be encouraged. There was no doubt, she was special. For sure, they had to try for another one. Millie might very well become a prima ballerina at the Royal Ballet, why not? Who knows what else they could produce: an astronaut, the next Steve Jobs, the person who finds the cure for cancer. Or even, simply a pleasant person who was nice to their neighbors, remained faithful to their partner, became an interested parent. It was life. Life! What was more important than that? You had to try, didn't you? You had to.

Millie danced every single day. She was crabby if she missed a class, even on holidays she carved out a couple of hours practice time. She was just six, but was that dedicated. It was astounding. Aspirational. Her existence was wall-to-wall pink tulle. When she started school she'd had meltdowns every day and, at first, Simon and Daisy had been confused and troubled as to why. "Do you have friends, Millie?', "Is your teacher kind to you?', "Do you like the lunches?', "Can you find your coat peg?" they'd asked, wracking their brains to imagine any possible irritation or upset.

"Yes, yes, yes, yes," she'd spluttered through distressed tears.

"Then what is the matter?" Simon had asked, exasperated, tense. He'd taken the morning off work to be with Daisy when they tried to persuade Millie to go into her classroom.

"The uniform is ugly!" She'd howled. "It's green. I want it pink." Her explanation, hiccupped out indignantly, had only made Simon laugh. Daisy ultimately solved the matter by sewing a pink ribbon all around the inside hem of Millie's school skirt. An act that Simon always thought was a display of pure brilliance and devotion.

"I feel very uncomfortable taking Millie into the consultation room," Daisy whispered. "She'll understand enough of what we are talking about to be interested. I don't want to get her hopes up that there's a sibling on the way." Because Simon had just been thinking about the hand sewn pink ribbon, he was more inclined to indulge Daisy.

"OK, well how about I go in first and hear what he has to say and then you pop in after me."

"Won't that take twice as long?" Daisy looked anxiously about her. There were two other couples in the waiting room. They may or may not have been waiting to see Dr. Martell. "I'd feel awful if we overran."

"We're paying for it, so you don't have to worry."

"It's impolite." Daisy had a heightened regard for being polite. Simon sometimes found that charming, other times he found it frustrating.

"Well what do you suggest? Leaving would also be impolite."

Daisy nodded. "I suppose."

At that moment a smartly-dressed nurse appeared, she had a clipboard and clipped tones; she oozed efficiency. "Mr. and Mrs. Barnes?"

Simon stood up, kissed Daisy on the top of the head. "Don't look so worried. This is the start of a wonderful adventure," he told her. "Love you."

Look for Lies, Lies, Lies *by Adele Parks*
available from MIRA Books June 2020